The Billionaire's Club

Meet the world's most eligible bachelors...

by Rebecca Winters

For tycoons Vincenzo Gagliardi, Takis Manolis and Cesare Donati, transforming the Castello di Lombardi into one of Europe's most highly sought-after hotels would be more than just a business venture; it was a challenge to be relished!

But these three men, bound by a friendship as strong as blood, are about to discover that the chase is only half the fun… as three women conquer their hearts and change their lives forever.

Return of Her Italian Duke

Available now!

And look out for Takis's and Cesare's stories, coming soon!

RETURN OF HER ITALIAN DUKE

BY
REBECCA WINTERS

All rights reserved including the right of reproduction in whole or in part in any form. This edition is published by arrangement with Harlequin Books S.A.

This is a work of fiction. Names, characters, places, locations and incidents are purely fictional and bear no relationship to any real life individuals, living or dead, or to any actual places, business establishments, locations, events or incidents. Any resemblance is entirely coincidental.

This book is sold subject to the condition that it shall not, by way of trade or otherwise, be lent, resold, hired out or otherwise circulated without the prior consent of the publisher in any form of binding or cover other than that in which it is published and without a similar condition including this condition being imposed on the subsequent purchaser.

® and ™ are trademarks owned and used by the trademark owner and/or its licensee. Trademarks marked with ® are registered with the United Kingdom Patent Office and/or the Office for Harmonisation in the Internal Market and in other countries.

First Published in Great Britain 2017
By Mills & Boon, an imprint of HarperCollins*Publishers*
1 London Bridge Street, London, SE1 9GF

© 2017 Rebecca Winters

ISBN: 978-0-263-92280-6

23-0317

Our policy is to use papers that are natural, renewable and recyclable products and made from wood grown in sustainable forests. The logging and manufacturing processes conform to the legal environmental regulations of the country of origin.

Printed and bound in Spain
by CPI, Barcelona

Rebecca Winters lives in Salt Lake City, Utah. With canyons and high alpine meadows full of wildflowers, she never runs out of places to explore. They, plus her favourite holiday spots in Europe, often end up as backgrounds for her romance novels, because writing is her passion, along with her family and church. Rebecca loves to hear from readers. If you wish to email her, please visit her website at www.cleanromances.com

To my darling daughter, Dominique,
a wonderful romance writer who has an editor's
instinct and insight to keep her mother's writing
on track and believable. She, too, is a Dumas lover.
We're both Francophiles at heart.

CHAPTER ONE

Castello di Lombardi, ten years ago

AT TWO IN the morning, Vincenzo Gagliardi, newly turned eighteen, quickly dressed in jeans and a hoodie he pulled over his black hair. The long sleeves covered the bruises on his arms. He could feel the welts still smarting on his back and legs as he slid his pack over his shoulders. Then he looked around his room one more time, glancing at the bed.

A vision of Gemma, the woman who'd been entwined in his arms there the night before, wouldn't leave his mind. After the pleasure they'd given each other despite his wounds, and the plans he'd envisioned for their future, it killed him to think he had to leave her at all. But the difficulties with his father made his flight necessary. Worse, he couldn't tell her where he was going or why. It was for her own protection.

Once his father, the acting Duca di Lombardi, started looking for him, he'd interrogate everyone, including Gemma, and he would be able to tell if she was lying or not. If the girl he'd grown up with from earliest childhood knew nothing about his disappearance, then his father would sense it and have to believe her.

Arrivederci, Gemma, his heart moaned. *Ti amo.*

Making sure no one saw him, he hurried through the fourteenth-century *castello* to Dimi's room in the other tower. His cousin had left his bedroom door open. Closer than brothers, they'd been planning Vincenzo's disappearance for a year.

Dimi was waiting for him. "You're late and must go now! I've been watching from the parapet. The guard with the dog won't be walking past the entrance for another seven minutes."

"This is it, cousin. Remember—when I'm established in New York, I'll contact you. Look for the phone number through an ad in the help wanted of *Il Giorno*'s classified section. Be sure to call me on a throwaway phone."

Dimi nodded.

"It won't be long before you turn eighteen. I'll wire you money so you can join me. And as soon as I reach my destination, I'll phone our grandfather so he won't worry." Both boys were the grandsons of the cancer-stricken Emanuele Gagliardi, the old Duca di Lombardi, who no longer could function and verged on death.

His cousin's eyes teared up. "*Che Dio di benedica*, Vincenzo."

He tried to clear his throat. "God be with you, too, Dimi. Promise me you'll keep an eye on Gemma."

"You know I will."

Vincenzo hated this situation that took him away from her, but there was no going back. He thanked his cousin for his sacrifice, hating their gut-wrenching separation and the horrible position he'd been put in. But they both agreed the danger was too great to do anything else.

As they hugged hard, Vincenzo realized that he could barely see through the tears. The deep well of shame and pain because he hadn't been able to protect his mother was something he would have to carry for the rest of his life. Gemma was better off without him.

Because of Dimi's loyalty, no one would ever know where he'd gone. This was the way it had to be.

Now that Vincenzo had been forced to cut himself off from the world he knew, the need to make money had taken hold of his life and had become his raison d'être.

Gemma lay in bed, wide-awake, at six in the morning, reliving the moments she'd spent with Vincenzo the night before last. When she'd heard he'd suffered injuries from a fall off his horse, she hadn't been able to resist slipping up to his tower bedroom to see if he was all right.

Despite his physical pain, they'd tried to love each other until he'd told her she needed to get back to her room. Gemma had wanted to stay the entire night with him and couldn't understand why he'd been so insistent she leave. She'd wanted to lie in his arms forever.

It was painful to have to tear herself away from him. After making sure no guards were watching, she slipped down the winding staircase at the back of the *castello* to reach the rooms where she and her mother lived behind the kitchen.

Yesterday after school she hadn't seen him at all,

and she feared his injuries were worse. If she didn't spot him in the back courtyard today after she got home, she'd go up to his room again tonight to find out why.

He was such an expert rider, it was hard to believe he'd been hurt so badly. While she suffered over what had happened to him, she heard a knock on her bedroom door. "Gemma? Get up and get dressed, then come in the main room quickly!"

She didn't normally get up until six thirty to start getting ready for school. Alarmed by the concern in her mother's voice, Gemma did her bidding.

When she emerged from the small room, she saw a sight she'd never forget. Vincenzo's father, the acting Duca di Lombardi, stood there while three policemen searched their rooms off the *castello* kitchen.

He and Vincenzo bore a strong likeness to each other, but there was all the difference in the world between them. The *duca*'s stare at her was so menacing, she shuddered.

Her mother grabbed her hand. "The *duca* wishes to ask you a few questions, Gemma."

He'd never talked to her personally in her life. "Yes, Your Highness?"

"Where's my son?"

She blinked. "I—I don't know what you mean," she stammered.

"If you know anything, you must tell him, Gemma."

"I know nothing, Mamma."

The police reappeared, shaking their heads. The *duca* took a threatening step toward her. "My son is missing from the *castello*, and I believe *you* know where he's gone."

Gemma froze. Vincenzo was gone? "I swear on my faith in the Holy Virgin that I have no idea where he would be."

His face turned a ruddy color. He shot a fiery glance at Gemma's mother, who crossed herself. "She's lying! Since you can't get the truth from her, I insist you leave the premises immediately and take your baggage with you." Gemma flinched. "I'll make certain you're never able to get another job again!"

He wheeled around and left. The police followed and shut the door.

Gemma ran to her mother and hugged her hard. Both of them trembled. "I swear I don't know anything about Vincenzo. I swear it, Mamma."

"I believe you. Start packing your bag. I'll do the same. We have to get out of here as soon as possible in case he comes back. I'll call for a taxi from the kitchen. We'll leave for the train station and go back to Florence."

Fifteen minutes later they assembled in the kitchen. The other cook and her daughter, Bianca, Gemma's best friend, were there, too, with their bags. The *duca*'s fury knew no bounds. As they hurried out of the service entrance at the back of the *castello* to wait, the *duca*'s words rang in her ears.

She's lying! Since you can't get the truth from her, you must leave the premises immediately and take your baggage you. I'll make certain you're never able to get another job again!

When the taxi arrived, Gemma climbed inside feeling as dead as last winter's ashes.

New York City, six months ago

After Dimi had phoned Vincenzo during the night with news that had come close to sending him into shock, he made calls to his two best friends and asked them to come to his Manhattan penthouse above his office ASAP.

Once arrangements were made, he told his assistant he wouldn't be in the office today and didn't want to be disturbed for any reason. Within two hours they'd both shown up using his private elevator.

The ultra-contemporary apartment suited Vincenzo perfectly. He liked the modern art on the white walls and the floor-to-ceiling windows that let in the light. Up here there were no dark reminders of the past. Here, he could breathe. Or he'd thought he could, until Dimi's phone call.

"Thanks for coming so fast," he said in Italian. "I'm just thankful you were available."

Cesare nodded. "You made it sound like life or death."

"It is to me."

His friend Takis eyed him curiously. "What's going on, Vincenzo?"

"Something that will surprise you. I'll tell you over breakfast. Come to the dining room."

Once they sat down and started to eat, Vincenzo handed them each a photograph of the massive Castello di Lombardi. "You're looking at the former residence of the Gagliardi family. From that family, two hundred years ago, sprang the first illustrious Duca di Lombardi, an important political figure in that region of Italy."

They stared at the photo, then looked at him in confusion.

"Why am I showing you this?" He read their minds. "Because there's more to me than you know. What I'm about to tell you could cause you to distrust me. You would have every right to walk out of here and never look back."

"Tell us what?" Cesare asked in total bewilderment.

"I haven't been completely honest about myself. You know me as Vincenzo Nistri, but my full name is Vincenzo Nistri Gagliardi. Nistri was my mother's maiden name."

Takis blinked. "So you're full-fledged Italian? For some reason you remind me of one of my Macedonian friends."

"That's what I thought, too," Cesare said. "Maybe Eastern Europe."

"Is that so?" Vincenzo grinned, amused by their honesty. "Not that I know of. The *castello* you're looking at was my home for the first eighteen years of my life." *And the woman I left behind there so cruelly is still the only girl I ever loved, though there've been women since.* "If a great tragedy hadn't happened to my family—one that caused me to flee—I would have taken over as the next Duca di Lombardi upon my father's death."

There was no question that he'd stunned his friends. Neither of them said a word. They kept staring at him as if he were an alien being speaking an unknown language.

"Let me tell you a story so you'll understand everything. My father and uncle did very bad things, evil things. At one point I realized my life was in danger."

When he'd given them details, he said, "The old *duca*, my grandfather, died nine years ago, leaving the way open for my father and uncle to bring down the house of Gagliardi. To start paying their debts, they sold off family treasures, including other properties that had been in the family for hundreds of years. Inevitably they let go the staff who'd served our family faithfully.

"Then a month ago my father was riding his horse through the forest behind the *castello* in a drunken rage. The horse reared and my father fell, breaking his neck. That left my uncle, Alonzo in charge.

"He has just been sent to prison, where he's now serving a thirty-year sentence for manslaughter, drunkenness, embezzlement and debt in the millions of euros. The family has now disintegrated, and the authorities have closed up the *castello*."

His friends shook their heads. "How could such a thing happen to a powerful family like yours?" Takis asked.

"There's one word for it. Corruption. Absolute and truly terrible. The family coffers had been raided for so long there was nothing left but staggering debt they'd accrued. They were like two bad seeds.

"My maternal grandparents died two years ago, and the only remaining family members on my father's side besides my imprisoned uncle are my cousin Dimi, who is like a brother to me, and his mother, Consolata. They live in a small palazzo in Milan given to her by her grandmother before her marriage to my uncle."

It was the only piece of property that neither Alonzo nor Vincenzo's father had been able to lay his hands on at the end.

"Dimi lives there quietly with her because she's in a wheelchair, suffering from dementia, and needs care." He eyed them directly. "Can you forgive me for omitting all of this until now?"

"*Si*—" both men said in unison. Takis's brows met. "Your life was in grave danger."

"But that's in the past. Now I'm faced with something I hadn't imagined, and I wanted to discuss it with you."

Cesare's solemn gaze played over him. "Tell us."

"The *castello* is now in receivership. I swore to God I would never return to Italy, but the thought of my heritage being sold to some foreign potentate to help the slipping Italian economy is anathema to me.

"My cousin Dimi is particularly concerned. He has an eye on what's happening everywhere. Both Italy's Villa Giulia museum in Rome, built by Pope Julius III, and the nine-hundred-year-old Norman palace in Palermo, the seat of former kings, are soon to be on the list to be sold off by the government, too.

"In view of such a frightening prospect, I wondered if you might like to go into business with me. Dimi will assist behind the scenes. Not only will my cousin and I be able to preserve our own family heritage, we'll transform the *castello* into a glorious hotel with a restaurant that could be the toast of Europe. It would mean the three of us would have to put our assistants in charge of managing our businesses when we're not in the country."

After a pronounced silence, both men let out cries

of excitement. For the rest of the day the three of them brainstormed.

"Now that we've talked things out, there's one favor I must ask. I intend to be the silent business partner in this venture and prefer to remain anonymous because of the family scandals."

Their solemn acknowledgment of his request warmed him and he knew they'd honor his request.

"Now, you can imagine that when word gets out that the *castello* has been sold and turned into a resort by two businessmen from the US, the press will be all over it. Dimi will send me the necessary information and put you in touch with the contact person to get the ball rolling.

"If we do decide to go into business together, I'll expect you two to do the negotiating. Naturally I'll supply the money needed so we can get started on the renovations right away."

Cesare smiled. "The *duca*'s return."

"No, Cesare. I don't want my title mentioned. That's not for public consumption." He couldn't escape the title he'd inherited by being his father's son, but in time he intended to renounce it legally through the court system. *And I'll find Gemma if it kills me.* Over the last ten years, no search had turned up any evidence of her.

"Understood." Cesare eyed him seriously. "When we first met at university, I always knew there was a lot more to you, but I couldn't put my finger on it and didn't dare ask for fear of insulting you."

"Now it's all making sense," Takis admitted. "Your English is too perfect, and you're far more sophisticated and knowledgeable than anyone else I know."

"Your friendship has meant the world to me. Let's hope for success in our new venture."

Takis sat back in the chair. "Edmond Dantes had nothing on you, Vincenzo Gagliardi."

Florence, Italy, present day

The bulletin board of the Florentine Epicurean School of Hospitality and Culinary Arts listed the latest career openings across four continents for their recent graduates to investigate.

At twenty-seven years of age, Gemma had finally received her long-awaited certification with the much-coveted first-place blue ribbon, and she hurried down the corridor toward the office. Everyone wanted to apply for the most prestigious position posted. She didn't know what her chances were, but it didn't matter. Her hard, grueling years of schooling were over, and she would find a position that guaranteed her a new life so she could prove herself.

She wanted to pay back her mother's family, who'd taken them in after they'd been thrown out of the Castello di Lombardi. Her relationship with Vincenzo years ago had put her family in such dire straits, it had ruined her mother's career. Gemma felt the responsibility heavily, because she hadn't heeded her mother's warnings that a commoner didn't mingle with royalty. But those days were behind her.

With students gathered around the bulletin board, it was hard to get close enough to write down the information. Later the lists would be put online, but she was too impatient and took pictures of the various announcements with her cell phone.

Her best friend Filippa Gatti, who'd gone through pastry school with Gemma, had the same idea. They made plans to talk later before she hurried off. Gemma found a bench farther along the corridor and sat down to study everything but gave up because she couldn't concentrate with so much noise.

Once outside, she got in her old blue car and headed back to her aunt's apartment two miles away. Her mother's sister owned the hundred-year-old Bonucci family bakery and ran it with her married daughter. When Gemma and her mother had fled to Florence, her aunt had let them live in the apartment above the bakery.

Her aunt was goodness itself and had put her mother to work. She had also helped Gemma get a scholarship to attend cooking school, because her mother's funds were so low. Her cousin was wonderful, too, and they all got along.

Once she had started culinary school, Gemma had helped out in the bakery every day after classes. The culinary school required ten years of apprenticeship. After high school she'd begun her training there. Now that she'd graduated, it was important she start paying her aunt back for letting them live there and helping to get them on their feet after being kicked out of the *castello.*

Today she dashed up the back stairs to the door off the porch. Gemma couldn't wait to call her mom and aunt and tell them she'd been chosen the top graduate in her class. After they'd shown such faith in her, Gemma was thrilled that her hard work had paid off.

But of course, it would happen that her mother and aunt had just left to go on a well-deserved vacation to the United Kingdom with friends, their first in years. They wouldn't be back for three weeks, because their trip included England, Scotland, Wales and Ireland. Such good news from the school had filled Gemma with joy. She would have to phone her *mamma*, Mirella, immediately.

Now that she'd received her certification, she was anxious to find a fabulous job and move out. She planned for her mother to go with her. They'd find a small, affordable apartment. Her mother could stop working and enjoy her life while her daughter earned the living.

After grabbing her favorite fruit soda from the fridge, Gemma sank down on the chair at the small kitchen table and phoned her *mamma*. Frustrated when she got her voice mail, Gemma asked her to phone her back ASAP because she had exciting news.

Next, she scrolled through her photo gallery to the information she'd recorded on her cell. To her utmost disappointment, none of the eighteen openings for pastry chefs were in France, the place where she'd had her heart set on working.

Both the French and the Italians thought they produced the finest chefs. As her mother and aunt had told her, because she was a woman, she'd have an even harder time breaking into a top five-star restaurant in either country. Women chefs still struggled for equality. One day she would get a position on the Côte d'Azur. But for now she needed a job right away!

Trying to manage her disappointment, she studied each opening one at a time: five in Spain, three in England, one in Liechtenstein, two in Australia, three in Japan, three in Canada, one in Italy.

Since it couldn't be France, nothing else thrilled her, but she studied the requirements for the various openings.

It wasn't until she came to the last posting, from Italy, that Gemma was shaken to the core. She thought she'd read it wrong. The shock had her jumping up from the couch. She read the words again, attempting to quell the frantic pounding of her heart.

> Location: Milan, Italy. Fourteenth-century castello and former estate of the deceased Duca di Lombardi, Salvatore Gagliardi. Grand opening of the five-star Castello Supremo Hotel and Ristorante di Lombardi, July 6.

July 6 was only four weeks away. She read on.

> Résumés for executive chef and executive pastry chef are being accepted. See list of requirements. Only those with the proper credentials need apply.

Gemma came close to fainting when she thought of Vincenzo. The fact that he'd disappeared without even saying goodbye had caused an anger in her that, even now, she was still trying to suppress. He'd told her he was in love with her and that one day they'd find a way to be married.

After he'd vanished, she'd felt so used. What a fool she'd been to believe he could love the daughter of a cook! How naive of her to think the *duca*-to-be would consider an alliance with an underling like Gemma. In her dream world they'd been equals and anything was possible. But once Vincenzo's father had tossed her and her mother out like a heap of garbage, she'd received the wake-up call of her life. It had shaken her world forever.

As she read the announcement again, something twisted painfully inside her. The *castello*, an icon over the centuries that had been her home until the age of seventeen, had now been turned into a hotel and restaurant. She tried to understand how such a thing could have happened to the family with its succession of *duchi* for over two hundred years.

Gone was their birthright and traditions. Vincenzo had disappeared along with his family. Last year she'd heard on television that Vincenzo's father was dead. And soon after that Dimi's father had been sent to prison for fraud. Beyond that there'd been no more news.

Now she was horrified to think the *castello* had been put up and sold for its commercial value in an increasingly mercenary world. Gemma considered it a form of sacrilege.

No doubt every new graduate would apply there first, but they didn't have a prayer of being hired. Only the most famous chefs throughout Europe and elsewhere would be allowed an interview at such a magnificent and famous landmark. Many considered Italy to be the vortex of gastronomic delight in the world. The competition would be fierce.

Even so, she was going to apply.

After her failed relationship with Paolo, she realized she needed to draw a line under the past. Until she discovered what had happened to Vincenzo and why, she knew in her heart she'd never be able to move on with her life.

If by some miracle she only made it to the first interview before being rejected, maybe she'd be able to find out where Vincenzo had gone. What had caused the demise of the Gagliardi family? So much had been hushed up in the press.

Pushing those thoughts aside, for the rest of the day she emailed her prepared résumé to Milan, Valencia, Barcelona, London and Vaduz in Liechtenstein. For some reason she couldn't attach her picture, but it was too late to worry about that now.

Filippa called to tell her she'd applied for all three jobs in Canada. She would have preferred to go to the States, but Canada was the next closest place with openings. Gemma wished her luck and told her what she'd done. They promised to keep each other updated on what happened.

The next day she started receiving emails back and learned that the positions in Vaduz and Valencia had already been filled. Barcelona and London were still open. To her satisfaction, they'd sent her a specific day and time to report for a personal interview.

But it was the email that came after lunch from the *castello* that almost sent her into cardiac arrest. She was told to report there at noon tomorrow! And to please let them know immediately if she couldn't make it.

Gemma had thought, of course, that being a new graduate, she wouldn't have been considered. Something on her résumé must have caused them to give her an opportunity.

Thank heaven her mother wasn't in Italy right now.

Gemma needed to see this through before she told her parent anything. The last thing she wanted to do was hurt her *mamma*. But for Gemma's own emotional health and progress, she had to do this! It might be her only chance in this life to find out about Vincenzo. If she didn't follow through, she knew she'd always regret it.

With hands trembling, she sent an email to let them know she'd be there at the correct time. If she left Florence within the hour, she could drive to the village at the base of the *castello* today and find a room for the night. That would give her time tomorrow to get ready before the interview.

Gemma phoned her cousin to let her know that she was leaving for a day or two to go job hunting. She made no mention that her destination was the *castello*. Her cousin had been so hurt for Gemma and her mother, she would have tried to persuade her to avoid more pain and not go. But this was something she had to do.

Without wasting any time, she showered and packed a suitcase that included her laptop. After dressing in jeans and a blouse, she set off on the three-hour drive to Milan full of questions that might get answered after all this time. It would be a trip of agony and ecstasy, since she'd never once been back.

By seven in the evening, she'd arrived in the busy city and took the turnoff for the village of Sopri, where she'd gone to school with a few children of the other estate workers. Even after all this time, Gemma knew where to find a *pensione* with reasonable rates.

But sleep didn't come well. She tossed and turned

for hours. Memories of Vincenzo and the night they'd been together in his bedroom kept her awake. Lying in his arms she'd felt immortal, but he hadn't let her stay with him all night, something she'd never understood.

How she'd loved her life at the *castello* with him! For years since his disappearance she'd tried to discover his whereabouts, but he'd vanished as if into thin air. Over time it finally sank in that she hadn't been good enough for him. That's what her mother had been trying to tell her without putting the painful message into actual words. Gemma believed it now!

When she wasn't hating Vincenzo, she feared that something terrible had happened to him. The possibility that he might have died was insupportable to her. Combined with her pain over the loss of Vincenzo was her outrage for what his father had done to her and her beloved mother. The great, cruel Duca di Lombardi! There were times when the memory of that morning still tormented her.

Once they'd moved to Florence, she'd never heard anything about Vincenzo or Dimi. Where had his cousin gone? She'd once hoped that if she could even find Dimi, she'd get answers to all her questions. But it was as if the Gagliardi family had been erased from life. It was too strange… She missed Dimi. He'd been such a wonderful friend all those years ago.

Now she was going back to the place where she'd known such joy…and pain. What if by some stretch of the imagination she got the job? How would she feel? How would her mother feel to realize her daughter had graduated with honors from the top cooking school in Italy and was going to make it despite what the *duca* had done to them?

Wouldn't it be the height of deliciousness to be hired there, of all places on earth? Such sweet revenge after being kicked to the gutter.

Gemma was relieved when morning came. After washing her hair and showering, she dressed in a peach-colored two-piece suit, wanting to look her best. At ten she ate breakfast at a trattoria before leaving for the *castello* ten minutes away. She'd planned to get there early enough to look around and ask questions. Surely someone would be able to tell her about Vincenzo.

For him to disappear on her was a betrayal so awful, she hadn't been able to put her trust in another man for years. Even after she'd starting dating, the memory of that horrible time when it became clear he'd never be back still haunted her nights.

It had taken until a year ago for her to have her first serious relationship with a man. After a month of dating, Paolo wanted to sleep with her, but she couldn't. Her heart wasn't in it. She explained to him that in another eight months she'd be graduating and looking for a position, hopefully in France. There could be no future for them. She had to follow her own path.

After breakfast Gemma opened the car window and breathed in the warm June air as she drove past the familiar signposts, farms and villas toward the massive Castello di Lombardi.

The ocher-toned structure, with its towers and crenellated walls sprawled over a prominent hilltop, had its roots in ancient times. So many nights she and

Vincenzo had walked along those walls with their arms around each other, talking and laughing quietly so none of the family or guards would see or hear them.

Closer now, cypress trees bordered her on either side of the winding road. Memories came flooding back. Because of Vincenzo, she knew all about its history. The remains of a Romanesque church standing in the inner courtyard dated back to AD 875. But the *castello* itself had been built in the fourteenth century to protect the surrounding estate from invasions.

Many owners had possessed it, including the House of Savoy. By the mid–eighteen hundreds it had become the residence of the Gagliardi family. Although it was the first Duca di Lombardi who was considered illustrious, as far as Gemma was concerned that right would have belonged to Vincenzo. That was, until he'd plunged a dagger in her heart by disappearing.

The visitor parking beneath the four flights of zigzagging front steps held no cars. Her breath caught to see the profusion of flowers and landscaping done to beautify everything. New external lighting fixtures had been put in place. At night it would present a magnificent spectacle to guests arriving.

After taking it all in, she drove down a private road that wound around to the rear entrance where in the past the tradesmen used to come. Beyond it was a large parking area that she remembered had been used by the staff.

There were a dozen vans and trucks, plus some elegant cars, clustered in the enclosed area around the door. From the front of the *castello* the entire place had looked deserted, but that clearly wasn't the case.

Once she'd gotten out of her car to walk around, a male gardener planting flowers called to her. "The lady is lost, perhaps?" he asked in Italian.

She shook her head. *Anything but.* "I'm here for a job interview."

"Ah? Then you must go around to the front. The office is on the right of the entrance hall."

"Thank you." It seemed that the day room she remembered must have been converted into an office. She could never have imagined it. "Tell me—do you know why the *castello* was sold in the first place?"

He hunched his shoulders. "*No lo so.*"

With her hair swishing against her shoulders, Gemma nodded and walked back to her car, realizing she'd get nothing from him. Her watch said eleven forty-five. She might as well arrive a few minutes early to show she was punctual. She backed her car around, retracing her short trip back to the main parking lot, where she stopped the car and got out.

How many hundreds of times had she and her childhood friend Bianca—who'd had a crush on Dimi—bounded up these steps after getting off the school bus looking for Vincenzo and his cousin?

They would enter the *castello* through a private doorway west of the main entrance and hurry down the corridor to the kitchen. Once they'd checked in with their mothers, they'd run off to their hiding place in the back courtyard, where hopefully the two Gagliardis would be waiting.

To her surprise the old private entrance no longer existed. The filled-in stone wall looked like it had been there forever. Gemma felt shut out and could well believe she'd dreamed up a past life.

But when she entered through the main doors, she had to admit that whoever had undertaken to turn this into a world-class resort had done a superb job of maintaining its former beauty. Many of the paintings and tapestries she remembered still adorned the vaulted ceilings and walls on the right side of the hallway.

The biggest difference lay in the bank of floor-to-ceiling French doors on the left. They ran the length of the long hallway she used to run through on her way to the kitchen. Beyond the mullioned glass squares she could see a gorgeous dining room with huge chandeliers so elegant it robbed her of breath.

On the far side of the dining room were more French doors that no doubt opened on to a terrace for open-air dining. Gemma knew there was a rose garden on that side of the *castello*. And though she couldn't see it from here, there was a magnificent ballroom beyond the dining room to the south.

She was staggered by the changes, so exquisite in design she could only marvel. Whoever had taken over this place had superb taste in everything. Suddenly she realized it was noon and she swung around to report she was here.

The enormous former day room had been transformed into the foyer and front desk of the fabulous hotel, with a long counter, several computers and all the accoutrements essential for business. She sat down on one of the eighteenth-century sage-and-gold damask chairs with the Duca di Lombardi's royal crest and waited to see if someone would come.

Just as she was ready to call out if anyone was there, she saw movement behind the counter that revealed an attractive brown-haired male, probably six foot two and in his late twenties. Strong and lean, he wore trousers and shirtsleeves pushed up to the elbows. When his cobalt-blue eyes wandered over her, she knew he'd missed nothing.

"You must be Signora Bonucci."

CHAPTER TWO

GEMMA CORRECTED HIM. "I'm Signor*ina* Bonucci."

"Ah. I saw the ring."

"It was my grandmother's." Gemma's mother had given it to her on her twenty-first birthday. Her grandmother had also been a great cook, and the hope was that it would bring Gemma luck. Now Gemma wore it on her right hand in remembrance.

As for the name, Bonucci, that was another story. Once Gemma and her mother had left the *castello*, Mirella had insisted Gemma use her maiden name. She'd hoped to be able to find work if the *duca* couldn't trace them through her married name, Rizzo.

One corner of his mouth lifted in a smile. "Now that we have that straightened out, I'm Signor Donati, the one who's late for this meeting. Call me Cesare." With that accent the man was Sicilian down to his toenails. "Thank you for applying with us. Come around the counter and we'll talk in my office."

She got up and followed him down a hallway past several doors to his inner sanctum, modern and in a messy state. Everything about Cesare surprised Gemma, including the informality.

"Take a seat."

Gemma sat down on one of the leather chairs. "I have to admit I was surprised that you would even consider a new graduate."

He perched on the corner of his desk. "I always keep an open mind. I had already chosen the finalists and the field was closed, but when your résumé showed up yesterday, it caught my eye."

"Might I ask why?"

"It included something no one else's did. You said you learned the art of pastry making from your mother. That was a dangerous admission and made me curious to know why you dared." He was teasing her.

"It *was* dangerous, I know." For more reasons than he was implying, but the *duca* was dead now. "To leave my mother from my résumé would make me ungrateful."

She felt his gaze studying her. "For you to mention her means she wasn't just an average cook in your eyes."

"No. She came from a family of bakers. To me, her pastry will always be the best." Gemma owed her mother everything after her sacrifices.

The man cocked his head. "It shows you're willing to give credit where it's due. But being the daughter of a cook doesn't always make the daughter a cook, no matter the genes nor how many classes at school."

"No one is more aware of that than I am, but I would be nothing without her. She helped me go to cooking school in Florence."

He folded his arms. "The best in Italy, where you received the highest award during your ten year apprenticeship there. It's a stringent education, but the most prestigious culinary schools require that much training to turn out the best cooks. She guided you well. Bravo."

A compliment from a man who knew the culinary business well enough to be in charge of staffing this new hotel came as a complete surprise.

"If I hadn't been born her daughter, I would never in this world have decided on a career that keeps you on your feet all day and night, that will never pay enough money and that is unfair to women chefs in general. In truth I'm shocked you allowed me this interview, even if you are exceptionally open-minded."

She shouldn't have said it, but she'd spoken without thinking. Incredibly he burst into laughter.

"Signorina, you're like a breath of fresh air and have won yourself one chance to prove if there's genius in you. Report to me at ten in the morning and I'll put you to work making what you do best."

Gemma stared hard at him. "You're serious..." Was it really possible?

His brows lifted. "When it comes to cooking, I'm always serious. You'll be sharing the kitchen with another applicant who is hoping to become the executive chef. All the ingredients you need will be provided, and you'll both have your own workspace. When you're finished, you will leave. Any questions?"

Yes. She had a big one, but now wasn't the moment. It had to be another test to see how well two different chefs got along under this kind of pressure. "None, Signor."

"*Bene.* When your pastry has been sampled by the people in charge tomorrow evening, an opinion will be made. The next day you'll be phoned and informed of their decision. Please see yourself out."

Now she was scared. She'd heard back from her mother last night and had been able to tell her about receiving the top marks for her certification. Her mother and aunt had been overjoyed. Gemma had told them she planned to apply at quite a few places for work, but she'd left out the position offered at the *castello*.

There was no need for her mother to know about it since Gemma had no real hope of getting it. Instead she'd asked them about their trip and they'd talked for a long time. Her mother had sounded so happy, Gemma hadn't wanted to say anything to take away from her enjoying the only trip she'd had in years.

Deep in painful thoughts, Vincenzo strode down the portrait-lined *castello* hallway toward his deceased grandfather's private dining room. Even after being back in Italy for a half year, it was still hard to believe this had once been his home.

All Vincenzo could think about was Gemma. Over the last ten years, he'd paid an Italian private investigator to look for her to no avail. For the six months he'd been in Lombardi, he'd doubled the search. Vincenzo's guilt over how his unexplained disappearance must have hurt Gemma beyond description had tortured him from the beginning. It matched his fear that he would never catch up to her again.

Though Dimi had promised to keep an eye on Gemma for him, fate had stepped in to change Dimi's life, too. The day that Vincenzo's father had gone on a rampage over his disappearance and had searched the countryside for him with the help of Dimi's father and the police, Dimi had realized the danger in staying at the *castello.* That very morning he'd left with his mother and taken her to her family's property in Milan, where they'd be safe and out of the way.

On his own, Dimi had searched for Gemma, but that path had led nowhere, either.

The thought filled Vincenzo with such profound sadness, gripping him to the point he couldn't throw it off. Echoes and whispers from a time when he'd known real happiness with Gemma haunted him and made his disconnect with the past even more heart wrenching.

His friends looked up when he entered. They must have heard his footsteps on the intricate pattern of inlaid wood flooring. Before he sat down at the oval table, Vincenzo's silvery-gray eyes—a trait of the Gagliardi men—glanced at the wood nymphs painted on the ornate ceiling.

Twenty-eight-year-old Vincenzo found them as fascinating now as he'd done as a little boy. One of them had always been of particular interest, because Gemma could have been the subject the artist had painted.

"*Mi dispiace essere in ritardo.* I was on the phone with Annette."

The savvy real estate woman he'd been involved with before leaving New York had wanted to plan her vacation to be with him for the opening. Deep down he knew she was hoping for a permanent arrangement. But since Vincenzo had stepped on Italian soil, memories of Gemma had had a stranglehold on him. He knew he wasn't ready to live with anyone, let alone get married.

Maybe after the opening he'd be able to relax and give it more thought. He enjoyed Annette more than any woman in a long time. But he had work to do and had told her he would call her back when he had more time to talk. The disappointment in her voice when he said he had to hang up because he was late for a business dinner spoke volumes. It was the truth.

Cesare smiled at him. "*Non c'e problema.*"

Greek-born Takis grunted. "Maybe not for you, Cesare, but I didn't eat lunch on purpose, and now I'm famished."

Vincenzo nodded. "I held back, too. Tonight is the night we make decisions that will spell the success or failure of our business venture. Let's get started."

"Just so you know, a fourth pastry chef applicant has created a sampling of desserts for us this evening."

"A fourth?" Vincenzo frowned. "I thought we were through with the vetting process."

"I thought so, too, but this one came in at the last minute yesterday with amazing credentials, and I decided to take a chance."

Takis groaned. "So we have to eat two sets of desserts?"

"That's right, so don't eat too much of any one thing," Cesare cautioned them.

On that note Vincenzo used his cell phone to ring for dinner. Tonight was the final night in their search to find the perfect executive chef and executive pastry chef for their adventure. The right choices would put them on the map as one of the most sought-after resorts in the world.

They'd narrowed the collection of applicants down to three in one category and now four in the other, but they were cutting it close. In one month they would be opening the doors and everything would have to be ready.

Their recently hired maître d', Cosimo, came up on the newly installed elevator and wheeled in a cart from the kitchen with their dinner. If tonight's food was anything like the other two nights, they were in for a very difficult time choosing the best of the best. The battle between the finalists was fierce.

For the next half hour they sampled and discussed the main course and made the decision that the French applicant would become their executive chef.

With that accomplished, Vincenzo rang for the desserts. Cosimo brought in the tray of delicious offerings from the third pastry chef.

"Remember," Cesare reminded them, "we have one more round of desserts from the fourth pastry chef to sample." He passed them a dish of water crackers. "Eat a few of these now so you'll be able to appreciate what's coming." They drank tea with the crackers to help cleanse their palates.

Cosimo wheeled in the last offerings of the night. As he placed the tray on the table, Vincenzo took one look at the desserts and thought he must be dreaming. *All* of them were Italian, and there were so many of them! They made up the parts of his childhood. He couldn't decide what to try first.

Unaware of his friends at this point, he started on *sfogliatelli*, his favorite dessert in the world, layered like sea shells with cream and cinnamon. When he'd eaten the whole thing he reached for the puffed dome of sweet panettone, the bread his family had eaten on holidays. When he couldn't swallow another bite, he lifted his head. His friends were staring at him like he'd lost his mind.

Takis nudged Cesare. "I believe we've found our executive pastry chef."

"But first we must get Vincenzo to a hospital. He's going to be sick."

Their smiles widened into grins, but he couldn't laugh. All these desserts were too good to be true and tasted like the ones prepared by Gemma's mother years ago. But that was impossible!

He eyed Cesare. "Who made these?"

"A graduate from the Florentine Epicurean culinary school."

Vincent shook his head. "I need to know more." At this juncture his heart was thumping with emotion.

Their smiles receded. Cesare looked worried. "What's wrong?"

"Tell me this person's name."

"Signorina Bonucci. I don't remember her first name. It's on her résumé in my office."

The name meant nothing to Vincenzo. "How old is she? Early sixties?" Had Mirella, Gemma's mother, seen the advertisement and applied for the position?

"No. She's young. In her midtwenties."

How could anyone reproduce desserts identical to Mirella's unless she knew her or had worked with her? If that were true, then perhaps she could tell him Gemma's whereabouts!

"What's going on, Vincenzo?"

For the next few minutes he told them about one of the cooks at the *castello* years ago. "Her pastry was out of this world. She had a daughter who was a year younger than me. We grew up together on her mother's sweets. She was my first love."

"Ah," they said in a collective voice, clearly surprised at another one of his admissions.

"I have no idea what happened to either of them. In fact, over the years I've spent a large sum of money trying to find them, with no success. I want to meet this applicant and find out how she happens to have produced the same desserts."

He jumped up from the chair and hurried out of the room to the elevator at the end of the hall. Once on the main floor, they walked through the lobby and congregated in Cesare's private office. His friend pulled up the résumé on his computer for Vincenzo, who stood next to him to read it.

Seeing her first name nearly gave him a heart attack.

Gemma Bonucci
Age: 27
Address: Bonucci Bakery, Florence Top student in the year's graduating class of pastry chefs.

He was incredulous. His search had come to an end. He'd found her!

Vincenzo had known her as Gemma Rizzo. So why Bonucci? So many questions were bombarding him, he felt like he'd been punched in the gut.

"This must be Mirella's daughter, but there's no picture of her."

"It wasn't attached to her application," Cesare explained, "but her cooking is absolutely superb."

"So was her mother's. I can't comprehend that she was in the kitchen earlier cooking our dessert."

"You look a little pale. Are you all right?"

Vincenzo eyed Cesare. "I will be as soon as I get over the shock. You don't know what these last ten years have been like, trying to find her and always coming to a dead end…"

"Do we agree she's our new executive pastry chef?" Takis asked.

Vincenzo looked at both men. "Don't let my overeating influence you in any way. I have a terrible Italian sweet tooth, but we need to consider the various preferences of all patrons who will come through our doors. I'm sorry that you haven't been able to vote your conscience because of my behavior."

"It wasn't your behavior that decided me," Cesare insisted. "That was the best tiramisu I've ever eaten."

"Don't forget the baba and the baby cannoli," Takis chimed in. "Every dessert was exquisite and presented like a painting. When the guests leave, they'll spread the word that the most divine Italian desserts were made right here."

"Amen." This from Cesare. "But Vincenzo, did you have to eat all the *sfogliatelli* before we could sample it? Cosimo had to bring us more. It was food for the gods."

It was. And the lips of the loving seventeen-year-old girl Vincenzo had once held in his arms and kissed had been as sweet and succulent as the cinnamon-sprinkled cream in the pastry she'd prepared for this evening.

"Takis will make the phone calls now and tell our two new chefs to come to the office at noon for an orientation meeting." Cesare's announcement jerked Vincenzo out of his hidden thoughts.

"I'm glad the decisions have been made. As long as I'm in your office, I'd like to see the résumés of the other pastry finalists." It was an excuse to take another look at Gemma's.

"Be my guest," Cesare murmured. "Those desserts finished me off. I may never eat again."

"You're not the only one. I'm going to my office to make the phone calls."

But for the stunning realization that tomorrow he would see Gemma—the chef who'd turned them all into gluttons—Vincenzo would have laughed.

He walked around the desk and sat down in front of the computer screen to look at it. Her training had been matchless. She held certificates in the culinary arts, baking and pastry, hospitality management, wine studies, enology, and molecular gastronomy. She'd won awards for jams, preserves, chocolate ice cream. Mirella's chocolate ice cream had been divine.

The statement she'd made to explain her desire to be an executive pastry chef stood out as if it had been illuminated. *I learned the art of pastry making from my mother and would like to honor her life's work with my own.*

His eyes smarted as he rang Cesare.

"*Ehi, come va*, Vincenzo?"

"Sorry to bother you. What was it about Signorina Bonucci's résumé that decided you on allowing her to compete? I'm curious."

"You know me. My *mamma*'s cooking is the best

in the world, and I never make a secret about it. When I read about her wanting to honor her *mamma*'s cooking, I decided it was worth giving her a chance. On a whim I told her to report to the *castello*. I did the right thing in your opinion, *non e vero*?"

He closed his eyes tightly. "You already know the answer to that question. If you'd ignored her application, I doubt I would ever have found her." His throat closed up with emotion. "*Grazie, amico.*"

"I'm beginning to think it was meant to be. Before I hang up, there's one thing you should know, Vincenzo."

"What's that?"

"I didn't tell you before because I didn't want you or Takis to think I was biased in picking her for personal reasons."

His pulse sped up. "Go on."

"The signorina is beautiful. Like the forest nymph on the dining room ceiling you were staring at tonight. You know, the one leaning against the tree?"

Yes. Vincenzo knew the one and felt his face go hot. One night when he'd been kissing Gemma, he'd told her she reminded him of that exact nymph painted in the room where Vincenzo had spent many happy times talking to his grandfather. Cesare had noticed the resemblance, too.

"*A domani*, Cesare."

"*Dormi bene.*"

Vincenzo turned off the lights and headed for his old bedroom in the tower. No renovations had been made here. Guests would never be allowed in this part of the *castello*. It was too full of dark memories to open to the public.

He removed his clothes and threw on a robe before walking out on the balcony overlooking Sopri at the foot of the hillside where he'd run away. Where was she sleeping tonight? Down below, near to where she'd once attended school? Or in Milan?

Vincenzo knew her deceased father's last name had been Rizzo. Everyone called her mother Mirella. He'd heard the story that her husband, who worked in the estate stables, had died of an infection in his leg. After that, Mirella moved up from the village where they'd lived before his death and was allowed rooms in the rear of the *castello* with her little girl, Gemma.

One of the cooks who'd lived there, too, had had a child of the same age, named Bianca. Vincenzo couldn't remember when he and his cousin Dimi had started playing with them on the grounds of the estate. They were probably four and five years old.

Strict lines between social classes were drawn to prevent them from being together, but like all children, they found a way. He remembered his eighth birthday, when Gemma entered the courtyard where he and Dimi had been practicing archery with his new bow. She gave him a little lemon ricotta cheesecake her mother had baked just for him. He'd never tasted anything so good in his life.

From that day on, Gemma found ways to slip sweets to him from the kitchen. They'd go to their hiding place at the top of the tower and sit outside, straddling the crenellated wall while they ate his favorite *sfogliatelli*. When he looked down from that same wall now, he realized they could have fallen to their deaths at any time.

An hour later he went to bed, but he couldn't turn

off his thoughts. When he'd had to leave Europe in the dead of night, he hadn't been able to tell Gemma why and hadn't dared make contact with her. Days, weeks, months and finally years went by, but she'd always lingered in his memory.

To think that while he'd been in New York buying and selling businesses and building new companies over the last decade, she'd been in Florence working heaven knew how many hours, day in and day out, before ending up back at the *castello* as executive pastry chef. *Incredibile!*

CHAPTER THREE

GEMMA HAD BEEN in a state of disbelief since last night. A Signor Manolis, the business manager, had called to tell her she'd been hired to be the executive pastry chef at the Castello Supremo Hotel and Ristorante di Lombardi! She was to report to him at noon today.

Things like this just didn't happen, not to a new culinary graduate. But it was, and it meant she didn't have to leave Italy. By some miracle she was going back to where she'd known years of happiness…being friends and falling in love with Vincenzo before that dreadful moment when she'd learned of his disappearance.

Don't think about that terrible morning when the duca *destroyed your life and your mother's. That part of your life was over a long time ago. Let the memories go...you're the new pastry chef. And now it's possible you can find out what happened to Vincenzo.* One of her new bosses had to have information.

But a huge new problem beset her.

How was she going to tell her mother about this? Her dear mother, who was in England and knew nothing yet.

Gemma flew around the room in a panic. How

would her *mamma* react to this after all the many sacrifices she'd made for her daughter over the years? Would it be like pouring acid on a wound? Or could Gemma make her see that this might just be the way to turn the ugliness around?

And what greater triumph than for Mirella's daughter to arrive at the *castello* as executive pastry chef? Gemma's mother had been hired by the old, beloved *duca*, Vincenzo's grandfather. Now Mirella's daughter would be following in her footsteps. Best of all, her mother wouldn't have to leave Italy and could stay in Florence if she wanted to. These thoughts and more filled her mind while she tried to convince herself this could work.

After showering, she decided to wear her other suit, consisting of a navy skirt and a short-sleeved white jacket with navy piping and buttons. Though she swept her wavy hair back with a clip when she cooked, today she left it to hang down to her shoulders from the side part.

Being five foot seven, she mostly wore comfortable flats for cooking. But on this special occasion she wanted to look her best and slipped on strappy navy heels. Tiny pearl studs were the only jewelry she wore besides her watch and her grandmother's ring she would always wear in remembrance of her.

Gemma didn't need blusher. Excitement had filled her cheeks with color. With a coating of frost-pink lipstick and some lemon-scented lotion, she was ready and walked out to her car without her feet touching the ground.

After stopping at the same trattoria for breakfast, she headed for the *castello*. Four days ago she'd been upset that she couldn't apply for a position in France. But she hadn't known what was awaiting her at the former ducal residence in Milan.

Yesterday she'd worked alongside another applicant who was hoping to be chosen executive head chef. The five-star hotel he'd come from in Paris was renowned throughout Europe. To be stolen to work here meant he was the best of the best.

Gemma had taken French and English all the years she'd ever gone to school. Her mother had insisted on it, which had turned out to be advantageous for her. Some of her classes at the culinary school had been taught by various French experts, and she'd been thankful she didn't have to struggle with the language.

After they'd been introduced, she wouldn't say Monsieur Troudeau was rude. If anything he treated her as if she were invisible. No chitchat. Naturally he was shocked that such a young woman was vying for the pastry chef position. She'd ignored him and had concentrated on the pastries she'd planned to make.

The newly renovated kitchen with state-of-the-art equipment had been a dream. If only her mother could have worked under such unparalleled conditions...but that was in the past. Perhaps her mother could come to the *castello* and see the way it had been renovated. And instead of the ducal staff and family, Gemma would now be making pastry for the jet set, royals, celebrities and dignitaries of the world. She still couldn't believe it.

This time when she drove up to the front of the *castello*, she saw a black Maserati parked there. Maybe it belonged to the business owner with the strong accent who'd phoned her. Gemma got out of her car and hurried up the steps. When she entered the lobby of the hotel, she saw a fit, dark blond man, maybe six foot one and thirtyish, waiting for her behind the counter. His hazel eyes swept over her.

"You must be Signorina Bonucci. I'm Takis Manolis."

"How do you do?" She shook his hand. The signor was another good-looking man, dressed more formally in a suit and tie. This one had rugged features and probably needed to shave often. He spoke passable Italian and reminded her of some of the guys she'd met at school, possibly Turkish or Greek.

"I'm still trying to come down from the clouds since your phone call."

He flashed her a quick smile. "Congratulations."

Her eyes smarted. "I'm so happy I could burst."

"We're happy, too. Now that we've found you, we can get going on the preparations for the grand opening. If you'll come back to my office, we'll start the paperwork and sort out all the little details to make this a happy working experience for you."

Once again she found herself walking around the counter and followed him to one of the offices down the hallway. He kept his room tidy and asked her to sit down while he took his place behind the desk.

When they'd finished, he told her to report for work the day after tomorrow at nine in the morning. All staff would be assembled in the grand ballroom off the dining room for an orientation meeting to meet the new owners. Throughout the day there would be sessions to discuss policies, after which she would meet with the newly hired kitchen staff. "Do you have any questions?"

"Just one, but it doesn't have anything to do with the position. Would you be able to tell me how it is that the Gagliardi family no longer lives here? I once lived here with my mother, who cooked for the old *duca*. I find it impossible to believe that this magnificent monument, if you will, has been turned into a hotel after centuries of being the ducal seat of the region."

He studied her for a moment, but it gave her a strange feeling. "You'll have to speak to the only man who can answer that question for you."

At last there was someone who knew something. "Do you have a phone number where I can reach him?"

"I can do better than that. If you'll wait here, I'll send him in to you." He got up from the chair and left the room.

Her heart began to thud while she waited. Maybe this man would be able to tell her where she could find Vincenzo. Perhaps this man could tell her where he'd gone that night or where Dimi was. It seemed impossible for a family to just vanish.

What if he's not alive? That question had haunted her for years. *No, no. Don't think that way.* By now he was probably married to a princess and had children he adored.

Gemma couldn't bear to think that he might have found someone else. *Oh, Gemma. You're still the same lovesick fool from years ago.*

Vincenzo was on the phone with Annette when Takis walked in on him. "She's in my office waiting for you," his friend whispered before leaving him alone.

His pulse sped up. Gemma was only a door away.

"Vince? Didn't you hear me?" Annette asked him.

He sucked in his breath. "Yes," he said in English, "but someone just came in and it's important. I promise to call you by this evening, my time."

"I hope you mean that."

"Of course."

"We haven't been together for five weeks. I miss you terribly."

He just couldn't tell her the same thing back. "I have to go. Talk to you later."

He rang off and got to his feet, dressed in trousers and a polo shirt. To see Gemma again meant facing demons he'd tried to repress for years. Too many emotions collided at the same time—anxiety, excitement, curiosity, pain, guilt. Terrible guilt.

She'd been with him the night he'd been at his most vulnerable. The night after that, he'd been forced to flee before more tragedy could befall the family. The two of them had only been seventeen and eighteen, yet the memory of those intense feelings was as fresh to him right now as it had been ten years ago.

Since he'd returned to Italy, thoughts of Gemma had come back full force. At times he'd been so preoccupied, the guys were probably ready to give up on him. To think that after all this time and searching for her, she was right here. Bracing himself, he took the few steps necessary to reach Takis's office.

With the door ajar he could see a polished-looking woman in a blue-and-white suit with dark honey-blond hair falling to her shoulders. She stood near the desk with her head bowed, so he couldn't yet see her profile.

Vincenzo swallowed hard to realize Gemma was no longer the teenager with short hair he used to spot when she came bounding up the stone steps of the *castello* from school wearing her uniform. She'd grown into a curvaceous woman.

"Gemma." He said her name, but it came out gravelly.

A sharp intake of breath reverberated in the office. She wheeled around. Those unforgettable brilliant green eyes with the darker green rims fastened on him. A stillness seemed to surround her. She grabbed hold of the desk.

"Vincenzo—I—I think I must be hallucinating."

"I'm in the same condition." His gaze fell on the lips he'd kissed that unforgettable night. Their shape hadn't changed, nor the lovely mold of her facial features.

She appeared to have trouble catching her breath. "What's going on? I don't understand."

"Please sit down and I'll tell you."

He could see she was trembling. When she didn't do his bidding, he said, "I have a better idea. Let's go for a ride in my car. It's parked out front. We'll drive to the lake at the back of the estate, where no one will bother us. Maybe by the time we reach it, your shock will have worn off enough to talk to me."

Hectic color spilled into her cheeks. "Surely you're joking. After ten years of silence, you suddenly show up here this morning, honestly thinking I would go anywhere with you?"

He'd imagined anger if he ever had the chance to see her again. But he'd never expected the withering ice in her tone. Her delivery had debilitated him.

"Four days ago I applied for a position at this new hotel. Yesterday I was told I'd been hired, and now you walk in here big as life. I feel like I'm in the middle of a bizarre dream where you're back from the dead."

That described his exact state of mind. "You're not the only one feeling disoriented," he murmured. He felt as if he'd been thrown back in time, but they were no longer teenagers, and she was breathtaking in her anger.

"How long have you been in Milan?"

"Over the last six months I've made many trips here from New York."

"New York," she whispered. A crushed expression broke out on her face.

"When Dimi told me the *castello* had gone into receivership, two of my friends in New York and I decided to go into business with Dimi and turn it into a hotel. We couldn't let our family home be seized by the government or sold off to a foreign entity."

"It's yours by right, surely, unless that was a lie, too."

"It *was* mine by right…once. But that's a long story."

She shook her head. "I tried to imagine where you'd gone. I'd supposed you had friends somewhere in Europe, but it never occurred to me you would leave for the States." Gemma rubbed her hands against her hips in a gesture of abject desolation.

Vincenzo pushed ahead with the story he'd decided to use as cover. "I'd turned eighteen and decided it was time I made my mark and proved myself by making my own money. But my father would never have approved, so I had to leave without his knowledge."

"Or mine," she whispered so forlornly it shattered him.

"I couldn't do it any other way." He didn't dare tell her the real circumstances. She'd suffered enough. Vincenzo's guilt was so great, he was more convinced than ever that she'd been better off without him and still needed protection from the hideous truth.

"Are you trying to tell me that there wasn't even one moment in ten years when you could send me as much as a postcard to let me know you were alive?" Her voice was shaking, partly with rage, partly pain. He could hear it because pain echoed in his heart, too.

"I didn't know where to write to you, let alone call you. Dimi didn't know where you'd gone and looked endlessly for you. You'll never know how I've suffered over that."

He heard another sharp intake of breath. "Are you honestly trying to tell me that you looked for me?"

The depth of her pain was worse than he'd imagined. "Over the last ten years I've had private investigators searching for you. I've never stopped."

"I don't believe you." It came out like a hiss. "Has Dimi been in New York with you, too?"

"No. He lives in Milan with Zia Consolata."

Her face paled, and a hand went to her throat. A nerve throbbed at the base where he'd kissed her many times.

"I've heard all I need to hear."

In the next breath, she moved toward the door. Before he could comprehend, she flung it open and raced down the hall to the lobby. He'd never seen her in high heels before. She moved fast on those long gorgeous legs of hers.

Vincenzo started after her, noticing her hair swish and shimmer in the sunshine with every movement. He didn't catch up until she'd reached her car. Too many questions about her life were battering him at once. He wanted to make up to her for all the pain he'd put her through by disappearing without a word. Vincenzo couldn't let her get away from him. Not now.

"Where do you think you're going?"

She ignored him and opened the car door. He was aware of a lemon scent coming from her that assailed his senses. Right this minute her fragrance and femininity wrapped around him like they had done years ago, and his desire for her was palpable.

Once seated, she slammed the car door. Through the open window he saw her put the key in the ignition.

"We have to talk, Gemma!"

Her cheeks had turned scarlet with anger. "That's how I felt for days, weeks, months, even years until the need was burned out of me."

"You don't mean that," he ground out.

"Let me explain it this way. Remember our discussion about one of the films of the *Count of Monte Cristo*? If you don't, I do. Mercedes had waited years for Edmond Dantes, the man she loved. But when he suddenly appeared years later, he'd changed beyond recognition and she said goodbye to him.

"I related totally to her feelings then and now. I celebrate your return to life and all the billions of dollars you've made in New York, Vincenzo Gagliardi. I wish you well. Please tell the business manager that

I've changed my mind and won't be taking the job after all. *Arrivederci*, signor."

Wild with pain, Gemma backed away and flew down the road leading to the town below. Her eyes stung. By the time she reached the *pensione*, she realized she'd lashed out for all the years she'd been crushed by his silence.

And for his being so damned gorgeous it hurt to look at him. In ten years he'd grown into a stunning man. Standing six foot three with hard muscles and hair black as midnight, he was the personification of male beauty in her eyes.

She could hardly breathe when he'd walked into Signor Manolis's office. No wonder she hadn't been able to go on seeing Paolo. The memory of Vincenzo had always stood in the way. *He* was the reason she hadn't been able to find happiness with another man.

When they'd been together for the last time, he'd imprinted himself on her. She'd read about such things in books of fiction, but the love she'd felt for him had been real and life changing.

To think she'd suffered ten years before learning that he'd left Italy with the sole desire to earn money! Being the *duca* apparent wasn't enough. All the time they'd been growing up, he'd never once shown signs of greed in his nature. But it turned out he was just like his father!

The moment he'd reached legal age, he'd disappeared like a rabbit down a hole to add more assets to the massive family fortune. Apparently if you were a Gagliardi with a title, you could never have enough!

She couldn't credit it. And no one had known where he'd gone except Dimi.

Because of Gemma's involvement with the *duca*'s son, her mother had paid a huge price the night he'd taken off without telling his father. Shame on her for believing in something that had been a piece of fiction in her mind and heart. How many times had her mother tried to pound it in her head that she and Vincenzo would always be worlds apart?

She could hear her mother's voice. She and Vincenzo hadn't just been two ordinary teenagers indulging in a romantic fantasy. She was from the lower class, while he was an aristocrat who would one day become the Duca di Lombardi.

Any woman he married would have to be a princess, like his aunt and his mother. Day in and day out, her mother had cautioned her against her attachment to Vincenzo, but Gemma hadn't listened, so sure she was of his love.

After she reached the *pensione*, her troubled cry resounded in the car's interior. If she hadn't applied for the position at the *castello*, they would never have seen each other again in this lifetime.

You simply can't let what he's done destroy your life.

For a few minutes she struggled for composure so the *padrona di casa* wouldn't know anything was wrong. Then Gemma went inside to gather her things before driving back to Florence. Her cousin wouldn't have to know what had gone on. Gemma could simply tell her she was still looking for a position but that it would take some time.

While she packed her toiletries in the bathroom,

there was a knock on the door. Gemma told the *padrona* to come in.

"*Scusi*, signorina." She shut the door. "There's a gentleman outside from the *castello* wishing to speak to you in private."

Her heart knocked against her chest, but she kept packing and tried to feign nonchalance. "Who is it?"

"Signorina—" She ran over to her with excitement. "I would never have believed it, but it's the dashing young Duca di Lombardi himself, all grown up."

She trembled. "Surely you're mistaken." What else could she say?

"No, years ago the police looked for him and circulated pictures." Gemma remembered those policemen. "I would know him anywhere. He has the Gagliardi eyes."

She moaned. Those silvery eyes were legendary. Had he decided to use his title with the *padrona* to get what he wanted? Gemma hadn't thought Vincenzo would go so far as to follow her here, but like his father, he did whatever he wanted. Well, he couldn't force her to work at the restaurant!

Now that Gemma had shown up on his radar, it seemed he'd decided it was all right to fulfill the role destined for him from birth. Though she wanted to ask the *padrona* to tell Vincenzo she wasn't available, she couldn't do that. The older woman wasn't a servant, and Gemma didn't want her involved.

"Thank you for telling me. I'm leaving now and going back to Florence. I've left your money on the table. You've been very kind."

Gemma picked up her bag and walked outside to find Vincenzo lounging against the front of her car with his strong arms folded. The *padrona* smiled at him one last time before disappearing back through the doors.

Gemma put her bag in the rear seat. "Why did you follow me? I thought I made it clear that I can't accept the position of pastry chef. You're crazy if you're trying to expunge your guilt this way. Perhaps not guilt, exactly... A *duca* doesn't suffer that emotion like normal people, right? Yet he's known to give payment to someone like the cook's daughter for past services rendered. However, I can assure you that it's wasted on me."

A little nerve throbbed at the side of his compelling mouth, a mouth she'd kissed over and over before he'd told her she had to leave. "Is that what I'm doing?" he fired in a wintry voice.

"Yes! I'm quite sure you didn't offer the new executive chef a room at the *castello*, but Signor Manolis was told to offer me one."

The brief silence on his part upset her even more, because he didn't deny it.

"I knew it! The truth is, I don't deserve this job. The offer was too good to be true. I sensed there had to be a catch somewhere. I just didn't realize *you* had everything to do with it."

"Would it be so terrible of me to want to do something for you after the way I left without telling you? Let me make this up to you."

"I don't want anything from you, Vincenzo."

"If you're worried about the bedroom at the *castello*, I promise it won't be the back room behind the kitchen where you and your mother once lived."

"It's a moot point, but I wouldn't mind if it were."

"Nevertheless, all of that area was renovated along with the kitchen. The offer for you to stay at the *castello* will always stand."

"Why aren't you listening to me? I was shattered that you didn't say goodbye, that you didn't even let me know you were alive, but as for the rest, you owe me nothing!"

"That's not true."

"Think back to that night! Because you were in too much physical pain from that terrible fall from your horse, we didn't make love, even if we came close. Let's not forget I was as eager as you. Those moments happen to teenagers all the time! I had the hots for you, as they say in the US."

He grimaced. "Where did you learn that expression?"

"I picked up some American slang from the students at culinary school. So forget trying to fix what can't be fixed. I don't want to be compensated with a position of this magnitude or the extra perks that come with it. I understand there are two other applicants you can choose from."

"Three, but that's not the issue here."

She hadn't known that. "Then there's no problem."

Lines darkened his striking features. "You're wrong, Gemma. As for your expertise as a chef, the desserts made by you overwhelmed the committee. You have to know the decision to hire you was unanimous."

"I'll never really know, will I?"

His chest rose and fell visibly. "What do I have to do to convince you? Both Takis and Cesare are connoisseurs of fine food and wine. They recognize what will bring heads of state, kings, princes and world celebrities to the hotel over and over again. They chose you."

"Does it matter? I have interviews with two restaurateurs in Barcelona and London. If one of them hires me, I'll know I got the job for my cooking ability, nothing else."

She climbed behind the wheel. At least he didn't try to stop her.

"Where are you going?"

"Back to Florence."

"To the Bonucci Bakery? I saw the address on your application."

"Yes."

He stood there with his legs slightly apart, piercing her with those fabulous eyes. "You'll be driving in heavy traffic."

Since when had that become a concern? For the last ten years he hadn't known if she were dead or alive. He'd been flying from New York to Milan for the last six months on business. Her temper flared again.

"Vincenzo—I haven't been a teenager for years and I love to drive." She started the engine.

He moved closer. "Before you leave, tell me about your mother. How is she?"

Her bitter laugh shook him to the core. "She's alive and well, not that you'd care or be the least bit interested. Now I really have to go."

To her profound relief, he stepped back so she could drive away. Through the rearview mirror she saw his incredibly male physique standing there until she rounded the next corner.

The irony of running away from him after looking for him all these years wasn't lost on her. She drove back to Florence feeling as if she'd jumped off a precipice into the void.

CHAPTER FOUR

VINCENZO REACHED FOR his phone and left a message for the guys to say that he wouldn't be back at the *castello* until late. There were other calls from his assistant and his attorney in New York on his voice mail. None of them sounded urgent. He would deal with them later. But Annette's latest message demanded his attention. Earlier that morning he'd promised to call her back.

After putting on his sunglasses, he climbed in his Maserati and followed Gemma to Florence. The satellite navigation would lead him to the Bonucci Bakery. There was no way he would let her turn things around and disappear on him. He needed the chance to talk to her. The depth of her pain had caused him to reel. This was worse than anything he'd imagined if he'd ever seen her again.

While he was en route, he phoned Annette.

"Is it possible you've found some time for me?" she teased, but he heard her underlying impatience and didn't blame her.

"I'm sorry, but I've had business that has taken priority."

"Vince, you seem different. What's wrong?"

There was no way to explain to her what was going on inside him right now. But Annette deserved to hear how he felt even if it was going to hurt her. "You've asked me before if there was a special woman in my life. I've told you no and would never lie to you about that. But in my youth I fell in love with an Italian girl I haven't seen or heard from in ten years. Today I met up with her by accident."

He was still trying to recover.

After an ominous quiet, she said, "So what are you saying? That after all this time you find you're still in love and don't want me to come for the opening?"

He took a deep breath. "I'm saying that a big portion of my past caught up with me today. To be frank, I'm reeling." It wouldn't have been fair to lie to her.

"I sensed there was someone else all this time. She must have a powerful hold on you for those feelings to have lasted over a decade."

"Annette, I can't honestly tell you where this is headed."

What he did know was that seeing Gemma again had stirred up longings in him more intense than he could ever have imagined. To find out that Gemma wasn't married yet was a miracle. But her anger had been so intense, he needed to talk to her about it.

"Neither can I," Annette murmured. "Under the circumstances, I don't intend to wait for calls from you that might not come."

"I haven't meant to hurt you."

"I realize that, but on my part I always felt something was holding you back. If you ever figure it out and find yourself whole of heart, you know where to find me."

Even deeply upset, she had a graciousness and maturity he had to admire. "I'm sorry, Annette. Give me some time and I'll get back to you."

"I won't be holding my breath, Vince."

He heard the click.

Though Vincenzo hadn't wanted to cause her pain, his sense of relief that he didn't have to pretend with her had removed a burden. He'd told her the only truth he knew, since he needed time to deal with his emotions.

The reality of seeing Gemma again, the incredible coincidence that she'd applied for the pastry chef position, had knocked the foundations from under him.

At ten after six, he entered Florence at the height of evening traffic and found the Bonucci pastry shop. After searching everywhere for her old Fiat, he drove around the corner into an alley. Her blue car sat beside a stairway leading to the second floor of the bakery.

He found another spot along the crowded one-way street. Once he'd parked his car at the rear of the *pasteria* next door, he took the steps two at a time to the little porch outside her door. To think all these years since leaving the *castello* this place had been her home. How could he or Dimi have known?

He knocked twice.

Soon he heard, "*Chi e?*"

He was glad she didn't automatically open the door. Anyone could be out here. "It's Vincenzo. I would have phoned you I was coming, but I wasn't sure you would answer."

There was a long silence. "Go away!"

"I can't. Surely you can see that," he fought back. "I never expected any of this to happen. Even if you refuse to come to work for us, how could you think I would just let you drive away?"

"I'm not going to open my door. Go back to your home, Vincenzo."

What home? He hadn't known that feeling in the ten years since he'd last been with her. He broke out in a cold sweat. So much damage had been done, he didn't know if he could repair any of it, even if he told her the real truth of everything.

"Would you deny your time to any other person you knew well in the past who wanted to get reacquainted after a long period of separation? Since I've come all this way and am starving, let's have dinner at the *pasteria* next door. We'll order some wine and reminisce over a time when life was wonderful for both of us."

"That would be a mistake."

"You don't recommend the food? If anyone would know whether it was good or not, you're the one."

"Be serious, Vincenzo," she snapped.

"I'm trying to be. You have no idea how isolated I've felt all these years. Dimi and I are the only ones left who can talk about that other life and relate. Our fathers kept us under virtual lock and key, with bodyguards controlling everything we did. You better than anyone know that they only allowed us to have a few friends they picked.

"But all these years there's been a huge hole, and you know why. Because that other life included you. I need a few hours with you, Gemma." His voice shook. "Will you grant me that much?"

He waited for her response. "You're not the person I thought you were, Vincenzo. Otherwise you wouldn't have left without so much as a goodbye. I was never good enough for you, we both know that. We've led separate lives since your disappearance, and we were never the same people growing up."

His eyes closed tightly, but her pain kept her talking.

"You're from one world and I'm from another. A little while ago the reminder came from the *padrona*, who said the Duca di Lombardi was standing outside waiting to see me. There's no need for us to talk or be with each other again, Vincenzo."

She knew where to thrust through to the gut. Her mother had done a sensational job of indoctrinating her over the nonsense of ancient class distinctions he couldn't abide.

"If I swear on my mother's soul to leave you strictly alone, will you accept the position at the *castello* to see us through the first three months? Takis and Cesare will be the ones working with you. I'll stay out of your way unless there's a professional reason why I have to talk to you about something."

Was she even listening?

"You can put me on probation, Gemma. If I make one mistake, you can leave immediately, no questions asked. If at the end of the three months you still want to leave, you'll receive impeccable recommendations and be given a generous severance package of your choosing."

"Why would you enter into an arrangement like that when you know how I feel?"

"Because your expertise as a pastry chef is unparalleled. My partners will be bitterly disappointed to learn that you've refused the position because you can't forgive me for my past sins."

"It's not a matter of forgiveness. The trust is gone."

Vincenzo couldn't take this much longer. "*They* trust me. You have to understand that I asked them to go into business with me. But for me they wouldn't be here. Not only my integrity, but their financial lives and reputations are on the line. Like me, they want our business venture to work."

"As you told me earlier, you have three other applicants eager to work there."

"My friends don't want anyone else and are convinced that with everything we've put in place including your cooking, we'll succeed beyond our wildest dreams. I *know* we will, because I grew up on your mother's delicacies that you've perfected. You have no equal, Gemma."

"Please leave."

"I only have one more thing to say. You don't have to make a decision this very minute. I'm on my way back to Milan." *I've got to stop and see Dimi.* He wasn't going to believe Gemma had been found.

"Gemma? If you don't show up for your first orientation meeting with rest of the staff the day after tomorrow, then I'll tell my partners you found you couldn't accept the position after all because of a family emergency at the bakery. Naturally we'll choose one of the other pastry chef finalists."

She still said nothing.

His pain had reached its zenith. "*Arrivederci, tesoro.*"

Gemma gasped. The night in his bedroom when they'd been wrapped in each other's arms, he'd called her his treasure. While her world spun in reaction to that endearment, she watched out the window. His car traveled down the street until she couldn't see him anymore.

Surely to accept his offer would mean that she had no self-control, that all he had to do was summon her in his inimitable, seductive way and she'd come running.

What else could she expect when Vincenzo's immoral father and uncle had been his role models? He might not think he could ever behave as they'd done, but the precedent had been set for decades. Once he married a princess and had children, the need for distraction would come.

With business enterprises on either side of the Atlantic, he'd have ample opportunities to be with women his wife wouldn't know about. Or would pretend not to know about. Who better than the adoring daughter of the former cook to fill the position as one of his mistresses and provide him amusement during secret getaways when he was in Italy?

Gemma, unmarried and childless, wouldn't have a life while she waited for those moments of rapture with him. Little by little his need for her would grow more infrequent while she went on getting older and more unfulfilled. Over the centuries, women of the lower class had done as much in order to be with the titled men they'd loved, but Gemma refused to be one of them!

She'd been afraid he'd break her down with words like this. Somehow he was succeeding despite her determination not to listen or be moved. Tears dripped from her eyes while she called Filippa, who'd just come out of a bad relationship.

Her friend knew Gemma's history. When she heard Vincenzo was back in Gemma's life, she cried out in shock. For the next hour Gemma told her everything.

Before they hung up, Filippa asked her one salient question. "Did he ever do anything in his past that caused you not to trust him until the day when you learned he had disappeared?"

"No. But we're grown up now, and he's the *duca*. I can't see our lives together in any way, shape or form."

"From what you've told me, he hasn't asked for more than a three-month probationary period to help him get their restaurant off the ground. He wants you to have this position because you were the top applicant. Naturally he wants to make it up to you for leaving without an explanation."

"I know."

"Remember that he said he needed to make money and couldn't let his father find out his plans. That sounds like a strong reason for what he did. And don't forget he said he looked for you over all these years. So what more can he do to make you feel any better? You *did* sign on with them in good faith, and they did, too."

Gemma sniffed. Put that way, there was no argument. "You're right."

"If I were you, I'd agree to his offer. He promised to leave you alone away from work, and he would be a fool if he reneges. Just think, Gemma—the opportunity to be the head pastry chef there will give you entrée anywhere in the world when you leave. With a five-star recommendation, you'll have carte blanche with whichever wonderful restaurant in France you'd like and you could realize your dream."

Filippa made it sound possible, even easy. But she'd never met Vincenzo Gagliardi and had no comprehension of the man Gemma had always loved. Every day of those three months she worked at the *castello*, she'd be in agony thinking about him, desiring him. Was he on the premises, or was he in New York? How soon would the media reveal breaking news about the fiercely handsome, dashing Duca di Lombardi coming back home? Which gorgeous princess would be the one to catch his eye and become his bride and the mother of his children?

"Gemma? Are you still there?"

She blinked away the moisture. "Yes, of course. I was deep in thought. Sorry."

"So what are you going to do?"

"I'm not sure, but I love you for listening to me and helping me sort through my pain."

"You've done the same thing for me too many times to count. I've got to go right now. Let me know what you finally decide."

"I will. Ciao, Filippa."

"Ciao, *amica*."

While Gemma fixed herself an omelet, she reran their conversation over in her mind. By the time she went to bed, her pragmatic side had taken over. She needed a job and had been offered one that would make her the envy of everyone at her school. There was no way she could turn down his offer.

When she gave her mother the news, she'd tell her it was only for a three-month period. But she'd wait to tell her *mamma* anything until Mirella got back from her vacation. By then Gemma would have lined up another job so that when the three months were up, they'd leave Lombardi and the *castello* behind.

With a top recommendation, she would be set up to find a great restaurant in the South of France that would hire her. In time she could accrue enough savings to put down roots.

Gemma had dreamed of buying a little villa in Vence or Grasse with a garden and some fruit trees overlooking the Mediterranean. She'd won an award for her jam. Since her mother would be living with her, maybe they'd make their own and sell it locally. Anything could happen. Filippa had made her see that.

For now she would have to trust Vincenzo to keep their bargain. As she'd told her friend, she'd trusted Vincenzo in the past. It would be her own fault if she couldn't remain strong and stay away from him.

Grateful for her friend's advice, she woke up early the next morning and got busy house cleaning. When her mother and aunt returned from England, they'd find the place spotless. At four that afternoon, she left with her large suitcase and went down the steps to her car parked in the alley. It was best her cousin didn't know where she was going until Gemma had told her mother everything first.

When she reached Sopri, she called on the *padrona di casa* and told her she would like to stay at the *pensione* for a three-month period because she'd be working at the new hotel. Would that be possible?

The older woman couldn't have been more delighted and they settled on a good price. "You'll be working for the *duca*. Any arrangement you want is fine." On that note she let Gemma into the room she'd had before with a huge smile. Such was Vincenzo's effect on every female, young or old.

Gemma got settled in and pulled out her laptop. She needed to send emails to London and Barcelona and thank them for setting up appointments with her. In her note she told them she was sorry but she'd found another position. If by any chance it didn't work out at the *castello*, she wondered if they would allow her to reapply?

Once that was done, she got ready for bed and lay back against the pillows. Tomorrow morning she'd be meeting with Signor Donati at nine for the orientation meeting. The newly hired kitchen staff would also be present. Being part of a hotel, the restaurant would serve meals throughout the day and evening as well as provide room service. Such organization required a genius at the head.

Vincenzo.

Because he was the one who'd masterminded everything, he would always have input. She expected that. Naturally they'd see each other coming and going, much the same as they'd done ten years earlier. But this time everything would be different. In order to survive, she was forced to put on her armor and leave the sweet innocence of their youthful love in the past.

After confiding in Dimi the evening before, Vincenzo had worked through the night on his personal business affairs here in Italy. Establishing Nistri Technologies in the south of the country consumed a lot of his spare time, but that was good. He existed on coffee, trying not to think about what would happen if Gemma didn't show up today. He hadn't told the guys anything, not wanting to alarm them.

His cousin didn't have great hopes where Gemma was concerned. She was an unknown entity at this point. Vincenzo didn't like hearing Dimi's opinion but appreciated that his was the voice of reason.

After a shower and shave, he put on a business suit and tie before leaving his tower room to go downstairs. His watch said it was ten to nine, and already the ballroom appeared full. But as he looked around, his worst nightmare was confirmed, because Gemma was nowhere in sight.

His fear that she'd left Florence and he'd never see her again came close to paralyzing him, but for the guys' sake, he had to pull himself together. He'd wanted to hire security to keep an eye on her but had resisted the impulse. That's what his father had done to him and Dimi. He knew Gemma had already accused him in her heart of being like his father. He didn't dare make that mistake.

At their first break in the morning schedule, Vincenzo would take his partners aside and give them the bad news. While they ran the next segment without him, he would have to go to his office and contact their other applicants. If none of them were available, there was more work to do.

A blackness had descended on Vincenzo as he joined Takis in front of their awaiting audience. He was on the verge of asking him about Cesare when the Sicilian entered through the tall double doors.

Gemma followed him in. At the first sight of her, Vincenzo's heart kicked him in the ribs so hard he almost moaned aloud. Somehow she'd managed to put aside her hurt and anger enough to accept his proposition.

She'd come dressed in a fabulous peach-colored suit. It was a miracle he had any breath left. He couldn't take his eyes off her as she found a chair on the end of a row halfway toward the front. Vincenzo was still in a state of shock when Takis stood up with the microphone in hand.

"Welcome, everyone! Take a look around. The success of the new Castello Supremo Hotel and Ristorante di Lombardi is in your hands. By the end of the day it's our hope you'll feel like family. It's the only way our enterprise will work."

Vincenzo had hoped everyone they'd hired would feel like family. After all the work he and his partners had done over the last six months, he couldn't help but be proud of what they'd accomplished so far.

He was happy that he'd asked the guys to employ as many local staff as possible, especially those who hadn't been able to find work lately. It was a way to give back to the community that had been harmed because his father and uncle had been such bad people.

For a long time he'd been worried that he'd involved his friends in a project that could have professional as well as personal repercussions if things didn't go well. But Gemma's appearance a minute go went a long way to help calm some of those fears. With both of them together again in the same room, he felt an odd sense of rightness.

"At your interviews, you were given a small history of the *castello*. For as long as you work here, guests will ask you repeatedly about this iconic hundred-years-old structure. As you've learned, it was the home of the first Duca di Lombardi of the house of Gagliardi in the eighteen hundreds.

"Today I'm honored to introduce one of the owners and chief operating officer for the estate, security and publicity, Vincenzo Nistri Gagliardi, seated on my right."

A collective sound of surprise was followed by resounding applause that filled the room. With the media calling for information at this point, Vincenzo had given Takis permission to offer public disclosure of their three-owner enterprise. He'd felt it was time he embraced his name again. But there'd be no mention of the family title.

"I'm Takis Manolis, one of the owners and general manager of the hotel. On my left is Cesare Donati, the other owner and general manager for the restaurant." More clapping ensued.

Takis finished talking and handed Vincenzo the mic.

Vincenzo only intended to say a few words that would put the floating rumors to rest. "Some of you may know this was my home for the first eighteen years of my life. Though I've spent the last ten years in New York City, my roots are here."

The girl who made it my own private heaven is seated among you.

"My business partners and I hope this will become a desired destination for locals and tourists from around the globe. If we all work together, I know it will be a great success. Thank you."

This time everyone got to their feet and kept clapping. He handed the mic to Cesare and sat down.

His friend took over the reins. When the noise subsided, he introduced their head chef, Monsieur Maurice Troudeau. Then he turned to Gemma.

"In the words of Schiaparelli, 'a good cook is like a sorceress who dispenses happiness.' That would describe the Italian desserts of our executive pastry chef, Gemma Bonucci Rizzo. Please stand, signorina."

There was more applause.

Vincenzo's pride in her accomplishments brought a lump to his throat. At the same time he couldn't stop his eyes from fastening on the lines of her beautiful figure.

Cesare continued to introduce the entire kitchen staff that also included the sous chefs, dishwashers, and front of house staff. Takis followed by introducing the front desk group, the head of housekeeping and the laundry staff. Then it was Vincenzo's turn once more to present the estate manager and gardeners. The security men made their own presentation.

After a ten-minute break, his partners met with the employees under them to get down to specifics on the job, including the hours they would work. That left Vincenzo to circulate.

He visited Takis's group first and added a few words. Then he walked to the kitchen, where Cesare laid out the hours for each shift and their duties, which included room service and the dining room. Vincenzo refused to look at Gemma. After saying a few more words of greeting, he made certain he stayed on the far side of the room away from her.

Gemma and Maurice had been asked to make out a day's worth of sample menus for the three meals they'd serve the day of the grand opening. Cesare looked them over before passing them to Vincenzo for his opinion. Since he didn't want to give Gemma any fuel to leave and never come back, he took the menus and walked to his office.

After sitting at his desk for a few minutes, he realized that having to distance himself from her was going to be the hardest thing he would ever have to do in his life. The key was to focus on work.

He spent the next few minutes studying her dessert choices, including the rolls, breads, preserves and jams she'd suggested to accompany Maurice's entrées and specialty dishes. They were both masters at what they did. He put his seal of approval on them.

But thoughts of Gemma made it impossible for him to stand his own company any longer. He walked to Cesare's office to give him the menus. His friend wasn't around. Vincenzo left them on his desk and went in search of Takis, who was still in the ballroom directing some of the newly hired staff to put the chairs away.

He waved. "*Ehi*, Vincenzo—all in all, I think it went well."

"I agree." But it would have been a disaster if Gemma hadn't shown up.

"Want to have drinks on the east patio later?"

"Sounds good, but I'll see. I have to run an errand, but I should be back soon."

Vincenzo hurried out of the *castello* to his car, too restless to stay put. After getting behind the wheel, he took off and drove aimlessly. He had a hunch Gemma had spent last night at the same *pensione* as before. If he returned by way of Sopri later, he assumed he'd see her car parked in front. But much as he wanted to find out where she was staying, he didn't dare.

Instead he ended up in the little village of Cisliano, only three miles from Sopri. He passed in front of the Rho Bistro. The owners had had the unique idea of waiting for all the customers to arrive. Then they started cooking the same menu for everyone and served it at one time.

Vincenzo had eaten there several times in his youth after a bike ride with Dimi, always being followed by a guard his father had hired. On his eighteenth birthday, he and Dimi had slipped away from their tutor and the guard. They'd arranged to meet Gemma and Bianca here.

He remembered that Friday as if it had been yesterday. Bianca's mother had taken pity on him and his cousin. She'd dropped the girls off and come back for them two hours later without telling Gemma's mother, who would have been upset.

The memory of that red-letter day had taken hold of him. Wanting to relive it, he decided to go in, but parking was difficult. He ended up driving around the corner to find a spot. For the moment all he cared about was soaking up those moments when he knew they'd been crazy in love with each other.

As usual, he discovered the noisy, unpretentious place was filled with summer customers at the dinner hour. There was one empty table in the corner partially separate from the others, probably available for any overflow. He grabbed it and was served coffee while everyone waited to be served.

CHAPTER FIVE

AFTER HER LAST meeting for the day, Gemma left the *castello* experiencing so many emotions, she didn't know where to go with all her feelings. Cesare's comments about her in front of the whole assembly had been very touching. She'd enjoyed the various sessions and had gotten on well with Maurice. But overriding everything was the realization that Vincenzo was back in Lombardi.

Along with his partners, they'd turned the *castello* into a hotel and restaurant that would definitely be the envy of other resorts in Italy. She'd felt the camaraderie among the people hired and had heard their praise for the new owners. The favorable whispers about Vincenzo would have pleased him.

Part of her had wanted to go to his office and thank him for this opportunity, but it was too difficult for her to be in such close proximity to him. She feared she wouldn't be able to fight her attraction to him. But the other part of her would always struggle, because he hadn't felt she was good enough to confide in before he'd disappeared. He'd created a deep wound that would never heal.

Where was the Vincenzo she would have done

anything for? On his eighteenth birthday, she'd dared to eat a meal with him at a restaurant outside the *castello*, even knowing they could both get into terrible trouble.

Caught up in the memory, she drove to Cisliano and found a parking place at the end of the street near the Rho Bistro. She and Bianca had spent two divine hours here with Vincenzo and Dimi. The need to recapture that moment took her inside, but the place was packed. As she looked around, her gaze suddenly collided with a pair of silver eyes staring at her between black lashes.

Vincenzo—her heart knocked against her ribs. He was here?

She watched as he got to his feet and walked over to her. "It appears you and I had the same idea this evening. As you can see, the whole world is here. You're welcome to join me at my table. I think I have the only free one left."

Gemma couldn't believe this had happened, but to turn him down would be churlish at this point.

"Thank you. I have to admit I'm starving."

No sooner had he held a chair for her to sit down than the waiters started bringing the food. The menu included antipasto, risotto, sautéed mushrooms, roasted polenta and potatoes, with a dessert of *limoncello* and iced cookies.

After a few bites she said, "I had no idea you were here."

"That works both ways." He sipped his coffee. "Seeing you again has made me nostalgic for my happy past, and I found myself driving here. The meal we enjoyed on my birthday will always stand out in my mind."

"Truthfully, I'll never forget it, either," she confessed. "On the way back to my flat, I decided to drive by and see if this place still existed. We were fed so much food, I didn't think I would ever eat again."

"You're not the only one."

"I was frightened someone from the *castello* would find out and word would get back to my mother. She would have grounded me forever."

"Three weeks after my birthday, I was in New York, ending our one and only over-the-*castello*-wall experience."

Over the wall was right! But Gemma didn't want to think about the past and changed the subject.

"After the last meeting in the kitchen, Cesare told us to go home and get a good sleep before we report in the morning ready to dig in. I didn't expect to see you here, but since we have bumped into each other, I'd like to thank you for giving me the opportunity to be the pastry chef. It *is* the chance of a lifetime."

"If anyone should be doing the thanking, it's me," he came back unexpectedly. "When I saw you walk into the ballroom this morning, I was able to breathe again. Later in my office I started looking over the menus. You and Maurice stimulate the brilliance in each other. There's no doubt in my mind the food at the Castello Supremo Ristorante will bring the world to our door."

"Coming from you, that's a great compliment." But Gemma wished he'd stop being so…so nice and charming the way he'd been years ago, the way he'd been today during the orientation meeting.

He kept talking. “Cesare is the true expert. The light in his eyes after he’d studied the menus and handed them to me told me all I needed to know about how excited he is about our new chefs.” He drank more coffee.

“That’s very gratifying to hear.”

He flashed her a penetrating glance. “I can’t believe you aren’t married.”

She drank her *limoncello* too quickly and started coughing. Had he been hoping she’d found a man? Would it make him feel less guilty for disappearing from her life? Why not turn things around on him?

“What about you, Vincenzo? You’ve been in New York all this time. I don’t see a ring on your finger.”

His mouth tautened. “I’ve been too busy conducting business to think about getting married.”

No woman could resist him, so he couldn’t have suffered in that department. But there probably weren’t that many available princesses on the East Coast of the US to consider marrying. For that, he’d have to return to Europe. No doubt there’d been a short list compiled years ago for Vincenzo to consider.

She cleared her throat. “Labor-intensive work *does* have a way of interfering. Being an apprentice at the school hasn’t allowed me the time to consider marriage. They require nine to ten years from you. That doesn’t give you a spare moment to breathe.” Except for that one month with Paolo, which was a mistake.

“Understood. As long as we’re together, would you be willing to answer a question for me? Your last name is Rizzo, yet you used Bonucci on your application. Why?”

They were wading into dangerous waters now. “That’s a long story.”

“Is there some secret?”

Her eyes closed tightly. If he only knew.

“Bonucci is mother’s maiden name. When we moved to the apartment above my aunt’s bakery, Mamma told me to put Bonucci on my application. That way when I attended pastry school, it would be an easy identification with her family’s bakery.”

“Mirella was an intelligent woman and was always very kind to me and Dimi.”

Just hearing him say her mother’s name made her eyes smart. She nodded. “People love her. I love her terribly.”

“Gemma,” he murmured. “Don’t you know I’ve missed that old life more than you can imagine? I know she’s your whole world and you are hers. Interesting that after you left the *castello*, no one knew you as Gemma Rizzo. That’s why neither Dimi nor I could find you.”

Oh, no. She clenched her fists beneath the table. “Mamma would have done or said anything she could to—” Gemma stumbled “—to increase my chance to succeed.”

She knew by the flicker in his eyes that he’d caught her correction. Vincenzo was a shrewd, brilliant businessman, and she was afraid he wouldn’t let it go. “Your *mamma* got her wish. My colleagues have been praising your expertise.” Heat crept into her cheeks again, but this time anger wasn’t the culprit.

“That’s very nice to hear. Now I’ve got to go so I’ll be fresh for tomorrow.”

"Gemma," he whispered. "What aren't you telling me?"

The tone in his voice reminded her of the old Vincenzo. Slowly, steadily, he was breaking her down. His magic was getting to her. *Damn, damn, damn.* Her heart pounded so hard, she was certain he could hear it. "I don't know what you mean."

"You forget I've known you since you were four years old. When you're nervous or afraid, your voice falters. You did it just now. You said that your mother would have done or said anything to…to what, Gemma? You left out something of vital importance. What was it?"

She felt sick inside. "You're wrong."

"Now your cheeks are red. They always fill with color when you're not telling the truth." He wouldn't stop until he'd wrung it out of her.

Vincenzo, Vincenzo. "Mamma said I had to say my last name was Bonucci in order to…protect me."

His handsome face darkened with forbidding lines. "From whom?"

"I—it was a long time ago and doesn't matter."

He let out an oath, and his brows formed a black bar above his eyes. "Did you get into trouble that night after you left my room? I still had to stay in bed the next day, so I didn't see you."

Gemma was thrown by the haunted sound in his voice. "No," she answered honestly.

"Why don't I believe you?"

"Vincenzo, I promise. After looking out the door that night, I snuck down the back staircase when I knew a guard wouldn't be there. No one saw me."

"Do you swear before God?" A vein stood out in his neck.

She sensed an unfathomable depth of anxiety here. It wasn't something he could hide. "Why have you asked me that?"

His body tensed. "Because if I thought my father had been waiting in the hall and did anything to you..."

"No one saw me." It was her turn to shudder at the degree of his concern. "I swear, nothing happened to me, Vincenzo."

"Keep talking to me, Gemma. There's still something else you haven't told me."

She stirred restlessly. Now was her chance to reveal every single cruel thing his father had done to her and her mother. But looking into his eyes and seeing the pain, she found she couldn't..

"Did you get questioned after my father found out I'd gone missing?" he demanded.

Give him some of the truth so he'll be satisfied.

"He and the police commissioner interrogated everyone at the *castello*, one at a time. No one knew anything about your disappearance. At that point they looked elsewhere for answers."

"Grazie a Dio."

She heard the tremendous relief in his voice, but by the way he was staring at her, she could tell he was far from finished with her, and she started to be afraid.

"When were you let go at the *castello*?"

Her pulse raced. "Does it matter? It's all in the past."

He shook his dark head. "Did it happen after my *nonno* died?"

"Yes," she said quietly, because with that question Gemma realized he really didn't know anything that had happened. Neither did Dimi, otherwise his cousin would have told him.

His sharp intake of breath was alarming. "You're lying to me again."

She jumped up from the chair. "I can't do this anymore. Thank you for letting me eat with you. Now I have to leave."

He looked up at her. "Where are you going?"

"Back to the *pensione*."

"If you leave now, you'll never know the true reason behind my sudden disappearance and why it had to be carried out in complete secrecy."

Stunned by what he'd just said, Gemma clung to the back of the chair. *The true reason?*

"On the strength of the years you and I spent together as children and teenagers who fell in love, isn't learning the whole truth worth something to you?"

"I thought you said you left to make your own fortune and name."

"That was a by-product of the real reason I left, but I didn't tell you the truth in order to spare you more grief. I can see now that I've been wrong to do that."

Along with everything he was saying, his confession that he'd been in love with her a long time ago was almost too much to bear. Gemma couldn't talk, couldn't think.

"I don't ever remember you running out of words before, so I'm following you home." He put some bills on the table. "We need privacy because we're not finished talking, but we can't do it here. People are watching."

"You made a promise."

"I would have kept it, but you've just told me another lie. If you don't want to work at the *castello* then I'll have to live with it, but I need the truth from you first. Let's go."

With her heart in her mouth, Gemma left the restaurant and walked to the end of the street to reach her car. She started the engine and pulled into traffic. Soon she was headed for Sopri.

Through the rearview mirror she could see the Maserati following closely behind. Adrenaline gushed through her veins. Finally she would know what had happened all those years ago. It didn't take long to reach the *pensione*. Vincenzo pulled up behind her and parked his car.

Without looking at him, she went inside, leaving the door open. He followed, closing it behind him.

"Come in and sit down. Take your pick of one of the chairs or the love seat."

Vincenzo did neither. First he looked around at the small, well-furnished flat. From the living room he could see part of the bedroom. Then he walked into the kitchen, where she was clinging to the counter.

This evening, the fear that he was losing his grip on Gemma had made him realize he had to tell her the painful truth about his disappearance if he ever hoped to have a chance of keeping her in his life. All the guilt and the shame would have to come out. He'd wanted to protect her, but it was too late for that now.

But first he needed to hear what had happened to her after he'd left. He sucked in his breath. "The truth,

Gemma. All of it! How soon after I disappeared did you and your mother leave the *castello*?"

She was trembling. "The second your father learned you were missing, he came with the chief of police and guards to our rooms at six that morning, demanding to know where you were. I told him I knew nothing. They searched our rooms before the police chief said he believed me.

"Your father told my mother to get out and take her baggage with her—meaning me, of course. Your father's outrage was frightening. The idea that his son, who would one day become the Duca di Lombardi, was enjoying life below the stairs with one of the cooks' daughters put him into a frenzy.

"He vowed to make certain she never got a job anywhere else. He threw Bianca and her mother out that same morning before he left with the police to start searching the countryside for you. That's why Mamma made me use the Bonucci name, so he couldn't find us."

Vincenzo's pain bordered on fury. He fought to stay in control. "What he did was inhuman. You should never have been forced to live through such a nightmare, and all because of me. I can never hope to make this up to you."

"It's over, and he was a sick man."

His jaw hardened. "More than sick. You don't know what a frenzy is until you've seen him raging drunk. My uncle was the same. Dimi had to get away, too."

She swallowed hard. "You said he lives in Milan with his mother."

He nodded. "They left the same day as you and

your mother did, while my father was out with the police hunting for me."

"When I first met your aunt Consolata, she was in a wheelchair. I always worried about her."

"I know you did. She always spoke of you with fondness, but she isn't well and has lost her memory."

"That's so sad."

This was the girl he'd remembered and dreamed about. She'd always had a sweetness and kindness that made her stand out from any woman he'd ever known.

"Did you ever hear how she ended up in her wheelchair?"

"Mamma told me she had a disease."

"No, Gemma," he ground out. "That was a story the family made up to cover the truth. My father and my uncle Alonzo were the ones with the disease."

"What do you mean?"

"They are alcoholics. Alonzo drove Dimi's mother home from a party when he was drunk out of his mind. She begged for someone else to drive her, but he became enraged and dragged her to the car. En route home, there was a terrible crash. The man in the other car was killed and Dimi's mother was paralyzed from the waist down, unable to walk again. But as usual, my father had it hushed up to protect the family honor."

Tears splashed down her cheeks.

"Just know that since my uncle has been imprisoned, Dimi and my aunt have been able to live in peace. But there's a lot more you need to hear in order for you to understand my sudden disappearance."

"A lot more?"

His fear for what his father might have done to her

triggered other thoughts. “The night we almost made love, you thought I’d been recovering from a fall after I’d been out horseback riding.”

She nodded. “That’s what they had been gossiping about down in the kitchen. I snuck upstairs that night to see how bad your injuries were.”

“My bruises and welts weren’t because of an accident, Gemma.”

A cry escaped her lips. She looked ill. “Your *father* was responsible?”

“*Si*. He beat me almost to a pulp.” Gemma winced. “But he did worse to my *mamma*, and she died because of it.”

“Oh, Vincenzo—no—” Hot tears spurted from her eyes. “Why would he do that? She was a wonderful person.”

“My parents’ marriage was a political arrangement with a lot of money and land entailed. But my grandfather Count Nistri, the one who lived in Padua, didn’t trust his new son-in-law. Even back then my father had a reputation for drinking and gambling. But he came from a family of great wealth and was a business wizard.

“To make certain his daughter, Arianna, my mother, always had security, he’d put a fortune in a Swiss bank account for her alone.”

“He sounds like a loving man and father.”

“He was, but my father resented me having any association with him. Still, he couldn’t stop me from visiting him from time to time. My grandfather had the foresight and the means to help me get away when the time came.”

“How did he do it?”

"Through a secret source, he learned my father had been badgering my mother for her money. At that point he gave her the information to access it and passports for both of us so we could escape."

Another gasp flew out of her.

"During the last year before she died, my father started hitting her when he couldn't get at her money. She couldn't withstand all those beatings." His eyes stung with tears. "Do you have any idea what I went through, hearing her cries while I was held back by the guards so I couldn't help her?"

Gemma covered her mouth in horror.

"I was helpless. He was the acting *duca*. He was the law. No one questioned him or his authority. If I'd sent for the police, they wouldn't have stopped him. Mamma needed me, but I failed her as her son."

"Of course you didn't!" Gemma cried. "Don't say that! Don't even think it!"

"For a long time she'd begged me to take the money and escape because she feared for my life. That's when I started to plan my disappearance, but I would never have left her behind. As far as escaping, I had to be an adult and couldn't go anywhere until I was of age.

"My uncle had no reason to stop his brother, since he was in worse trouble financially and was fighting to stay out of prison. To escape my father, I had to get as far away from Italy as possible. The US suited my plan perfectly."

She shook her head. "What plan?"

"The one Dimi and I devised a year before I left."

"A whole year, and you never once told me?" Her voice shook with pain.

"I didn't dare until I knew it was safe for you. But when that time came, you were nowhere to be found in Italy. Dimi hunted endlessly for you, too. When I escaped, our family had been unraveling at the speed of sound, Gemma, but until I turned eighteen and Mamma passed away, I couldn't do anything about it. If my father had gotten wind of anything, that would have been the end of me.

"Worse, if he'd found out that you knew where I'd gone, there's no telling what price you might have had to pay. As it was, your mother paid dearly for my disappearance. Thank heaven you got away without him beating you, too."

"This is a horror story."

"After Mamma's funeral, my father followed me to my room. He'd been drinking heavily. This time he beat me with his horse whip after I'd gone to bed."

At this point Gemma was quietly sobbing.

"He thought he could force the truth from me and get his hands on Mamma's fortune. As you know, he was a tall, powerful man. He would have succeeded in killing me if he hadn't been so drunk.

"Somehow I held him off. The next night was when you came up to my room looking for me. Your loving comfort and kisses held me together. But I was afraid my father would be back. That's why I couldn't let you stay the whole night with me. I was afraid if he found us, I wouldn't have the strength to protect you."

She'd buried her face in her hands. "I understand now."

"I'll always be in hell because I couldn't protect my mother."

She lifted her head. "Thank heaven you got out of

there alive. I remember the menacing look in your father's eyes. No wonder you were running for your life."

"The night after we were together, I made my getaway with Dimi's help. But leaving you without telling you anything was the hardest thing I'd ever had to do in my life. My cousin had to take the brunt of everything, and I asked him keep me informed about you. He was frantic because he didn't know where to look for you."

"I was so hurt and angry at you, I didn't even try to say goodbye to him. I'm so sorry now. He didn't have any way of knowing where we'd gone."

Without conscious thought Vincenzo wrapped her in his arms, and they clung while she sobbed. He wept in silence with her. After her tears subsided, she said, "Tell me what happened the night you left. I want to hear everything from the moment you left your room that night."

CHAPTER SIX

A MIRACLE HAD HAPPENED, because Gemma wanted to keep talking. Vincenzo kissed her hair and forehead.

"Let's go in the other room, where we can be comfortable." He walked her trembling body to the love seat, where she sat down, then he pulled the chair closer to be face-to-face with her.

"After I got up and dressed, I snuck to Dimi's tower room at two in the morning. We hugged and then I stole down the back staircase and through the old passage no longer used to reach the outside."

"I remember it."

"Knowing the guard wouldn't be able to see me yet, I raced through the gardens to reach the forest on the estate property without problem. The family cemetery plot was a good spot to rest. Then I ran past the lake and stables to the farthest edge of the property and hid up high in a tree until another guard had passed around the perimeter and disappeared."

"The dog didn't give you away?"

"It wasn't with him. That was another miracle. I stayed free of detection for twenty more minutes before climbing the fence. You should have seen me. I ran like hell down the hillside."

A little laugh escaped. "I can just see you!"

"My destination was a farm, where I waited behind a truck for the sun to come up."

"That must have been so scary."

"Not as scary as worrying that I'd be spotted before I jumped the perimeter fence. When I saw more activity on the road, I started walking to the village."

"Did anyone recognize you?"

"I put on a baseball cap and sunglasses."

She smiled. "I would have loved to see that."

"It did the trick. A half hour's walk and I reached the bus stop that took me into central Milan, where I got off near the main train station. After buying a one-way ticket to Geneva, I boarded a second-class car and found a group of German backpackers to sit by."

"Naturally you struck up a conversation with them. I know your royal tutors taught you four different languages, including German."

"My education came in handy during that four-hour train ride to Switzerland."

"Weren't you worried someone would recognize you?"

"I was lucky and made it to Geneva without problem."

"Thank heaven."

"Around three in the afternoon, the train arrived in Geneva. I said goodbye to the other backpackers and took a taxi to the Credit Suisse bank in the town center. I'd planned every step with Dimi and only withdrew enough cash to fly to the States and get settled."

"I often wondered about those secret meetings you had when Bianca and I weren't included."

"Now you know why. After showing the banker

my passport and the letter from my grandfather verifying the origin of the funds in my account, I took a taxi to the airport."

Her eyes lit up. "You really were free at last."

"Except that you weren't with me."

"Let's not talk about that. Tell me what happened next."

"I bought a one-way ticket to New York. As it took off, I saw the jet-d'eau at the end of Lake Geneva and the Alps in the distance. You know I'd traveled through Europe before and had been to Switzerland on several vacations. But this time everything was different."

Shadows marred her classic features. "I can't imagine it."

His body tautened. "That's when I realized I had left you behind for good. You wouldn't be able to come to me, nor I to go to you. My ache for you turned into excruciating pain." Hot tears stung his eyes. "Gemma—I swear I didn't know how I was going to be able to handle the separation."

Hers filled with tears, too, revealing the degree of her pain.

"You and I had grown up together and lived through everything. I was tortured by the knowledge that until the situation within my own family changed, our separation would have to be permanent."

"When I first heard you'd gone, I thought I was going to die."

He reached for her hand, enclosing it in his. "I would have given anything to spare you that pain. There was no way to know how soon we'd ever be able to see each other again."

She gave his hand a little squeeze before removing hers.

"You can't imagine my panic. I feared you would hate me forever for my inexplicable cruelty in telling you nothing. There'd be no way you could forgive me. But I didn't know how else to keep you safe from my father's wrath. To my sorrow, you didn't escape it entirely."

"You know what hurts the most, Vincenzo? To realize our teenage love wasn't strong enough in your mind to handle telling me the truth before you ever left Italy."

"I thought I was protecting you."

"I realize that now, but why did you lie to me again the other day about your reasons for leaving?"

"Again, I wanted to shield you from so much ugliness."

"Did you think I'm not strong enough to handle it?"

"I know you are, Gemma. Forgive me."

"Of course I do," she cried. "Finish telling me about New York."

"It was a different world. I checked into a hotel and called my grandfather Emanuele to let him know where I was, knowing he wouldn't tell my father. After talking with him, I phoned my grandfather in Padua to thank him for all he'd done for me...all he'd tried to do for my mother."

"He must have been so thrilled to hear from you."

"When he knew I had escaped, you should have heard him weep."

"Oh, Vincenzo. To think he'd lost his daughter at your father's hands. It's so terrible."

He could feel her grief. "It was over a long time ago, Gemma. Later I placed an ad in *Il Giorno*, needing to talk to Dimi. Four days later the call came. The first thing I demanded was to hear news of you!"

She'd buried her face in her hands. "What did he tell you?"

"Dimi couldn't give me any information. He said that while an intensive search of the countryside had been going on for me, he'd arranged to leave the *castello* that morning with Zia Consolata. He realized that if he didn't get them out of there, he would be my father's next victim."

"I can't bear it, Vincenzo."

"The news was devastating to me. He'd promised to watch out for you. Instead you were gone, and he had to leave, too."

"I'm so sad that you and your cousin will always carry those scars."

He took a deep breath. "I cringed to realize the suffering my disappearance had brought on everyone. And worse, knowing I couldn't comfort you. Neither could Dimi. He tried looking for you."

She dashed the tears from her eyes. "I can hardly stand to think about that time, but I have to know more. How *did* you survive when you got to New York? You'd never been there before."

Her interest thrilled him, because until he'd told her the truth, she'd refused to listen to anything.

"Don't forget I'd been making plans for a whole year. As soon as I arrived, I checked into a hotel Dimi and I had picked out, then had my funds electronically transferred from Switzerland to a bank in New

York. Two days later I applied to take the SAT college entrance test."

"You're kidding—"

His brows lifted. "You can't go to college without sending in the results."

He felt her eyes play over his features. "With your education, you must have been a top candidate."

"Let's just say I did well enough to get into NYU, but I didn't receive the results for eight weeks. During that waiting period, I purchased a town house in Greenwich Village."

"What was it like?"

"The architecture is nineteenth-century Greek Revival, with three bedrooms. I wanted to have enough room for Dimi when he was able to join me. But of course that never happened because he didn't want to move my aunt, who preferred being in her own palazzo."

"Of course. I'm so sorry. Tell me about the university. What courses did you take?"

"Business and finance classes. Thanks to my grandfather Nistri, who was my business model growing up, I started buying failing companies with his money and turning them around to sell for profit."

She let out a cry. "Nistri Technologies is your corporation!"

"One of them. My *nonno* was brilliant and taught me everything he knew. Little by little I started to build my own fortune and planned to pay him back every penny once I'd made the necessary money. But he died too soon for that to happen."

"You're a remarkable man." Her voice shook.

"No, Gemma. Just a lucky one to have had a

mother and grandfather like mine. He had a contact at NYU who taught an elite seminar for serious business students. This revered economics professor formed a think tank for his most ambitious followers and told us to visualize our greatest dreams."

"Is that where you met your friends?"

"*Si.* For different reasons, Takis and Cesare came to the States from Greece and Sicily to study and work. Like me, they wanted to make a lot of money. This seminar that brought us together was a complete revelation to the three of us. We grew close, and they went on to become wealthy, highly successful hotel and restaurant entrepreneurs."

"As did you. Why was this professor so effective?"

"No particular reason except he was brilliant. We learned it wasn't good enough to want to make money. You've got to know how to get it, how to deal with brokers, renovate, assess the value of property, how to buy, sell and secure a mortgage. He sounded just like my grandfather."

"Was that period of your life good for you?"

"Very good in some ways. Our mentor drummed into our heads how to cut costs, decide how much risk to assume in investments and balance our portfolios in order to impress anyone. His final rule was ingrained on my psyche. 'You must find out if your friends can be loyal.'"

"You and your partners must be very close."

"I trust them implicitly. That means everything. When I brought them together with my idea to buy the *castello*, I hadn't seen either of them in at least two months and had missed them. They got excited when I showed them pictures."

"There's no place like it." Her eyes glistened with unshed tears. "After the pain you and Dimi endured at the hands of your fathers, I'm glad you've found friends like that."

"So am I."

"When I met them, I didn't know they were owners and your partners. Both of them have made me feel comfortable. Some of the people in the culinary world are hard to deal with, but your friends aren't stuffy or full of themselves."

"So you like them?"

"I do. They have a lot of charm and sophistication. Before I knew what was going on, I thought that whoever owned this hotel knew what they were doing to employ them."

"They're the best, and they'll be pleased when I pass on what you said."

She cocked her head. "Do you mind answering another question for me?"

"Ask away."

"You may not be married yet, but is there someone waiting for you to return to New York?"

Vincenzo was in a mood to tell her the whole truth. "Yes and no."

He saw her swallow. "What do you mean?"

"I've been away from Annette five weeks this time. Yesterday on the phone she told me I sounded different. She wanted to know why. I told her about the Italian girl I fell in love with in my youth, the girl I hadn't seen or heard from in ten years until two days ago."

If he wasn't mistaken, he heard a moan pass her lips.

"I explained that meeting you was a complete accident. Annette wanted to know more. All I could tell her was that a big portion of my past had just caught up with me and I was still reeling. I know she wanted more reassurance, but I couldn't give it to her."

She averted her eyes.

"What about you, Gemma? There has to be someone in your life." He braced himself for what might be coming.

"I dated a little after moving to Florence. But the only important relationship I had with a man was a year ago."

The blood pounded in his ears. "Did you love him?"

"I tried. My feelings for Paolo were different than those for you, but I felt an attraction. He was a writer for *Buon Appetito*, a nationwide food magazine, and had covered the school for an article. His interview with me turned into a date, and we started seeing each other.

"After a month he wanted me to sleep with him. I thought about it, hoping it would help me forget you, but in the end I couldn't do it. He was very upset, so I told him I couldn't go out with him anymore because it wouldn't be fair to him. He accused me of loving someone else even though I'd told him there'd been no important man in my life for years."

Vincenzo's breath caught. He'd hoped for honesty from her and her confession brought out his most tender feelings. He now had his answer to why she'd come to this particular restaurant tonight. Her ache for him had grown worse, too. They suffered from the same pain.

"Paolo said he wanted to marry me, but I told him

no because I didn't love him the way he needed to be loved. I couldn't even sleep with him. For both our sakes, I knew we had to stop seeing each other and get on with our separate lives. I'd lost my heart to the man I'd grown up with."

"Gemma…"

"After this long, it had to be unbearable to relive the ugly truth of your family's tragedy to me tonight, Vincenzo. Thank you for your courage, for forcing me to listen to the last page in the book. You were right. I needed to hear the ending so I can let go of my anger. Now I can close it."

This intimacy with Gemma, the knowledge that all the secrets were out, had changed his world forever. They'd been brought together again, and he loved her with every fiber of his being. The rush of knowing she'd been the constant heart in their relationship filled every empty space in his soul.

He grasped both her hands, ignited by the desire to be her everything. "Since we're past the age of eighteen, I have a simple solution to our problem that has been out there for the last ten years."

"What are you saying?"

"Marry me, Gemma."

With those words, everything changed in an instant. A stillness seemed to envelope the room. Her complexion took on a distinct pallor that revealed more than she would ever know.

"A *duca* doesn't wed the cook."

Somehow he hadn't expected that response. He'd thought that because a miracle had brought them together at last, they'd gotten past every obstacle. After baring his soul to her, Vincenzo couldn't sit there any longer knowing she was more entrenched in that old world than he would have believed. She still saw him as the son of the evil *duca*. Like father, like son?

Cut to the quick, he let go of her hands and got to his feet. "This *duca* won't be a *duca* much longer. Enjoy the rest of your evening, *bellissima*."

He flew out of her flat to his car. As he accelerated down the road, he could hear her calling to him in the distance, but he didn't stop. After believing that telling her the truth would make them free to love each other as man and wife, the opposite had happened.

A duca *doesn't wed the cook.* The words that came out of her had been so cold, it frightened him. He felt as if the bottom had dropped out of his world once more. But by the time he'd pulled up to the front of the *castello*, his sanity had returned.

Vincenzo should have been ready for that automatic response—after all, Gemma had learned it from her mother at a very early age. He'd known how Mirella had always tried to guide Gemma and put distance between them because they were from different classes. But tonight his heart had been so full, he couldn't take the answer she'd thrown back at him.

The class divide was a more serious obstacle to a future with her than anything else. He planned to deal with that issue soon, but first he needed to leave for New York and take care of vital business. When he returned, he'd be able to concentrate on Gemma and their future. Because they *were* going to have one!

No sooner had Vincenzo gone than Gemma's phone rang. But she was so fragmented after her conversation with him, she ran into the other room and flung herself across the bed. Great heaving sobs poured out of her.

Something was wrong with her. Since the moment he'd entered Takis's office, appearing like a revenant, she seemed to have turned into a different person, one she didn't know. Nothing she'd said had come out right. Every conversation after that had ended in disaster. Either she ran out on him or he walked out on her.

Marry me, Gemma.

That's what he'd asked her moments ago. And what did she do? Throw his proposal back in his incredibly handsome face! *That's because you've been on the defensive from the moment he came back into your life, Gemma Rizzo!*

No wonder he'd walked out on her. Why wouldn't he? Didn't he know she loved him with all her heart and soul? But he was a *duca.* And that made a marriage between them out of the question, even though it was what she wanted more than anything in the world. While he'd been holding her hands, her body had throbbed with desire for him.

Gemma lay there out of her mind with a new kind of grief. All these years she'd misjudged him so terribly. Now the truth of his revelations burned hot inside her. At this point she knew she was more in love with him than ever.

But the woman who owned the *pensione* had recognized Vincenzo as the new Duca di Lombardi. That revelation was the coup de grâce for Gemma. His title created a chasm between them that could never be bridged. His marriage proposal thrilled her heart, but she couldn't marry him. In fact, everything was much worse.

While she worked at the *castello*, she would have to keep her distance from him. That she'd been crazy in love with him and they'd grown up spending as much time together as possible made it all the more difficult.

He had a potent charisma she found irresistible. Gemma didn't trust herself around him. Vincenzo had a way of crooking his finger and she'd come running no matter how hard she fought against it.

But she couldn't allow things to end this way. It was up to her to repair the damage and reason with him so he would understand. She hadn't told him that her mother didn't know about her new job yet. If Mirella had any idea he'd asked Gemma to marry him, there'd be even more grief, and Gemma didn't want to think about that.

Unfortunately it was too late to see him tonight. Tomorrow after work she'd find him and ask him if they could go somewhere private and talk this situation out.

After she'd cried until there were no tears left, she went to the bathroom to get ready for bed, then she returned Filippa's phone call. Her friend was excited because she'd received an affirmative response from one of the restaurants in Ottawa. "I'm flying to Canada tomorrow for the interview."

"That's wonderful." Gemma was thrilled for her. "Call me when you get there and tell me everything. Just think. You'll be closer to New York."

"It's very exciting. Now tell me, what's the situation on your end?"

"You don't want to know and I don't want to burden you when you're so happy."

"Let me be the judge of that."

Gemma spent the next while telling her all the shocking truths Vincenzo had revealed. "Although I've forgiven him, and I do understand, I'm still hurt he couldn't tell me the truth before."

"He was only eighteen, remember? And tonight he finally told you the whole truth."

"But you haven't heard it all yet. He's asked me to marry him."

"What?"

"Yes, and because I know a marriage to him is so impossible, I told him a *duca* doesn't marry the cook!"

"Oh, Gemma…you didn't! No wonder you're a mess."

"I am. During those early years we never had trouble communicating. Not ever."

"But you want something that isn't possible, because you're not teenagers anymore."

"I was more sane as a teenager than I am now. Forgive me for not making any sense tonight."

"You've been in shock since his return. I'm pretty sure he's in the same condition. Give it all time to sink in."

"I don't have another choice. Promise to call me from Canada and tell me everything."

"Don't worry. Now try to get a good sleep."

"I don't know if I can. Be safe, Filippa, and good luck!"

"Thanks. Be nice to Vincenzo. He could use it. Ciao."

Those words couldn't have made Gemma feel

guiltier, but she knew her friend hadn't intended anything hurtful. Quite the opposite, in fact. Filippa always made good sense. With a plan in mind to talk to Vincenzo tomorrow, Gemma got ready for bed and was surprised she didn't have trouble falling asleep.

The next morning, she got up and ready for the day. With the formal meetings with the owners and staff out of the way, she dressed for regular work in a short-sleeved top and pleated pants rather than a skirt. Before she left Sopri, she would buy a few groceries to put in the mini fridge for future meals. In fact, while she was shopping, she'd buy a pool lounger to take out to the lake behind the *castello*.

Until the opening of the hotel, she and Maurice would be working midmorning hours on menus and ordering the staples. But for a few more weeks there'd be free time in the afternoons before the intense work began and she earned her keep.

In the past there was nothing she'd enjoyed more than watching the swans, especially when Vincenzo had joined her. She assumed the water fowl were still there and would be an attraction for hotel guests. For now, she could lie in the sun and read a good thriller before leaving to drive back to the *pensione*. Maybe she could ask Vincenzo to meet her out there later in the day so they could really talk.

Though she followed through with her plans, she discovered that Vincenzo had flown to New York and wouldn't be back for a while. The news made her ill. She kept busy, but inside she was dying. He could have left Italy for personal as well as legitimate business reasons. She'd never know and speculation didn't get her anywhere.

Four days later she was in the depths of despair when she overheard Cesare and Takis talking in the kitchen. Vincenzo would be arriving at the airport at eight thirty that evening. She hugged the information to herself, trying not to react to her joy so anyone would notice.

After she finished the day's work with Maurice, she drove back to the *pensione* and kept busy until evening. Once she'd showered and changed into a sundress, she drove back to the *castello*. To her relief she saw the Maserati parked in front. Thankful Vincenzo was back safely, she hurried up the steps to find him.

One of the security men, Fortino, let her in the front entrance. This was the first time in ten years that she'd been here at night. The place was quiet as a tomb. Maybe because it was a Friday night and Vincenzo's partners had gone out. It was too early for anyone to be in bed. Gemma had no idea about their personal lives, though she remembered Vincenzo telling her that they were both single.

She wished she had his cell phone number, but he hadn't given it to her. If he wasn't in the kitchen, he might be out with Takis and Cesare. Then again, he was probably exhausted after his long flight and could be up in his tower room.

A long, long time ago, she'd gone looking for him there after hearing he'd suffered a terrible fall from his horse, or so she'd been told at the time. Desperate to make certain he was all right, she'd made her way to his aerie at the top of the *castello*, afraid one of his father's guards would see her. His door had been ajar and she'd heard him moan.

Summoning her courage tonight, she stole through the massive structure and made the same trek as before up the stone staircase at the rear. It wound round and round until she arrived at the forbidding-looking medieval iron door. This time it was closed. She held her breath while she listened for any sound.

Nothing came through except the pounding of her own heart.

Gemma knocked. "Vincenzo? Are you in there?" She waited.

Still no response.

It was here—away from everyone, away from any help—that Vincenzo's father had attacked him. A little sob escaped her lips to think something so terrible had happened to him. Yet he'd survived. She loved him desperately.

Desolate because he wasn't there, she turned to go back down when she heard the heavy door open behind her and whirled around.

"Gemma—" His deep male voice infiltrated her body. "What are you doing up here?" He was half-hidden by the door.

"I heard you were back from New York and I've been waiting to talk to you in private. I know it's late, but I need to apologize for my cruelty to you the last time we were together."

"Growing up I memorized your mother's views on class distinctions like a catechism. Your answer to my marriage proposal shouldn't have come as a surprise, although I'd hoped for a different response."

She bit her lip. “That’s why I came up here. To talk about this like an adult.”

“My problem is, I’m in an adult mood. If you cross over my threshold, I won’t be accountable for my behavior. Is that honest enough for you?”

Thump, thump went her heart. “Vincenzo—I’m so sorry—”

“For what?”

“For throwing your proposal back in your face like I did.”

“Are you saying you didn’t mean it?”

“Yes—no—I mean—”

“You can’t have it both ways,” he broke in on her.

“This isn’t a black-and-white situation.”

“So you admit there’s some gray area where we can negotiate?”

She let out a troubled sigh. “I shouldn’t have come up here.”

“Are you saying good-night, then? I can assure you I’d much rather you came in my room the way you did a long time ago, but the decision is up to you.”

Close to a faint from wanting to be with him, she turned to go back down the stairs. The next thing she knew, Vincenzo had caught her around the waist with his strong arms. “*Oh*—”

“Is this what you want, Gemma? Yes or no?”

Heaven help her. “Yes—”

CHAPTER SEVEN

VINCENZO PULLED HER into his room so her back was crushed against his chest.

"After our troubled reunion days ago, I didn't expect a welcome home like this. I love this dress, by the way. You're not so covered up." He kissed her neck, sending curls of delight through her body.

There was a playful side to him that seduced her. Though he was still dressed in trousers, Gemma could tell he was shirtless. His male scent and the faint aroma of the soap he used were intoxicating. She struggled for breath. "I didn't know if you were up here or not."

"I'd barely arrived and was getting ready to drive to the *pensione* to find you." He buried his face in her hair like he'd done so many times in the past. "You have no idea how beautiful you are. I couldn't get back fast enough. When did you let this profusion of silk grow out?"

"Mamma liked it short, but I got tired of the style."

"It's breathtaking and smells divine."

He'd always said wonderful things to her. "I don't remember your voice being this deep."

His low chuckle excited her. "Yours is the same."

"I think you're taller than you once were."

"So are you, in high heels. I don't think I ever told you how much I love your long legs." He turned her around so he could look into her eyes. "Do you think we're through growing up?"

In the dim glow of a lamp she saw a glimmer of a smile hover at the corners of his compelling mouth.

"I don't know. You're still the tease I remember."

"And you still blush. Give me your mouth, Gemma, so I'll know not everything has changed."

She put her hands against his chest with its dusting of black hair. "Please don't kiss me again, Vincenzo. I was simply trying to find you so I could explain what I meant the other night after you followed me to the *pensione* to talk. Everything came out wrong. I'll go downstairs while you finish getting dressed and meet you in the lobby, where we can have the conversation we should have had."

Gemma tried to pull away from him, but he held her firmly in his grasp. "The last time you came to this room, I had to let you go too soon because I was afraid you could be in danger. That's not the case anymore, and I've waited too long for this moment."

He lowered his mouth to hers and began kissing her. A kiss here, a kiss there, then one so long and deep her legs started to give way. Vincenzo picked her up in his arms and carried her past the square hunting table in front of the fireplace to the hand-carved bed.

The suite had been redecorated in nineteenth-century decor with every accoutrement befitting his title. But Gemma wasn't aware of anything except this man who was kissing her senseless. No longer the eighteen-year-old she'd adored, he was a man already making her feel immortal.

When she'd come to his bed ten years ago, he'd been suffering, in pain, and they'd had to be so careful how they kissed and held each other. Not wanting to make it worse, Gemma had had to be the one to make it easier for him to get close to her and caress her.

Tonight that wasn't their problem. With one kiss Vincenzo had swept her away to a different place, exciting her in ways she hadn't thought possible. He rolled her over so he could look down at her. His hands roamed her hips and arms as if memorizing her.

"I could eat you alive, *bellissima*." He kissed every feature of her face before capturing her mouth again and again. One kiss turned into another, drowning her in desire. Vincenzo was such a gorgeous man, she couldn't believe he was loving her like this. "I know this is what you want, too. You can't deny it. You're in my blood and my heart, Gemma."

"You're in mine," she cried softly. "I can't remember a moment when you weren't a part of me."

"I want you with me. It's past time we were together."

She cupped his striking face in her hands. "That's what you say now."

He kissed the tips of her fingers. "What kind of a comment is that? You think I'm going to change? Wouldn't I have already done that over the years we've been apart? I've already asked you to marry me. What more proof do you need? That's a commitment to last forever." He plundered her mouth with another heart-stopping kiss.

Gemma moaned. "All lovers say that. If you were a normal man, I could believe it."

He raised up on one elbow, tracing the outline of her lips. "You don't think I'm normal? We've been apart too long. Spend the night with me and you'll find out the truth."

"I don't mean that kind of normal, and you know it."

"With you lying here in my arms, your lambent green eyes as alive with desire as your body, I'm in the mood to humor you. I hunger for you, Gemma."

"You're not thinking clearly, Vincenzo." She fought tears. "I can't marry you."

Lines marred his arresting features. "Of course you can. A *duca* can do whatever he likes, choose whatever woman he wants, just like any other man."

"I know," she whispered, turning her head away. Oh, how well she knew after learning the dark secrets inside the walls of the *castello*. His father's and uncle's proclivities for other women had been one of the great scandals in all Lombardi.

He caught her chin so she had to look at him. "Let's get something straight once and for all. I have despised the class system all my life and fought against it growing up. The idea of finding the right princess to marry in order to gain more power and money is revolting to me. Your love sustained me growing up. It means more to me than any riches or possessions."

She eased away from him and sat up, smoothing the hair off her forehead. "You say that now."

"I'll say it now and until the end of our days together."

"Vincenzo—" A sob escaped. "You just don't understand."

"Then help me." He tugged on her hand so she couldn't get off the bed. She'd never heard him sound so dark.

"You're the most wonderful, remarkable man I've ever known. But you were born with a special destiny."

"No. I happened to be born the son of a *duca*. That's not destiny. It's an accident of birth."

"Please listen. I'm going to tell you something you never knew. One time when your grandfather was out in the back courtyard in his wheelchair, I was sent out to take him a sweet. He loved Mamma's zeppole. I gave them to him.

"After he thanked me, I started to hurry away, but he called to me. 'Come back here, *piccola*,' he said and reached for my hand. 'I've seen you with my grandson. You've been a good friend to him and I can tell you like him. And I know why. Can you keep a secret?' I nodded.

"'There's a reason everyone likes him. One day he'll grow up to be the finest *duca* of us all. With his princess he'll raise future *duchi*, who will have a wonderful father to look up to. But I'm afraid I won't live to see it.' He kept hold of my hand and wept.

"Even though I was young, I realized that he was letting me know how lucky I was to be in your company. When I ran back to Mamma and told her, she said it was a sign from heaven that I should always respect my friendship with you. To think of wanting anything more would be sacrilege."

* * *

"*Santa Madre di Dio!*" Vincenzo got off the bed, putting his hands on his hips in a totally male stance. "So *that's* the reason for all this talk! Gemma—if it will ease your mind, I've heard your opinion on the subject before. Your mother shared her beliefs because she loves you and wants to protect you."

"Still, my temper sometimes gets the best of me."

"I remember," he murmured. "That time you and Bianca went swimming in the lake without your clothes. You thought Dimi and I had been spying on you and had taken them. I confess we did spy with my binoculars from a tree at the edge of the forest."

"Vincenzo—"

"But it turned out we weren't the culprits. The dog of one of the guards ran off with your clothes. We chased it down and brought your things back to you, but I don't recall you thanking us."

She shook her head. "We were too embarrassed to talk. That was so humiliating, you can't imagine."

"You were our wood nymphs come to life. Dimi and I thought it was the most wonderful day we'd ever spent."

"You would!" But even across the expanse separating them he detected a half smile.

"I'll tell you another secret. My mother was very fond of you. But because she was a princess, she believed any feelings I had for you would come to grief. Like your mother, Mamma had also been raised in a different world of rigidity within the titled class."

Gemma sat on the edge of the bed. "Her words were prophetic."

"Not completely. Dimi and I broke rules all over

the place. It's a new world now. Because of a reaction to the misuse of noble titles in our country, you'll notice a trend among legitimate aristocracy in this last decade to refrain from making use of their titles."

"I didn't realize."

"What's important is that you and I have found each other again and I'm no longer in danger from my father or uncle. The powers that be are gone."

"Thank heaven for that, Vincenzo. But what did you mean when you said you wouldn't be a *duca* much longer?"

He hadn't meant to tell her this soon, but right now he was desperate to get closer to her. "Since my return to Italy, there are men in the government who know of my business interests in the US and here. I'm not blind. Because of my title they want me to get on board with them to play an economic role in the region's future. It's all political, Gemma. The title corrupted my father and uncle. It turned their souls dark. I refuse to let that happen to me."

"You don't know if the title did that to them, Vincenzo. I watched you grow up titled, remember? I never once saw you do an unkind thing in your whole life." She stared hard at him. "You can't change who you are."

"Oh, but I can."

"How?"

"By renouncing my title. Once that's done, it's permanent. If I have a son or sons, they won't inherit it, and any daughters I might have can't inherit it anyway. The beauty of it is that an Italian title of nobility cannot be sold or transferred. In other words, the abuse stops with me. My male children and their children and the children after them won't be burdened."

Her eyes widened. "If you do that, won't the title fall on Dimi through his father?"

"Yes, but he's taking the same steps."

"You'd both stop the title from progressing after centuries of succession?"

Vincenzo nodded. "There are so many dreadful things my father and uncle did in the name of that title, seen not only in the scars that Dimi and I carry. You know the head gardener who was introduced at the orientation meeting?"

"Yes. I met him out in back the first day."

"Years ago, my father got angry at him for planting some flowers Mamma wanted. He told him to get out and never come back. He didn't give him a reference or any severance pay. While Dimi and I were looking up old employees, we found him.

"That's just one of a hundred stories I could tell you of my father's cruelty. If he and my uncle hadn't been born to a *duca*, they wouldn't have felt they had the right to treat people like animals. The only way to end the corruption is to rid ourselves of the title and restore the honor of those noble Gagliardis from the past by preserving the *castello*."

"*That's* why you turned it into a resort," she whispered.

"What better way to make restitution than by allowing the public to enjoy its heritage, thereby giving back something good and decent to the region."

Her features sobered. "You loved your grandfather Emanuele. He was a great *duca*. How would he feel about this?"

"I can't speak for him, but if he's looking down on us now, he couldn't be pleased with what his sons did while he was dying. Being born with a title gives some men dangerous ideas."

"But not you, Vincenzo. Emanuele adored you. I don't think he'd want you to do this."

He frowned and got to his feet. "For someone who came close to bearing the brunt of my father's dark side, I'm surprised to hear this coming from you. I thought you of all people would be happy to see this kind of inequality come to an end."

"But you're a different breed of man and shouldn't have to give up what is part of you."

"I'm a man, pure and simple. Don't endow me with anything else. This isn't an idea I just came up with on a whim. When I was five, maybe six, I saw my father kick one of the young stable hands to the ground because he didn't call him Your Highness. It sickened me. That was the day my plan was born. Now I can see it through to fruition."

The way she shook her head filled him with consternation. What could he say to get through to her?

"Years ago I told you I'd find a way for us to be married. A few days ago I asked you to be my wife because there'd be no barrier between us. But there *is* one. It goes so much deeper than I realized."

His words caused her to flinch, alarming him.

"When you said you and I weren't the same people growing up, I didn't understand how fully you meant it." His chest felt tight. "It's clear you don't love me the same way I love you, no matter what I do. I can tell you would rather I keep the title, the very thing you think prevents us from ever getting married."

He started pacing in frustration, then stopped. "Is this because of what my *nonno* said? It's no wonder you don't think you can marry me."

"I didn't mean to upset you. I thought if I told you about that experience, you would begin to see."

"I see, all right," he muttered. "Mirella deliberately interpreted it so you would only worship me from afar. She didn't want you getting any ideas about a real relationship with the future *duca*. After all this time, it's still working."

"You can scoff about this all you want, Vincenzo, but it was very serious to me. He was a prayerful man. I saw him go to Mass in the private *castello* chapel every day before I left for school."

"He wasn't a priest destined to be cardinal one day, Gemma. Who do you think administered the Mass to him every morning?"

"You don't have to be a priest to be a godly person. Everyone felt that way about the old *duca*. I know you loved him."

"That's beside the point. He knew he was dying. All he was doing that day was expressing his sentiment about me to a sweet girl who'd brought him his favorite dessert baked by the best cook around. But to see that as a sign from above..." He shook his head.

Gemma slid off the bed. "My mother was raised in a good Catholic family."

He raked a hand through his midnight-black hair. "Heaven help me, so were you."

"That's why she honored the traditions here."

"You're right, but she went too far. Without giving me any voice at all, she made me out as the untouchable one, the future *duca* whose word was law.

It's that old divine right of kings business and it disgusts me."

No one could confuse her like he could with his logic.

"It's time to put the past *in* the past, where it belongs. There's no room in the modern world for it. I'm a normal guy, Gemma. Warts and all."

"You don't have any."

Vincenzo leaned against the door with his strong arms folded. "Of course I have flaws and imperfections, like every other man. Think about it—until I called my friends together about buying the *castello*, they didn't know my last name or the fact that I inherited a title. Do you see them treating me any differently? Have they once shown me a special kind of deference?"

"Actually, no," she said with her innate honesty.

"Good. Maybe that will convince you. Please hear me out. We need to be spending time together as adults, not as those teenagers from the past having to live by ridiculous rules that constantly divided us in your mind. It's important—in fact, it's *vital*—that you throw away the blinders while we explore the world we're living in now as equals in all things and ways."

Gemma could hear what he was saying, but it was so hard to silence her mother's warnings after all these years. It meant throwing off old fears and conceptions that had dominated her thoughts forever.

"I'm in love with you. Isn't it worth it to you to find out if you can see me as a typical man you've met and want to get to know better?"

Vincenzo was the most atypical man she'd ever

known, but he couldn't see it. He wasn't a woman. She hugged her arms to her waist. "You already know what's in my heart."

"I do?" he quipped, making her smile. "Then prove it. Here's what we're going to do."

She recognized that no-nonsense tone in his voice. When he went after something, he was impossible to stop. Gemma knew she had to get away from him. "There's nothing to do, Vincenzo. I have to leave."

With a few long strides, he stood in the front of the doorway so she couldn't walk out. He was such a breathtaking male, her legs turned to mush.

"The second I learned you didn't have a husband, I planned for us to take a vacation together. That's why I left that night for New York. There were loose ends I needed to tie up first so we wouldn't have anything standing in our way."

"That's a fantasy you need to let go of. For one thing, you just employed me. I can't take a vacation."

"There's still enough time before the grand opening for us to be gone a couple of weeks. My partners will handle everything, and you've already done the most important work with Maurice. When was the last time you went off on a real trip anywhere? Be honest."

Her eyes closed tightly. "I don't remember."

"That's what I thought. I need a holiday badly, too, but I never felt like taking one because the woman I wanted with me wasn't available. My fear that you were happily married and living somewhere in Italy with your husband and children tortured me more nights than you'll ever know."

Gemma had battled the same fears about him and had suffered endlessly for years.

"We'll leave in the morning. Go home and get packed. I'll come by the *pensione* at eight. We'll drive to the airport and have breakfast on the plane."

He was serious. It frightened and thrilled her at the same time. She moistened her lips. "Aren't you too tired to go anywhere after coming back from New York?"

"When we get to the beach, we'll sleep, relax and play in the water to our hearts' content."

It did sound out of this world.

"If—if we go," she stammered, "I don't want us to sleep together. When we're in each other's arms we communicate as a man and woman, but—"

"We certainly do."

Heat filled her cheeks. "You know what I mean. I didn't think of you as the *duca* while we were on the bed, but at other times—"

"I get where you're going with this," he broke in. "You want to see us as that man and woman no matter what else we're doing."

She nodded.

"So do I, so I'll try to keep my hands off you. But I'll warn you now, it's not going to be easy." He walked over to the massive dresser and pulled out a knit shirt he put on. "I thought I'd better cover up before I walk you out to your car. Fortino's a man and would understand, but I don't want him to get the wrong idea about you."

"Thank you."

His deep chuckle reverberated through her body as he caught her face between his hands, kissing her long and hard. Like old times, they wrapped their arms around each other and started down the winding staircase. Vincenzo stopped every so often to give her another kiss. She didn't think they'd ever reach the bottom and didn't care.

They crossed through the *castello* to the front entrance. "It feels like we're the only two people on earth."

"Don't I wish," he whispered against her throat. They nodded to Fortino and went down to her car. "Let's exchange phones so we can put in our numbers. I want you to call me the second you reach the *pensione*."

She nodded. When that was done, he crushed her against him. "*Ci vediamo domattina.*"

If she wasn't dreaming, then she would be seeing him in the morning. Taking the initiative, she pressed a kiss to his lips and climbed in the car. "Tomorrow."

Vincenzo packed a bag, then phoned his cousin before getting in bed. "Dimi?"

"Are you back from New York?"

"Yes, and I'm going away again, but I wanted to call you first. How's Zia Consolata?"

"Failing a little more each day."

"I'm so sorry. When I get back from this trip, I'll come and spend a few days with her to give you some relief."

"Where are you going?"

"I've had a breakthrough with Gemma." He'd always told his cousin everything. For the next little while he explained what had gone on this evening.

The part about her conversation with their grandfather Emanuele came as a shock to him.

"You're right. That gave Mirella more ammunition. But I'm worried. You sound too excited, Vincenzo. The zebra doesn't lose its stripes."

Vincenzo didn't want to hear that. "But she has agreed to go on vacation with me."

"Just be warned. You've been in hell for years. Two weeks with her might still not be enough to make her see the light."

His breath caught. "Thanks for your optimism."

"I just don't want you to end up in more pain that could last for the rest of your life."

He didn't want that, either, and worried about his cousin. Vincenzo wished there was more he could do for him. Dimi had relationships with various women, but his prime concern was to take care of his mother.

"I love you for caring, Dimi. Talk to you soon. Ciao."

CHAPTER EIGHT

WHEN MORNING CAME Vincenzo dressed in chinos and a sport shirt, then met early with Cesare and Takis to tell them his plans. With everything settled, he phoned Gemma to say that he was on his way to Sopri in one of the hotel service vehicles. He'd parked his Maserati around the back of the *castello*.

When he pulled up in front, she came out with her suitcase. His heart rate picked up speed. She looked fabulous in white sailor pants and a sleeveless white top. He wondered how long it would be before the sight of her didn't send adrenaline pounding through his blood.

He jumped out of the car to help her in and put her case in the back. Those luscious lips of coral were too much of an enticement. By the time he'd finished kissing her, there was no more lipstick left.

"The *padrona* was watching out her window."

"Are you ever going to stop worrying about being with me?"

Her chest heaved. "I promise to try not to let my fears get the best of me."

"That's all I can ask." He tucked some strands of honey-blond hair behind her ear.

"Where are we going?"

"First we'll fly to someplace I haven't been before. Have you ever traveled to Bari along the Adriatic?"

"No."

"Good. I want to explore the coast."

"Ooh. That sounds exciting. Are we taking the ducal private jet?"

"No. We're flying commercial, like two ordinary people."

Her head turned toward him. "Are you teasing me?"

"Does that mean you're disappointed?"

She blushed. "Of course not."

"We're simply two people on holiday together, doing whatever we feel like."

By two in the afternoon, they'd arrived at Bari international airport and rented a car. Vincenzo was starting to feel in the holiday mood. They stopped at a deli to buy some wine and a bag of Italian sausage and egg pies.

He looked over at her. "Having a good time?"

"This is the best. Can you imagine how much fun we would have had if you'd been able to drive us around years ago?"

"I've tried hard not to imagine what joy that would have been. In truth, if I'd driven off in a car with you, no one would have seen us again. My father knew that if I got behind the wheel of any car, I'd disappear."

"No, you wouldn't have. Like you told me, you'd never leave your mother."

He squeezed her thigh. She remembered everything.

"When did you learn to drive?"

"After I got to New York and bought my first car."

"What kind?"

"A white Sentra, perfect for a college guy. I have pictures I'll show you."

"I want to see and know everything that happened to you."

"We've got the rest of our lives, Gemma."

She didn't respond, but he wasn't worried. She'd come with him and today was only the first day. They whizzed along, chatting and eating. They explored Puglia before coming to the medieval town of Polignano a Mare, scattered with white buildings.

"Oh, look, Vincenzo. This whole area is built on sheer cliffs."

"This is where we're staying tonight. Years ago the guys told me about this place. I've been anxious to see it ever since." He turned in to the Grotta Palazzese Hotel built from the local stone. "We can't see it from here, but there's a cave restaurant below where we're going to eat tonight."

"I've heard about it. I can't wait to see it! A real cave."

"Yes. Seventy or so feet above the water. Let's check in and get our room, then walk around some of those narrow streets until we get hungry."

Gemma's heart raced when Vincenzo asked the concierge for a key to their room. Except for the night she'd crept up to his room all those years ago, and last night, she'd never been in another man's bedroom.

There were several couples checking in. She wished she could be nonchalant about their situation. After they reached their room and closed the door, Vincenzo put their bags down and pulled her into his arms. They kissed hungrily.

"Relax. It'll get easier." He knew everything going on inside her. "Go ahead and freshen up." She passed the queen-size bed on the way to the bathroom. This was all so new to her, she had to pinch herself.

Before long he took her out to play tourist. She had the time of her life as they meandered through the ancient streets hand in hand. No woman they passed could take their eyes off Vincenzo. One of the clerks in a tourist shop fell all over herself to get his attention.

But he'd fastened his attention on Gemma. He constantly teased and kissed her all the way back to the hotel, where they dressed for dinner. In their youth they'd had to plan every move to be together so no one would find out. It had been as if they were caged. Little could she have imagined a night like this with him. To be free and open to show their love was intoxicating.

A cry escaped her lips when they went down the steps to the limestone cave restaurant below. In the twilight, the individual tables had been lit with candles. The whole ambience had a surreal feeling with the warm evening breeze coming off the Adriatic.

They were shown to a table for two and served an exquisite meal of prawns and swordfish. She looked into his silvery eyes. "You can hear the water lapping beneath us. This is an enchanting place."

"The guys were right. You can't find a more romantic spot anywhere in Italy."

"I agree. A restaurant without walls. It's incredible." Near the end of their meal, the waiter came over. "No more wine for me," she said. "One glass is all I can handle."

Vincenzo declined a second glass, too. "Shall we take a little walk before going to bed?"

The thought of being with him all night sent a wave of delight through her body. "I'd love it."

An hour later they returned to the hotel and headed for their room. Vincenzo waited for her to get ready for bed. While he was in the bathroom, she climbed under the covers, dressed in the only long nightgown she owned. She wasn't quite as full now, but the food had stimulated her. She doubted she'd be able to sleep at all lying next to him.

He entered the darkened room in his robe and opened the window to let in the sea air. When he got into bed, he turned on his side toward her and drew her around so she faced him.

"Do you know that since we've been together again, all we've done is concentrate on me? I want to talk about you. I want to hear everything that happened to you from the morning you had to leave the *castello*."

She tucked her hands beneath her pillow so she wouldn't be tempted to throw them around his neck. "That was the worst moment of our lives. Mamma was so quiet I was frightened. We left with Bianca and her mother in a taxi early in the morning. At the train station in Milan, we all said goodbye. They were going back to Bellinzona in Switzerland, where their family came from."

He let out a groan. "So that's why Dimi couldn't find her, either."

"I cried for days. Bianca and I promised to write,

but it didn't last very long, because they moved again and one of my letters came back saying *return to sender*."

Vincenzo stroked her hair with his free hand.

"As for Mamma, she at least had her sister and niece in Florence. They offered us a home over the bakery. I loved them and we were very blessed, really. She was able to work in the bakery immediately to start earning money."

"Thank heaven your aunt was so good to you. I'd give anything to make it up to your mother for the pain. Not only couldn't I protect my own mother, I couldn't do a thing for yours."

Gemma heard the tears in his voice. "Please don't worry about it. My aunt knew Mamma had to use the Bonucci name so your father couldn't track her down. Everything worked out.

"On our first weekend there, Mamma took me to the cemetery to see my *papà*'s grave. I never knew him, so all I could feel was sadness for that. But for the first time in years, I watched her break down sobbing. I'd been so fixated on my own problems, I never realized how much she'd suffered after losing my father.

"Their married life had been cut short and she didn't have any more babies to love. My selfishness had caught up to me and I determined to be a better daughter to her from then on."

"You were the best, Gemma! I was always impressed by how close you were to her. How did you end up going to cooking school? You never talked about it to me. I didn't know that's what you wanted to do."

"I didn't, either. I assumed I'd to go college. One time when you and I were together, I told you as much in order to impress you."

"After I went to New York, I'd hoped that was what you would do."

"The trouble was, I didn't know what I wanted to study. Two weeks after we got to Florence, the family sat me down. I sensed they were worried about me, and they said they thought I might have been suffering from depression."

Vincenzo reached for one of her hands and kissed the palm.

"They told me I should attend cooking school. If I didn't like it, I didn't have to keep going. But since I'd already learned how to cook by watching Mamma, I'd be way ahead of the other students applying there.

"It sounded horrible to me, but everything sounded horrible back then." Her eyes stung with tears. "I'd lost all my friends."

"That's exactly how I felt when I arrived in New York," he whispered.

"Oh, Vincenzo—" She tried not to cry. "Over the years Mamma had saved a little money, but not enough to go toward my schooling. Yet I never felt deprived."

"You were loved, and that kind of wise frugality puts the sins my father and uncle committed to shame. Now keep telling me how you became a cook."

"So my aunt who runs the bakery knew someone in the administration at the Epicurean School, and I was given a scholarship. When she said that it was close enough for me to take the bus there, I realized they were all telling me I had to go and try it. I knew it was what my mother wanted. She'd sacrificed everything for me, so I did it."

"Did you hate it in the beginning?"

"No."

He smiled. "That's interesting."

"It was a surprise to my family, too. On the first day I met a girl named Filippa Gatti, who was from Florence. She reminded me of Bianca, and we became friends right away. She said she was tired of academic studies and wanted to do something different. After buying an expensive slice of ricotta cheese pie that tasted nasty, she thought, 'Why not be a pastry cook? Anyone could cook better than this!'"

"Why not?" Vincenzo laughed.

"With so many classes together, we hit it off, hating some of the teachers, loving others."

"You mean the same way Dimi and I felt about our tutors."

"Exactly."

"I'd like to meet her one day."

"She'd pass out if she ever met you."

"Ouch."

Gemma chuckled. "You know what I mean. There's no man like you around anywhere." He kissed her again. "She helped me deal with my pain over losing you, and our friendship got me through those nine years as an apprentice."

"I'm glad you have her in your life."

"So am I. You'd love her. She's darling, with black hair like yours and the most amazing sapphire-blue eyes. She's fun and *so* smart. After work we'd go to movies and eat dinner out and shop. Sometimes we took little trips along the Ligurian coastline. We'd visit lots of restaurants and check out the food."

He grinned. "Were there any good ones?"

"I found out you can't get a bad meal in Italy, but we determined to invent some fabulous dishes that would become famous someday. The truth is, Mamma was the creator in our family, better than my aunt or my grandmother and great-grandmother, who started the bakery. All I could do was try to match her expertise."

"You've succeeded, Gemma. Is Filippa as good a cook as you?"

"Much better, and that's the truth. She's innovative, you know?"

"I saw your résumé. You were named the top student in your class."

"That's because Signora Gallo, the woman on the board, loved my aunt and knew it would make her happy to give her niece the top ranking. It should have been Filippa."

"Where is she now?"

"In Canada, applying for a pastry chef position in Ottawa."

"Could you have applied there?"

"Yes, but I wanted a position in France. That is, until I saw the opening advertised at the *castello*."

"It was our luck we got you first. Finders, keepers. Cesare believes you applied for the position because it was meant to be. But I hope your friend gets what she wants."

"Me too. She always wanted to work at a restaurant in New York City and be written up in some glossy magazine as Italy's greatest cooking sensation. I'm kidding. She never said that, but I know she wanted to work in New York. In time I know she will, and I hope she becomes famous."

"I could put in a good word for her with Cesare. He owns an excellent restaurant chain."

She put her fingers to his lips. "No favors. We're going to be ordinary people right now, remember? But thank you for being so kind and generous."

"Gemma…an ordinary person can recommend someone for a job without being a *duca*."

"You don't know Filippa. She's intensely proud. The only way she would take a job would be for her to prove she's the very best at what she does. To be given a chance through a friend wouldn't go down with her at all."

"Sounds like your soul mate."

"Vincenzo—"

"Does she have a boyfriend who's going to miss her?"

"She *had* one. He let her down in a big way, but she's over the worst of it now."

"That's good. Now come here and let me kiss you the way I've been wanting to. We've talked long enough."

"I don't dare."

"Then will you do me a favor and turn on your other side? I can't promise not to reach out for you during the night. I have no idea what I do in my sleep."

"Then we're both in trouble. *Buonanotte*, Vincenzo. I've had the most wonderful day of my life."

"Guess what? We have two weeks of wonderful

days and nights ahead. Tomorrow I thought we'd fly to the island of Mykonos."

"You're joking. Aren't you?"

"Is that excitement I hear in your voice?"

"Yes! I've never been to Greece."

"Neither have I. Ironic, isn't it? I've traveled all over North and South America, parts of Asia. I've been to many of the states in the US—Hawaii, Alaska—and I know New York City like the back of my hand. But the rest of my education is still lacking."

"So is mine," Gemma murmured after she'd taken in what he'd just told her about his travels.

"Both Takis and Cesare say I have to see the Greek islands. Once you go there, you'll never want to travel anywhere else. I've arranged for us to stay at a small hotel with a restaurant, Gemma. It's on a white sandy beach where the waters are blue and crystal clear. You step right out of the room onto the beach. If you want, you can walk to town from there."

She let out a long sigh, picturing the white Greek architecture. "In my opinion, to live and be surrounded by water is true paradise. That's the one thing missing in Milan and Florence. They're both landlocked. Eating by the sea tonight inside that grotto was sheer enchantment. No other restaurant could compare."

"Being with you made it magical. Tomorrow morning we'll fly straight from Bari to Paxos. Sleep well, *il mio adorabile cuoca.*" He leaned over to give her a tender kiss, then rolled on his other side.

Vincenzo had just called her his adorable cook.

"You're too good to me, you know. I haven't done anything for you but cause you trouble."

"If you want to make it up to me, all you have to say are four little words besides *I love you.*"

I know.

"We're doing fine, aren't we? We're a man and a woman enjoying life together, right?"

"Yes." Her voice wobbled.

"You sound like you're going to cry."

"How do you know me so well?"

"Maybe because we met from the moment we were out of the cradle. You're as familiar to me as Dimi. No one else was in my world. I saw you in every mood and circumstance, just as you saw me."

"Our deep friendship is unique. On the strength of it, will you tell me the truth about something? When you went back to New York this time, did you see Annette?"

"Yes. We went to dinner and I told her she wouldn't be seeing me again because I was so madly in love with you, it was as if we'd never been apart."

"But—"

"No buts, Gemma. I can read your mind. If you can't commit to me by the end of our vacation, my feelings for Annette won't be resurrected. I can't imagine being a good husband to any woman when my heart has been yours from the age of five."

Now the tears started.

"Maybe that was the problem with my father and my uncle. Both of their marriages were arranged. They didn't have the luxury of already being in love with the women chosen for them. Our poor mothers had no choice, either."

"But they had you and Dimi to love."

"Still, what a shame they weren't lucky enough

to have grown up with the sweetest little girl on the planet. If I had to look for a reason for their notorious philandering, that might be one of them. I'd have fought dragons for you."

"I would have nursed your wounds." Her words came out ragged.

"That's what you did the night you came to my room. I ought to be thankful for what my father did to me. Though you didn't know he was the reason I was hurt, the news brought you to me."

"I still can't believe what he was capable of."

"It's over, and we were able to have that precious time together before I had to leave the country. The memory of that night was the only thing that has gotten me through the years—and Dimi, of course."

"Has he met a woman he loves?"

"He's had girlfriends, but no one special. My uncle is still alive and in prison. Work is Dimi's panacea to stave off the demons. With his contacts and resources, he's helped us put the details of the *castello* transaction together. He and the guys have developed a strong friendship already."

"You can't help but love Dimi. I've missed him terribly. Does he ever go to see his father?"

"Not yet. He's does a lot of his business at home to be with my aunt. She has several health care workers who provide relief for him. He says her doctor doesn't give her much longer to live."

"How hard for him. How hard for you. Forgive me for talking my head off."

"It's music I'll never grow tired of, Gemma. We were parted by too many years of silence. I'm greedy for all the time I can get with you."

She lay there bombarded by shock waves of feelings and emotions. Gemma didn't need any more time to know she wanted to be his wife. She'd always wanted to belong to him. What she had to do now was believe that even if he was the *duca*, he would stay this normal man who made her feel so complete she could die of happiness.

In that regard every woman wanted to believe that about the man she married. She wanted proof that he would always love her and never change. But no power on earth could give you proof like that. Her faith in him had to be enough. She *did* have faith in this man. Since she'd been with him again, it had been restored to new heights.

He's back now, Gemma.

He's back now, so what are you going to do about it?

Ten days playing on the beach beneath the Grecian sun had turned both of them into bronzed facsimiles of themselves. The shiny hair on Vincenzo's wood nymph reflected golden highlights that hadn't been visible before their trip. He never tired of watching Gemma or the voluptuous mold of her body.

She lay in the late-afternoon light on a lounger by the pool wearing a new turquoise-and-blue bikini.

"We've invented a new phrase, Gemma. Beach potatoes."

She lowered the thriller she was reading and broke into serious laughter, the kind he remembered from long ago. The nervous, worried woman he'd started out with on their flight to Bari was no longer visible. He loved this new Gemma, who seemed carefree and relaxed.

But she hadn't broken down, letting him know she wanted him to make love to her. The signs that she was ready to give him the answer he was waiting for hadn't come.

The zebra doesn't lose its stripes. Dimi's warning had haunted him throughout the night.

He'd decided to speak his mind now. There was no sense in putting it off, especially since the phone call he'd just received from Dimi.

Their loungers were placed side by side. She turned her head toward him. "I can see that look on your face."

"What look is that?"

"The one that says you've got something important to say."

"I can't hide much from you, can I?"

"Do you want to?" Her anxious question startled him. Well, well...beneath her calm facade she wasn't calm at all.

"No, Gemma. I was teasing. What I wanted to tell you was that while you were out in the sea a few minutes ago, Dimi phoned me."

"I didn't realize." She looked alarmed. "Is your aunt worse?"

"No. He called me because he just got word that my uncle died of liver failure in prison last night. They rushed him to the hospital, but it was too late."

Gemma sat up and slid her feet to the patio. "I hardly know what to say."

"That makes two of us."

"I'm sure he needs you right now."

Vincenzo nodded. “I’ve already made the flight arrangements for morning. When we reach Milan, we’ll drive to his villa.”

“In that case I’d better start getting packed.”

“Wait—before you go in the room, there’s something else I must tell you. I’ve been hoping you’d break down and talk to me about the thing I want most to hear. Since you haven’t, I’ve decided you need another nudge.”

“I don’t understand,” she cried softly.

“I’m renouncing the title right away. My uncle’s death convinces me even more it’s the right thing to do. Now Dimi and I can wipe the slate clean and be done with it. Even your mother would approve and give you her blessing. I’m looking forward to talking to her.”

A gasp escaped her lips.

“Why the consternation? It’s what you’ve always wanted so we could be together. Deep down it’s what I’ve wanted, too. These days with you have been the happiest of my life. I’m not going to let anything change that now.”

He got up from the lounger to pick up the towels and carry them into the room. She followed with the sunscreen and her book, but when he looked at her, she reminded him of a person suffering from shellshock. Good! The situation couldn’t go on this way any longer.

“While I’m at the front desk making arrangements for an early-morning drive to the airport, why don’t you decide where you want to go for dinner? I’ll be back in a little while.”

"To be honest, I'm not hungry. We had a late lunch."

"Then I'll stop at the deli for some snacks in case you change your mind later." He put on a sport shirt and left the room.

Gemma put her book down and sat on the bed, alarmed.

Vincenzo was going to renounce his title! He honestly believed that by getting rid of it, he'd be freed of the curse and Gemma would be happy. Her poor darling Vincenzo believed it would open up the way for her mother's blessing on their marriage.

But Gemma wasn't happy. Not at all.

She didn't want him to give up something that was part of him. He was already proving to be a wonderful *duca* through his vision of the *castello* and by all the great things he'd done to this point to restore the family's good name.

Unfortunately, until he could accept the whole of himself—until he could trust himself the way she trusted him—how could they be married? How could she live with herself knowing he was tearing himself and the fabric of his life apart just to be with her?

Gemma couldn't let him renounce the title, she just couldn't. She wouldn't let him. Somehow she had to find a way to stop him.

Oh, help! Her mother wasn't even home from her trip yet. She didn't know Vincenzo was back in Gemma's life! Gemma hadn't told Mirella about the job at the *castello* yet, either. She thought Gemma and Filippa were out together looking for jobs.

Propelled by anxiety, she headed to the bathroom

for a quick shower. Then she started packing, trying to sort out her thoughts. She wouldn't be able to work on Vincenzo tonight, not when he had Dimi's family on his mind. In a few days she would find the right time to beg him to listen to her, but it couldn't be right now.

As for her mother, Gemma would wait until she returned from England before she told her the news that would shake her *mamma*'s world once more.

An hour later Vincenzo returned and could see Gemma had showered. Her bags were basically packed and now she was in bed looking a beautiful golden honey blond. Though she'd opened the same book she'd been reading earlier, the page never turned.

Before they'd come on this trip, she'd claimed to be all mixed up. But these days in Greece had proved to him they were divinely happy doing the kinds of things other couples did on vacation. So why had the announcement she'd wanted to hear caused her to lose her concentration? Whatever was going on, he intended to get to the bottom of it.

She looked up at him with those dazzling green eyes. "Hi."

"*Buonasera.* I bought a few spinach rolls in case you want them."

"Thank you. Maybe I'll try one in a little while. Vincenzo? When you talk of marriage, do you even know where you'd want to live? You have a huge business empire in New York and are building one here. Once the resort is running smoothly, do you intend to go back and forth to the States? Are you and your friends going to put other people in charge at the *castello*? Don't they have to get back to New York, too?"

He unbuttoned his shirt before getting ready to shower and flashed her a piercing glance. "Don't you think I need an answer to *my* question first? The most important one I'll ever ask?"

Without waiting for a response, he went into the bathroom. When he came out later wearing his bathrobe, he discovered her, white-faced, sitting on the side of the bed in her nightgown, waiting for him.

"Vincenzo—I *can't* answer your question."

They'd been through this before. He shuddered. "Why not?"

"Because I've thought long and hard about it, and I don't want you to renounce your title. Not for me. I couldn't live with it."

"I'm not doing it for you. I thought you understood me. Isn't that what our whole trip has been about? Enjoying life like normal people?"

She got to her feet. "But you're not an ordinary man."

He shook his head. "Thank you for your nonanswer. I finally understand the meaning of déjà vu." After shutting off the lights, he climbed in his side of the bed. "I'm tired, Gemma. We have an early-morning call."

So saying, he turned away from her, unable to deal with this right now. Dimi's words were screaming in his head.

Just be warned. You've been in hell for years. Two weeks with her might still not be enough to make her see the light.

CHAPTER NINE

GEMMA HADN'T SLEPT at all and was numb with pain. Vincenzo's rare show of sarcasm last night, followed by his silence, was worse than any visible anger.

On Friday morning he rented a car at the airport in Milan and drove them to an area off the Duomo with a few secluded properties of the wealthy. She wasn't surprised when he pulled into the courtyard of a small, exquisite nineteenth-century palazzo. This represented the world he intended to give up.

After what he'd told her last night, she believed him. Her opinion *didn't* enter into his decision to give up the title. He'd hated it all his life and didn't want anything to do with it, period!

But in her heart she felt it was wrong, because he was the best thing that had happened to the Gagliardi family in two hundred years. Though she couldn't convince him of this, maybe Dimi would listen before it was too late.

Vincenzo helped her out of the car and walked her to the front entrance. To her surprise the double doors opened and his black-haired cousin stood there, almost as tall as Vincenzo. In trousers and an open-necked white shirt, he'd turned into one of the most attractive Italian men she'd ever seen. He too had the Gagliardi build and silver eyes, though his features were his mother's.

"Dimi!" she cried. The world stopped for a moment as a myriad of memories from their youth passed through her mind. He held out his arms and she ran into them. After he'd swung her around at least three times, she cried for him to put her down. "You look so wonderful!"

He wiped his eyes. "I swear I never thought to see you again in this life. Come with me." She felt his arm go around her shoulders. "We'll go out to the garden to talk."

"I'll look in on Zia Consolata while you two get reacquainted."

"*Perfetto*, Vincenzo."

Together they walked through a palazzo filled with treasures, leaving Vincenzo behind.

"How beautiful!" she exclaimed when they reached the sunroom that led to the outside patio. The rose beds were in full bloom. Dimi sat down beside her next to the wrought-iron table with an umbrella to shield them from the hot sun.

"Mamma loves it out here."

"Of course she does."

He hadn't lost that sweet smile. "Let me take a good look at you." His eyes played over her. "Short or long hair, you're a vision, Gemma. That's an extraordinary tan you and Vincenzo acquired in Greece. Your body was so white that day at the lake when—"

"Don't you dare say another word!"

Dimi burst into laughter. The sound took her back years. "I see my cousin told you about that."

"I'd rather not think about it." She reached over and grasped his hand. "He's told me all about your mother...and now your father."

His features sobered. "To be honest, I'm surprised his diseased liver held out as long as it did."

She squeezed his fingers before letting him go. "I understand your mother isn't aware of what has happened."

"No. Besides Alzheimer's, she has developed bradycardia, a slow heartbeat. The doctor inserted a pacemaker, but her body has rejected it. She's close to death now and never leaves her room."

"Would it be possible for me to talk to her?"

"That wouldn't be a good idea. She gets agitated by anyone who comes. But you're welcome to look in on her before you leave."

"Thank you." A lump had lodged in her throat. "Dimi, how can we help you with your father's funeral? Vincenzo couldn't get here soon enough."

"That's the way it has always been between us. If you want to know the truth, there's little to be done. My cousin and I are planning on the priest giving a blessing at the grave site tomorrow morning behind the *castello*. That's where all the Gagliardis are buried. No one will be invited."

"Not even me?" she asked in a small voice.

Gemma knew the location well. It was located in a special section deep in the forest. Vincenzo had met her there several times and had given her a history of the Gagliardi line. There was one spectacular monument among the headstones where the first Duca di Lombardi was buried. But she hadn't visited the family cemetery since coming to the *castello*. Duca Emanuele would be buried there now.

A strange sound came out of Dimi. "He doesn't deserve anyone as kind and loving as you being with us to say goodbye."

"Your father gave you life." Tears filled her eyes. "I can't imagine my youth without you. For that, I'm grateful to him. Something in his brain had been wired wrong, but look how you've turned out. You've been the greatest blessing to your mother, who has always adored you."

Dimi got out of the chair and paced for a few minutes, reminding her so much of Vincenzo when he had something painful on his mind. She stood up and walked over to him, putting her hands on his arms.

"You and Vincenzo are the greatest of all the Gagliardi men. I know, because I grew up with you for seventeen years and never saw anything but goodness in either of you."

He shook his head.

"I beg you to listen to me, Dimi. Don't let the actions of your fathers stain your lives and prevent you from doing the extraordinary things you were meant to do. You've both risen above the evil and corruption that entrapped them. Can't you see it's within your power to restore the good name you inherited?"

His features hardened, just like Vincenzo's did. It was uncanny. "That's a tall order, Gemma."

"Of course it isn't! Look at me." He lifted his eyes to her. "Vincenzo doesn't believe in destiny. He says your titles came as an accident of birth. Does that matter? You could raise the bar above everyone else. In fact, you've already started."

"What do you mean?"

"I've heard Vincenzo's partners talking. The two of you have hired dozens and dozens of local workers who've been unemployed to help restore the *castello* and grounds. Vincenzo started Nistri Technologies in southern Italy, putting over five hundred people to work. And Cosimo told me in private that you've started a huge new charity for Alzheimer's victims in honor of your *mamma*.

"You've done amazing things and opened doors only you could with your money and your positions as leaders. Please promise me you'll think about it and talk to him before he makes a mistake I can't bear for either of you to make."

He stared at her through narrowed eyes. "What happened to the girl who couldn't see past the title that divided you?"

She drew in a deep breath. "She grew up and is standing in front of you with no more blinders on. On this trip Vincenzo has shown me he can be a *duca* and the most wonderful man who ever lived, all at the same time. I'm so proud of both of you and all you've accomplished. It's made me see clearly at last. But he needs to believe it, too. You both do."

Gemma couldn't tell if she was getting through to Dimi or not. "Will you let me do something for you?"

"What would that be?"

"Stay with your *mamma* while you bury your father? It will be my way of showing my respect. She was a lovely woman and so kind to me. I realize she won't know me, but I can be in the room while you and Vincenzo do your part in the morning. In a small way it will make me feel connected again. If my mother weren't away on her trip, she'd want to be with the *principessa* at a time like this, too. Everyone loved her."

A mournful sigh escaped before Dimi drew her into his arms. He rocked her for a long time without saying anything. Suddenly Vincenzo's shadow fell over them.

"Zia Consolata is asleep. I'm going to run Gemma to her *pensione* right now, but I'll be back."

Dimi let her go. "I haven't even offered you something to eat or drink."

"We ate on the plane. See you soon."

Gemma waited for Dimi's answer, but he didn't say anything as he escorted her and Vincenzo through the palazzo to the front entrance. Dimi's eyes locked with Gemma's. "You have no idea what it meant to see you today."

"I feel the same way. *Piu tardi*, Dimi." She kissed his cheek and hurried out to the car. Vincenzo joined her for the twenty-minute drive to Sopri.

"Is Consolata as bad as Dimi said?"

"Worse. I can't see her lasting long now. We may have another funeral before long."

"Thank you for taking me with you to see him. I love him."

"That was quite a hug he gave you."

Within a few minutes Vincenzo pulled up to the *pensione* and helped her take in her bags. She stood at the door. "I told him I'd like to stay with Consolata in the morning. Will you let me know if he'd like that?"

His lips had formed a thin line. "I'll call you later after I've talked to him."

Gemma bit her lip as he walked back to the car and drove away. No sooner had she shut the door than her phone rang. Hoping he had regretted his hasty departure, she clicked on without checking the caller ID. Her heart was thudding. "Vincenzo?"

"No. It's Filippa."

The world spun for a moment and then settled back just as quickly. "It's great to hear your voice. Did you get the job?"

"No, I'm no longer in Canada. Instead of returning to Florence, I flew straight to Milan to see you. Do you mind if I come by the *castello* to talk? I've rented a car."

"I just got home from a trip with Vincenzo and am at the *pensione* alone. By all means, come!" Gemma knew in her heart Vincenzo wouldn't be by again today, and she needed her friend. "We'll eat lunch here and catch up."

"Thank you. You'll be saving my life."

"Let me give you instructions how to get here. My car will be out in front."

"I'll find you."

Half an hour later her darling friend came running to the door and they hugged.

"Come and sit down on the love seat. You're the last person I expected to see for a long time." She sat on the chair across from her friend, whose shoulders were shaking while she tried to hold back tears. "Talk to me, Filippa."

"Oh, Gemma—"

"I can't believe you didn't get the position."

"I did get it—but I was so homesick, I knew I

couldn't live there. If I'd had a chance to work in New York, I know it would have affected me the same way. All this time I thought I wanted to go to someplace new in the world and make my mark. By the time my orientation was over, I had to tell the owner I couldn't take the job."

Little did she know Gemma had told Vincenzo she couldn't accept the position. Twice, in fact! But not for the same reason.

"I felt terrible about it, but he was very nice. Do you know what's funny? He'd moved there from Hong Kong to start a new restaurant that's very successful."

That *was* funny, but Gemma didn't laugh and moved over to put an arm around her. "I'm so sorry."

"I'm okay, but I'm embarrassed to go home and tell the family their daughter who's never going to get married is a great big baby."

"No, you're not. Vincenzo and I have spent the last nine days in Paxos on a beach. If I thought I had to go there alone, beautiful as it is, and cook at a restaurant with no friends or family for thousands of miles, I couldn't do it."

"That's not true."

"I wouldn't lie about something like that."

Her brows lifted. "This trip you took. Does it mean—"

"No. We haven't been together like that. I'm not sure we ever will be now, but I'll talk to you about it later. Let's concentrate on you. You're welcome to stay with me on the couch for as long as you want."

"I wouldn't do that to you, but if you're willing to put me up for one night, I'll leave for home tomorrow."

"You've got to stay a couple of days at least. I don't have to be to work until Monday."

"You always make me feel good."

"Ditto. To be truthful, you couldn't have shown up at a better time for me. Vincenzo and I had to come home early from our vacation. His uncle died and he has to be with Dimi to plan the funeral. Come in the kitchen. I made a salad for us."

"Oh, it's so great to see you! What on earth was I thinking to go off, when the world I love is right here?"

"That's what I'm trying to convince Vincenzo of. He's planning to renounce his title, something that's part of him. I don't want him to do that, not for me nor for himself.

"Filippa—he doesn't think he's a whole man because of it. Somehow he's got to develop faith in himself that he can be a good man and a good *duca* at the same time. I couldn't marry him knowing he was giving it up partly because of me. The problem is, I've agreed to stay on at the *castello* for three months no matter what happens. I'm praying that in that amount of time he'll begin to see what I see."

They ate and later went to a movie. After they got back around nine, her phone rang. It was Vincenzo. With her hand shaking, she picked up and said hello.

"Gemma? I've been busy making arrangements for the burial and haven't talked to Dimi yet. If you haven't heard from him by now, then I would imagine he has decided against your staying with my aunt. I'll see you at the *castello* on Monday. Takis is calling a meeting."

She pressed a hand to her heart. "I'll be there." She

fought the tremor in her voice. "Thank you again for the trip of a lifetime, Vincenzo."

"I'm glad you enjoyed it. *Buonanotte.*"

Click.

Gemma made up a bed for Filippa on the couch, then pulled back the covers to get into her own bed. There'd been no life in Vincenzo's voice. Her grief had gone way beyond tears.

As she slid beneath the bedding, her phone rang again. This time the caller ID reflected an unknown number. She answered it with a frown. "*Pronto?*"

"Gemma? It's Dimi." She couldn't believe it. "I've decided I would like you to be here with Mamma while I'm gone. I called the *castello* for your address and phone number." *Not Vincenzo?* "I'll be by for you at eight o'clock in the morning."

Joy. "I'm honored and I'll be ready."

After she got off the phone, she ran into the living room and told Filippa. "I want you to stay. I won't be gone for more than a couple of hours."

"All right."

Like the night before, Gemma didn't get much sleep. The next morning she showered early and put on the one black dress she had in her wardrobe. It had capped sleeves and a slim skirt. Nothing fancy, but she felt it was appropriate.

Her friend had gotten busy in the kitchen and fixed them a delicious breakfast. When Dimi came for her, she didn't know who looked more surprised, him or Filippa.

It was very interesting to feel the aura that surrounded two stunned, beautiful people before Gemma introduced them. Dimi wore a black mourning suit. Filippa had put on a summer dress in a small blue-and-white print, bringing out the intensity of her blue eyes.

When Gemma explained why Filippa was there, he turned to her friend. "Please come with us so Gemma doesn't have to sit alone."

"I don't want to intrude in such a private matter."

"You're her best friend. We have no secrets and it's no intrusion. If you're ready, let's go."

They walked out to the black limousine with the insignia and coat of arms of the Duca di Lombardi. When they got in the back, Dimi placed himself across from them with his long legs crossed at the ankles. All the way to the palazzo, Gemma sat there in wonder as he and Filippa talked quietly, sharing small confidences so naturally, it surprised her.

By the time they reached their destination, Gemma was convinced something of consequence was happening between them. Dimi's eyes never left her face. As for Filippa, her expression had to have mimicked Gemma's the first time she'd seen the dashing, grown-up Vincenzo in the office at the *castello*. If any man ran a close second to Vincenzo, it was his cousin.

He led them inside his mother's bedroom. A health care worker sat beside the bed. Dimi showed the two of them to comfortable upholstered chairs in a corner of the room. He made arrangements for food and drinks to be brought to the small table if they wanted them.

Gemma squeezed his hand. "God bless you today, Dimi."

He kissed her cheek. "Thank you for doing this."

His eyes swerved to Filippa. The look he gave her friend was a revelation. “Thank you for coming with her. I won’t be long.”

A cloudy sky above the opening in the forest didn’t allow the sunlight to shine on the casket. Vincenzo and Dimi stood side by side holding long-stemmed yellow roses while Father Janos delivered the funeral prayer.

“Here we have gathered in memory of Alonzo Trussardi Gagliardi, second in line to the Duca di Lombardi, so that we may together perform one final duty of love. As an act of remembrance, we have gathered to place his remains here in this sacred resting spot. In so doing, we trust that somehow what was best in his life will not be lost, but will rejoin the great web of creation.

“May the truth that sets us free, and the hope that never dies, and the love that casts out fear be with us now until dayspring breaks and the shadows flee away. We have been blessed by life—go in peace. Amen.” He made the sign of the cross.

Dimi placed his rose on the casket, then Vincenzo. They both thanked the priest and had just started to walk away when Dimi said, “Let’s go over to your father’s grave before we drive back to the palazzo.” He pulled two more long-stemmed roses from a planter vase for them.

Vincenzo hadn’t visited it since he’d been back in Italy. He hadn’t ever planned to take a last look, but something fundamental had changed in him since he’d been with Gemma. All their long talks about the past had forced him to delve deep inside himself for the first time in ten years. Perhaps it was time.

His father's grave was behind a nearby tree. They looked at the writing on the headstone. Was it possible that all the evil had been buried with him and hadn't been handed down to Vincenzo? He wanted to believe it. He wanted to believe Gemma, whose soul had been in her eyes when she'd begged him to keep the title and do great things with it. If he thought he could…

Dimi turned to him. "Gemma gave me a piece of advice earlier."

Gemma again, Vincenzo mused. She'd had a profound effect on both of them.

"She said not to let our fathers' misdeeds stain our lives. Though my father was never the *duca*, he'd always hoped to be one day. But no matter what, being the offspring of the old duca didn't make him or your father who they were. It was a flaw in them. She was right, you know?"

With those words he placed his rose at the base of the stone. Clearly Dimi had forgiven both their fathers.

Gemma had forgiven them, too. She'd seen the example of the old *duca* and she believed in Vincenzo. That belief caused an epiphany in him.

As he stood there, he realized his faith in himself had been restored. Stunned and humbled, he put his own rose by the headstone. Then they walked back to the limousine. Vincenzo had come to the cemetery in his car parked behind the limo.

"I'll follow you to the palazzo, Dimi. I don't want you to be alone today."

His cousin eyed him oddly. "I won't be. Gemma

and her friend are there. I picked them up early this morning so they could sit with Mamma."

Vincenzo reeled from the news. "What friend?"

"Filippa. I'm sure she's told you about her."

"Yes, but I thought she was in Canada interviewing for a pastry chef position."

"It seems it didn't work out and she came back last evening."

"A lot has gone on since I dropped Gemma off yesterday."

Dimi nodded. "I told you we talked while you were with Mamma. Something she said, plus what Father Janos said today, has decided me against renouncing the title."

Vincenzo knew the line he was talking about. It had struck a chord with Vincenzo, too.

"Remember the part, 'We trust that somehow what was best in his life will not be lost, but will rejoin the great web of creation'? Gemma convinced me there's a lot you and I can do if we keep our titles to create something really good to repair the damage. In my soul I know she's right." He opened the rear door. "I'll see you back at the palazzo, cousin."

Vincenzo stood there for a few minutes pondering everything. Little did Dimi know he'd been preaching to the converted. In time he broke free of his thoughts long enough to jump in his car. He took off behind Dimi, intending to talk to Gemma as soon as possible.

Dimi was waiting for him in the courtyard when he pulled in. "Have you ever met Gemma's friend?" Dimi asked as they went inside.

Vincenzo hadn't expected that question. His cousin's decision not to renounce his title had been superseded by something else—like the fact that Dimi had a woman on his mind when they'd just laid his uncle to rest.

"Not yet."

Once they entered the palazzo, he followed him through the house to his aunt's bedroom. There he found Gemma and her friend talking quietly to one of the health care workers.

The older woman said Consolata had been resting comfortably all morning, which was a relief. Vincenzo tore his gaze from a pair of green eyes to a pair of blue ones. He had to agree with Gemma's assessment—with that coloring, Filippa was a knockout. Dimi told them to come to the sunroom. When they stood up, he noticed Signorina Gatti was a little shorter than Gemma, but just as curvaceous.

Outside in the garden, formal introductions were made. The maid served them iced tea and sandwiches. Dimi wasn't inclined to talk about the funeral service. If anything he seemed intrigued by Filippa and asked her about her trip to Canada.

Vincenzo took advantage of the moment to get Gemma alone. "We need to talk. How long is your friend going to be with you?"

"She's driving back to Florence tomorrow."

"I'll take the two of you to your place as soon as you're ready to leave. Hopefully we'll find time to be alone tomorrow after she's gone."

Before he could hear her answer, Dimi had walked over. "I've told Filippa I'd like to drive her back to the *pensione* later. What are your plans?"

This day wasn't going the way Vincenzo had imagined at all. He'd thought he might be able to console his cousin, but it didn't look like he needed it. Under the circumstances, nothing could have suited Vincenzo better than to get Gemma alone without offending her friend. He had something vital to tell her.

Gemma gave Filippa the key to the *pensione*. They all said goodbye and Vincenzo walked out to his car with Gemma. But when they left the heart of the city, he turned onto the A8 motorway.

Her head jerked around. "Where are we going? This isn't the way to Sopri."

"First you need to answer a question for me. What magic did you weave on Dimi that has caused him to want to keep his title? He has spent a lifetime telling me he despised it."

"I'm glad he feels that way." She sounded overjoyed.

He gripped the steering wheel tighter. "Was that your plan? To get him on your side so he'd try to influence me?"

"I'd do *anything* to get you on my side! I've finally realized why you don't want to keep the title. You think you can't be a whole person unless you renounce that part that has pained you. But don't you see? You've already done so many things for the community, for your country since you've come back. You're an extraordinary man by being exactly who you are. I don't want you diminished in any way, shape or form. I love you, Vincenzo, title and all."

He didn't know where to go with his emotions. It seemed he didn't have to explain how his feelings had changed about the title and the good he could do with it. "I'm glad you feel that way, because I've decided to keep it. Does that mean you'll marry me?" This was the last time he was going to ask.

"Yes, yes, *yes*!"

CHAPTER TEN

JOY ROCKED VINCENZO'S WORLD, but he groaned aloud. "*Gemma*—what a time to tell me! I'm driving and can't pull over right now. The summer traffic will be bumper to bumper like this all the way to Lake Como."

"That's where we're going?"

"If we can ever get there. Everyone's trying to leave Milan at the same time."

An infectious giggle came out of her, a happy sound he hadn't heard in years. "We've practiced self-control for the last few weeks. Another hour won't kill us."

"You mean *two*. It's *killing* me, you beautiful witch." He reached for her hand and clung to it.

"I want to marry you, Vincenzo. I'm crazy, madly, terrifyingly in love with you. I'm sorry it's taken me so long to get my head on straight. Please—while you can't touch me and I can't make love to you—tell me where we're going to live. I want to know everything. Will we fly back and forth from here to New York every few months? The suspense is killing me."

"One answer at a time. We're going to live here permanently."

"You really mean it?" That was pure happiness he heard in her voice. "Where is here, exactly?"

"That's what I want to show you."

"You mean at Lake Como?"

"The first night in Greece, when we were on the beach, you said that to live surrounded by water would be paradise. I've always wanted to live by water, too. There's a place I've had my eye on for the last six months, never dreaming I'd find you again. And it's not too far from the *castello*."

"I've never been to Lake Como. Have you already bought it?"

"No. The Realtor has been holding it for me, but my time is almost up."

"What town is it in?"

"Cernobbio, in the foothills of the Alps, where the scenery truly is magnificent."

"Is it as fantastic as I'm imagining it is?"

"You'll have to wait and see. I'm sure your mother will love it. She'll be living with us, wherever we are. When the traffic is light, it's only a little over an hour's drive from Milan. There's a private dock on the lake, so we'll have to buy a boat."

"She doesn't know about us yet."

"I didn't think she did. When will she be back from her trip?"

"Tomorrow."

"That's perfect. We'll drive to Florence tomorrow and tell her we're getting married. She loves you enough to want what you want. I'll spend the rest of my life proving to her our marriage will work. But the ceremony has to happen before the grand opening, so we only have a few days left to plan it."

"I'm so happy, I feel like I'm going burst!"

"Don't do that while we're still in this traffic."

She grabbed onto his arm. "When we're married, if the traffic is too horrible to drive home, we can always go upstairs to the tower room, and we'll hibernate while I feed you *sfogliatelli*. No one will know where we are."

Vincenzo didn't know how much longer he could last without pulling Gemma onto his lap. "The one thing we won't have at Lake Como is a beach. Almost no property has beachfront."

"There's only one beach I want. It's in Greece. You've spoiled me. I know I'm dreaming. Do you care if I keep working?"

"I want you to be happy, whatever it takes."

"Will you be happy living away from New York?"

"I have a confession to make. I was never happy there."

"Honestly?"

"I'm an Italian. I was homesick."

Gemma let out a cry. "Filippa said the same thing. That's why she's back."

"Good for her. Where would you like to get married, *bellissima*?"

"I think that should be up to you."

"Then I say we ask the priest to marry us in the *castello* chapel."

"That would make me the happiest woman on earth." Tears ran down her tanned cheeks. "It is so beautiful. I remember looking inside when your grandfather was in there. I thought it was the closest place to heaven."

"Have you considered what he was trying to tell

you that day out in the courtyard might have had a different meaning? My belief is that he knew you were my soul's delight and saw you as the princess I would marry one day."

"Do you really think that?"

"Yes. I'm going to tell your mother that. She'll have to be happy for us."

Gemma's eyes filled with tears. "I'll treasure what you've said all my life."

"You're *my* treasure, Gemma."

"Oh, I can't wait until we get there."

Another few minutes and they passed through Como. Cernobbio was only a little farther up the lake. When they reached it, Gemma gasped. "I didn't know scenery like this existed on earth. There are dozens of incredible villas!"

He wound around until they came to one that jutted out into the lake. At the sign—Villa Gagliardi—he slowed to a stop on the private road.

Gemma took it in with disbelieving eyes before she turned to Vincenzo. "This villa belonged to your family?"

He nodded. "Until my father gambled it away. I've negotiated to buy it back. It's ours if you want it."

"If I *want* it?" She launched herself at him, throwing her arms around his bronzed neck. "I want you forever, any way I can have you. I'll take anything that comes with you."

For the next little while, they tried without success to show each other how much they loved and wanted each other. It was impossible within the confines of his Maserati.

"How can you do this to me?" he whispered against

her lips. "For nine days you held me off. Now you're giving yourself to me and I can't do a thing about it until we find a place to be alone."

"I know. I'm sorry, but I promise I'll make it up to you."

"Let's get married the day after tomorrow. No man ever needed a wedding night more than I do."

She buried her face in his neck. "How can we do that? Wouldn't you have to get a special license?"

"Yes. But I'm the Duca di Lombardi. I'm the person who makes these things happen." His smile melted her bones.

"I presume Father Janos will perform the ceremony whenever you say."

He nodded.

"Won't he think it's too soon after the funeral?"

"Not at all. He'll be happy we're making a dream come true in the midst of so much sadness."

She kissed every feature of his face. "Is there anything you can't do?"

"No."

"Vincenzo—" She hugged him harder. "Be serious. You want to get married the day after tomorrow?"

"Don't you? With your mother coming back tomorrow, there's no reason to delay it a second longer."

"I love you, *il mio amore*."

"Then we need to drive back to Milan immediately and make all the arrangements. Besides your mother, I want Dimi and my partners there."

"I'll tell Filippa she can't leave for Florence until after the ceremony. She can stay at the *pensione* until then."

"Kiss me one more time, Gemma, so I know I'm not hallucinating."

"I plan to kiss the daylights out of you after we say 'I do.' But since I shouldn't be bothering you while you're driving, I'm going to call Mamma right now and tell her everything. She can think about it on her flight back to Florence."

He squeezed her arm. "I'll talk to her, too, and tell her we've just come from the home where we want her to live with us."

Gemma was euphoric as she pulled out her phone to reach her mother. No matter her parent's first reaction, Gemma would talk her down, because there was no one like Vincenzo. She planned to be his wife, and her mother had to understand that.

The phone rang a few times until Mirella picked up. "Oh, Gemma—I'm so glad it's you. I'm tired of traveling around and am anxious to come home."

"I can't wait for you to get here, but please don't be too tired, Mamma."

"Ah? What's wrong?"

"Everything is so right, I don't know where to start."

"You must have gotten a wonderful job."

"Oh, I did!"

After a pause, her mother said, "I haven't heard you this happy since..."

"Since we once lived at the *castello*?" she answered for her.

"Gemma? What's going on?"

"Vincenzo is back in my life! That's what's going on." She smiled into his eyes of molten silver. "You're not going to believe why he really disappeared or why he's back now. We're going to be married the day after tomorrow."

"But he's a *duca*!"

She smiled at Vincenzo through her happy tears. "Yes, and I'm going to be his *duchessa*. That's why you can't be too tired. Tomorrow we have to buy me a wedding dress and a beautiful dress for you. Filippa will need one, too. The ceremony is going to take place in the *castello* chapel by Father Janos. You remember him?"

"Lentamente, mia bambina—"

"I'm too excited to slow down. Tomorrow I'll tell you all the details while we're looking for dresses."

Vincenzo took the phone from her. "Mirella? We want your blessing. No one knows better than you how much I love your daughter. The day you made that little lemon ricotta cheesecake for me when I was eight was the day I fell in love with you, too. Here's Gemma back."

Tears were rolling down her cheeks as she took the phone from him. "Mamma? Did you hear what Vincenzo said?"

"I did," she answered in a croaky voice. "Tell him that if I hadn't loved him, too, I wouldn't have made it for him."

Gemma could hardly breathe. "I'll tell him. I love you, Mamma. See you tomorrow. Fly home safe."

The minute she heard the click, she told him what her mother had said. His eyes filled with tears before she broke down sobbing for joy.

When Dimi arrived at the *pensione* in the ducal limousine at three o'clock, Gemma walked outside with

Filippa, leaving the place in a complete mess. She wore the white wedding dress her mother and her friend had helped her pick out in one of the shops in Milan earlier that morning.

The skirt was a filmy chiffon that fell from the waist and floated around her legs. Lace made up the bodice and short sleeves. Instead of a veil or a bouquet, she wore a garland of white roses and a single strand of pearls with matching earrings that had been delivered that morning by courier. Vincenzo's prewedding gift.

Filippa had helped her put them on and handed her the enclosed card.

Ti amo, squisita.

You are my treasure.

The little makeup she wore was ruined by her tears, and she had to rush to repair the damage.

Gemma had wanted a simple wedding outfit that would still look bridal. If they'd been getting married in front of several hundred people, she would have chosen a long dress with a train and veil. But she was happy with their perfect little wedding.

Dimi took pictures with his camera first. Gemma insisted on taking some of him. Within minutes he helped her into the back of the limousine, where her mother was waiting in an ivory lace suit and pearls. Then he assisted Filippa.

He looked marvelous in a dark blue suit with a white rose in the lapel. Her friend wore a pale pink silk sheath with a corsage of pink roses and looked stunning.

As the limousine drove away, Gemma looked across at Dimi. She squeezed her mother's hand. "I've been thinking back through the years when we were just little children."

"Now you're all grown up." Mirella smiled at them.

"I can't believe this is really happening, Mamma."

Dimi grinned. "Neither can my cousin. He's been waiting for this day for so long, I hope he's still holding it together. I told his friends to do whatever was necessary to help him make it through to the four o'clock ceremony. It's your fault he's in this state, Gemma."

"I've been in a state since I applied for a job at the *castello*, battling my old demons."

"Vincenzo and I know all about those. But yours are gone, right?"

Filippa spoke for her. "I can promise you that my dear Gemma is the most divinely happy woman on the planet. I ought to know. For the last nine years I've listened to her pain over losing Vincenzo."

"Oh—" Mirella threw her hands in the air. "I prayed every night the pain would stop."

Gemma's friend chuckled. "The minute I heard he was alive and back at the *castello*, I actually sent up a special prayer of thanksgiving."

Dimi nodded. "I did the same thing when he told me you'd applied for the pastry chef position. It was your recipes, Mirella, that put Gemma over the top with Vincenzo's partners. Do you know that from the moment he arrived in New York, I've heard nothing but grief from him where Gemma was concerned?

Today I'm the happiest man on the planet to know that this torturefest is about to be over."

The four of them laughed.

"I love Vincenzo so much. When he walked in the office, I almost fainted."

Dimi leaned forward and patted her hand. "When you two met, we couldn't have been more than four or five. Even then it was as if no one else existed. He followed you around like a puppy dog. You teased him and provoked him, but he just kept coming."

"He teased me back constantly. His growls were terrifying when he chased me around the old ruins. I laughed until I fell down and couldn't catch my breath. Every day when I woke up, I knew I was going to see him and there'd be a new adventure. Nothing else mattered.

"But I want you to know something, Dimi. I loved you, too. So did Bianca. I don't think there were four happier children anywhere."

"I agree. What I want to know is, are you ready to be chased around the *castello*'s secret corridors and chambers for the rest of your life?"

"Yes. I can't wait!"

"Gemma!" Mirella cried, but she knew her mother was only pretending to be shocked.

"I'm warning you. He hasn't outgrown certain tendencies." His wicked smile reminded her of the old Dimi.

"Neither have I, but don't you dare tell him."

When she looked out the tinted windows, she realized the limousine had pulled up in front of the *castello* steps. She gripped her mother's hand. "This is it."

Dimi got out and held the door open for the three of them. "Be sure you want to go inside, Gemma," he teased. "Because when you do, you'll never be the same again."

"I know." She gave him a hug. "I'll be Signora Gagliardi. Don't have a heart attack, Mamma."

Her mother only laughed, the most wonderful sound Gemma had ever heard from her parent. eh.

"Well, here goes!" She took off alone and rushed up the steps, breathless to find Vincenzo, who was inside waiting for her. Never had there been a bride as eager as she to seal her fate.

Cesare stood at the entrance in a becoming tan suit. He too wore a white rose in his lapel. "Your husband-to-be has asked me to do the honors and escort you to the chapel." He kissed her on both cheeks.

"Thank you so much."

He gave her his arm and they walked through several long corridors to reach that part of the *castello*. "I had no idea when I interviewed you that you were the person who ruined every woman for Vincenzo all those years ago."

"That's not quite true. I know of one special woman, very recently in fact."

He shook his head. "No, no. If she'd been the one, he would have brought her with him. Did you know he wanted you to stay in the tower room of the former *principessa*?"

Warmth traveled up her neck to her cheeks. That had been her favorite room in the whole *castello*. "He was only joking."

Cesare laughed. "Denial becomes you."

They reached the closed chapel doors, where Takis

stood, dressed in a beige suit, also wearing a white rose. He hugged her before Dimi introduced Filippa and Gemma's mother to the other men.

Cesare gave her a special smile. "So you're the *mamma* responsible for raising our new executive pastry chef. She gave all the credit to you on her résumé. I understand why. The pastry she made for us was beyond compare. I'm honored to meet you." So saying, he gave her a kiss on both cheeks. Gemma loved him for showing her mother such deference.

Dimi turned to Filippa. "This is where I leave you to join Vincenzo, but Takis will take good care of you." Dimi's gaze swerved to Gemma's. "You're sure you want to go through with this?"

"*Dimi—*" she cried softly in exasperation.

"Just checking."

He took more pictures of all of them, then folded her mother's arm over his and they moved inside the chapel.

Gemma looked at Takis. "Have you seen Vincenzo? Is he in there?"

"*Si.*"

"And Father Janos?"

"*Si.*" With a poker face, he added, "In case you can't tell them apart, Vincenzo is the tall guy wearing the gray suit and white rose. The short, portly father is wearing...well...let's just say he's dressed in splendid robes for this once-in-a-lifetime celebration of your marriage."

Her eyes smarted. "Thank you for being his dear friends. Your friendship saved him at the darkest moment of his life."

Takis cocked his head. "Someday we'll tell you

just how dark our lives were when we arrived in the States. Meeting Vincenzo was the best thing that ever happened to us. Isn't that right, Cesare?"

The Sicilian nodded and lent her his arm. "It's four o'clock. Time to begin."

Takis opened the doors and walked Filippa down the aisle. Gemma followed with Cesare. For such a small chapel, the interior was breathtaking, with wall and ceiling frescoes still vibrant with color.

This was where she'd seen Vincenzo's grandfather worship. Now Emanuele's two grandsons stood on either side of Father Janos, waiting for Gemma. She feared her heartbeat could be heard throughout the incense-sweet interior. With each step that took her closer to Vincenzo, it seemed to grow louder.

Except for the absence of the father she'd never known, Gemma couldn't imagine a more perfect setting for their intimate wedding. The most important people in the world were here in attendance.

Cesare walked her to the front, where Vincenzo reached for her hands. Beneath his black wavy hair, the bronzed features of his striking face stood out against the frescoes. The candles beneath the shrine cast flickering shadows, revealing to Gemma the impossibility of his male beauty.

They both whispered, "*Ti amo...*" at the same time.

Father Janos bestowed a thoughtful smile on them. "I understand this moment has been in the making for many years."

She nodded. Vincenzo must have told him everything.

"That is a good long time for you to have loved each other and should give you the faith that your union will be blessed by the Almighty. Vincenzo? Take her right hand in your left and repeat after me. 'I, Vincenzo Nistri Gagliardi, Duca di Lombardi, take Gemma Bonucci Rizzo for my beloved wife. I will love her, cherish her, protect her for the rest of my life.'"

Gemma heard him repeat the words in that deep, thrilling voice of his.

"Now, Gemma. Repeat these words."

She looked into Vincenzo's eyes. Between the dark lashes they gleamed pure silver. "I, Gemma Bonucci Rizzo, take Vincenzo Nistri Gagliardi, Duca de Lombardi, for my beloved husband, who has always been beloved to me." The last part of the sentence was her own addition. It brought a smile to Vincenzo's lips.

"I will love him, cherish him, support him and honor him for the rest of my life." The honor part was another deviation from the script, but she wanted him to know how complete was her commitment to him.

"Because you have taken these vows, I pronounce you man and wife. In the name of the Father, the Son and the Holy Spirit. Amen. Vincenzo? Do you have a ring?"

"I do."

"You may present it to your wife.

She was his wife!

His fingers were sure as he pushed home a diamond in a gold band on her ring finger.

"Do you have a ring, Gemma?"

"She does," Dimi said and came forward. He handed her the gold band she'd picked out for Vincenzo during their shopping spree with her mother.

"You may present it to your husband."

Vincenzo helped her put it on, then pulled her into his arms and kissed her. It went on for a long, long time. Gemma forgot everything and everyone. Somehow she'd been given her heart's desire, and nothing mattered but to pledge her heart and soul to him in the most intimate way she knew how.

"I love you, Gemma. You just don't know how much."

"But I do, *amore mio*."

They kissed each other once more. When he finally lifted his mouth from hers, she realized they were the only ones left in the chapel. "Oh, no—even the priest has gone."

He gave her that white smile to die for. "Father Janos was a man before he wore the robes. That should answer your question."

"There's no one like you. It was a perfect wedding."

Vincenzo wrapped his arms around her. "There's more. Much as I want to take you upstairs, our friends are waiting in my grandfather's small dining room to celebrate with us. I'm excited, because Cesare's contribution has been to make the meal for us. He learned to cook from his mother, just the way you did. It'll be an all-Sicilian menu tonight."

She put her arms around his neck. "I love your friends. I adore Dimi, and I love my dear friend Filippa. I've decided her timing in coming back to Italy was meant to be, as was Mamma's. Now I guess we'd better not keep them all waiting."

He kissed her eyes, nose and mouth. "They understand and will enjoy the vintage Sicilian wine until we get there. One more kiss, *sposa mia*."

Twenty minutes later they walked arm in arm to the second floor. When they entered the dining room, Gemma could smell the beef fillet in brandy before she saw the paintings of wood nymphs, all in a serious state of undress. Her face turned scarlet.

Everyone clapped. Vincenzo walked her to the table and sat down next to her, putting his hand on her thigh beneath the table. Heat coursed through her body.

Dimi raised his glass. "To my cousin and his wife. To Mirella. None of you have any idea how long I've wanted to say that. I don't know when I've ever been this happy." His eyes were smiling. So were Filippa's.

Cosimo waited on them, bringing one delicious dish after another. Caponata...*arancini*...pasta with urchin sauce.

When the meal concluded, Gemma got to her feet. "This is joy beyond measure to be surrounded by our friends and my beloved mother. What can I say about our bridal feast? The six-star award goes to Cesare for the best meal I've ever eaten in my life. *Grazie* with all my heart."

Cesare beamed. "*Di niente.*"

Vincenzo stood up and put his arm around Gemma's waist. "I can't improve on anything my bride said. And now I must tell you we have a pressing engagement elsewhere and ask to be excused, but we know you will understand."

The men's deep laughter filled the room while Filippa and Gemma exchanged a secret smile. With her friend planning to stay at the *pensione* for a few more days, everything was working out perfectly. On a whim, Gemma removed her garland of roses and tossed it to Filippa, then tossed her mother a kiss. She would be staying in the tower room of the *principessa* until after the hotel's grand opening. Vincenzo couldn't do enough for her.

"Come with me," her husband whispered.

She needed no urging. Her desire for him had reached a flashpoint.

Vincenzo rushed her through the hallways to the back of the *castello*. When they came to the winding steps, he picked her up in his arms and carried her to the tower room. His strength astounded her. When they'd reached the bedroom, he wasn't even out of breath.

"I've dreamed of doing that for years. Help me, Gemma. I want you so much I'm shaking."

While he was helping her out of her dress, she was trying to take off his suit jacket. Somehow they managed and kissed their way to the bed. He lay down with her and crushed her in his arms, entwining his legs with hers. After suppressing their needs for the last two weeks, the freedom to love each other made her delirious with longing.

Each touch and caress ignited their passion. Vincenzo had lit her on fire. The right to show her husband everything she felt and wanted was a heady experience too marvelous to contain. They drank deeply from each other's mouths, thrilling in the wonder of being together like this.

Far into the night, they gave and took pleasure with no thought but the happiness and joy they found in each other. Gemma hadn't known the physical side of their lovemaking could be this overwhelming. Her rapture was so great that at times she cried afterward and clung to him.

When morning came he began the age-old ritual all over again. They'd suffered for so long, they thoroughly enjoyed becoming one flesh, one heart.

Toward noon, they lay side by side, awake again. Vincenzo smiled at her. "I feel like I've just been reborn."

"I know. I've had those same feelings."

He suddenly pulled her on top of him. "I'm too happy, Gemma."

"Can there be too much happiness?"

"I don't know. Promise me it will always be like this."

She searched his eyes. "My love for you just keeps growing."

Rolling her over, he kissed her fiercely. "I want to make love to you all over again, but I know you must be hungry. Are you?"

"Yes. For you!"

"I'm serious."

"So am I."

"Cesare told me yesterday he'd have food brought up to us. I'm pretty sure it's outside the door now."

"Then we'd better eat it. I don't want to hurt his feelings." Her darling Vincenzo. He was starving, but he didn't want to admit it. She loved this man beyond description. "Why don't you go look and see?"

He pressed a kiss to her throat. "I'll be right back. Don't go away."

"Where would I go?"

"Never disappear on me, Gemma. I couldn't take it." Lines had darkened his face.

She couldn't understand it and pulled him back. "Someone once said, 'Don't give in to your fears. If you do, you won't be able to talk to your heart.'"

"That was Paulo Coelho."

Gemma caught his handsome face in her hands. "You're disgustingly intelligent, my love, but you need to take his advice. Don't you know I plan to cling to you forever?"

"I'm besotted with you, Gemma." He hurried to the door in his robe and came back with a tray of food that smelled divine. "Cesare has really outdone himself."

She took it from him and put it on the bed. "Let's eat fast so I can love you all over again."

His smile melted her bones. "I'm planning to keep you locked up here forever."

She leaned across to kiss his jaw. He needed a shave. "That's fine as long as you let me out in time for the grand opening. It'll be here in a few days. I was hired to cook, remember?"

Those silvery eyes blazed with fire for her. "Do you think I can ever forget anything since you came back into my life?"

He ate his cheese-and-ham strata in record time, displaying the appetite she always associated with him. Then he put the tray on the floor. After taking her in his arms again, he buried his face in her neck.

"We were meant to be together from the beginning. Love me, *sposa squisita.* I was hooked from the first time I saw the cutest little honey-blonde girl on earth come running out to the ruins to play hide and go seek. Her eyes were greener than the grass and her smile was like sunshine. My five-year-old heart quivered, and that has never changed."

"*Vincenzo—*"

EPILOGUE

THE MORNING OF the day before the grand opening, Gemma worked with her team as they prepared everything. While she was supervising the tiramisu desserts, Cesare walked in the kitchen and came over to her.

"*Per favore*, will you stop what you're doing and come out in the hall? This will only take a minute."

"Of course." She washed her hands and wiped them on her apron as she hurried after him. Once through the doors she came to a full stop. *Paolo!*

Cesare said, "I understand you two know each other."

"Yes. It's good to see you, Paolo."

He gave her a slight nod. "I understand you're Signora Gagliardi now. I get why it didn't work out for us. The Duca di Lombardi was the man you could never forget."

"You're right."

"Congratulations on your marriage."

"Thank you."

"*Buon Appetito* magazine has sent me out to cover the grand opening of the restaurant tomorrow and write up my opinion. Knowing that *you're* the new executive pastry chef has blown me away. Signor Donati told me I could say hello to you if I waited out here. I realize how busy you must be, so I won't keep you. *Buona fortuna*, Gemma."

She felt his sincerity, though that didn't mean he wouldn't be brutal if her food didn't measure up to his idea of five-star dining. "To you, too, Paolo. *Grazie.*"

Two mornings later

While Gemma lay wrapped in her husband's arms, both still exhausted from all the work of the grand opening, she heard a knock.

"Vincenzo, get up and see what I've slipped under your door."

At the sound of Cesare's voice, both of them came awake. *The reviews!*

"Grazie!"

"Stay there, *caro.*" Gemma bounded out of bed first and grabbed her husband's robe to put on. Half a dozen computer printouts had been pushed through. She reached for them and ran back to the bed.

By now Vincenzo was fully awake. He threw his arm around her shoulders while they read the glowing reviews. Then his cell phone rang. He saw the caller ID and picked up, holding the phone so Gemma could hear, too.

"Dimi?"

"Have you read everything yet?" His cousin sounded ecstatic.

"Almost."

"Our cup has run over today."

"I agree."

"I'm bringing Filippa to the *castello* with me later on today and we'll celebrate."

"That sounds perfect. Ciao."

He hung up and they began to read Paolo's article.

A new star is born in Lombardi!

Ring out the bells for the Castello Supremo Hotel and Ristorante di Lombardi. From its hundred-years-old ducal past has emerged a triumph of divine ambience and cuisine so exquisite to the palate, this critic can't find enough superlatives. One could live forever on the slow-cooked boeuf bourguignon and the *sfogliatelli* Mirella dessert alone. This critic thought he'd died and gone to heaven.

It deserves six stars. Bravo!

Gemma put it down and threw her arms around Vincenzo's neck. "You and Dimi and your partners did it, *amante*! You did it!" She broke down crying for joy.

"We all did it, including your wonderful *mamma*."

"Was it your idea to name the dessert after her?"

He studied her features before kissing her passionately. "It was Cesare's. An Italian loves his mother. After hearing your story, he knew your *mamma* deserved the credit on the souvenir menu commemorating the opening."

"That's so sweet of him. When Mamma sees this, she'll die."

"I have a better idea. Let's frame it, along with a menu, and give them to her for a special present. Cesare was touched that you loved your mother so much you talked about her on your application. I already know how sweet you are.

"The day you came running outside with the lemon ricotta cheesecake she made for my birthday, you ran straight into my heart and never left. You'll always be there. *Ti amo*, Signora Gagliardi."

"*Ti amo*, Your Highness."

"Don't call me that."

"It's the highest honor I can give you, Vincenzo. You're the greatest Gagliardi of them all."

* * * * *

Look out for two more stories in
The Billionaire's Club coming soon!

You might also enjoy Rebecca Winters'
MONTINARI MARRIAGES *Trilogy*

THE BILLIONAIRE'S BABY SWAP
THE BILLIONAIRE WHO SAW HER BEAUTY
THE BILLIONAIRE'S PRIZE

“No, that’s good. I’m glad you’re all mine—”

All his?

“Not *all mine*,” he said in a hurry, amending it. “I’m glad there isn’t anyone but the colonel on your to-do list because you’ll have your hands full with just her.”

“With her and your shoulder rehab,” Kinsey reminded.

“Yeah, sure… that, too,” he conceded.

Was he just the slightest bit flustered?

It amused Kinsey to think so but she tried not to let it show.

He opened the door and went out with her when she stepped onto the landing.

“I’ll see you tomorrow,” she said. “And you, too, Jack,” she told the dog, petting his head and inadvertently brushing Sutter Knightlinger’s arm when she did.

Then she headed for her car, wondering why that bare hint of contact had had the same effect as the first time she’d set eyes on him just shortly before— that odd sensation that had made her skin tingle.

Another chill? she wondered.

That had to be it.

Certainly it couldn’t have been Sutter Knightlinger.

Because no matter how attractive he was, a marine was still a marine to her.

And towering and muscular and handsome as all get-out or not, there was no place in her life for another one of those.

* * *

Camden Family Secrets:
Finding family and love in Colorado!

THE MARINE MAKES HIS MATCH

BY
VICTORIA PADE

All rights reserved including the right of reproduction in whole or in part in any form. This edition is published by arrangement with Harlequin Books S.A.

This is a work of fiction. Names, characters, places, locations and incidents are purely fictional and bear no relationship to any real life individuals, living or dead, or to any actual places, business establishments, locations, events or incidents. Any resemblance is entirely coincidental.

This book is sold subject to the condition that it shall not, by way of trade or otherwise, be lent, resold, hired out or otherwise circulated without the prior consent of the publisher in any form of binding or cover other than that in which it is published and without a similar condition including this condition being imposed on the subsequent purchaser.

® and ™ are trademarks owned and used by the trademark owner and/or its licensee. Trademarks marked with ® are registered with the United Kingdom Patent Office and/or the Office for Harmonisation in the Internal Market and in other countries.

First Published in Great Britain 2017
By Mills & Boon, an imprint of HarperCollins*Publishers*
1 London Bridge Street, London, SE1 9GF

© 2017 Victoria Pade

ISBN: 978-0-263-92280-6

23-0317

Our policy is to use papers that are natural, renewable and recyclable products and made from wood grown in sustainable forests. The logging and manufacturing processes conform to the legal environmental regulations of the country of origin.

Printed and bound in Spain
by CPI, Barcelona

Victoria Pade is a *USA TODAY* bestselling author of numerous romance novels. She has two beautiful and talented daughters—Cori and Erin—and is a native of Colorado, where she lives and writes. A devoted chocolate lover, she's in search of the perfect chocolate-chip-cookie recipe.

For information about her latest and upcoming releases, visit Victoria Pade on Facebook—she would love to hear from you.

Chapter One

"Come on, marine, come home!" Kinsey Madison said as she glanced down the street hoping for an approaching car. Then, hearing her own words, she laughed a small, wry laugh and said, "Same old tune."

But on this November day in Denver, she wasn't waiting for her brothers to come home. Instead, she was waiting for the man who was scheduled to interview her for a job.

Dignified old homes lined both sides of the street, shaded by enormous trees all bursting with red and gold leaves. But scenic or not, she'd been sitting there for over half an hour.

She was slated to meet Sutter Knightlinger, son of retired marine colonel Geraldine Knightlinger, who was in need of Kinsey's services as a home–health care nurse. He'd texted that he was delayed at the hospital with his mother but would be there as soon as possible.

She wouldn't have stayed, but this was a job she really wanted. It came with a particular opportunity she hoped to mine. An opportunity that fit into her own secret agenda.

She'd left Denver and her former job almost a year ago to return to her small Montana hometown. Her own mother's health had been failing and with all three of her brothers deployed overseas, she was the only choice to take care of her mom.

Alice Madison had passed away a month ago. A short-term job as a private duty nurse had helped Kinsey transition from Northbridge back to Denver. When that job ended, her employer's fiancée, Livi Camden, had recommended her for another home–health care position.

And just like that, when Kinsey had been fretting about losing what little contact she'd gained with the Camdens through Livi, another way had fallen into her lap via the Knightlingers.

Filling time, she pulled down the sun visor in front of her to look in the mirror that was hidden on the underside. She wanted to make sure she remained interview ready.

Her dark brown hair was long. It fell to the middle of her back when she wore it down, like she had today—parted just off-center and swept somewhat away from her oval face.

Makeup was something she kept to a minimum but she did use a little mascara to darken the lashes around her cobalt blue eyes, and blush to highlight her high cheekbones.

A barely-colored lip gloss moistened lips she pressed together before checking straight teeth to make sure nothing was stuck in them.

She craned up higher so she could see the high collar of the cream-colored blouse she'd worn today under a cinnamon-colored cardigan to go along with tan slacks.

All in all, she judged herself presentable for the interview and again just wished Sutter Knightlinger would get there so it could begin.

So a lot of things could begin. Things her brothers were opposed to her doing at all.

A big black SUV came down the street just then and pulled into the driveway. Kinsey got out of her car and opened the door to her backseat, leaning in to retrieve the leather satchel that contained her résumé and patient forms along with her medical supplies and instruments.

By the time she'd done that, a deep, deep male voice was calling across the yard, "Are you Kinsey Madison?"

Drawing out of the car she closed the door and looked over the top of it to say "I am." And to stop short at the sight of the very fine specimen of man who had gotten out of the SUV.

Tall—at least six foot three—he had broad shoulders, a narrow waist and long legs that no doubt did much justice to his uniform when he was wearing it. As it was, he certainly wasn't putting shame to the checked sport shirt and unfaded denim jeans he wore. Not even the fact that his left arm was in a sling detracted from the image.

To top off the impressively muscular build was a face that could have graced recruitment posters to help attract women to the service. Ruggedly handsome, he had hair the shade of wet sand that was cut short on the sides and just long enough on top to comb back. He had deep-set, piercing teal eyes, a longish nose that was a hint hawkish, a great mouth with a full lower lip and an angular jawline that culminated at a squarish chin with the sexiest dimple right in the center of it.

And all of a sudden Kinsey felt the oddest sensation, as if a small electrical charge rippled through her.

Maybe she'd caught a chill.

Whatever it was, she ignored it and told herself to be professional. This *was* a job interview, after all.

She locked her car and rounded the front end to head up the walkway as he came from the driveway.

At the front door, Kinsey paused while he punched in a series of numbers on a keypad to unlock it. Opening it with his uninjured right hand, he said, "Come on in. I apologize for the delay. It couldn't be helped."

He didn't sound at all contrite, just matter-of-fact and he offered no explanation. She'd known he was an officer in the marines, and his attitude showed he was accustomed to laying down orders and expecting them to be followed by lesser ranks whether they liked it or not, whether they understood it or not.

"No problem," she assured, having a lot of experience with that mindset and taking no offense. Kinsey followed him into a living room, the whole way accompanied by the sound of vigorous barking coming from another room.

"Jack! Quiet!" her host commanded, making Kinsey fight a smile when the order was completely disregarded.

"Just a minute. I have him crated in the kitchen and he won't stop until I go get him."

The man who still hadn't introduced himself left her. Kinsey took the opportunity to look around.

The inside of the house was like the outside—no-nonsense. The walls were paneled, the floors were hardwood, the furniture was all dark leather, the draperies were formal and the tables were antique. Heavy, dark and distinguished, there wasn't a single thing that was light, airy, frivolous or fun. Or particularly homey or welcoming, either.

The barking stopped and the sound of four skittering paws announced the wire-haired fox terrier puppy that suddenly charged into the room. The pint-sized white, black and brown pup came straight for Kinsey, jumping up on her and wagging his tail eagerly.

"Jack! Down!" was the second command the dog ignored.

Kinsey leaned over to pet the adorable terrier. "Hi, Jack."

"I'd put him in the backyard but he'd just bark his head off until I let him in again."

"He's fine," Kinsey said, laughing as Jack started wrestling with her pant leg, growling with puppy ferocity.

Her host bent over and scooped the animal away from Kinsey's slacks, holding the little wriggler under his arm like a football.

"I'm Sutter Knightlinger, by the way," he said finally. Then, nodding in the direction of the leather sofa, he added, "Have a seat."

He waited until she was sitting to take one of the tufted leather wing chairs across from a mahogany coffee table coated with a layer of undisturbed dust. He situated Jack beside him and the pup promptly began gnawing on the big hand keeping him prisoner until Sutter distracted him with a chew toy.

He began the interview saying, "Livi told me about your credentials—registered nurse with physical therapy training and experience both in hospitals and in home health care. She also told me what you do as a home–health care provider, so we don't have to go through that—you're well qualified. But I'm not sure how much you know about the situation here."

"I know a little," Kinsey said. "Livi told me that you're a cousin to her cousins? That your mother and her aunt by marriage were sisters?" The key part to this for Kinsey, though she couldn't admit that to Sutter.

"You'll need to address my mother as Colonel—if you call her anything but that you'll get off on the wrong foot," he advised. "But yes, the colonel's sister Tina and Howard Camden were married, making Seth, Cade, Beau and Jani Camden my cousins."

"Livi told me that your dad passed away a couple of months ago," she continued. "I'm sorry for your loss."

He acknowledged that stoically, with only the raise of that dimpled chin.

"Livi said that you were injured in Afghanistan and in a hospital when your dad died so the memorial service was postponed until last week, when you could get back. But your mom—the colonel—had a mild heart attack in the middle of it. I know that she's since had a pacemaker put in, that she needs some recovery care, and that you, too, need physical therapy on that arm and shoulder."

"For starters," he said as if that was all only the tip of the iceberg. "Livi speaks highly of you," he added, those teal eyes steady on her. "She says you go above and beyond the call of duty."

Why did she automatically go to thoughts of doing completely inappropriate things with him? That wasn't the way he'd said it—he was all business.

Kinsey pushed the thoughts aside, saying, "Above and beyond the call of duty in what way?"

His well-shaped eyebrows arched as if he'd just realized what she might be thinking and he was quick to say, "I'm not talking fraternizing." He glanced at Jack, now gnawing on his toy, and when he looked at her again he was expressionless. The military blank face—Kinsey knew that well, too.

"I've had some shocks in the last two months," he said then, all business again. "There were a lot of things the colonel didn't tell me—first and foremost that my father was in the hospital. I had no idea anything was going on here. Then I got notified of his death, long after it had happened..."

That did not sit well with him because boy, could that handsome face scowl!

"Left on her own, without my dad around, the colonel..." He shook his head. "At work, at home, she's always had subordinate staff to take care of things—she was a lawyer and then a judge—"

"Did she have help at home other than your dad?"

"No, at home my dad took care of everything."

Which made him subordinate staff?

"The point is," Sutter continued, "my dad looked after everything around here. Including the colonel. Without him, the house, the yard, have gone downhill. And so has she. She's always tended to hole up, get lost in her books, the journal she'll probably turn into a memoir one day or her old war movie DVDs."

Sutter shook his head in what seemed like some frustration. "She doesn't cook, never has—so as far as I can tell all she's been eating are cheese puffs and candy bars, and not much of those. She hasn't kept the house up at all."

"I would imagine your mother spent a lot of time at the hospital with your father while he was there," Kinsey said. "Tough to keep up on home maintenance and do that, too."

"Sure. But my dad died two months ago. When I got home, no one had checked the mail in weeks. There were condolence floral arrangements dead in their vases outside the front door. The refrigerator had rotten food in it."

"Did she forget about those things?" Kinsey asked in case what they were discussing was the onset of dementia or Alzheimer's.

He knew what she was asking, though, because he said, "The colonel is as sharp as she's always been. It isn't that. She's slowed down over the years but she doesn't have any major physical or cognitive problems. This is more about her needing to…"

He raised both hands in frustration. "She needs to change!" he said.

His movements gave Jack just enough freedom to jump down. The adorable puppy went to the basket of toys, ignored its contents and instead began waging war against the basket itself, dragging it into the center of the room. Sutter left him to it.

"I have people coming in to clean the house, to work on the yard. I can set up automatic payment for the bills, set up a grocery delivery. But without my dad, she'll just keep herself cut off from everything outside of her den—I think some nights she doesn't even bother to go up to her bedroom to sleep. She didn't let in anyone who came to pay respects after my dad passed—she wouldn't even come to the door."

"Everyone reacts to grief in their own way," Kinsey offered.

"Sure, but this isn't grief, it's how she's always been. Day-to-day life has never been what she deals with.

Her work, the military—that's been it for her. Except for me and my dad."

"And now with your dad gone, there's just you," Kinsey said.

"And I'm on extended leave until my shoulder heals, but then I need to rejoin my unit in Afghanistan. I can't leave her the way she's been living."

Kinsey nodded her understanding.

"Somebody has to convince her to take better care of herself. Maybe if someone other than me, someone with some professional medical standing, gets on her about it, it'll bring it home to her."

"I can do that," Kinsey assured.

"And she needs a network of support. She has to have people in her life, whether she knows it or admits it or not. She has to have human contact and she certainly won't go find it for herself."

"What about an assisted living facility—"

Another firm, definitive shake of his head stopped her from going on with that. "This house has been in her family for four generations, she won't leave it. And she's only accepting having you here until she gets back on her feet. I offered to get her live-in help and she blew a gasket—"

"I know it isn't much comfort but what you're describing isn't all that uncommon. So what *exactly* are you wanting me to do beyond her recovery?" Kinsey asked.

But his frustration level was too high to give her calm, concrete answers. "Anything! I want you to do anything you can to get her out of her rut, to make her let people into her life, to take care of herself!"

It was an outburst that Kinsey could tell was out of the ordinary for him. He took a deep breath and exhaled to get himself under control. Then he went on unemotionally again. "Livi said you have a lot of good ideas. And if they come from someone other than me—" He heaved a sigh that was somewhere between frustration and disgust. "She won't take suggestions from me. I tried talking to her about this stuff again yesterday and she actually pulled rank on me and just shouted for me to quit meddling in her life."

Kinsey didn't suppress her smile this time. "Are you sure she won't figure she outranks me, too?" she joked.

Sutter actually laughed. He was even more good-looking when he did.

Not that that was something that mattered. She was just glad to have eased some of his tension.

Then, in a more confidential tone, he said, "And whatever you do, you can't let her know that we even talked about this. If the colonel thinks I put you up to socializing her or networking her or whatever, she will dig her heels in and that'll be it."

"So you need me to work a miracle transformation on your mother and her life before you have to leave again—and not let her know you put me up to it," she summarized.

"Yes."

The wheels of Kinsey's mind began to turn.

He was recruiting her for a conspiracy. A conspiracy to get him something he wanted. To reach a goal.

Could she do the same with him?

It would mean taking him into her confidence, something she was hesitant to do. But if she did, how much closer could she get to her own goal?

The chance to build a relationship with the Camdens was the whole reason she wanted this job. If Sutter could provide her with more direct contact with them, things could move along much quicker.

Or he could just throw her out when he found out her true motives.

Was it worth taking the risk?

"What you're asking *is* above and beyond the call of duty," she reminded him, deciding to take a chance. "But I'd be willing to give it a try if you might be willing to help me with something, too."

"Like what?"

"I'd like to get to know the Camdens better."

"You already know Livi," he pointed out.

"We're *acquainted*, yes," Kinsey hedged. "But I'm interested in more than that. I mean I've met all of them—I went to one of their Sunday dinners but just in the role of nurse to my last patient. Everyone was nice and said hello, but that was it."

"And you want more than that?" He sounded suspicious.

"I do. You're an insider—"

"And you want to use that—me—to get close to them and do what?"

Oh, yeah, he was suspicious all right. She could understand why. The Camdens were one of the wealthiest families in the country thanks to their massive chain of superstores. There was probably no shortage of people who wanted to get close to them to take advantage in some way. But Kinsey wasn't interested in their money or prestige.

"I'm not after anything but the chance to get to know them. For them to get to know me—"

"Why?" he demanded.

Should she inform him of something she hadn't told anyone except her brothers?

"I'll tell you here and now," Sutter said sternly, "I don't give a damn what you might be able to do for the colonel, I won't help you work some kind of scam or angle on the Camdens."

"That's not what this is about! I told you, I don't want anything from them but to get to know them."

"To gain their trust and then what?"

Oh, he was thinking the worst of her—it was there in those penetrating teal eyes that were boring through her.

She realized that she was going to have to tell him the whole truth now just as damage control. Otherwise, she had no doubt that he'd do everything in his considerable power to make sure she never got within a mile of a Camden ever again.

So she steeled herself and said, "You're part of the Camden family…" *Deep breath. Exhale...* "And so am I. Mitchum Camden was my brothers' and my biological father."

It didn't look like Sutter believed her.

"We had no idea until recently," she went on. "My mother only told me in her last days. Then there was a letter her lawyer gave me when she died. There isn't any question but I'd welcome DNA testing…"

She paused. It wasn't easy to be convincing when there was so little she knew herself. "I don't know if any of them know we exist—my mother said they didn't. But I'd like it if, before I approach the subject, they got to know me a little. If maybe they liked me a little. If they did, they might be more receptive to the news—"

"For what? So you can hit them up for money?"

"No! We don't need that! There already *is* money—a lot of it. Part of why my mother told me the truth after all this time was to explain the money I'd be finding when she died. For me it's just about family—maybe having some around instead of always being on my own."

His well-shaped eyebrows were pulled into a frown but there was something about his expression that seemed to have softened around the edges. "What exactly do you want me to do?"

"Tell me about them—whatever you know… I realize that my half siblings aren't from the side you're related to, but I've heard that they're a close-knit bunch and I'm thinking that if you're in with one of them, you're in with them all to some extent. And maybe you could bring me along if you're going to be with them—to the Sunday dinners, or whatever else you might be able to arrange. I'm not asking a lot—just for some information and to be around them as much as possible so I sort of become a familiar face."

Sutter gave her the hardest stare she'd ever endured but she didn't waver. Nothing she'd said was a lie so there was no reason for her to back down.

Until Jack leaped onto her lap, jabbed his nose into her bag and stole her stethoscope, taking it with him to jump off the sofa.

Even injured, Sutter's reaction time was quicker than Kinsey's and he nabbed the puppy before Jack got too far, retrieving the stethoscope.

Containing the terrier beside him on the chair once more, he handed it back to her. "Can you do something with this, too?" he asked, referring to the dog. "I got him so the colonel would have a companion but that's not working out very well, either."

"Actually, yes—I think I can get help with Jack."

Sutter returned to assessing her before he said, "Then you'll match-make my mother with the dog and with a support system, and you want me to match-make you with the Camdens?"

"That's about it," Kinsey confirmed.

Another long moment passed under his scrutiny.

"I'd be watching, you know. Like a hawk. And should anything make me think you're up to something to hurt the Camdens, I wouldn't hesitate to warn them. If that happened you'd never get anywhere near them again."

"Sure," she said.

More scrutiny before he seemed to come to a conclusion.

He sighed again, this one resigned. "You better be on the level…"

"So we have a deal? You'll help me while I'm helping you?"

"Yeah, I guess," he said as if he wasn't altogether thrilled with it. "But you'd better have a pretty good bag of tricks, lady. And you'd better not be working me."

Kinsey only said, "When do you need me to start?"

"I'm bringing the colonel home tomorrow, whenever she gets released. I can text you when we're about to leave the hospital and you can meet us here."

"Okay."

Sutter stood then, again holding Jack football-style.

Kinsey took that as her cue to go and stood, too. "Tomorrow I'll just take your mom's history, check her vitals and settle her in, start to get to know her. Then we'll go from there."

The towering marine agreed with an outward jut of his chin. "Brace yourself, she's not a warm and fuzzy little old lady," he warned.

"She's the colonel—got it," Kinsey said.

"And you think you're a Camden," he mused.

"It's what I'm told," Kinsey countered, heading for the door with him following behind.

"So how does this work hour-wise?" he asked along the way.

Her fee had been discussed when they'd initially arranged this meeting, but her hours hadn't.

"The colonel is my only patient so I can be here as needed—morning till night. Unless you don't want me around that much."

"No, that's good. I'm glad you're all mine—"

All his?

"Not *all mine*," he said in a hurry. "I'm glad there isn't anyone but the colonel on your to-do list because you'll have your hands full with just her."

"With her and your shoulder rehab," Kinsey reminded.

"Yeah, sure, that, too," he conceded.

Was he just the slightest bit flustered?

It amused Kinsey to think so but she tried not to let it show.

He opened the door and followed her onto the landing.

"I'll see you tomorrow," she said. "And you, too, Jack," she told the dog, petting his head and inadvertently brushing Sutter's arm.

Then she headed for her car, wondering why that bare hint of contact had made her skin tingle.

Another chill? she wondered.

That had to be it.

Certainly it couldn't have been Sutter Knightlinger.

Because no matter how attractive he was, a marine was still a marine to her.

And towering and muscular and handsome-as-all-get-out or not, there was no place in her life for another one of those.

Chapter Two

As a career marine, Sutter had long ago become accustomed to rising early. But not quite as early as the following morning. By sunrise, he was already showered, shaved and dressed and had had breakfast, fed Jack and was on his second cup of coffee.

Now Jack was in the backyard and Sutter was standing at the sliding glass door in the kitchen, watching him.

Sutter had had a restless, nearly sleepless night.

Kinsey Madison had better be the marvel Livi thought she was, otherwise he was worried that the nurse wouldn't be able do what he needed done. Especially in the small amount of time before his shoulder was usable again and he was sent back overseas, leaving his mother to her own devices.

The colonel was a tough nut to crack and Kinsey

was going to have to damn near work a miracle to effect any change in her.

But he didn't know what else to do. His father had had a way with the colonel. He'd been able to finesse her into socializing and keeping up a healthy routine. Sutter didn't have that same knack with her. Every suggestion, every recommendation he made, just set off her temper.

But letting her have her own way was no solution. Merely looking out at the condition of the backyard was a testament to that.

The accident that had ultimately cost his father his life had happened at the start of August and the lawn hadn't been mowed since. Amos Knightlinger's prized raspberry bushes were laden with unpicked fruit that had withered on the branches.

The sight of that twisted something up inside of Sutter.

He and his father had been close.

"If I'd known what was going on, Dad, I would have busted my ass to get home. To see you…" he said, looking at those bushes, remembering how happy his father had been when the colonel had retired and they could finally settle in a place they could really call home. A place where his father could watch something grow year after year. His father had babied those bushes and reveled in the berries they'd produced every summer, eating them as if they were a great delicacy.

If I had been here, I would have picked them for you and brought them to you in the hospital...

But picking his father raspberries and bringing them to him was hardly the only thing that Sutter hadn't been able to do one last time. And all because of the way his mother had handled things. There was a lot he would have—*should* have—had the chance to do, to say, in those last weeks and days.

Instead he hadn't even known his father was at the end of his life. And it pissed Sutter off something fierce.

Maybe that was part of why he and the colonel were at odds. Maybe he wasn't hiding his feelings, his frustrations, as well as he thought he was.

But he couldn't help resenting that the colonel had robbed him of any opportunity to say goodbye to his father. After all the years that his father had been there for him while the colonel was halfway across the world or just busy with one case or another; after all the years that his father had bent over backward to make every move, every transition, every new school as easy as possible for him; after so much time that he and his father had spent together, *just the guys*, the colonel had kept him from being there for his dad.

"Not the right call, Colonel," he grumbled.

But what was done was done and now he had to deal with things the way they were. With the colonel the way she was. He had a mission here at home.

He and Kinsey Madison had a mission.

Kinsey Madison—also part of what had kept him up most of the night.

Her agenda.

Should he have agreed to help her get closer to the Camdens?

His gut said no.

He counted his cousin Beau as his best friend—more like the brother he'd never had. It had been that way since they were kids. But not only were Beau, Seth, Jani and Cade family, Sutter had strong feelings for all of the Camdens. GiGi had always treated him like her eleventh grandchild. They'd been good to him and he wouldn't do anything that might cause them any harm.

But it was Livi who had recommended Kinsey, so they did already know her, he reasoned. And the way Livi had talked about Kinsey made it clear that Livi thought highly of Kinsey, so any overtures she made on her own *would* likely pan out with or without him.

He just didn't like that, because of this *deal* he'd struck with her, he could be playing a part in anything that might bite them in the ass.

On the other hand, he thought, this did make it possible for him to keep an eye on her and what she was doing. It positioned him to protect them—maybe that was better than if she managed to sneak in on her own.

But he'd meant what he'd told Kinsey—if he got any inkling that she was up to something ugly, he'd sound the alarm and put a stop to it.

And he'd be careful about what information he did feed her. Nothing that wasn't public knowledge or on public record.

But what about her claim to be half sister to Beau's cousins?

As much as Sutter cared for and respected the Camdens of now, as sure as he was that they were all honest, trustworthy, ethical people, he also knew that the generations that came before had bad reputations. Bad reputations that the colonel said they'd earned.

She was open about the fact that she'd been leery of her sister's marrying into the family at the time. She'd said that the men couldn't be trusted, that H.J.—the founding father of the Camden empire, GiGi's father-in-law—had been a modern-day robber baron, and that he'd instilled the same principles in his son and his two grandsons, the fathers of the current generation. That more than a fair share of the Camden fortune had been ruthlessly built on the backs of people who were swindled or hoodwinked or used without conscience.

If that was true, if the earlier Camdens were those kinds of men, was it a big leap to think that Mitchum Camden had cheated on his wife? That he could have had a second, secret family in the wings?

Sutter knew what the colonel would say—that it wouldn't surprise her.

And to be honest, Kinsey Madison's appearance also supported the claim. She didn't look *un*like a Camden. She was built like the rest of the Camden women—not too tall, maybe only three or four inches over five feet, and compact with just enough curve to her to make it rough for him not to take notice.

And she had the same coloring they all shared—her hair was as dark and rich a brown as the black coffee in his cup. She wore it longer than any of the Camden females, though—all the way to the middle of her back. Shiny and silky and thick…

And along with the hair, there was her fair skin and blue eyes—those blue eyes especially made it seem likely to him that she was telling the truth. Those eyes that people called the Camden blue eyes—so blue they almost didn't seem real. Kinsey definitely had those.

She also had one of the most beautiful faces he'd ever seen. With flawless skin and a fine, delicate bone structure, with a perfect nose and lush, begging-to-be-kissed lips.

He'd grown up with the Camden females, tormented them alongside Beau the way he would have tormented sisters of his own, seen them through every awkward stage. So to him Lindie and Livi really were family the same way Jani was. But he recognized that his cousin and her cousins were beautiful women. As for Kinsey… he thought she had them all beat. By a mile.

But yes, she *did* resemble them.

Of course the likeness *could* be only a coincidence that she was trying to capitalize on. People could look like other people and *not* be related to them.

But she *had* claimed to be willing to do DNA testing. In fact there had been something that sounded like eagerness for it in her voice.

Or maybe he'd been sucked in by her. Maybe because she *was* such a knockout. He'd actually felt an impact from just sitting across from her—until he'd snapped himself out of it.

Kind of like he needed to do right then.

That just wasn't how things were going to be around here, he told himself forcefully.

He'd said no fraternizing and he'd meant it. There wasn't going to be anything personal between them. They would complete the mission—if the mission *could* be completed—and he'd be off again, far away and forgetting all about her.

But damn, she was hot…

"No fraternizing!" he commanded himself out loud, trying to put her in the same category he would one of his marines.

And failing because everything about her shouted soft and warm and sweet and certainly not marine.

It would probably help once he got the colonel home today. Then he wouldn't be alone with Kinsey. Kinsey would just do her job, the lines would be clearly drawn and he would keep his distance.

Except that she needed to do his physical therapy.

And he'd agreed to answer questions about the Camdens.

And help her get close to them.

He could already see lines blurring and when it came to distance, there was going to be precious little of that.

But he was a marine, he reminded himself.

He was trained to persevere, to withstand anything he needed to withstand.

Anything..

Even if what he needed to withstand were the most beautiful blue eyes in the world and a beautiful face and hair and body to go with them…

"It's entirely up to you, Colonel. Your doctors want you on oxygen at night but if you don't want to do it, you have that option," Kinsey said to her new patient.

She'd been at the Knightlingers' house since late afternoon when Sutter had finally gotten his mother home. Oxygen tanks and equipment had been delivered and set up in the colonel's bedroom, and Kinsey had done her own intake routine, interviewing, examining, taking the colonel's full medical history and getting to know her.

Kinsey was not surprised to find that the colonel was obviously accustomed to being in control and in authority, and unwilling to give up any of that control and authority to anyone else.

There was nothing weak about the seventy-six-year-old's will. She had a strong personality, she was blunt and obstinate and she was obviously dissatisfied at finding herself physically weakened to the point where she was forced to contend with a pacemaker, a regimen of medications and the prescribed nighttime oxygen usage. She clearly did not like feeling fragile or unwell, or being treated as if she was.

But she *was* fragile and recovering from a heart attack in addition to the procedure to clear four blockages in her heart and a minor surgery to implant the pacemaker.

She was also somewhat vain and with good reason—her face sported only shallow lines and wrinkles that did little to diminish what had no doubt been great beauty in her youth and middle age.

Between her high rank in the marines and those looks, Kinsey was reasonably sure that the colonel was accustomed to always getting her own way. Which told Kinsey that trying to force anything on her was a mistake.

"Here's my recommendation," she said. "Give it a week. See if you don't get used to the feel of the tubing and sleep better and feel more rested in the morning. If none of that happens, then we'll forget it. I'll call and have it picked up and taken out of here. The choice is yours. You always have the right to refuse any medical advice or treatment."

"Yes, I do," the colonel said, aiming that bit of mulishness at her son, who stood in the doorway watching the interaction between them. Sutter had already tried arguing with her and gotten nowhere.

Then, to Kinsey, the colonel said, "I'll give it a week. But don't think I'm some pushover old lady who'll just give up the fight. If I don't like it, it goes!"

"No question," Kinsey confirmed.

"Now if you're finished," the colonel said as if they'd exhausted her patience, "both of you get out of my room so I can read my book and get some sleep without somebody waking me up a hundred times during the night."

"If you need anything—" Sutter began.

"If you hear a thud that sounds like I've hit the floor, come running. Otherwise I can take care of myself."

"Or you can call me if there's anything you need," Sutter said anyway.

The colonel shooed them out of the room.

But as Kinsey headed for Sutter and the door, she still said, "I'll be back in the morning."

The colonel's only response was, "Catch that dog! He has my bookmark!"

Sutter nabbed Jack before he could slip past him and retrieved the bookmark, handing it to Kinsey to pass to the colonel.

"Insubordinate animal!" the colonel muttered disapprovingly.

"I'm going to take care of that, too," Kinsey assured her.

But the colonel did not respond and Kinsey didn't wait for her to. Instead she went with Sutter out into the hallway, closing his mother's bedroom door behind them and following him down the stairs to the first floor.

When they reached the entryway he said under his breath and facetiously, "And that would be my mother."

Kinsey laughed. "Basically what I expected," she said.

"She didn't fluster you," he observed with some surprise in his tone.

"I was raised by a retired marine, I have three brothers serving right now." She laughed again. "I hate to tell you, but you all run a pattern that I'm pretty familiar with."

His eyebrows arched. "Are your brothers here or—"

"They're all overseas."

"Ah, that makes more sense. You said yesterday that you wanted to get to know the Camdens to have family around. I wondered what that meant if you had three brothers."

"It means that I'm all there is here," she said. Then, offering no more than that, she switched gears. "You texted that you need stitches removed?"

"It's been more than ten days since the second surgery and they're pinching bad. I'd do it myself if I could find any scissors around here but I can't. I tried to get a nurse at the hospital to do it—I figured they were in and out of my mother's room every five minutes anyway, why couldn't they? But no chance of that. They were going to send me to the emergency room to see a doctor and waste my whole day."

"I need a look at your injury anyway to figure out an approach for your physical therapy. If the stitches are ready to come out, I can do it. I brought another kit for that but it's in my car. I'll run out and get it while you take off the sling and your shirt."

"You want to do it in the kitchen?" he asked.

Take out his stitches in the kitchen, Kinsey mentally amended when her mind went to another meaning of *doing it*. What was it with her brain making everything risqué?

"Wherever I'll have the brightest light," she said as she shoved her thoughts onto the right track and left him in the entryway to step into the evening air.

Where she could cool off.

Really, what's going on when it comes to this guy?

Maybe the same thing that had caused her to debate about what she wore and how she did her hair for this initial meeting with his mother.

Kinsey was disgusted with herself for the amount of time and consideration she'd put into her appearance today. Since she wasn't affiliated with a home–

health care company, there was no dress code. It was her choice whether to wear scrubs or street clothes. She used whatever she would be doing on any particular day as the decider—something messy, scrubs. Something not messy, street clothes.

Today, the first day of meeting a difficult patient whose respect she needed, she knew she had to go with her lab coat over business attire.

Yet something in her had wanted to dress casually, in something cute. And that impulse had come complete with the image of Sutter Knightlinger in the back of her mind.

Okay, so he was a good-looking guy. So what? She couldn't let it interfere with her job with his mother or her goal with the Camdens.

That's what she'd told herself as she'd stood in front of her closet and it was what she told herself again now.

Of course it had only *partially* worked earlier.

She *had* put on the tailored navy blue pantsuit she wore as business attire, with the lab coat over it.

But then, instead of putting her hair up to make her look competent and efficient, she'd worn it down, losing that battle with herself completely. Along with the one against using a little eyeliner and a touch of highlighter on the crest of her cheekbones above her blush.

It was ridiculous, she told herself as she reached across the driver's seat to retrieve her kit from the passenger side. He was a career marine, and that was the only thing she needed to know to count him out of any kind of personal relationship. She could work for him, he could be one of the means to her ends with the Camdens, but that was it!

So no more of this silliness, she vowed as she relocked her car. From here on, her clothes, her hair, were going to be chosen without him as any part of the equation. And if there were any more temperature changes due to being around him? She'd ignore the phenomenon until it went away.

She found him in the kitchen, having done what she'd told him to do—he'd removed the sling from his left arm and taken off his shirt.

As a nurse she'd seen more male torsos than she could remember and never once had there been one that did to her what that first sight of Sutter did. Suddenly she was hot *and* cold and felt as if everything inside of her had gone a little spongy.

Because despite the bandage wrapping his left arm and shoulder, her view was of bulging biceps, shoulders a mile wide, a superbly broad chest, super flat abs with more than a six-pack—she counted eight rows of sinew that went down to his waistband—and all of it astonishingly sexy. Fortunately, he was draping his shirt over the back of a chair so he didn't notice her reaction.

She took a very deep breath, thinking that she could have used some of the colonel's oxygen at that moment, and exhaled, all the while telling herself to snap out of whatever this strange reaction to him was.

Then she went the rest of the way into the kitchen, set her kit on the table and said, "Let me wash my hands."

*Breathe... Breathe... Stop being stupid...*she told herself.

Then, shoulders back and reminding herself that she was a professional, she dried her hands on a clean paper towel and turned to Sutter once again.

He was no less fabulous. And now she was going to get up close and personal...

"Okay, sit down and let's see what we have here," she said too merrily.

She removed the bandaging to expose a large incision and the remnants of his original wound.

Concentrating on sounding normal as she went to work on the stitches, she said, “So what happened to you?”

“Sniper fire. I was on a mission in Afghanistan.”

An answer with a bare minimum of information. Kinsey had had more than her fair share of responses like that from her brothers. She knew nothing she asked would garner additional details and before she could even try, Sutter changed the subject.

“Are you originally from Denver?”

“No. I was born and raised in a small town in Montana—Northbridge.”

“I know Northbridge. My cousin Beau and I have always been close. I went to the Camden ranch in Northbridge with him many times during the summers.”

So Sutter wasn’t opposed to opening up, just not about his mission in Afghanistan.

“Is this your first time living away from Montana?” he asked.

“No, I left to go to college at the University of Colorado, then stayed here for nursing school,” she said, wanting his attention somewhere other than his wound. He’d been right that the stitches were past ready to come out. The skin had healed around them and they weren’t easy to remove—something that she knew was painful.

Not that he so much as flinched. But still she wanted to offer him a distraction. And keep her own mind on the straight and narrow in the meantime.

“After nursing school,” she continued, “I got a position at Denver General Hospital. I worked there full-time until two and a half years ago—I went to half-time when my stepfather got lung cancer so I could go back and forth between here and Northbridge to help my mom take care of him."

"Did he make it?"

"For about eight months. Then six months after the funeral, I realized that my mom wasn't doing well. At first I thought it was grief but she just got worse and worse. I finally persuaded her to see a doctor and she was diagnosed with kidney disease and dementia. I had to quit my job here to take care of her full-time."

"Because there wasn't anyone else. What about your brothers? You said they're marines?" he asked then.

"Two out of three. My oldest brother is a doctor—"

"Navy, I'll bet, because there's no doctors in the marines, it's navy docs who patch us up. Are you about finished?" he asked as she yanked a particularly deep stitch. Apparently she'd come close to reaching his pain threshold.

"Sorry," she apologized. "You were right that this should have been done days ago. I think that one was the worst, though. They shouldn't be as bad from here."

"So after your mom passed, that was when you went into private nursing?" he asked, apparently wanting the diversion of her history to go on.

"Not intentionally. I was closing down my mom's house until my brothers and I can decide what to do with it when one of the Northbridge doctors called. He asked if I could do some home health care for neighbors of his—the Tellers. They needed help but they were also in the process of moving to Denver. The Northbridge doc knew I wanted to get back here so he thought I could start with the Tellers in Northbridge then transition along with them to Denver."

"And the Tellers are somehow hooked up with the guy Livi Camden is engaged to, right?"

"Callan Tierney, right. He was kind of a foster son of theirs. He was best friends with their son, and lived with the Tellers after his own parents died. When their son was killed in a car accident, Callan stepped in to see that they were taken care of, along with their granddaughter who is his godchild."

"And that's how you met Livi—nursing the Tellers. Livi, who you think is your half sister."

"And Livi recommended me to you, so I'm here on what's only my second home–health care job," Kinsey concluded.

"Do you like it?"

"I do," she said with some surprise. "I guess it lets me be sort of like family for a little while—and it's nice working in a home environment. Oh!" she said, startled when Jack suddenly attacked her foot. Then she laughed and added, "And I would never have had a terrier puppy trying to chew on me while I worked at the hospital, so what fun is that?"

"Jack! Stop it!" Sutter commanded the dog, who elected to go on doing what he was doing.

Kinsey stopped her work on Sutter's shoulder to kick the ball Jack had dropped nearby into the other room to distract him, too.

Jack took the bait and chased the ball so Kinsey could return to the stitches.

"You told my mother you were going to take care of the puppy problem, too—does that mean you have a plan? Because today she told me to take him back to the breeder," Sutter said ominously.

"Ohhh, poor Jack!" Kinsey said sympathetically.

"We've always had this breed, but it was my dad who trained and took care of them. I've managed to housebreak this terror, but that's it. I don't know how to fix the rest—training a whole platoon of men is easier than getting Jack to behave. And if I don't find a way to get him into shape before I leave, the colonel won't keep him."

A big tough marine daunted by a puppy—the idea of that amused Kinsey to no end.

"Actually," she said then, "there's an organization called Pets for Vets that pairs shelter animals and former military dogs with veterans. That way either the dogs already have military manners or the shelter dogs have been trained with them so they kind of fit a little more comfortably with a vet's lifestyle and expectations. An animal like that might have been a little more to your mom's liking at this point."

"I didn't even know that existed."

"But now that you have Jack, we can't give up on him—he's just a puppy being a puppy. I know someone who works for Pets for Vets and I called him. I thought he could teach us—and the colonel, too, if we can get her onboard—what to do with Jack."

Jack brought the ball back, dropped it and jumped against Kinsey's leg, jarring her into yanking too hard on the stitch she was removing and causing Sutter to flinch.

"Ooh, I'm sorry! Again," she apologized. "But that's the last one."

The only relief Sutter showed was in the cautious and slight rolling of that shoulder as if to ease the tension out of it.

"It looks good, though," Kinsey said, meaning his wound, though the movement caused her to notice once more just how good everything else looked, too.

"I need to do a little bit of an exam—can you wiggle your fingers? Make a fist? Squeeze my hand?"

He could, wiggling long, thick fingers, making an impressively tight fist and then taking the hand she offered, showing more strength than she'd expected.

And at the same time causing her to feel her temperature rising again.

She ignored her own reaction to him.

"Good," she said.

That seemed like signal enough for him to let go but he didn't until she told him he could. And even then it seemed as if there was a split second more of lingering.

She put him through a few more exercises, then she bent over and picked up the ball Jack had abandoned, handing it to Sutter. "You can start therapy with a few squeezes of this. Tomorrow when I come, I'll bring you one of your own and we'll add a few other things."

"It's all gonna work again, right?" he asked.

"I think we can get you back to a hundred percent range of motion. You're even healed enough to shower without being bandaged, but you might want the incision site covered just to avoid any irritation from the sling."

"Great, let's give it air tonight—I don't sleep in the sling, I just rest the arm on my chest. Tomorrow I'll slap some gauze over the wound after I shower in the morning."

So very many mental images ran through Kinsey's head, but she shoved them away, washed her hands again and then began to clean up as Sutter retrieved his shirt.

Being careful to keep her eyes to herself, she said, "Todd—he's the dog trainer—can come tomorrow evening after he leaves work if I give him the go-ahead."

"Sounds good to me. The sooner the better."

"Then I'll call and tell him. And maybe we can save Jack from exile."

She'd repacked her suture kit by then and—still without a glance in his direction—she told him she wanted to peek in on the colonel one last time before she left.

The colonel was asleep with her glasses on and her book resting on her chin, so Kinsey silently went into the room to remove both, managing not to disturb her patient in the process.

Sutter was waiting for her when she returned to the kitchen, his shirt on again but only one button fastened.

Kinsey tried not to look, instead noting that he'd replaced the sling, too, which told her that he still needed it. "The colonel is asleep," she informed him. "So unless you need anything else—"

"I don't."

"Then I'll get going and let you rest, too."

She leaned down to pet Jack where he was trying hard to open a cupboard door with his nose. "You rest, too, Jack, because you're in for a big day tomorrow."

Sutter surprised her by walking her to her car.

"Feel free to park in the driveway. Nearest to the house," he said as they reached her small sedan at the curb and she unlocked her door. "If I need to get out I can use the far side."

"Okay," she said, appreciating that he was trying to save her a few steps.

She tossed her purse and bag and suture kit across the console into the passenger seat and then glanced over the car's roof to Sutter. "You have my number—don't hesitate to call anytime during the night if there's any problem or you have any question—this is round-the-clock care even if I don't live in."

"We'll be fine."

"Just in case," she persisted, recognizing in herself a certain unfathomable lack of eagerness to leave.

But then Sutter said, "See you tomorrow," giving her no other option.

Kinsey nodded and got behind her steering wheel, closing her car door behind her.

But as she put the key in the ignition, she glanced in Sutter's direction once more, thinking to catch sight of him returning to the house. Instead he was merely taking slow steps backward. Slow enough that her view was of his belly button just above the waistband of his slacks. His very sexy belly button there amid those rock-hard abs.

And up went her temperature all over again before she turned on the engine, put the car in gear and hit the gas.

Telling herself to get away as fast as she could.

Chapter Three

"Oh, Conor, finally! I've been worried," Kinsey said when she connected for a video chat with her oldest brother on Friday morning. She'd been up since five waiting to hear from him. It was almost eight. "Is Declan all right?"

Declan was another of her brothers and a twin with her brother Liam. The twins were the middle children—older than Kinsey, younger than Conor.

Three weeks earlier Declan had been badly wounded when the Humvee he was driving in Afghanistan went over a hidden bomb. He'd undergone an initial emergency trauma surgery in Afghanistan, then been transferred to a hospital in Germany for more surgery this morning.

Conor was a navy doctor but couldn't treat family. So he'd taken leave to oversee Declan's care and travel with him.

"It was touch and go for a while," Conor admitted. "That's why I'm late getting to you—the surgery went on longer than expected. But he did okay and he's not going to lose the leg!"

"Thank God," Kinsey muttered, breathing a sigh of relief.

"I was just with him in recovery and I got him to move his toes, so it looks like everything is working," Conor continued. "They recasted his hand when we first got here and he's starting to be able to use his fingers. The rest of the bumps and bruises and cuts are under control now, too, and I think he's going to come out of this okay. The good news is that he'll be sent stateside to recuperate and rehab, and I've put in for reassignment to go with him—that means you could have two of us there for a while."

A while...

That was all she ever got with any of them.

"For how long?" she asked without showing her feelings.

"Can't say. But we'll be there, both of us in the states. Bethesda—"

"Maryland. Hardly right next door to Denver."

"Right. But you can meet us there. And once Declan is doing well enough to be on his own a little, I can get to you. Eventually even Declan will probably be able to travel and maybe stay with you so you can help with some of his physical therapy."

Kinsey nodded, knowing what her brother was getting at before he said it.

"This is a time for us to pull in—focus on each other and deal with our situations. So don't stir up that whole Camden mess," he added, just as she'd been expecting. "We don't need the complication right now."

Kinsey had broken the news of who their biological father was when she'd found out. All three of her brothers had had a different reaction than she had. Instead of wanting to reach out to family the way she did, they wanted to let sleeping dogs lie, certain that the Camdens would refuse to acknowledge them, leaving them—specifically her, who had put so much stock into this idea—with nothing but heartache and rejection.

"Now that you're finished with that job that put you around them, just let it go," Conor said.

"I don't want to do that," she responded, deciding not to mention that her new job put her in line for even more contact with the Camdens. That she'd struck a deal to create opportunities for it.

"Declan and I will be there!" her brother insisted. "We're all the family you need."

"You'll only be here for a while," she reminded him by repeating his words back to him.

"I know it's been hard on you, Kins," Conor said. "We all know it, even though you never complain. And we appreciate everything you've done standing in for us, not having us around to share the load with Mom and Hugh..." He shook his head. "But you have to think this through. The Camdens could already *know* we exist, meaning they've opted to pretend they don't—"

"I never saw any hint that Livi Camden knew we're related."

"They could know there's another family out there somewhere without knowing specifically who we are—do you think *nobody* missed all that money we've ended up with? That nobody ever knew it was paid to cover up a dirty little secret? A dirty little secret they don't want to put faces and names to, let alone acknowledge? And say they *don't* know we exist and you tell them.

Can you see that being anything but ugly? They'll probably call Mom a whore. And they're the ones with the legitimate pedigree—that makes us the mutts. Is that really how you want us to be thought of? Labeled as less worthy? The Camden bastards? Is that what you want? Because we don't."

"They seem like nice people, Conor. Maybe it wouldn't play out that way," Kinsey persisted. "And even if you and Declan and Liam don't want anything to do with the Camdens, that doesn't mean that I *can't* have anything to do with them."

"It's opening a can of worms, Kinsey. A *huge* can of worms. And I'm afraid it wouldn't have whatever happy ending you're hoping for. We're the living proof that this guy was an adulterer—how well can that go over with people who want to believe the best of him?"

"But maybe no matter how it came to be, they might want to know that they have three half brothers and a half sister out in the world. The Camdens are all about family. Maybe their grandmother might like to know she has four more grandchildren..."

"Or not," Conor said intractably. "Can't you date or something instead? Think about building a family of your own? *Something* else?"

"Connecting with other brothers and sisters, our grandmother, isn't a replacement for marriage and kids. I still want that, too. But I also want the Camdens. A grandmother. Cousins. Siblings."

"You *have* brothers," he said as if she'd forgotten.

"I haven't been in a room with you or Declan in three years, Conor. It's been closer to four for Liam."

"Liam is on an elite team—"

"I know," Kinsey said, cutting off one brother's defense of the other. "I understand. But you have to understand where I'm coming from, too—"

"I do," he said with some resignation, as if he'd been trying not to admit it. "It's not just what you had to do without our help with Mom and Hugh. Now they're gone. And if you get a flat tire you can't call one of your big brothers to fix it."

"I can change a flat tire and I have road service if my car breaks down, but yes! With you guys doing what you do, I sort of have family in name only—"

"Yeah, I know that's true," he conceded. "I know that's it for you—day in, day out, on your own, nobody to turn to, nobody around to blow off steam to, to ask for help or an opinion or to go to dinner or a movie, no family for holidays or birthdays. Nobody to come if you end up in an emergency room. None of us for anything… Believe me, we hate that."

"But hating it doesn't change it. And maybe being part of the Camden family could…" Kinsey said.

Conor grimaced. "Really think about it before you reach out to them, will you? Declan and I will be in the states shortly—plan for that instead. Look forward to that for now. Maybe the three of us can even have Christmas together this year. Liam is out of reach for the time being, but when we have contact again, I'll talk to him about putting in for leave. Maybe we could all meet at the farm, really talk this through while we pack things up there so you don't have to do that on your own, too."

That was so appealing—Christmas back on the farm, all four of them together…

But how many times had she hung her hopes on promises like that and had those promises broken? And even if the promises were kept, it only meant a brief taste of family before it ended and she was on her own once more.

She'd come to accept that that was the way it was with Conor, Declan and Liam, that it wasn't ever going to be any different. Her brothers were career military. They went where they were ordered to go. And none of them was likely to come out of the service until they were retirees like the colonel. Her brothers would always be far, far away.

But the Camdens—who were also family—weren't so distant, if only she could get them to open the door to let her in.

"Say you'll wait at least until the first of the year before you do anything," Conor prodded when she didn't respond to his Christmas proposal.

"I can't," she said honestly.

A nurse appeared in the screen behind Conor just then to tell him something Kinsey couldn't hear.

When the nurse left, Conor said to Kinsey, "I have to go. Declan is in some pain and I want to monitor what they're giving him for it."

"Sure. Good. Tell him I'm thinking about him and I love him."

"I will. We love you, too, you know?"

"I know," Kinsey said. "Love you, too."

"Think Christmas in Northbridge like when we were kids. And don't do anything rash."

Kinsey only nodded at that before they said goodbye.

Then she gave a little prayer of thanks for Declan having come through the surgery and not losing his leg before she went to take a shower.

But even as she took off her pajamas and got under the spray of warm water, her conversation with Conor weighed on her.

What if he was right and the Camdens knew there was another branch on the family tree but didn't want to acknowledge them?

If that was the case then none of them were likely to look kindly on her forcing the issue.

And even if they had no idea that Mitchum had been a philanderer with a second family, it certainly couldn't come as good news now. Plus yes, it was possible that there wouldn't be any love lost for that second family when they did find out.

But the Camdens *were* her flesh and blood—it always came down to that for Kinsey. And she just couldn't let go of that now that she knew it. She just couldn't let go of the hope that they might open a door for her to become one of them.

She recognized that a part of her hope for that might be coming from grief over losing the mother she'd loved dearly and been very close to. But that loss had also opened her eyes to the fact that she didn't have anyone else left, either.

Being completely overwhelmed with caring for her adoptive father and then her mother for the last two and a half years had made it impossible *not* to neglect her other relationships.

Friends had found mates and she'd missed meeting those new people in their lives, missed their engagement parties, their bridal showers, their bachelorette parties, their weddings. They'd had babies and she'd missed those showers, too, and then the births, and even a first birthday celebration. Her friends had become enmeshed in their own lives, and Kinsey just hadn't been able to keep up. So those friendships had gone by the wayside and left no meaningful place for her in any of them.

And now there was the potential to have sisters and

brothers, a grandmother, nearby. And that had become important to her.

Not that she didn't want to find a man and have a family of her own because she did, she thought as she finished her shower and began to dry her hair. The hardest thing she'd ever done was saying no to Trevor's proposal. But it had been the difficulty she'd had rejecting Duncan after Trevor that had told her that she needed to conquer her loneliness *before* she ventured into any other romantic relationships. She didn't want to end up with a man she didn't really love just because she was afraid of being alone.

She opted to leave her hair down again today and dressed in a pair of jeans that she knew fit her to perfection and two layers of T-shirts—a tight yellow scoop-neck over a white tank top. Glancing in the mirror, she realized that once again, she had dressed to impress not the colonel, but Sutter.

There was no denying that he was a hunk and a half. That he was sexy as all get-out and so handsome any and every woman would take a second look and go slightly slack jawed.

But he was wrong for her. As wrong for her as Trevor had been. And yet here she was, here she had been since she'd met him, thinking about him. Factoring him into her choice of hairstyles and clothes again today despite having told herself she wasn't going to do that again.

Loneliness was coloring her thoughts, her leanings. If not for that she was certain that the simple fact that Sutter was a career marine would have been enough for her to put him out of her mind.

But she didn't seem able to do that. Instead, she was filled with eagerness to see him again, even though it wasn't something she *should* be feeling. Something she doubted she'd be feeling at all if her life was fuller.

So it was better to focus on the Camdens, on the possibility of connecting with them.

And if—hopefully—that went well and she suddenly found herself a part of something bigger, *then* she could look for a mate of her own and trust that she was choosing wisely.

"With a little patience and a little effort, Colonel, you'll have a fine dog in Jack. He's just a pup—keep that in mind," Todd Runyun said.

Todd had been working for Pets for Vets since leaving the marines four years ago. Kinsey had met him through her brother Liam, who had done two tours with him. An injury during their last deployment had caused Todd chronic back problems. ffWhen those problems flared he called Kinsey for physical therapy that she'd provided gratis. Returning the favor, he'd come to the Knightlingers' house after his workday was over to teach Sutter, the colonel and Kinsey what to do with the rambunctious Jack.

Todd had brought his own dog Reggie, a former bomb-sniffing German shepherd he'd adopted when Reggie was retired from service. It had become clear during the two hours he'd been there that the colonel preferred Reggie to Jack and that was only confirmed when the colonel said, "How about you take Jack with you and leave me Reggie?"

Todd laughed. "Give young Jack here a chance—he's a new recruit who needs to be whipped into shape like all new recruits."

Then Todd wrapped up the training session with assignments as Jack tried to enlist Reggie into play, front paws outstretched, hind end in the air, tail wagging, at the ready for mischief while Reggie sat regally beside his master, pretending the puppy wasn't there.

"Jack is a good pup, he'll make a good dog," the trainer concluded.

The colonel huffed under her breath as if she'd have to see it to believe it.

What Kinsey could see was that the elderly woman was tiring, and since their lessons were over she thanked Todd for everything and suggested she get the colonel settled for the night.

As Kinsey and the colonel left, she heard Sutter asking about the Pets for Vets organization itself, lamenting that he hadn't known about the group when he had been looking for a dog for the colonel.

"Good man," the colonel said once they were in her room, referring to Todd.

"He is."

"Boyfriend?"

Not only didn't Kinsey mind answering most personal questions, she was glad to have any show of interest from this particular patient. The colonel wasn't one to make polite chitchat. If she was asking, it was because she wanted to know more about Kinsey, which was a sign that the colonel was warming to her.

"No, he's only a friend," she said, thinking as she did how true that was and wondering why, in comparison to Sutter, Todd's good looks had no impact on her whatsoever. He was an attractive guy, after all—tall, blond, Nordic-looking. But nothing about him had ever inspired in her what she was struggling with over the colonel's son.

"Todd is actually one of my brother's friends," she said, shying away from analyzing that phenomenon.

Instead she forced herself to concentrate on the colonel and went on to explain how Todd knew Liam.

That led to the colonel's asking about all three of her brothers and their military careers as Kinsey prepared the older woman for bed.

The fact that Kinsey had such close ties to the military in her brothers and her late stepfather—who had just retired from the marines when he'd met her mother—went a long way toward establishing greater rapport with the colonel, and by the time Kinsey was finished and the colonel was situated with a book and the remote control for her television, the atmosphere between them was considerably friendlier.

Friendly enough for the colonel to confide on the sly, "You know, I like a little brandy before bed..."

"I can't call your doctor for permission for that now, but I'll check with him first thing in the morning to make sure it won't interfere with any of your meds. If we get the go-ahead, I'm fine with that. Even though you seem to sleep without it, I'll tell him you need a little help and that should do the trick," Kinsey offered.

For the first time she saw a small smile cross the older woman's lips, apparently appreciating Kinsey's willingness to conspire with her. "You do that," the colonel said with the arch of one eyebrow.

Then, as Kinsey headed for the door after making sure the older woman didn't need anything else, the colonel said, "Glad your other brother made it through his surgery this morning."

"Thanks. Me, too. See you tomorrow."

Apparently Sutter had found quite a bit to talk to Todd about because he was just closing the front door as Kinsey came from the colonel's room. He had Jack slung under his good arm.

"Jack wanted to go home with Reggie?" Kinsey guessed as Sutter bent over to set the dog on the floor now that the opportunity to make a run for it was taken away.

"Yes. And I thought Todd might be tired of this puppy pestering his dog. I think there's some hero worship going on there," Sutter said. "Maybe Reggie can be his role model and Jack will work at improving himself to impress him."

"Looked more to me like Jack was trying to corrupt Reggie, but let's think positive," Kinsey said.

"The colonel's down for the count?"

"She's in bed but not asleep if you want to say goodnight, then we can do your physical therapy since we didn't get to it earlier."

"Yeah, we can't skip that," Sutter agreed with more enthusiasm than the prospect usually brought on in most of her patients. Not that that was a surprise to her—recovering meant he'd be able to return to combat, and her experience with her brothers had taught her that that was all the motivation a marine needed. "Meet you in the living room."

Jack followed Kinsey while Sutter went to his mother's bedroom. Once in the living room the puppy promptly leaped onto the sofa.

"Todd says you're not supposed to do that unless you're invited," she whispered.

Jack wagged his tail and stayed put.

"Come on, get down," she said before she recalled that she was to use one-word commands, and repeated only, "Down!"

Jack still didn't budge so she picked him up and set him on the floor while saying, "Down!" again and then adding, "I bought you a reprieve from going back to the breeder, you'd better use it wisely."

Jack wagged his tail again and she took that as encouragement. Until he jumped on the sofa again.

"Jack, down!" came Sutter's deep voice from behind Kinsey as he joined them.

This time the puppy actually got off the couch.

When Sutter didn't respond to that Kinsey whispered a reminder to him. "Praise..."

"Good boy!" Sutter said while Kinsey leaned over to pet the pup, too.

Then Sutter asked, "Shirt on or off?"

Oh, off, please!

He was wearing a pair of loose-fitting workout pants and a short-sleeved crew-necked gray T-shirt that could have been painted on him. It had been a terrible distraction to Kinsey all day and evening but since it didn't create much of a barrier now it wasn't really necessary for it to come off. Despite her every inclination to have him remove it.

Reminding herself that she wasn't supposed to notice things like those incredible shoulders and that mile-wide chest and those muscular pecs, she resisted the urge to have the shirt disappear, and said, "I think we can work with the shirt on. Just take off the sling." Then forcing herself into work mode, she said, "How's everything feeling today?"

"The incision feels better with the stitches out. The shoulder and arm? Doesn't seem possible for such a small thing but I can feel it all the way to my neck when I squeeze the ball."

All the way to that neck that was thick but not too thick.

"But you're able to squeeze the ball," she pointed

out. She'd watched him do it and—on top of everything else—realized that he had great hands, too. Big and strong and capable, with long fingers and thick wrists that led up to impressive forearms and those biceps…

Oh, those biceps...

Kinsey mentally took herself to task and again yanked her attention back. "Being able to squeeze a ball might seem like a small thing but it isn't."

And she needed to stop thinking about him squeezing more than the ball, squeezing parts of her…

Stop it right now!

"Why don't you sit down?" she said then, deciding she needed to do her job and get out of there.

He did as he was told, sitting on the coffee table in front of the sofa where Kinsey could go to work.

"Todd says there are a lot of organizations out there for vets," Sutter said as she did an initial warm-up of his arm and shoulder. "He works for Pets for Vets, but volunteers for a couple of others and has used the services of one or two more. Apparently getting back into civilian life can have complications for servicemen who decide not to be career military—I never really thought about it since I grew up surrounded by people who were either military-for-life or civilian employees of the military. I guess I just didn't think about anything in between."

"It can be difficult. Health, mental health, getting a job, a place to live, just getting used to *not* having the military calling the shots, and getting back into a civilian mindset—there's a lot involved for people when they get out, and it can be kind of a rocky road sometimes."

"You know this how?" he asked.

"Before I got swamped with my stepfather's and my mom's health problems I… Well, I was in a relationship that left me a whole lot of time on my own, so I did pro bono physical therapy for veterans who needed more than their benefits would cover—and more than they could pay for outside of their coverage. I saw and heard a whole lot of things that they and their families needed help with above and beyond what I could do for them."

"I really have just never thought about life outside of the military."

"Because you don't have plans to leave it?" Kinsey asked.

"I'm definitely a lifer," he confirmed.

His use of the term struck a chord with her. *A lifer.* She needed to not forget that.

"Is this what you've always wanted to do—be a marine for life?" she asked as she proceeded to guide him through his therapy.

"I can't remember ever even thinking about being anything else. My mother's family has never had a generation without at least one—and usually more than one—career marine in it. My dad was a marine, too."

"Is that how he and the colonel met?"

"It is. He served until he was injured in Vietnam a year after they were married. He had a head injury that left him with some weakness on one side that ended his military career or he would have been in right to the finish the way the colonel was. He still always considered himself a marine and between him and the colonel—"

"There was no question that's what you would be, too," Kinsey guessed.

"And it was what I wanted."

"Even as a little boy? You never wanted to be a cowboy or a fireman or a superhero?"

"Nothing but a marine. I think it's in my blood. That was even my Halloween costume every year."

He was a hopeless cause if ever she'd heard one.

"Rank?" she asked.

"Lieutenant colonel," he said with pride just before he melted into a flinch when she raised his arm slightly higher than she had before.

"So you have a college degree."

Kinsey knew that without a college degree opportunities to rise within the ranks were limited.

"I graduated from Annapolis, majored in economics—"

"But all degrees awarded there are bachelors of science because the courses of study are so intense that you come out well educated in the whole spectrum of math, science and engineering no matter what you major in," she finished for him. Then she explained her knowledge. "Two of my brothers—the twins—graduated from the academy, too. They're younger than you are so it would have been after you were out. My stepfather enlisted at seventeen and it was a big deal to him that my brothers go in with more opportunities than he'd had."

"Did your brothers always want to be marines?"

"We were all very young when Hugh came into the picture—my oldest brother Conor was eight when they started dating, nine when my mom married Hugh and he adopted us. My brothers' wanting to be marines evolved under his influence, so I don't think any of them would say that it was *always* what they wanted to be, but since it started when they were so little it seems that way."

"Was your stepfather old-school and against women in the military?"

"Because I didn't end up there, too? No, he tried to persuade me to do it."

"But you had other ideas," Sutter surmised, his expression showing some strain at the therapy.

"Just a little more," she assured before she said, "The military didn't appeal to me, no. How many times have you been deployed?"

"I'm on leave from my third. My troops are in Afghanistan as we speak."

"And you can't wait to get back to them."

"It's where I have an obligation to be," he answered simply.

"And not even three deployments has you thinking about getting out?"

"Nah. I told you, I'm a lifer."

Which meant that any woman who ever got involved with him had to know that there would come many days when she would kiss him goodbye, knowing months would pass before she saw him again.

And why, when Kinsey knew unwaveringly that that was not something she would ever accept in any man, was she suddenly wondering what it might be like to kiss him? To have him use his uninjured arm and hand to reach over and pull her down onto his lap...

"Okay, I think that's enough for today," she said, her voice the tiniest bit breathy as she escaped that lapse in her thoughts.

The hand she'd just imagined him using to pull her into his lap went to the upper biceps of his injured arm, cupping it, kneading the muscles.

And before she even knew she was going to utter the words, she heard herself say, "Let me do that."

Oh, if only she could call those words back!

He can rub his own arm!

But the words couldn't be recalled and there was

nothing she could do then but put her money where her mouth was.

So, using both hands, she performed a tender but firm massage that she swore to herself was therapeutic and professional, something she would offer any patient.

She started at his hand and went from there to his wrist, from his wrist to his forearm, and on up to his biceps where she spent the most time, pressing her fingers into those massive muscles until they began to relax. Then she skipped over his incision and went to work on his neck and trapezius muscles.

"Oh, yeah…" he groaned as Kinsey felt the tightness in him begin to ease.

It reassured her that she *was* doing something medically helpful. Even if, for some reason, she was more aware of the texture and warmth of his skin than she ever had been with any other patient.

Then all of a sudden he tensed up even tighter than he'd been before and bent over, maneuvering himself out of her grip, and using his uninjured hand to scoop the sleeping Jack up from the floor to set in his lap as he said in a hurry, "That's okay… I'm good now."

There was no question that he meant for her to stop but she was worried she'd done something wrong.

"Did I hurt you?" she asked, confused.

He laughed wryly. "Uh, no," he said as if that was out of the question. "I'm fine."

With a sleepy-eyed Jack stunned to have been awakened for lap duty.

Oh.

Kinsey was a little slow on the uptake but it finally occurred to her that the massage might have had somewhat more than therapeutic results for him.

Much the way it had affected her more than it should have.

Alarmed by herself then, Kinsey handed him his sling to put back on and busied herself gathering her purse and putting on her jacket with her back to him.

Which was better for her, too, because the simple sight of him kept getting to her even when she was trying so hard for it not to.

"So you have housecleaners and yard work going on tomorrow?" she said, seizing something innocuous to talk about.

"Crews for both," he confirmed in a clipped tone. "The colonel isn't happy about it—she doesn't like people in her house. But this place needs work whether she likes it or not."

"You also need a trip to the grocery store," Kinsey said, sticking to business. "You'll both get better faster with some more nutritious food. Neither of you should be eating a regular diet of what you've been ordering in, and your cupboards are pretty bare."

He cleared his throat and when he spoke again his tone was less agitated. "Is that something you're on board for? Helping me grocery shop and cook? Because I haven't done much of either of those."

"Sure. We can shop tomorrow and work on the food preparation together—"

"In other words, you're not our cook."

There was humor in his tone now and she heard him set Jack back on the floor so she assumed he had…things…under control. She was better, too, enough to turn and face him again as she said, "No, I'm not. But I like to cook and if we make it a joint effort—and include the colonel when she's up to that, too—then you both come away with some KP skills."

"That's either a demotion or a punishment, you know," he said in a teasing tone.

"But I think you'll probably live through it," she countered the same way. "Then—also when the colonel is a little stronger—I'll try to get her to the store, too, so she can get the hang of shopping and cooking for herself after you're gone."

"Yeah, she needs to know how to do that."

"Think about the kinds of foods the two of you like and we'll make a list tomorrow," Kinsey advised.

With the air seemingly cleared of whatever had inadvertently happened before, they headed for the front door. Sutter walked Kinsey to her car, parked in the driveway today.

"Thanks for getting Todd in here," Sutter said. "He thinks we can have Jack pretty well trained before I leave."

Which he would be doing, Kinsey reminded herself when she discovered that she was gazing up into that handsome face and once again thinking about kissing. He *would* be leaving. So no kissing. Or even thinking about it.

"We'll work on it," she confirmed. *On training Jack and on not thinking about kissing.*

Or on any of the rest of the things that kept tormenting her when it came to this guy.

She got behind the wheel of her car to avoid what was beginning to feel like some kind of gravitational field that kept sucking her closer to him and remembered suddenly and out of nowhere that there was something else she *should* have been focused on.

"Maybe tomorrow we can talk about the Camdens, too. And what you're going to do to uphold your end of our deal."

He nodded slowly, his expression blank. Probably to conceal that he wasn't eager for that.

But if he thought she wouldn't hold him to it, he was mistaken.

And tomorrow she'd make sure she kept her own goal at the forefront so she *didn't* spend so much time going gaga over him!

"'Night," she said, angry with herself for having let her goal go so completely by the wayside today. So completely that she hadn't even realized it until now.

"Drive safe," he advised, closing her door for her.

Unlike the night before when she'd looked up to find his belly button in view, tonight when she glanced out her side window he was returning to the house. Providing her with the sight of one of the finest rear ends she'd ever seen.

And yes, there she was, hating herself for just how much she appreciated the absolute perfection of his prime derriere.

She sighed heavily and started her engine to back out of his drive.

Then she took herself to task the whole way to her apartment, recommitting herself to ignoring how hellishly handsome Sutter Knightlinger was, and to refocusing on getting herself access to the Camdens.

Who would fill her life again and put her in the right state of mind to find a man, to get married and have a family of her own.

A man who would be so much better for her, so much more suitable, than Sutter Knightlinger ever could be.

Chapter Four

"Is there going to be a quiz later?"

"Huh?" Sutter responded to his cousin Beau's question.

Beau had called after Kinsey left on Friday night to invite Sutter to the Saturday morning workout he was hosting for family members. Sutter had seen a few opportunities in that invitation.

It would give him the chance to do some light work on his body as a whole and that appealed to him.

He could bring Kinsey along for her medical advice and begin to keep up his part of their deal by putting her in a room with several of the Camdens she claimed were her half siblings.

And most importantly of all, maybe whatever they did at Beau's gym would count as his physical therapy today so he could avoid her doing it later, when they were alone.

Like last night when the feel of her hands on him had broken through his defenses and his damn body had reacted like he was a hormonal teenager. Maybe if they worked on his shoulder in the company of other people he could have a little more control over himself.

So he'd texted her to ask if she wanted to go to Beau's and she'd readily agreed.

Which was how this morning had come about. And after doing his physical therapy and instructing him on the recommended dos and don'ts for the weights and lifts and exercise, she'd gone across the room to do the same for Beau's cousin—and potentially her half sister—Livi Camden. Livi was pregnant and wanted to know what kind of workout was acceptable to help keep in shape during the pregnancy.

And now Beau was asking if there was a quiz? What the hell was he talking about?

"You haven't taken your eyes off Kinsey since you got here," said his cousin, answering his *huh*. "Are you trying to memorize how she looks or what?"

"Assessing her skills," Sutter said curtly, as if there was nothing personal in it.

Beau laughed. They'd known each other too long for him to buy it. "Yeah, right," he countered. "You have a little thing for your nurse?"

Okay, yes, he did. There. He'd admitted it to himself. What else could he call it when he couldn't stop thinking about her? What else could he call it when the image of her was in his head when he closed his eyes to sleep at night? When he woke up thinking about her? When she touched him and he responded instantly?

A little thing—yeah, he guessed he might have a little thing for her.

But there was no way he was going to talk about it when she was just across the room.

So he said, "Nah."

Beau just laughed again. "I don't know who you think you're kidding—me or you." Then he left Sutter to his squats.

Squats he was doing with Kinsey directly in his line of vision so how could he *not* be looking at her?

Dressed in a pair of just-snug-enough jeans that made her rear end look fantastic.

Dressed in a red T-shirt that had sleeves to her elbows and a neckline cut at a weird angle like a lopsided V, and that fit her also just snug enough for him to get to see how just-right she was built.

Wearing that shiny, silky hair of hers in a ponytail that bared her small, perfect ears and a thin neck that he wanted to kiss…

Cut it out! he silently shouted, assigning himself twenty-five more squats to punish himself.

Too long without female companionship—that's what was wrong with him.

Maybe he should take it as a sign that he was on the mend, he thought. If he was having urges for Kinsey now maybe that was just an indication that he was close enough to full recovery for things to be percolating again. And that was good.

Well, not good exactly. Mostly embarrassing, really. But maybe it was a positive sign of good health.

And kind of torturous, too…

But like the pain in his shoulder when he'd refused any more pain medication, he was just going to have to tough out whatever this little thing was with Kinsey, he told himself. He wasn't a kid and he knew better than to indulge in something that was tantamount to a summer camp fling.

Which was all anything with her would be, since he wouldn't be staying in Denver for long. And she wasn't even a base secretary or another female officer or a reporter—the women he'd been involved with in the past. Women with the same mindset he had—away from home, family and friends, from anything with any permanence, and just looking for company and fun and relaxation for a while.

Kinsey wanted family, wanted connections—wanted to dig in roots somewhere and feel like she belonged. And that kind of permanent relationship was something he couldn't offer. Long, long ago he'd seen enough to convince him that, for him, it was either marriage to a woman or marriage to the military, but not both. And he'd chosen the military.

So it was just better not to mess with anything—or anyone—that could cause complications. Especially when he had enough of those to contend with thanks to the colonel.

*But damn, look at her...*he thought as he watched Kinsey smile at something Livi said.

And he found himself fighting the same reaction to her that he'd had the night before.

Pleased with the healthy dose of Camdens that Sutter exposed her to on Saturday morning, Kinsey returned with Sutter to his house and the colonel afterward.

Cleaning and lawn maintenance crews spent the day tackling the job of whipping the place into shape. Sutter oversaw the work and gave orders while Kinsey wrangled Jack and distracted the colonel.

Not responding to the colonel's grumbling, Kinsey

instead enlisted her to do some training with Jack. The terrier loved the attention, activities, praise and treats. And being cooperative and a fast learner helped him make a few strides toward winning over the colonel.

Enough so that the colonel allowed the puppy to nap next to her on the overstuffed chair where she sat to play cards with Kinsey when the training ended.

The colonel won most of their games and ungraciously rubbed it in. But the older woman's revelry at winning only made Kinsey laugh and concede to the colonel's superior card skills. That boosted the colonel's spirits and caused her to commend Kinsey for being a good sport.

In order to vacate the older woman's bedroom so the cleaning crew could work in there, Kinsey persuaded her to go for one of the short walks recommended by the cardiologist.

Taking Jack along wasn't easy but, recalling Todd's advice on the subject, Kinsey decided it should be done. He was not as amenable to the leash as he was to learning about sitting and staying. All his pulling and tugging and yanking amused the colonel who observed that it was Jack that was walking Kinsey rather than the other way around.

When the cleaning and lawn maintenance continued into the late afternoon, Kinsey volunteered to do the grocery shopping on her own. By the time she returned both crews were gone and Sutter and the colonel were on the back porch assessing the yard work that even the colonel agreed was an improvement.

Leaving them to it, Kinsey put away the groceries. Just as she finished the doorbell rang. She answered it to find an elderly, dapper-looking gentleman with a full head of wavy white hair standing on the landing, a plate of cupcakes in hand.

"Hi," she greeted him.

"I'm Sol Landrum from next door," he introduced himself. "My daughter brought me more of these things than I'll ever be able to eat and I thought the colonel might enjoy them—I saw the two of you out walking today and I just saw her in the back again now—looks like she's doing better and maybe could stand a visit?" He craned to look around Kinsey into the house, making it clear he wanted to be invited in.

So that's what Kinsey did.

No sooner had she closed the door after admitting him than the colonel's voice came from behind her.

"Army, what're you doing here?" the older woman said bluntly.

"Colonel," Sol countered before he went on to repeat the cupcake story, then added, "And I wanted to see how you're doing."

"Takes more than a measly heart attack to get me," the colonel grumbled because—as Kinsey had learned—any mention of her ill health aggravated her.

Sutter joined them then and, as he exchanged amenities with their neighbor, Kinsey tried to pay more attention to what was being said than to the way Sutter looked.

After Sutter's morning workout and physical therapy he'd come home, showered and dressed in a pair of jeans and another of those skin-tight crewneck T-shirts—this one crisp white with long sleeves that he'd pushed up to his elbows before adding the sling for his injured arm. All day long she hadn't been able to keep from staring when he wasn't looking.

"Colonel, why don't you and Sol sit down and have

a visit while Sutter and I get dinner started?" Kinsey suggested. Then, to the older man she added, "You're welcome to stay if you don't have other plans, Sol—we're just having pasta, salad and bread. And your cupcakes for dessert."

Kinsey was the recipient of two shocked and displeased looks from the Knightlinger mother and son, but she pretended not to see them.

"I'd love to stay!" the neighbor said, jumping at the opportunity. "I'm alone, too, you know, and now that you're well enough for visits, I'd be happy for the company for dinners or a movie or even if you just want a comrade in arms to do something with—doctors' appointments, outings, whatever. I play a mean game of backgammon and I'm fair to middlin' at chess, and if something happens over here—one shout and I can come running."

"How nice," Kinsey said while both Knightlingers just stood there tongue-tied. After asking what the colonel and Sol would like to drink she said, "Now you two go in and chat—I bought some crackers you can munch on while the pasta cooks. I'll be right back with everything." Then to Sutter who was now frowning, she said, "To the kitchen—remember, you're getting cooking lessons."

She had the impression that Sutter was reluctant to leave his mother alone with Sol because there was a distinct hesitation before he followed her. But he did finally come along as the colonel and her gentleman caller moved into the living room.

"Why'd you invite him to dinner?" Sutter demanded the minute they were out of earshot in the kitchen.

"To be polite," Kinsey said. "Why? Don't you like Sol? Is he the Hatfield to your McCoys or something?"

"He's a nice enough old geezer. He and my dad were friends. He was at the memorial service. But I think he's *hitting on* my mother!"

"I think so, too," Kinsey said with amusement.

"And you just gave him a free ticket."

Kinsey put the promised crackers and drinks on a tray and handed it to him. "Here, take these out to them and see how it's going. And remember, you wanted her to socialize and have a network of people in her life that she can depend on and turn to when you leave. Who better than a next-door neighbor? And if sparks fly? Then she'd have companionship—also what you wanted."

"I didn't think that meant getting her a *boyfriend*!"

"Let's call him a *special* friend," Kinsey suggested before pointing an index finger in the direction of the living room to send him to deliver the crackers.

Sutter wasn't much help in the kitchen after that. He was too intent on finding excuses to check on the elderly couple every five minutes. Kinsey indulged it, hoping that the more he saw, the more comfortable he might get.

During dinner it was mainly Kinsey, Sol and the colonel who talked, with Sutter barely interjecting a word here and there.

A considerate guest, Sol stayed only about half an hour after dessert and coffee, then thanked them for the meal and said he'd go so the colonel could get some rest.

Kinsey and the Knightlingers went to the front door with the older man so they all heard when he told the colonel that he'd check back with her and then said good-night.

"Well, that wasn't so bad," the elderly woman observed once the door was closed and before she added, "But I'm worn out."

Kinsey glanced at Sutter to see his response to that. He looked baffled and unnerved. Enough to make her smile as she jabbed a thumb toward the kitchen and said with some humor, “You can get started with cleanup now that you don’t have to be on patrol. I’ll be back after I help the colonel get settled.”

Sutter didn’t balk. He merely said good-night to his mother before he did as instructed.

He was only partway through the job when Kinsey got back to him. Before either of them said anything, Jack came in the doggy door from outside, covered in mud.

“No, no, no!” Kinsey exclaimed at first glimpse of the puppy, catching him by the collar before he got too far inside.

“The yard guys worked on the sprinkler system before they closed it up for winter,” Sutter said with a groan, explaining where the terrier had found mud.

“He’s going to have to have a bath.” No sooner were the words out of her mouth than Kinsey realized she was the only one in the house capable of doing that.

Apparently Sutter realized it at the same time because he slightly raised his arm and sling at once to point out the predicament. And now it was his turn to smile.

“Yeah, I know—you can’t do it with one arm,” Kinsey interpreted.

“And it’s too late to get him to a groomer,” he said. Then, the smile turning devilish—and devilishly handsome—he added, “Maybe you can get helpful Sol back over…”

“You do realize this isn’t in my job description and I could just let go of Jack to track mud all over your just-cleaned house, right?” she countered.

He laughed but skipped any more jibes and said, "Let's get him into the laundry tub."

Glad that Jack was small, Kinsey picked him up, holding him away from her to take him into the laundry room connected to the kitchen.

Once she'd set him in the washbasin he immediately tried to scale the side with scurrying hind legs. Kinsey had to slide him back down and keep him from another escape attempt by hanging on to him.

"Dog shampoo?" she asked.

"I didn't think of that. Can we use the dish soap?"

"I've seen it used in commercials to wash oil off ducks, so maybe."

Sutter went back into the kitchen and returned with the bottle of dish soap, setting it on the washing machine beside the tub and then stepping out of harm's way.

"Oh, no, you can't!" Kinsey said. "I'm not doing this alone. You have one good hand to hold him with while I do everything else."

"It was worth a try," Sutter muttered as he went to stand on the free side of the washtub.

He restrained the puppy while Kinsey removed Jack's collar and started the water. She got it to the right temperature and then rinsed Jack before soaping him up and rinsing him again. He squirmed and splashed, but Kinsey had known better than to expect to get out of this completely dry. And anyway, Sutter did a good job of holding him mostly in place.

When she was finished she turned off the water and said, "We need a towel," leaving to get one from the linen closet and returning in a hurry.

But in the time between Sutter releasing Jack and

Kinsey trying to reach him with the unfolded towel, Jack shook with abandon.

Kinsey had the towel between her and the puppy so she didn't catch any of the spray. But Sutter's white T-shirt took the brunt of it.

Tight, white and now a bit wet to cling almost transparently to the side of those pecs and abs not blocked by his sling.

She had no choice but to laugh at him, both to cover up her uninvited appreciation of the sight and because in fact his recoil was funny.

"Oh, he really isn't Reggie..." Sutter lamented, referring to the veteran service dog as he pulled on the bottom of his T-shirt to peel it away from his skin.

Kinsey's mind took it even further, mentally peeling the wet shirt completely off to expose his entire upper half and give her the full-on view she'd had the night she'd removed his stitches...

Until she forced herself out of that bit of daydream.

"All dogs shake when they get wet," she remarked as she wrapped the towel around the puppy, picked him up and set him on the top of the washing machine. Then she offered Sutter one end of the large bath towel to dry his shirt while she applied the other end to Jack, trying hard to focus on the dog alone.

"I'd better go block the doggy door so he can't get out and roll in the mud again," Sutter said when he'd done all he could with his shirt.

"Good idea," Kinsey agreed. It would keep Jack contained *and* with Sutter gone she could take a few deep breaths and work on getting some control of herself.

Minutes later, with Jack dried off, Kinsey called, "Is it safe?" before having it confirmed that the spaniel would not be able to get outside again.

She set the damp pup on the floor and went into the kitchen where they both picked up where Sutter had left off in cleaning the dinner mess.

"So why does the colonel call Sol *army*?" Kinsey asked.

"That's what he was drafted into out of high school," Sutter explained. "The colonel tends to call anyone who served by whatever rank they achieved or branch they served in. I think that registers with her more than their names."

"Was he career?"

"No, he served in Germany as an MP for some dignitaries, then did some time stateside and got out."

"Soo…because he's not a marine, he isn't good enough for your mom?" Kinsey ventured.

Sutter made a face that said that was silly. "I didn't say he isn't good enough for her. He's just…"

"Not your dad?" Kinsey guessed when Sutter stalled.

"My dad's barely gone," he said as if he seemed to be the only one in the house remembering that.

"I know it seems soon. But for two people more than halfway through their seventies there's not any time to lose if they happen to meet someone compatible—"

"Who said they were compatible?"

"Your mother said that tonight wasn't as bad as she'd thought it might be," Kinsey reminded. "And the clock is ticking for you, too, because you're leaving and you want a lot of things in place for your mom before you go—that doesn't fit with a long mourning period. Not that I think being friendly to Sol means she isn't mourning your dad because I'm sure she is. But having people around will help her, you know?"

"So you think hooking her up with the neighbor is the answer to everything."

"I think it might be one answer," Kinsey admitted. "He's nearby. She already knows him and is comfortable with him. And from things she said while I was helping her get ready for bed I think she's a little flattered that he seems interested in her."

Sutter scowled.

"Plus I think maybe Sol is lonely."

"He has *eight* kids—how lonely can he be with them all coming around? *Eight* kids—he's probably just an old horndog coming after my mother!"

Kinsey laughed again as she washed off the counters and Sutter finished loading the dishwasher. "In the marines, your mother had to have been one of very few women in a world of men. I'm sure she ran into more than her fair share of *horndogs*—"

"She never cheated on my dad."

"So what makes you think she can't hold her own with your next-door neighbor if he *is* a geriatric horndog?" Kinsey tried not to laugh as she said that.

Sutter sighed resignedly. "Yeah, she'd shoot me if she thought I believed she couldn't."

"Then why not just get out of the way and let whatever is going to happen, happen?"

Apparently he had a mental image of what *could* happen happening because his expression turned horrified and this time Kinsey couldn't keep from laughing before she advised, "Don't think about *that*."

"You never had any problem having a stepfather with your mother?" he asked.

"I was barely two when my mother married Hugh. He adopted me when I was four. I didn't know the difference. He was just the dad of the household."

"But you call him *Hugh* rather than dad?"

"Actually, we called him Gunny because—like the

colonel—he preferred it. To other people we referred to him as our father, but yes, when we talked—or talk about him even now—we call him Hugh. I think that's because my mother called him that when she talked to us about him. She never said *your father*."

"Isn't that weird if he adopted you?"

"I suppose. But that's just the way it was. From what my mom told me before she died, Mitchum Camden was the love of her life and maybe that was her way of not letting go of him. She said that she loved Hugh—and I know she appreciated all he did for her, for us kids—but she admitted that she never loved him the way she did our real father."

"So you didn't think of your adopted father as your real father," Sutter surmised, leaning a hip against the counter's edge.

Kinsey rested back against the facing counter's edge as she answered. "I thought of Hugh as my father…sort of. But I knew there was someone else who had actually fathered me—even if I didn't know who he was."

"And how did that happen? I mean how did your mother keep the idea of your birth father alive without ever telling you who that birth father was?"

Kinsey shrugged. "She just wouldn't say. Every time any one of us asked, she said it was Hugh who kept a roof over our heads and food in our mouths. Hugh who cared for us like any father would, and it was disrespectful and ungrateful to talk about our *real* father—that's all she'd say about it. And I think my brothers loved Hugh like a real father."

"But not you?"

Another shrug. "I loved Hugh, but he and I were just never close. He was never unkind or unfair or neglectful, but I wasn't interested in the military so I was just an afterthought. Someone for my mother to deal with while he *trained the boys to be men and marines*," she said, deepening her voice to sound like Hugh's on his perpetual catchphrase.

"Did you fantasize about having a father you *did* mesh with? One who doted on you as daddy's little girl and didn't want to turn you into a marine?"

"A little," she admitted. "I did always wonder if my *real* father would have taken more notice of me, more of an interest in me. If we would have had father-daughter moments that never happened with Hugh."

"If you wouldn't have just been an *afterthought* to him," Sutter put in. "And now you know—or think you know—who your real father is and you think you can get an idea of how it was to be his daughter through Livi and Lindie?"

"I just want to know what I can know," Kinsey said.

Sutter nodded slowly, watching her reflectively. "And how disappointed would you be to find out you *aren't* Mitchum Camden's daughter?"

"I haven't really thought about that because I know I am," she said definitively. "It wasn't just a fling between them—they were together for years."

"She had to have known he was married..."

"She had a lot of guilt over that. Even decades later when she told me the whole story, it tore her apart. But she said she still couldn't deny herself her times with him."

Sutter's eyebrows arched but he didn't seem to be judging her mother so much as conceding to the possibility of that kind of passion.

"She knew it was wrong," Kinsey went on. "I think that had something to do with her not telling us until the end. And she said she would never have done anything to break up Mitchum's marriage. But when it came to him, she couldn't help herself. It almost seemed kind of sad."

"Northbridge is a small town," Sutter pointed out. "There wasn't talk as you were growing up? No hints about who your father was?"

"Sometimes… It was harder for Conor, he was nine by the time Mom married Hugh so he remembers more about whispers and snubs and kids who weren't allowed to come to our house. We all ran into some of that, but less than Conor did and we were too little to understand it all. I guess marrying Hugh made an honest woman out of my mother and when he adopted us that helped change things—although there were always some people who looked down on us. But no one ever said anything about a Camden being our father. We had no idea and now that I've thought about that, I think that the Camdens' position as important people in Northbridge protected them and made the scandal all my mother's while the Camdens got a pass."

"Yeah, I guess it might have actually been a little dangerous to cross a Camden of that generation."

"And then, like I said, Hugh came on the scene. He was a force to be reckoned with, so once he was around I'm sure anyone who didn't mind their own business would have had him to face. I think, for the most part, after that, everyone—except the real moral sticklers—just let it go."

"And the secret of who fathered you all stayed hidden."

Yet another shrug from Kinsey.

There didn't seem to be any more to say on the subject so she changed it. "By the way, thanks for this morning," she said, not having had the chance to express her gratitude before this. "It was great to spend that kind of time with Dylan and Derek. And Livi, too. It helped put us on the road to getting to know each other, maybe. I appreciate that you included me."

Again Sutter only nodded before he said, "And tomorrow there's the Camden Sunday dinner."

"I got the colonel to agree to go," Kinsey told him. The older woman had been dragging her heels about the event until the bedtime ritual when Kinsey had pointed out that since the colonel had ended up enjoying Sol's company— she might also enjoy getting out and being around other people tomorrow night.

"Really?" Sutter said. "She seemed so against the idea earlier."

"Maybe she had to see for herself that she feels better when her horizons are broadened a bit."

"And you think Sol did that tonight?"

"I think she was in better spirits all the way around today just having a lot going on—and then enjoying Sol's company tonight."

"Well, I guess *I* owe *you* thanks for that."

"Maybe we made some headway all the way around with our deal," she said. Then she glanced at the clock and realized how late it had become. "I should get going… Unless your shoulder is bothering you and—"

"I'm fine!" he said, cutting her off.

"I'll just look in on the colonel and go then," Kinsey said, pushing off the counter's edge.

The colonel was asleep with the television on. Kinsey turned the TV off, then she left the colonel's room, expecting when she reached the foot of the stairs to find Sutter.

But he was nowhere to be seen.

Since the front door was open, she glanced through

the screen and discovered him outside, wielding a broom with his usable hand to brush leaves off her car.

Grabbing her purse and the satchel with her medical supplies, she went out to meet him.

"Don't worry about that," she said as she reached the sedan.

"No reason you should have to deal with the fallout from the tree being trimmed," he said, completing the chore as she unlocked her door.

She didn't get in, though, because he came to stand by her and asked, "So you're sure you're all right with tomorrow? I guess it qualifies as a split shift."

They'd discussed needing her to be there in the morning to get the colonel up and ready for the day. Then Kinsey would leave and return when Sutter and the colonel got back from the church service and their planned trip to visit the crypt where his father was interred.

Kinsey crossed both arms on the top of her door frame, bracing herself on it. "Doing a split shift is no problem."

"And you think the colonel is up to everything tomorrow?"

"Her doctor gave the okay and I think she knows her limits. If she gets too tired she'll let you know and you can just bring her home. Plus she's promised to nap when you get back."

He nodded, knowing everything she was telling him. "And you also got her the go-ahead for her nightcap?"

"I did."

"It won you points, that's for sure—she likes her brandy before bed."

"Since it doesn't conflict with any of her meds and

wasn't connected to her heart attack, why not? If you can't do what you like at seventy-six, when can you?"

He smiled a small, relaxed smile that made him all the more appealing.

So appealing…

Why did he have to be so appealing?

"I'm glad—we're *both* glad—you allow for a little wiggle room," he said then. "That you go with the flow and don't pass judgments. We appreciate it."

"I'm here to help, to make things better, not worse."

"Still… You're nice to have around."

"Even if I invite possibly horny neighbors to dinner?" she goaded.

His smile stretched into a grin. "Yeah, even then," he said with a sigh. He tilted his head slightly to one side as something seemed to occur to him. "I'll bet your mom was pretty, wasn't she? Because look at you… Too pretty for Mitchum Camden to ignore."

So he was getting more accustomed to the idea that Mitchum Camden might be her biological father.

And he thought she was pretty…

Kinsey didn't want to feel as good as she did about that.

Neither of them said anything for a moment as Sutter seemed lost in studying her.

And when his gaze lingered particularly long on her mouth, Kinsey wondered if he was thinking about kissing her.

After all, *she* was thinking about him kissing her. And about kissing him back…

He took a step nearer, near enough that he wouldn't have needed to do more than bend forward a little for their lips to meet. Near enough that she thought he might.

And did she rear back to give the *no* signal?

She should have. But she didn't.

Instead, he was the one who ended the moment by straightening up so tall and stiff that any notion of kissing was dismissed.

He cleared his throat, lifted the broom to tuck under his arm and said, "Get home safe and rest up—tomorrow you get full-on Camdens."

Kinsey swallowed and told herself she'd probably been imagining the almost-kiss.

"'Night," she said.

He closed her door when she was behind the wheel and then stood almost at attention as she started her engine and drove out of his driveway.

Thinking as she did that it was better that he *hadn't* kissed her. That there was no place for that.

Thinking, too, that it was a good thing that Sutter was staying on top of his end of the deal with the workout that morning and the Camden Sunday dinner the next night.

Because what she *wasn't* keeping on top of was asking him questions or learning anything about the Camdens when she was with him—one of the main reasons she'd taken this job.

And she wasn't keeping on top of it because when she was with him, she couldn't seem to think about anything beyond him.

Chapter Five

"There you are."

The mere sound of Sutter's voice washed over Kinsey exactly when she needed it.

She, Sutter and the colonel were at the Camden family home on Sunday night, where they'd been for the last three and a half hours. Kinsey was standing alone in front of a hallway wall of framed photographs of the Camden family that she'd passed on her way to the bathroom.

She hadn't been able to resist stopping to look. But the display had had an effect on her that she hadn't expected.

Sutter came up beside her to face the wall, too, as if they were at an art gallery. But when he joined her she went from looking at the display to drinking in the sight of him. It seemed like he got better looking every day. The dress code for the Camden Sunday dinner was casual, but no jeans. Kinsey had laboriously chosen a dark gray turtleneck sweater dress with an A-line skirt that ended two inches above her black stiletto-heel boots—all chosen more with Sutter in mind again than with the Camdens.

What Sutter was wearing was more laid-back—navy blue slacks and a white dress shirt with a navy windowpane check. But clothes just loved that body of his and, sling or no sling, he looked polished and crisp and just plain great.

"The colonel tells me she's ready to go," he informed her. "I think we'd better cut this short and get her home."

"I thought she looked like she was crashing. I was going to ask if she wanted to leave when I got back. She did a lot today," Kinsey agreed before nodding in the direction of the photos and saying, "You're in some of these."

"Yeah. Only as a kid, though—the more recent photos are in the den. How'd you recognize me in these?" he asked.

"The dimple," she said simply. That adorable dimple in his chin that had just been cute when he was a boy.

"And what about you?" he asked, his voice lowered considerably despite the fact that they were alone and too far from the living room to be overheard. "Are you seeing shadows of yourself? Your brothers?"

"My brothers for sure," she said quietly. She'd recognized a resemblance in the boyhood photographs of Dane, Dylan, Derek and Lang. There were a few of those early snapshots that could have been pictures of her brothers. And even now she thought that there were some similarities in more than the blue eyes they all shared.

"It's a full wall..." Sutter observed in a way that seemed pointed.

"It is," Kinsey agreed even more quietly.

"Are you standing here thinking that you and your brothers should be up there, too?"

Sadly that wasn't at all what she was thinking.

"More like how it's all so complete and there really isn't room for us. A place for us... I've been trying to figure out where in all of this we could fit in."

"Seems like you've been *fitting in* pretty well tonight..." he said, sounding as if he was leading to something.

"With your help," she responded.

He'd kept his part of their deal, including her as if she were his date. He'd brought her into every conversation he'd had, specifically targeting her possible half siblings, doing his best to find common ground between her and Dylan, Derek, Dane and Lang. He'd given her an opportunity to have some time alone with GiGi by asking GiGi to show Kinsey her collection of Hummel figurines. He'd also done a considerable amount of tending to his mother in order to free Kinsey to just socialize.

He'd definitely succeeded in giving her a different experience than when she'd gone to the Camden Sunday dinner as Maeve Teller's nurse. Tonight it had seemed far more as if she were one of the guests. And that had allowed her to mingle, to seek out her half siblings, to engage them a little on her own—something she hadn't felt she could do before.

"Have you thought of maybe just trying for what we need for the colonel—friendship?" he suggested then.

Ah, that's what he was getting at.

"Seems like you already might have an open door

for that," he added. "Especially with Livi and Lindie. Maybe it would be better all the way around if you just keep your secret for now and find another way to connect with them."

Kinsey rejected that idea with a shake of her head. "It wouldn't be the same. And even if I could get to be more than an acquaintance of Livi and Lindie's, how much of a friendship would I be likely to have with Dylan, Dane, Lang or Derek—wouldn't the women in their lives think it was weird if I was suddenly trying to start up some kind of relationship with them out of the blue? And what about GiGi—she and I couldn't just be friends. If they never know I'm a blood relation then these Sunday dinners still wouldn't be *my* Sunday dinners. GiGi and Livi and Lindie and Dane and Derek and Dylan and Lang still wouldn't be my family."

But looking at that wall of pictures had made her feel very melancholy and less optimistic about penetrating the close-knit group.

She waited for Sutter to point that out, to say that if she revealed who she was it might only accomplish her being spurned by them all.

But he didn't do that. Instead, as if he knew she was feeling a little down, his tone was soft and compassionate when he said, "Then I guess we'll just stay the course and hope for the best."

She doubted that he knew how much it helped to hear even the slight note of encouragement in his voice. It was the only bit of support she'd met with since she'd started this quest to connect with her family. Whether or not he agreed with what she wanted to do.

And while she didn't want—or need—a reason to like him even more, she suddenly had one. Kind of a big one to her because his support made her feel like she wasn't completely on her own. It was as if she'd called in the troops, but it wasn't her brothers who had come, it was Sutter.

"But for tonight we'd better get off the course and get the colonel home," Kinsey said, reiterating his words.

Then Sutter did one more thing that bolstered her flagging spirits—he reached over and squeezed her arm.

Molten honey went from that point of contact all the way through her and it made her forget for a minute everything except the feel of that big, capable hand on her.

Until he released her arm and said, "Let's go."

Kinsey took a deep breath, squared her shoulders and left that wall of Camdens and the past.

All the while aware of Sutter by her side, reminding her that she wasn't about to leave alone.

And that helped, too.

"Are you sure you're up to that?" Kinsey asked Sutter.

The colonel's fatigue had made her all the more cantankerous when she, Kinsey and Sutter had arrived home from the Camdens' Sunday dinner. As a result, it had taken Kinsey longer to get the older woman settled for the night, so it was after eleven o'clock before she was ready to leave.

That was when Sutter said he needed some exercise and proposed that he get it by riding with her to her apartment and walking back home.

"Am I up to walking a little over three miles?" he responded. "I'm a marine—I've done three—sometimes four—times that in boots, carrying a full rucksack. This'll be nothing but a little stroll."

"With Jack," Kinsey said because he'd also decided to take the dog.

"Look at him—he's been locked up most of the day and for hours tonight. He needs to be worn out."

The wirehaired fox spaniel *was* trying hard to pull the cast iron grate out of the fireplace. Only his tail end was visible through the opening of the fire screen but he was growling and yanking back and clearly determined to conquer it.

"But he's only a puppy. Three miles is too far for him, don't you think?"

"So I'll carry him when he gets tired—he's all of five pounds—that's nothing compared to a full pack."

Kinsey could see that there was no point in arguing.

"All right, it's up to you," she finally said.

Sutter pulled Jack's halter and leash out of his sweatshirt pocket and called the puppy. Who ignored him.

So while Kinsey gathered her things, Sutter went to the fireplace to pull Jack from his quest and put on the halter. Then, carrying the pup like a football under his good arm—while Jack held the leash in his mouth and shook his head back and forth—Sutter returned to the entryway and Kinsey.

"I'll be back before long, Colonel," he called up the stairs to his mother, who he'd already told of his plans. "I have my phone and you have yours if you need anything."

"Don't wake me when you come in," his cranky mother responded.

Kinsey led the way to her car, where Sutter got into the passenger seat with Jack while she got behind the wheel.

"Think you're going to get the colonel to stick with

that oxygen at night?" Sutter asked as Kinsey backed out of his driveway.

"I'll keep trying. I think she was just tired tonight so everything was a bigger deal to her than it really is. Eventually she should get used to the tubing and not even notice it. I just have to try to make her use it long enough for that to happen."

"You were a busy little bee tonight at the Camdens'," he mused then. "I heard you arranged for the colonel to play bridge with GiGi's bridge club? And GiGi is putting in a call to some woman who's part of a group of women vets to get the colonel and this other woman together?"

"Since the colonel was so much older than her sister—seventeen years, right?—I pointed out that GiGi and the colonel were more contemporaries than either of them were with your late Aunt Tina. I think GiGi had just gotten in the habit of thinking of the colonel as her daughter-in-law's sister rather than as someone in her own age group. It sort of went from there. They both love bridge, and talking about it reminded GiGi that someone in her bridge club just died so there was an opening. She asked the colonel if she might be interested in joining to fill the vacancy—"

"And the colonel agreed?" he said with some surprise.

"It took a little coaxing, but she said she'd give it a try. As for the other, it isn't actually GiGi who knows the retired woman vet—"

"Who is it?"

"Margaret—who I guess is not only GiGi's housekeeper but has been around so long they're best friends?"

"Margaret and Louie Haliburton—they helped GiGi

raise the ten Camden grandchildren when GiGi took them on."

"They do seem like family." And if the Camdens could incorporate two people who had begun as mere employees into their inner circle, was it really overreaching to think they would accept her and her brothers?

Kinsey hoped it was an indicator that they might.

"Anyway," she said, "Margaret has the retired military friend. And the colonel was pretty eager to connect with another woman vet and maybe the group of them. The colonel was so enthusiastic about that that Margaret promised to call her friend tomorrow to get something going. So that should give the colonel two outlets and two chances to connect with other *women* her own age," Kinsey finished the lengthy explanation, emphasizing the *women* part of that so as not to get him riled up about any more chances of his mother finding male companionship.

"Well you did some good work tonight," Sutter concluded. "The colonel and GiGi have always known each other, but there hasn't ever been any kind of camaraderie before this."

"I know GiGi isn't military but she's so down-to-earth and pragmatic that she and the colonel actually seem like-minded in some ways."

"Apparently it took you to point that out."

"Just keeping up my end of the deal," Kinsey said. Then she changed the subject to something that looking at the Camden family photos had made her curious about. "So did you grow up in Denver, near the Camdens, even though your mom was in the military?"

"Nah," he said. "We've always had the house that the colonel is in now—I think I told you it's been in the family forever. But we used it more like a vacation home. We lived on whatever base the colonel was assigned to. I grew up a marine brat, in more places than I can count, going to more schools than I can remember. We even lived for two years in Australia and a year and a half in Japan."

"But you've always been close to Beau Camden?"

"Like brothers. I came back here for weeks at a time during summer breaks, and he came to stay with us on base, too—he actually did a full year of school with me in Australia on an exchange program. Spending time on base is what gave him the bug to join the marines himself."

"But he wasn't career."

"He was until just recently when he decided it was time to take his place in the family business."

"And you don't approve," Kinsey guessed by his tone.

"I don't approve or disapprove," he claimed.

"But you think he should have stayed in the military," she persisted.

"It's my calling. I thought it was his, too. And no, I don't like to see the kind of training we've had the privilege of go to waste."

"Wow, you are marine through and through, aren't you?" Kinsey observed, thinking that it was a good reminder for her.

"I am," he said without equivocation. "So is Beau, so I'm not sure how he's going to do outside of the marines, sitting behind a desk. But now that he's getting married and taking on that baby his fiancée adopted, it's what he should do."

"Because your dad hated being essentially a single parent while your mother served the military and you hated being dragged around from base to base as a marine brat?"

"Who said either one of us hated anything?"

"Neither of you did?"

Out of the corner of her eye she saw him shrug. "Duty to my country was bred in the bone and the moving around was just part of it. Starting over in new schools wasn't my favorite thing as a kid, but I got used to it. After my dad got out of the marines he willingly followed the colonel wherever she was assigned—which changed as she moved up the ranks. He always said that by supporting her, we were serving in our own way."

"So both of your parents did the nontraditional thing—a woman is in the minority in the marines, especially back then. And your dad kept the home fires burning on base—there couldn't have been a lot of husbands doing that."

"No, there weren't. We were always surrounded by waiting wives. But my dad was dedicated to my mom's being able to stay in the marines as long as she wanted. He went back to school and got an accounting degree that gave him a job skill he could use wherever we went—usually on base, hired as a civilian employee."

"So if you all lived on whatever base she was assigned to while she practiced law, then there weren't long separations?"

Sutter chuckled at that notion. "The colonel's specialty was operational and international law. In wartime, operational lawyers are deployed with operational units—that happened twice. And even when she wasn't deployed, she went wherever she was needed, for however long a trial or a court martial took—all over the country and out of it since she's also an expert in international law. She had plenty of time away until she became a judge. But that wasn't until after I was long gone."

"So you were mainly raised by your dad."

"I was," he said.

His voice got a little gravelly as he added, "For the most part it was just me and my dad."

Kinsey could tell that he was feeling the passing of his father. "It must have been particularly hard on you to lose him," she said.

"No question about it," he confirmed gruffly, sounding like his mother. "Thanks in no small part to the colonel," he added under his breath.

Kinsey was stopped at a light and glanced at him. He was frowning out the side window.

"The colonel made it harder to lose your dad?" she asked in confusion.

"She didn't tell me what was going on here. She doesn't believe that anyone on deployment should be burdened with what's happening at home. So I didn't even know my dad had been in a car accident or was lying in a hospital bed for a month. If I had known, I'd have done whatever it took to get home, to see him before he died. As it was…"

She saw his jaw clench and she could tell that there was some anger at the colonel for this. It was her turn to just be sympathetic and supportive of Sutter, so Kinsey said simply, "I'm sorry, Sutter. You should have had the chance—any chance there was—to be with your dad at the end."

The light changed and they went the last two blocks to her apartment building in silence.

Even Jack must have sensed the tension in Sutter because when Kinsey parked her car, the puppy slinked from Sutter's lap to Kinsey's as if to escape some of it.

Kinsey gave Jack a comforting pet, waiting for the storm to pass.

Finally Sutter sighed and said, "Nothing to be done about it now."

"And no one can take away the time you did have with your dad all those years growing up," she reminded him.

"I do have good memories," he confirmed.

"He was a good dad?"

"He was. He wasn't as…military…as the colonel. He was more easygoing. A genuinely good man. Kind. Tough on me when I needed it, but a buddy when I didn't. Everybody loved him. He was such an upstanding guy that when we were living on bases, husbands would come to him and ask him to look after their wives while they were deployed. And he would. He'd be the shoulder they needed to cry on, the helping hand with stuff around the house or teenage kids who got into trouble—he even rushed one woman to the hospital in the middle of the night to have her baby. They named the baby after him. I can't think of anyone who ever *didn't* like my dad."

Remembering that seemed to make him feel better because he persuaded Jack to return to his lap with a few pats of his hand on his thigh. When Jack went, Sutter made peace by stroking him with that big hand that had reached out to her earlier.

Lucky Jack…

Kinsey was in no hurry to go up to her apartment. Refusing to consider why that might be, she merely angled in her seat, resting her back against the inside of the door so she could look squarely at him.

"So…" she said then, "if you were okay being a marine brat and your parents were happily married despite your mother being in the military and gone most of the time, why do you think your cousin *should* have ended his career as a marine now that he has a family?"

He raised his eyebrows in a response to her question. "The military is hard on marriages and families."

"Sure," she said because that was a given.

"Growing up on military bases I saw *how* hard it is on them. I saw a lot..."

"Of?"

"Of people struggling on their own when their partner was away. A lot of unhappiness. Sometimes all-out depression. And loneliness—a *lot* of loneliness and missing the service member off doing their duty. Don't get me wrong, there are a whole lot of strong, stoic people like my dad who do it well. But it can take a pretty big toll."

"A toll you witnessed," Kinsey prompted.

"And lost my innocence to."

She hesitated to comment on that, surprised by his candor. *If* he meant what that sounded like he meant.

Then she decided the only way she was going to know for sure was to ask, so she said, "Innocence as in virginity?"

"No, not as in virginity," he answered with a laugh. "That went to a girl in high school—Zoey Dubois—who was also a marine brat. Her dad was a JAG officer like the colonel."

"If not your virginity, then innocence as in..."

"Innocence as in overhearing too many wives telling my dad how sick and tired they were of the separations and sacrifices. I saw too many marriages crumble under the pressures and loneliness, plus the funeral of the mother of one of my friends when she committed suicide because she couldn't stand the life of a military wife anymore. Another wife reached a low point and… Well, she would have taken my virginity if I'd been willing."

He shook his head, then added, "And it wasn't only that side of it. I also saw how hard it was for the marines—I saw my mother feeling like the odd woman out when she got back and life had gone on without her. I saw marines depressed from missing so many things with their families—birthdays, holidays, graduations, problems they should have been there for. That baby named for my dad was eighteen months old before his dad *met* him. Like I said, it takes its toll."

"That *is* a lot of innocence lost," Kinsey confirmed.

"And the conclusion I came to from it all was that a man should marry the military or marry a woman, but not both," he said bluntly. "So now that Beau will have a wife and baby, that's what he needs to pay attention to."

"While you stay married to the military," she finished.

He shrugged again. "It's the choice I made a long time ago. A policy I adhere to."

Kinsey nodded, telling herself how important it was for her to keep that in mind.

Then he switched gears, raising his dimpled chin at her. "How are you doing after your own bout with being the odd woman out tonight?"

Kinsey laughed slightly at the connection between how she'd felt standing at the gallery of Camden family photos and how his mother had felt returning home after long absences.

"I'm okay. I was actually just thinking a few minutes ago that if the Camdens can let Margaret and Louie in, why not me?"

He nodded slowly, his expression making it appear

that he was torn about something even before he said, "Should I say that it might be different because Margaret and Louie didn't come as proof of a pretty big deception and betrayal by one of their own?"

"No," she commanded.

He laughed and after seeing him as down as he'd been earlier over his dad, it was music to Kinsey's ears.

Or maybe it would have been that regardless because it was such a good, deep, rumbling-from-his-impressive-chest laugh.

"Then I won't," he assured. "Instead, how about I tell you that I laid the groundwork for a doggy playdate with Jack and Lindie, Lang and Dane's dogs to get you a little time with them." He laughed again at how that had sounded and amended it. "A little time with Lindie, Lang and Dane, not with the dogs—who came from the same litter Jack did."

"Oh, good," Kinsey said. "I thought I heard them talking about how badly behaved their dogs are, too. I considered suggesting things Todd taught us, but there just wasn't the opening for it since I was really only eavesdropping. And because Jack isn't my dog. But a playdate you bring me along on would be great!"

"Then you do still want to go after this thing?"

This thing being her heritage.

"Yeah," she said, her conviction a little shaken but still intact.

"Then I'll try to arrange it."

"Thank you," she said. "For that and for tonight and for being in my corner on this—even if you do think maybe I shouldn't do it. You're the first to support me on this."

"What about your brothers?"

She shook her head. "I told you they were closer to

Hugh than I was, and I think going after this makes them feel kind of disloyal to him. And they don't want our mother called ugly names. Or us, either..."

"But you want it enough to risk all that," he said as if it were something he was coming to understand about her.

"I do. I hope bad things don't come of it, but I'm willing to take that risk for a shot at having a family I can count on," she said quietly.

Jack started to whine the way he did when the doggy door was blocked and he couldn't access the yard. They both knew what it meant so Sutter opened the door and got out with him.

Slightly resentful of the terrier cutting her time short, Kinsey got out, too, taking her things with her and locking the car as Sutter took Jack over to a patch of grass in front of her parking spot.

"This is your place, huh?" Sutter said, glancing at the three-story apartment building.

"There." She pointed. "I'm on the second floor, the southern side. See that wilting plant in the window? Apparently it does better with northern exposure."

It seemed only polite to ask him in now that they were there.

At least that's what she told herself. And that it wasn't because she was still so reluctant to have the evening end.

"Want to come up?" she heard herself ask.

He didn't answer immediately. Instead he looked at her windows and seemed to consider it. Then he did the military straight-as-a-stick posture as if it helped him resist an urge and said, "Thanks, but I don't think Jack would be a good guest anywhere right now. We'd better hit the road."

"You're still sure you want to hike all the way home?" she asked as he brought the puppy from the grass back to the pavement.

Sutter laughed and nodded toward the terrier who was straining the leash to the very end trying to get moving. "I think it's probably for the best," he said as if Jack wasn't the only reason, his gaze fixed on her.

"If you can't make it all the way home, call and I'll give you a lift," she offered.

He again gave her the smile that let her know she was fretting about nothing. Then he humored her and said, "Sure. If I can't make it I'll call you."

He was standing not far in front of her, continuing to look at her, deeply into her eyes.

"You really *are* on the level with this Camden thing, aren't you?" he said quietly.

Kinsey recalled his suspicions of her on that first day they'd met.

"I am," she answered.

"You're willing to take it to the end even if it gets you hurt."

"I just hope that doesn't happen."

"Yeah…" he said, nodding as if that was what he hoped, too, his gaze still locked on her.

He switched the leash to the hand that poked out of the sling and grasped her arm again the way he had earlier at the Camdens' house.

"But if at some point, for any reason, you change your mind and want to back out, you don't have to worry that anyone will ever hear anything about it from me. Your secret's safe should you decide to keep it."

And she thought that, like his dad with the lonely wives on military bases, she could trust that he would be there for her to cry on his shoulder because—also like his dad—he just seemed to be such a good guy…

"Thanks," Kinsey said, not doubting the truth in his promise.

And not feeling at all safe even if her secret was, because she was once again looking up into that face of his, with those blue-green eyes and his supple mouth.

And wishing for something she shouldn't want.

He still had a hold of her arm and his thumb was rubbing it through the sleeve of her sweater dress in a way that had nothing to do with moral support. He was massaging her arm sensuously. And looking down at her with an expression that drew her in…

Then he came closer, pulling her toward him with that hand on her arm, and she knew he was going to kiss her.

Don't let him…

Ha! As if she had the willpower to resist.

She tipped her head back and—in spite of herself—waited so eagerly for it.

For nothing but a kiss on the cheek.

He hadn't been headed there all along—she knew it. But at the last minute that's where he'd made himself go. Disappointing her to no end.

"Do what's best for you," he whispered in her ear after that tiny peck.

Kinsey's initial thought was that what was best for her might be to grab him and kiss him the way she'd been hoping he was about to kiss her!

Until she curbed her impulses and reminded herself that kissing him would be very unwise under the circumstances. All the circumstances. And so, instead, she only nodded her acceptance of his advice.

Then there was a parting squeeze of her arm as he pulled back and said, "See you tomorrow."

Kinsey nodded again, a little speechless with frustration, and managed to mutter a faint, "Good night."

Then she headed for her building and forced herself up the stairs and into her apartment without looking back at him.

But once she was inside, her will weakened all over again and the first thing she did was go to the window that faced the parking lot.

Expecting to find Sutter and Jack at least half a block away, she didn't spot them at all.

Until she looked down at the parking lot again.

Sutter was still standing where she'd left him. Looking up at the window she'd told him was hers.

Catching her looking for him.

But she thought she was catching him, too.

With something in his expression that might have been indecision and regret.

Before he raised his chin at her, then turned and headed home with Jack in tow.

As she watched him go, nothing could truly convince her that it was better that he *had* only kissed her on the cheek.

And if the look on his face had been regret of his own for that?

Good!

Chapter Six

"She hasn't been gone that long and you know she's coming back. You—and the dog—don't have to wait for her at the door, you know." The colonel admonished Sutter in a teasing tone.

It was late Wednesday afternoon. They'd had a visit from Louise Turner, the retired navy captain friend of Margaret's. Louise was a talkative woman and her visit had lasted so long that Kinsey had had to excuse herself in order to get to the colonel's cardiologist's office before it closed—the doctor had samples of a medication he wanted the colonel to try.

Louise had stayed forty-five minutes after Kinsey had left and had just now departed herself. Sutter had walked her out but she was long gone and he and Jack *were* still standing in the doorway, looking for signs of Kinsey's return.

But he wasn't going to admit that to his mother, so he said, "Just getting some air," and then closed the door.

"Uh-huh..." the colonel muttered facetiously.

They went into the living room where the colonel sat in a wing chair as if she needed a rest.

"What did you think of Louise?" Sutter asked as he took a seat on the sofa.

"She's a talker. But I liked her," the colonel answered.

"Think you might go to one of her group's lunches when you're feeling better? See if you like the other women vets? She said you're on her way and she can swing by to get you every week..."

"I told her I would. And yes, I will go to GiGi's bridge club, too, and there's Sol next door—think you can calm down now?"

"Calm down?" Sutter repeated. "I'm perfectly calm."

"You don't fool me, Light Bird," she said, using the slang term for his rank of lieutenant colonel. "You've had your feathers all ruffled about me being alone and on my own once you ship out again. I'm fine and I'll be fine, but if me playing bridge and having lunch with some other vets makes you feel better and gets you back to your unit, then that's what I'll do. I'll even keep that pain-in-the-neck puppy—that had better shape up."

So she'd seen through his maneuvers.

"You're humoring me?"

"I like to play bridge and it won't hurt me to be around some other ex-military women."

"And from the looks of it you didn't hate having Sol here last night and the night before."

"Doctor's orders," the colonel said as if that was the only reason she'd taken the after-dinner strolls with the next-door neighbor. But the doctor hadn't given any orders for her to ask Sol in both nights to continue chatting when their walks were finished and she'd done that, too.

Sutter didn't say that or that she'd seemed to enjoy her time with the charming neighbor, though. The colonel might want it to look as if she was only socializing for her son's sake or to follow the doctor's instructions, but Sutter kept a close enough eye on her to see for himself that she liked Sol's attentions. And Louise Turner hadn't been the only one of them whose chattiness had lengthened today's visit.

"And now you're weaning yourself off using your sling," his mother went on then, "what's the plan for you getting back to duty?"

"The plan is to take the leave I need." Both his medical leave to heal and his family leave to make sure the colonel could be safely left behind. But rather than set off more of her insistence that she didn't need help he only said, "I'll have to have medical clearance before I can report for duty again."

"You *do* need to report back for duty," the colonel persevered as if she were giving a command.

"There's no question," Sutter responded, unsure why she seemed to think he needed the reminder.

"No?" the colonel challenged. "You've been with Beau Camden for two days—doing what? Talking about resigning along with him?"

Sutter had spent Monday and Tuesday with Beau because his cousin had asked for his input. But also because spending time with Beau meant time he wasn't spending with Kinsey. He'd hoped the distance would help him get control over himself when it came to her. He definitely seemed to have precious little of that. And on Sunday night the urge to touch her, to kiss, had won out. Not completely—he *had* only touched her arm, and he *had* only kissed her cheek when he'd wanted to do a whole lot more than that. But it was evidence of a lack of discipline that he couldn't—wouldn't—tolerate in himself.

Not that keeping his distance had helped. He'd still had Monday and Tuesday evening with her, doing his physical therapy, answering her questions about the Camdens, just being with her. And after two nights of that he was barely holding on to his discipline.

But his mother was suspicious of his time with Beau and it was that that he addressed.

"I haven't been talking to Beau about resigning. I've been listening to him worry about being a civilian again himself. But mainly I've been with him for the last two days because he asked me to brainstorm with him. He's going to set up programs through the family stores and business and start a Camden foundation to help vets. So he wanted to run some things by me."

"You mean the things you told Louise about—the plans for store discounts, credit lines, job programs, etc.," the colonel said, referring to a lengthy conversation he'd had with her guest.

"Yes."

"And what about her son? Louise said he works with veterans. Are you going to call him?"

"I'll call him to arrange for him and Beau to meet. Her son's group does financial aid, assistance and planning for vets—"

"And with your military background and degree in economics, you're just what he's looking to hire—yes, I heard it." And she obviously wasn't happy about what she'd heard. "Plus I'll bet your cousin Beau would give you a job in a heartbeat, wouldn't he?"

"He talked about wishing I was here to run the foundation once he gets it started, about things I could do if I retired my commission. So what? I'm not leaving the marines."

His mother didn't say anything for a moment but she stared long and hard at him.

Then she said, "You can't keep your eyes off Kinsey."

True. He couldn't keep his mind off her, either.

Or his hands when she was doing his physical therapy and he found excuses for any contact he could get.

And again, there was that kiss Sunday night…

But he automatically said to his mother, "Don't be silly."

"Don't think you can put something over on me," the colonel countered. "I see you looking at her. I hear the sound of your voice when you talk to her or about her. And I can tell you're thinking about her all the time."

He started to protest but the colonel cut him off. "Don't get me wrong, if you're willing to back down from that 'marriage to the military or marriage to a woman but not both' policy of yours, I'm all for it. I never agreed with the idea that it's unreasonable to have both—"

"Of course you didn't."

"Your father and I did all right," she defended.

But did his dad die wanting him there? Feeling let down by him because he wasn't? Because *he* felt as if he'd let down his father in favor of the service. And as bad as that was, Sutter thought it would be even worse to disappoint a wife and kids who depended on him. To disappoint them over and over again.

"It takes special people to make the kind of sacrifices Dad did for you to serve. And there was plenty you missed out on. My policy stands."

"Then if you're thinking of divorcing the marines in favor of the nurse, we have a problem."

"There's no problem." Except the trouble he was having fighting his attraction to Kinsey.

"You know," his mother said, "I believe that as long as you're able to serve your country you should. But the same way you don't want me to be alone, I don't want you to be alone, either."

That surprised Sutter. His mother had never pushed him about getting married or having kids. He'd assumed that didn't matter to her. And it had certainly never occurred to him that she might be thinking about him being on *his* own.

"Kinsey is from a military family," the colonel continued. "She has to know what it takes and I think she could handle things as well as your dad did. Maybe you should think about making an exception to your rule."

His mind went back to the sad woman who had tried to seduce him as a teenager because she'd been so lonely and unhappy. And the funeral for his friend's desperately despondent mother.

"The policy stands. I'm fine alone."

"You think it's different for you because you're a man? You think you won't get where I am someday?" she challenged once more. "Because you're wrong. Look at Sol—man or not, he needs some company just the way you think I do. And you better believe you'll get where I am. Only if you don't break that rule of yours, you'll get here with nobody to look out for you when you need it."

Sutter didn't want to think about that so he said jokingly, "Maybe when I retire and move in here, one of Sol's daughters or granddaughters will come over and bring me cupcakes."

"In the meantime your stubbornness could be costing you a good life and a family with a girl who's set off a spark in you," his mother persisted.

"But I come by that stubbornness naturally," he shot back pointedly as he stood and called for Jack to come.

"Jack needs a walk," he decreed, leaving the colonel to get the dog's leash before heading for the front door.

Reminding himself along the way of all the reasons he'd formed his marriage policy in the first place and all the reasons he was still committed to it, too.

Reminding himself that he was strong enough to resist the damn attraction he had to Kinsey.

And hoping that last bit was true…

"I knew it!" the colonel ranted as Kinsey helped the elderly woman get to bed for the night. "If that dog isn't underfoot then he's into mischief. Here I was thinking maybe he was behaving because he didn't bother anyone while Louise was here. But what was he doing? Stealing everything he could find and taking it outside!"

"Sutter is getting flashlights. We'll go out and bring everything back in," Kinsey assured.

They'd begun to notice that things were missing during dinner—a dishtowel, the hot pads. Then the colonel hadn't been able to find the gloves she wore to take her walk with Sol. Or the socks she wore to bed. Or her book.

By then Sutter had realized he was missing several things, too—just as the terrier slipped through the doggy door with one end of a roll of toilet paper in his mouth, unwinding almost the entire roll from the downstairs bathroom through the kitchen to get it out.

That was when a glance through the window over

the kitchen sink revealed that the yard and bushes were littered with things that didn't belong there.

"Jack is a puppy and puppies do get into mischief," Kinsey said. "But think of how enterprising he has to be to do what he did."

"And now I don't have my book to read tonight. He's probably chewed it to bits out there," the colonel grumbled.

"I'll turn on that TV show you like. And tomorrow I'll stop at the bookstore on my way and get you another copy of the book."

"Nuisance!" the colonel muttered under her breath.

"He's so cute and funny, though."

The elderly woman didn't deny it. That was a first and Kinsey took it as encouragement.

"Here's your brandy," she said, handing the colonel the small snifter. "Your cardiologist asked me about this today. He wanted to make sure we knew it has to be only in moderation. But I told him it was, so we're still in the clear."

"Good girl!" the colonel praised as if they were sharing a victory over a fierce adversity. "Now get out of here and go find my things!"

Kinsey laughed, said she'd check back before she went home tonight, and left the older woman's bedroom.

Sutter was waiting for her in the kitchen downstairs with two flashlights.

"Just in case, I think you should use the sling while we do this," she told him. "We don't want you jolting that shoulder if you trip over something in the dark."

Plus seeing him more and more out of the sling the last few days only made it harder for her to ignore her attraction to him. Like tonight, when he was wearing a navy blue mock-turtleneck T-shirt with a marine insignia riding the well-developed pectoral that would otherwise be hidden behind the sling.

While he put the sling on she kept herself from watching by gathering the trail of toilet paper Jack had left and throwing it away. But she knew better than to hope that ignoring Sutter would keep him out of her thoughts…or her dreams.

The dreams about him weren't the only things haunting her, though. She'd been struggling since Sunday night. Two simple touches of his hand on her arm, a dumb little kiss on the cheek and she was a mess. Thinking things she didn't want to think. Wanting things she didn't want to want. Noticing even more about him that only made it worse.

Monday and Tuesday it had been a relief to not have him around. But at the same time she'd been miserable because he wasn't around. And missing him, for crying out loud!

It was all just so confusing and aggravating.

So at least put on the sling and give me a little reprieve.

Although it didn't do anything to blunt the effects of the jeans he was wearing that made his rear end look divine.

Still, it was something…

Once the toilet paper was cleaned up, Kinsey went into the hallway to put on her jacket. It was a short leather jacket that she ordinarily only wore out for dates or special occasions. But she'd put it on today, along with her best jeans and the cashmere sweater set that were hardly work wear either, because she'd known that Sutter would be home.

"Ready for the hunt?" Sutter asked when she returned.

So much for the sling helping anything—one look at that sandy-colored hair and those piercing teal eyes and that chiseled face, and she was still sunk.

It was hopeless.

"Ready," she answered, handing him a plastic grocery bag and taking one for herself to use for the collection before accepting one of the flashlights.

Jack went out with them, excited to have company in the yard. The puppy proceeded to prance around the debris as if he was proud of his accomplishments.

Until he realized they were picking up his prizes, then it became a game of him trying to snatch things out of their grip and run with them.

They tried shutting him in the house but that only caused him to bark incorrigibly, which they both knew would aggravate the colonel. So the end result was a race to collect all the things Jack had snuck outside before he could steal them and dash out of reach.

In the process, Kinsey said, "So I think today went well—the colonel and Louise seemed to hit it off."

"She knows, though," Sutter said.

"Who knows what?"

"The colonel. She knows I'm trying to get her out into the world and find her some companionship and support. She had to make sure I didn't think I was 'putting anything over' on her."

"Was she mad?"

"No, she's going along with it to get me to go back to my unit."

"Does that mean she won't keep up with her new friends once you're gone? That she plans to turn into a hermit again?"

"I don't think so. I think, whether she wants to admit it or not, she's discovered that she feels better when she gets out a little and socializes. That's to your credit, though, because you're handling her with more finesse than I've ever managed and it seems like that's getting her to see what she needs for herself."

"So *are* you getting close to going back?" Kinsey asked, hating how much she didn't want to hear his answer.

"Clos*er*, I'd say." He paused as he picked up a sock to put in his bag. "The weird thing is that the colonel is thinking the same things about me that I've been thinking about her."

"That *you're* a hermit?"

"That I'm going to end up alone, without anyone in my life."

"Well, she has a point. Have you thought about that?"

And why was there something rushing through her that almost felt like hope? There was no cause for that. What would she be hoping for?

"I actually hadn't considered it, no. I guess I have the colonel's streak of self-sufficiency that makes it seem like I can do everything myself."

"For what it's worth," Kinsey said, "I think your mother is right, but so are you. If you stay married to the military and never marry a woman, who *will* you have when your career is over? But on your side of it—I haven't been a wife or a kid left behind for military service, but I am a sister in that spot, and it *isn't* easy."

"And being fully aware of that, would *you* sign on as a military wife?" he asked in a purely academic way.

"No," Kinsey answered without hesitation. "It's actually a big, fat, firm *no* for me."

He laughed. "A *big, fat, firm* no—no question about it? You'd rather eat worms than marry a military man?"

"You're joking but the two run about neck and neck for me—"

"Absolutely no chance you would ever even consider it?"

"Absolutely no chance," she confirmed. Which was why she really was fighting the growing attraction she had for him.

"Even if, say, you get in thick with the Camdens and end up with family coming out of your ears? With plenty of them around to help with anything that ever comes up?" he said as if offering a theoretical scenario. "You still wouldn't—"

"I still wouldn't," she answered before he even finished. But she didn't want to go into more of her reasons why so she said, "But that's just me. My brothers run into a fair share of women who *want* a military man—"

"Any of your brothers married?"

"No. But there have been some hot pursuits."

"By military groupies? Yeah, they're around. I don't know why anyone would want a wife who was only attracted to the uniform and not the person inside of it."

"But there are other people—like your dad, for instance—who can be happy, content military spouses. Have you ever thought about finding someone who *could* withstand the absences and would be willing to do what it takes at home with or without you?"

"No, because that goes back to the part where I don't want to be the one leaving someone else to do all the work. Back to where I don't want to miss my kid's birth or first word or baseball games or graduations. I guess the same way you're sure of what you want and don't want, so am I."

And they were exact opposites of each other in what they were both committed to for their futures.

Sutter leaned over to pick up the colonel's book and Jack came out of nowhere to snatch it and run before his master could get to it. But keeping a joyful eye on Sutter, the terrier ran in Kinsey's direction, so she lunged to grab him to prevent him from getting away.

"Oh, nice catch!" Sutter cheered.

But he'd spoken too soon. Jack leaped out of Kinsey's grasp, causing her to overbalance and fall.

"Ja-ack!" Kinsey lamented with an embarrassed laugh.

"Bad dog, Jack!" Sutter reprimanded. But while there was a rebuke in his words, Kinsey could tell he was suppressing a laugh.

And he was still fighting a smile when he came to hold out his free hand to her. "Are you all right?"

"I'm fine," she said.

She didn't need the help of his outstretched hand and knew without question that she shouldn't take it.

But there it was and she just wanted too badly to feel his touch again to deny herself. So she slipped her hand into his as if it was meant to be there.

He pulled her up with a little too much strength and she landed against his slinged arm and chest with some force.

"Oh!" she said reflexively, veering back instantly. "Did I hurt your shoulder?"

He was still holding her hand so she hadn't gotten far away and he was standing tall and rock solid, looking down at her with a full smile this time. "Killed me," he said facetiously.

"Seriously," she insisted.

"Seriously," he lied with the raise of one eyebrow. "I'm in horrible pain. What are you gonna do about it?"

"Amputate?" she countered because it was clear he was just being ornery.

He did laugh at that. "That's a little drastic, don't you think?" he said in a voice that had gone deeper all of a sudden.

He was looking into her eyes and somehow the distance she'd put between them closed to a bare inch.

Kinsey could feel the heat of his body and all she wanted to do was melt against him. But she fought it.

"No kidding, I slammed into you," she said, her own voice slightly breathy for no reason that had to do with anything except being that near to him. "Is your shoulder okay?"

"Perfect," he answered, this time honestly but with a hint of something in his voice that made it seem as if he was talking about more than his shoulder. Those eyes of his dropped to her mouth for a split second before returning to hold her gaze locked in his.

Something in the atmosphere around them changed and a moment later she realized his good arm had snaked around her. There wasn't any space at all between them again. In fact, one of her breasts was nestled in the crook of his slinged arm.

Then his expression sobered just before his head bowed slowly toward her and his mouth pressed to hers.

It was a simple, soft meeting but it went straight to Kinsey's head anyway. Her eyes drifted closed and she kissed him back. Savoring every moment as she melted into him and that kiss that she'd wanted even more than she'd thought. So, so much more…

And then it ended all too soon. There was once again space between them. Only that inch, but he felt miles away.

He took a deep breath, exhaled and shook his head. "That was probably out of line," he muttered.

"Only if I say it was," she said quietly.

He opened his eyes and smiled a smile that was more tender now. "Are you going to?"

"I should…"

"Go ahead," he challenged.

"That was out of line," she said by rote, clearly not meaning it.

"Court martial offense?"

"Yes. But the judge would likely be biased," she answered with a nod toward the house where the colonel who had presided over many of those was.

"So just more KP duty?" Sutter concluded.

Or more kissing...

"More KP duty," Kinsey ordered.

"Worth it," he said.

Then do it again...

For a moment it looked like he might.

Then Jack trotted over with the colonel's paperback and dropped it at his master's feet.

Sutter bent over and picked it up—wet, ragged and needing to be trashed—and when he stood again he was farther away.

No treats for you, dog!

"It's getting late. If we missed anything out here I'll get it in the morning when it's light," Sutter said as he dropped the book into his bag.

Kinsey nodded and retrieved her grocery sack and flashlight from the ground where they'd fallen.

"You've done your exercises?" she asked as they headed for the kitchen. She was no longer handling his physical therapy now that he knew what to do himself.

"Yes, ma'am. Doing them every chance I get."

"Don't overdo it," she said, knowing that it wouldn't matter. She'd told him to do the therapy twice a day but she knew he had increased that in order to get his shoulder back into shape sooner.

Which helped remind her that getting back to duty was his real goal. To continue on the path he'd just told her tonight he had no intention of veering from. He was a marine and he was staying a marine.

And she didn't want any part of that.

Regardless of how much she might want a part of him.

Once inside she went upstairs to look in on the colonel, who was watching television and waved her off.

Then she headed for the front door where Sutter was waiting.

Would he kiss her again now? she wondered.

Hoping he would.

Knowing she shouldn't let it happen.

But no sooner had she reached the entryway and gathered her purse and satchel than the colonel shouted from upstairs, "Damn dog, he has my remote! Get him!"

"I'll do it," Sutter volunteered. "Go ahead and go home."

And that was that, Kinsey said good-night and left while Sutter chased Jack who was headed for the doggy door with his latest prize.

So there wasn't even a chance for another kiss.

Which was for the best, Kinsey told herself as she left.

But that didn't stop her from reliving every nuance, every moment of the kiss that shouldn't have happened while she drove home.

And tonight she knew she would be reliving it in her dreams.

Knowing she should not be fostering these feelings.

And completely incapable of stopping herself.

Chapter Seven

"Oh, Declan, I hope you feel better than you look," Kinsey said around a lump in her throat, blinking back tears that had come the instant she'd seen her brother.

Conor had arranged a video chat on Friday morning, this time including the injured Declan from his hospital bed in Germany.

As a nurse Kinsey had seen people in bad shape. But those people had not been her brother. And Declan was in some of the worst shape she'd ever seen.

Even logy and weak, one eye swollen shut, the other lid too heavy to lift all the way up, he said in a thick, sluggish, exhausted voice, "Don't sweat it, twerp, I'm fine. A little rest and I'll be back to my unit. Don't think I should even have to come stateside—"

"You *do* have to spend some time stateside," Conor put in from off-screen.

Declan made a derogatory noise but he fell asleep halfway through it.

Conor turned the laptop around so that Kinsey was seeing him now rather than their battered brother.

"That's as good as it's gonna get, *twerp*," Conor said, using Declan's nickname for her, something he'd begun calling her when he was a teenager and she was an annoying preteen. "He's on so many meds that he sleeps most of the time."

"But he's doing okay?"

"He is. The leg looks all right—circulation's good, response and movement of his toes are all normal. He's just pretty banged up."

"And he *still* doesn't want to come home," Kinsey said sadly, more to herself than to Conor.

"He's out of it, Kins—he doesn't know what he's saying and he won't even remember he talked to you when he wakes up next. Orders are in to get him to Bethesda as soon as he can make the trip, though. And my leave to go along has come through, too, so we'll both be there before you know it."

They'd be there and then they'd be gone again.

But Kinsey didn't say that, she only nodded.

"How are you holding up?" she asked Conor instead. "You have bags under your eyes. Are you sleeping at all? Eating?"

"I've just been sleeping in the chair in Declan's room. Wanted to be close by. But I think he's finally stable enough for me to hit a call room tonight and sack out. Food is hospital food—what can I say? You'll have to cook me something good when I get there."

No time soon. But Kinsey knew he was trying to give her something to look forward to, so she didn't call him on it.

"How about you? You doing okay?" he asked.

"Sure. Just working. My patient is a retired marine colonel—Geraldine Knightlinger. I don't know if you've ever run across her or heard of her."

"I have!" Conor said. "I operated on a master gunnery sergeant who she got off some charges in Japan when he was a private. Talkative older man. I guess it was looking bad for him until she got there. He said I was the second person to save his life, that she was the first," he finished with a laugh.

"She's an interesting woman," Kinsey agreed.

"And keeping you busy."

"Busy enough," she confirmed.

"So you haven't had the time to do anything about the Camdens, right?"

"Not yet," she said, omitting the fact that since their previous video chat she'd been with them for Sunday dinner. She didn't want to tell her brother and risk revealing the feelings that had come out of that dinner. She knew if she showed Conor any doubt about the course she'd set for herself he would press her again to let her plans drop.

"Just keep thinking about Declan and me being on our way there," he said.

"Sure," she repeated. "Have you heard anything from Liam?"

"No. But I got word out to him about Declan so when he's able, I'm sure I will hear from him."

Something behind the screen caught Conor's eye and when he looked at Kinsey again he said, "I'm gonna have to go. One of Declan's machines is flashing—he needs a refill of pain meds. I don't want it overlooked."

"Take good care of him," Kinsey said.

"I am. And he's doing fine. He really is, no matter how bad he looks."

"Take care of yourself, too," Kinsey said.

"We love you, twerp."

"I love you guys, too."

Kinsey closed her computer and sank back into her couch cushion, closing her eyes. It wasn't yet six and she was still in her pajamas. She could have gone back to bed.

But she knew she wouldn't be able to fall asleep again so she just rested there, thinking.

How many mornings had she had like that—rising before dawn in order to connect with one of her brothers in a distant time zone? In order to connect with Trevor when he was away?

Too many to count.

She'd always been willing to do it, to go to any length to talk to one of them, to see them if that was possible. But it wasn't the same as them being there with her. It just wasn't. And afterward—every time—she was still faced with going on with her day, her week, her month, her life, on her own. Like she would today.

And even though that didn't feel dreary and lonely to her on this particular day because she was eager to see Sutter, she hadn't forgotten all the other days that had felt all the more empty to her after one of these calls that gave her only a few minutes' taste of family. A few minute's taste of the relationship she'd had with Trevor, too.

Absentee family. Absentee fiancé. Somehow touching base with them highlighted the loneliness she felt when the call was over.

And there Declan had been, lying in a hospital bed,

so hurt and still so eager to get back to his unit. To return to being a marine.

Just like Sutter was doing.

Sutter was so determined to recover and return to duty that he was working through his physical therapy exercises like no one she'd ever seen before—so many times a day she'd had to warn him to slow down.

He was forgoing the sling more and more, not to mention working out alone on Beau Camden's equipment every day to keep the rest of that gorgeous body in fighting shape.

All with one goal: to go back to his unit.

And that's how it would always be, Kinsey told herself, because Sutter was just like her brothers. Just like Trevor.

Going away was what they did.

Leaving behind people who cared about them.

So regardless of how much she kept thinking about Sutter; regardless of how much she'd liked kissing him or how much she liked being with him, talking to him; regardless of how much he made her laugh or how good he made her feel, she absolutely could *not* pin on him a single hope for anything.

It was a fact, pure and simple. And she knew it.

Yet he *did* make her laugh and feel alive and lighthearted. He *did* keep her on her toes in a way that was exciting—mentally and physically. She *did* like talking to him and joking with him and even being teased by him. And oh, she *really* liked kissing him, and she wanted him to kiss her again.

Despite knowing with every fiber of her being that it was only temporary—like visits from her brothers—she couldn't stop the way she felt.

This was temporary when what she wanted was permanence!

She'd actually shouted that at herself in the shower yesterday morning.

But nothing changed.

And she was getting tired of fighting it.

Fighting a losing battle.

So maybe she should stop fighting. Maybe she should just take the chemistry between her and Sutter for what it was.

A self-regulating situation.

Sutter was going to leave. That was inevitable.

And when he did, the rest would end on its own. It would have to—he wouldn't be around for her to talk to, to joke and laugh with, to tease or goad or ogle or kiss.

Any time with him—like any time with her brothers—had its own limited life span.

When her brothers came, she blocked out that time to do nothing but be with them so they could catch up, so they could tell old stories and relive those things she shared only with them, so they could reconnect.

All the while knowing it was going to end.

Could she do something like that with Sutter?

Maybe she could look at it—at this time with him—exactly the way she looked at visits from her brothers. A fleeting thing that she should enjoy while it lasted.

Always, always, always keeping in the back of her mind that it wouldn't go anywhere beyond right now.

She hadn't done that with Trevor. She'd held out hope that they could have a real life together. She'd fed the fantasy that things would change because they were going to get married. And that had been her downfall, ending her short-lived engagement and leaving her hurt and frustrated and angry.

All because she hadn't been realistic.

But her eyes were wide open now. And she knew better than to expect any more from men like her brothers, like Trevor, like Sutter.

And if she couldn't conquer this fixation she had on him, maybe she should just go with it. Give in to it. For now.

She certainly wasn't getting anywhere doing the opposite. Actually, her attraction to him was growing stronger and stronger by the minute in spite of her fight against it.

So maybe letting it run its course—and keeping constantly in mind that its course was a flash in the pan—was a better idea.

As long as she never let herself think for even a split second that anything more could come of it.

And as long as she continued to work toward getting to know the Camdens, toward a time when she could reveal who she was and hopefully have a lifetime relationship with them.

Then, with a family foundation to stand on and the itch for Sutter scratched, she could move on to finding a man, a husband who would be around, who would be there for her, every single day.

A man who she knew without question wouldn't be Sutter.

And Sutter could just be a memory of a tryst she'd had en route to the life she was aiming for.

Not that she would drag him to bed the next time she saw him. But she *was* going to ease up on herself and let this play out to its natural end.

She breathed another sigh, this one of a sort of relief—like finally giving in to a craving and eating the last chocolate doughnut in the box.

She'd been struggling so much against the draw of Sutter and now she gave herself permission to just let it pull her in without a battle.

It was liberating.

Within limits.

The limits being that she not forget that an end was looming and would ultimately and inevitably come.

"She can walk just fine on her own, you know."

Kinsey laughed at Sutter's muttering under his breath.

Friday was Veterans Day. With a slow pace and multiple rests to accommodate the colonel, Kinsey, Sutter, the colonel and next-door-neighbor Sol had gone to the parade, the remembrance ceremony and then the festival in Civic Center Park.

As they approached the event, Sol had offered the colonel his arm. And she'd taken it.

Walking behind them, Sutter watched it happen, and it provoked his muttering.

"She's doing better every day, but don't forget that she's still a little weak," Kinsey said quietly, amused by his brooding. "And remember that this is part of what you want—for her to have company."

Sutter frowned down at her. "So I can't yell *no touching*?"

Kinsey laughed. "No, you can't."

A growl rumbled in his throat that also made her grin.

"Just chill out," she advised. "He's only offering her a little help. It's not as if they're holding hands. He's just being a gentleman. You marines are supposed to be all about that, aren't you?"

"He's army."

Kinsey bumped Sutter's side with her hip. "Get over it," she commanded with another laugh.

He turned his handsome face toward her to glare at her, but there was enough of a hint of a smile playing around the corners of his mouth to let her know she'd succeeded in distracting him from some of his disapproval.

"If they get married you'll have to give away the bride because I won't," he warned with mock sternness.

"Happy to," Kinsey declared.

He beetled his brows at her and made her laugh yet again.

With Sol's support, the colonel lasted longer than Kinsey had expected. And once Sutter got over seeing his mother on the arm of a man other than his father, he got into the swing of things, too.

They toured the vintage military vehicles on display from the parade and watched uniformed men and women pose for pictures.

There was a beer garden where they took a long rest midafternoon and enjoyed a sampling from small local breweries. They tried food from several of the trucks, listened to live music and watched some of the games being played. They also made the rounds to all the vendors and booths.

Sutter showed particular interest in those booths offering resources, services and information on services for veterans, taking it all in and collecting brochures and pamphlets.

"I had no idea there was as much need as there is for help for returning vets," he commented when the day was done and they'd returned to his SUV.

"It can be rough," Sol responded, jumping into the

conversation. “With the drawdown reducing active duty forces, there’s a lot of people coming back.”

The older man helped the colonel climb into the backseat as he went on. “It’s rougher on some than others. I volunteer a day a week down at the DAV and you’d be surprised at all the troubles that I run across. Problem is, sometimes there’s more need than resources… or people willing to help.”

Sol got in after the colonel and closed the door as Sutter reached for the handle on the passenger door.

Before he could open it for Kinsey, she whispered, “See, he volunteers. He’s a nice man.”

Sutter leaned over and whispered in her ear, “Horndog.”

Then with a grin that said he was joking, he opened the door and waited for a chuckling Kinsey to get in.

They went for a light dinner at a pizza place a few blocks from home, where Sol talked about two of his own sons’ return from serving in the military. About how jobs hadn’t been easy for them to find because their military experience wasn’t the background employers were looking for. About how both sons had needed to live with him for a time because they hadn’t been able to afford civilian housing. And even once they’d had jobs, they’d had difficulties finding financing for homes because of their limited credit histories. All of that was on top of the other mental and emotional struggles they’d faced readjusting to civilian life.

“I had no idea,” Sutter repeated as he pulled into the driveway once dinner and the conversation was done.

It was after nine o’clock by then and even Sol was showing signs of fatigue. Sutter had won a seven-layer chocolate torte at one of the festival’s game booths where proceeds went to benefit retiring vets. The plan had been for everyone to come inside and have it for dessert, but Sol begged off and bid them all good-night at the car.

"I'm thinking along those same lines," the colonel said as Sol crossed their yards to his own house. "I just want my brandy and my bed. You two eat the cake."

Inside Kinsey sent the colonel upstairs while she took off the jacket she'd worn over jeans and a double layer of T-shirts—a green V-neck over a paler green tank top with tiny crocheting at the top edge.

Then she headed to the colonel's bedroom while Sutter went to deal with the yipping Jack.

The older woman was already in her connecting bathroom when Kinsey got there so she turned down the bed, arranged the oxygen tubes and poured a small amount of brandy to have it waiting when the colonel came out in her flannel pajamas. She was also using a knit headband that held her hair back, keeping it from entangling with the oxygen tubes when she slept—Kinsey's solution to the colonel's latest complaint against her nightly prescribed treatment.

"I'm beat," the elderly woman proclaimed as she got into bed.

"I'll bet. How are you feeling otherwise, though?" Kinsey asked.

"All right," she answered with some satisfaction.

Kinsey listened to her heart, took her blood pressure and pulse, then handed her the oxygen tubing as she sat back against her pillow.

"But just keep telling my son that I need to take Sol's arm for support if that makes *him* feel better," the colonel went on a few minutes later as if there hadn't been any interruption.

Kinsey was amused by the slyness in the older woman's tone. "You have hearing like an elephant's, huh?"

The colonel gave a smug smile. "It's always been good. Luckily Sol's isn't as sharp so he didn't hear that 'no touching' thing this afternoon. You're right, though, Sol *is* just being a gentleman. No harm in it."

"No, there isn't. I think Sutter realizes that—he just has to adjust a little."

"And you're also right about it being nice to have a little company my own age," the colonel said. "I didn't think so before, but it's good to talk to someone who's like-minded and sees my point of view without thinking I'm an old relic."

"Sure," Kinsey agreed.

"What about you?"

"Me?" she said with some surprise.

"My son could be a good catch, you know. For the right woman. And the two of you seem to be getting along pretty well—private jokes and what have you..."

Clearly the colonel wanted it known that nothing avoided her notice. But Kinsey's only answer was, "He has some strong opinions about that."

"I know. Change his mind."

Kinsey laughed but for the first time today it didn't hold much humor. "I don't think that's possible, Colonel."

"Anything's possible," the older woman muttered as she opened the new copy of the book Kinsey had brought her, picked up her brandy and proceeded as if Kinsey had already left.

Still, as she did every night, Kinsey said on her way out of the room, "I'll check on you before I leave."

Then she went to the kitchen where she could hear Sutter chastising Jack.

"What'd he do now?" she asked as she joined them.

"One step out of the crate, on his way to the doggy door, and he still couldn't just go out without making any trouble, he had to try snatching the keys I dropped. I barely caught him or we'd be outside with the flashlights again."

"Stinker! Go outside and run around," Kinsey said affectionately to the puppy.

As if he understood, Jack did just that, giving a little bark when he was through the door to announce himself to the yard.

"Cake?" Sutter said then, nodding at the baker's box on the counter that held his prize.

"I never turn down chocolate."

As he cut wedges of cake, she got two small plates for him to put them on and said, "I see the sling is off again but I'm glad you wore it today."

"Nurse's orders," he said as if he'd only been humoring her.

Minus the sling he had on jeans and a cream-colored Irish fisherman's rib turtleneck sweater. And as usual, he was something to see.

"Your shoulder is feeling okay even going without the sling?"

"Better every day."

Kinsey wasn't sure if that was true or if it was just a marine's bravado like she'd heard from Declan this morning. But she knew there was no sense pursuing it.

"I'm tired from being on my feet today, though," he said as he handed her the dessert and picked up his own plate. "Let's go sit in the living room with these."

Kinsey led the way, sitting on the sofa, making sure to hug one end in her efforts not to encourage anything with him. She may have decided to stop fighting her attraction, but she wasn't going to pursue Sutter. He'd have to decide for himself if he wanted something to happen between them.

But Sutter sat in the center of it and, as big a man as he was, that put him not far away despite her best efforts.

They each tasted the seven layers of cake and ganache. Sutter judged it good but rich, while Kinsey considered it just plain wonderful.

After her second bite she decided she was going to broach something she'd begun to consider today.

"You know, I took you at your word when you told me about the reasons for your 'marriage to the military or marriage to a woman but not both' thing. But now that I keep seeing how antiromance you are with the colonel, I'm beginning to think maybe there's more to it."

"I'm not antiromance," he claimed.

"None for you, none for your mother," she pointed out.

He smiled a crooked smile. "Who said none for me? I said no *marriage* for me," he qualified. "That doesn't mean no women or relationships."

"There's someone in your life?" Kinsey asked, alarmed that he might have kissed her while he was involved with someone else.

"Not now. Not recently. But I'm not a priest. And I'm not made of stone."

He just had a rock-hard body…

But Kinsey put that out of her mind and said, "I just started to wonder if—in addition to what you saw living on the bases as a kid—you'd been hurt and that turned you sour on things, too."

"I've always been really clear about not looking for marriage so I've never let myself get in deep enough to have my heart broken, no," he said between bites. "But I did have my own experience early on with breaking someone else's heart and that sealed the deal for me."

"Whose heart did you break?"

"Her name was Mandy Brisbon. My father had an old marine buddy who taught at the academy. He sort of adopted me while I was at Annapolis—invited me to family dinners, for holidays if I couldn't get home, that kind of thing. Freshman year I met his niece at one of the dinners."

"Mandy Brisbon."

"Right. She lived near campus and we started seeing each other whenever I had the chance. Dating. It lasted the full four years, all the way to graduation. Which was when she thought a marriage proposal was due."

"Did she not know about your marriage policy? Or was it not really a policy with you before that?"

"It was and I'd told her—early on, before we'd even been on our first date. But I was young and it didn't occur to me that I needed to say it again—"

"Ooh," Kinsey commiserated with the young Mandy. "You told her before the two of you even knew each other and then spent *four* years dating?"

"Yeah. It was a lesson I learned—as time went by, she thought our relationship was serious enough that it had canceled out my concerns."

"And she was willing to be a military wife?"

"Temporarily. For some reason she'd also switched things around in her mind to believe that I'd do my active duty obligation after graduation and then leave the marines so we could have a regular civilian life—not that we'd ever talked about that, because we hadn't or I would have made where I stood clear again. I honestly didn't intend to mislead her, but I guess the fact that I kept coming around—"

"For *four* years."

"Yeah, she thought that said more than what I'd told her before we'd gotten to know each other. So while I thought everything was cut-and-dried—"

"She thought the two of you were headed for the life she wanted," Kinsey concluded for him. "And you set her straight and broke her heart."

"No choice," he said, an edge of guilt sounding in his tone.

"Was she willing to be a marine wife forever?"

"No. Which helped a little. I didn't have to convince her of the strain our relationship would take after ten or fifteen years of my life as a marine because the course I was on was not what she saw for her future even five years down the road. But it didn't help much. It was an ugly breakup. And it wrecked my dad's friendship with her uncle, too. Like I said, it was a lesson I learned."

Kinsey nodded, seeing by the lines the mere memory drew on his face that he'd beaten himself up for it in the years since even though he hadn't intentionally caused the hurt.

"And after Mandy Brisbon?" Kinsey asked.

"I've made sure since then not to let anything ever get far enough for that to happen again—and I make absolutely sure that any woman I date knows where I stand."

"So since college you just sleep around? Love 'em and leave 'em as fast as you can?"

If that's the kind of man he was, it might alter her perception of him as a stand-up guy. And that could change things for her regardless of the decision she'd made to let whatever was happening between them play out.

"I do not sleep around or 'love 'em and leave 'em' as fast as I can, no," he said as if she'd insulted him.

"Then what do you do?" she asked bluntly.

He'd apparently eaten all he was going to of his cake—about two-thirds of it, leaving behind the thick layer of ganache that frosted the top—and he set the plate on the coffee table.

When he sat back he angled more in her direction than he had been, and stretched a long arm along the sofa back.

"There can be things between love 'em and leave 'em as fast as I can and marriage, you know. First and foremost, I follow regulations," he said. "I have not ever and would not ever get into any kind of personal relationship with anyone under my command."

"No fraternizing."

"None," he said firmly.

"But..." Kinsey prodded as she finished her own cake—crumbs and all—and set her plate on the coffee table, too. Once her hand was free, she swiped her finger through that ganache layer he'd left. No sense in having it go to waste.

Something about taking that one last bite made him smile as he watched it, before he said, "But there are women who exist who *aren't* under my command—"

"Women who aren't the military groupies you told me about before?"

"Women who aren't military groupies but are civilians. Or civilian personnel. There are military women in units apart from mine. I was involved for a while with a reporter on assignment overseas."

"All romances of convenience?" Kinsey asked when that occurred to her. That would also give her pause, since she didn't want to be a mere convenience, now that she thought about it.

He laughed. "There is pretty much nothing about getting involved with me that's convenient. I'm married to the military, remember? I've made extra sure since Mandy that any woman I'm with knows duty comes first."

"And that you're antimarriage."

He made a face. "I'm not that, either. I'm just—"

"Married to the military instead."

"And upfront about it. So if I meet someone who isn't completely onboard with what I'm about, I steer clear..."

Kinsey wasn't sure why his own words seemed to give him pause—as if they'd made him think something unexpected—but he did pause and his brows pulled together.

She wasn't going to get to know what had gone through his mind, though, because then he went on with what he'd been saying.

"Hurting Mandy was like what I saw growing up—misery one person caused another because that person had to answer the call of duty—and I honestly don't want to be responsible for doing that to anyone."

"But if a short-term relationship is okay with them, then—"

"Most of the relationships I've had haven't been *too* short-term," he amended. "I saw Bethany—the reporter—for over three years while she had the overseas assignment. And there have been others that went on for a while, too—a year, more than a year, another that was almost two years. As long as we know where things stand, it's all good. We have some time together when it can be arranged around my schedule and theirs, and when the time comes for us to part ways, we say goodbye—no harm, no foul."

"As easy as that?"

"It has been..."

Past tense? And why did that make his brows pull together like they had before?

Again Kinsey had the impression that the wheels of his mind were turning in unexpected directions.

But she doubted he was going to enlighten her this time either, so she ignored it and said, "And no one's changed their mind after getting in under your terms?"

"No," he said, coming out of his momentary lapse to answer her. "Every woman I've been involved with has had her own career or interest or duty to serve, so my kind of relationship has been what works best for them, too."

"So you aren't antiromance but your relationships are still more friends-with-benefits than love connections," Kinsey said.

"I'd consider some of the women I've been with good friends by the end, yeah. But while things are happening between us, we're not just friends who sleep together. I've cared about them and I think they've cared about me."

"Just not too much."

He frowned and laughed at the same time. "Are you just looking for me to be a creep?"

Maybe, she realized. Not that she wanted him to be a creep, but maybe she was looking for something—*anything*—that might give her pause about him.

Before she could answer his question he went on. "I've genuinely cared about the women I've been with," he said defensively. "There's just been something bigger that we both have to do, and knowing that from the start, we've enjoyed what we've had while we could and then gone our separate ways to do that bigger thing."

"Are you sad at all when it ends?"

"Sometimes. But when you know from the get-go that it *will* be ending, I think you're prepared for it and that makes it easier to deal with."

"And it's never been different than that? Prepared or not, you've never reached an ending and discovered that you just didn't want to say goodbye?"

"I haven't," he said candidly.

"It's just 'this has been fun, thanks for a good time, maybe we'll meet again'?"

"I don't think I've ever said those particular words or had them said to me, but the essence of them has been there. Coming *at* me as often as *from* me."

Kinsey nodded, getting the picture more and more clearly—he only risked relationships with women who had enough on their own agendas not to make him any more their priority than they were his.

"And you're not ever sorry that you don't get closer to anyone than that?" she asked. "You never want more?"

"There are days," he admitted.

She didn't know why he was looking so pointedly at her but he was.

"But I've made a commitment to serve," he said then, almost as if he was reminding himself. "And a commitment not to put anyone through what families left behind go through in the process."

Kinsey nodded her understanding again but said sadly, "I don't know...that doesn't sound very satisfying."

He gave her the wicked grin again. "Depends on how you do it," he said in a voice full of sexy innuendo, lightening the tone as he reached for a strand of her hair to let it curl around his fingers.

"I think," he said in a quieter voice then, watching his hand toying with her hair, "that if there aren't any illusions, consenting adults can have an enjoyable time being consenting adults. And short-lived or not, it can be good."

"I suppose that's true." Kinsey had to agree because she'd just that morning told herself that if she kept her eyes wide open with him, she could stop fighting against the exact things that were coming to the surface in her even now.

Now when she could feel the heat of his hand near her face, the idea of giving in was more tempting than ever.

She wasn't sure whether he had on a very light cologne or if it was his soap, but he smelled like crystal clear mountain air. And of course there were those blue-green eyes and that face that was all masculine and chiseled.

And there was that dimple in his chin.

Right below those fine, fine lips...

And she wanted what she'd wanted from the moment he'd stopped kissing her the last time—she just wanted him to kiss her again.

"God, you're beautiful..." he said even more quietly just before he stopped fiddling with her hair and combed his fingers through it to cup the back of her head. Cradling it, he brought her toward him as he leaned in and closed the distance between his mouth and hers just the way she'd been wishing he would.

Her first thought was that no, she hadn't been imagining it—he did kiss better than anyone she'd ever kissed.

And then her mind went blank and she just let herself drift completely into the warmth of parted lips and his sweet breath, and kissed him back.

His other arm came around her, strong enough despite his injury to pull her closer, for her to feel the strength in the big hand that splayed against her back.

She did something else she'd been wanting to do, pressing her own hands to his chest, careful of the side that was hurt but drinking in the feel of honed pectorals encased in that sweater.

His mouth opened wider and she followed his lead, happy when his tongue made its maiden voyage, her own coming out to meet and greet it with playful abandon that made him smile a smile she felt in their kiss.

He pulled her more forcefully to him then, capturing her hands between them until she let her arms snake around to his back where she did her part in keeping breasts to chest in a way that felt so good she couldn't resist pressing herself against him.

And that was how they stayed, mouths meeting and parting only to meet again, exploring and clinging together as if they were two teenagers who'd snuck away for a frantic make-out session in whatever bit of precious stolen time they had.

Kinsey wasn't sure when she'd made out like that in recent history—so intensely, so passionately that she completely lost herself in it. That she completely forgot about everything else.

They kissed for so long that she began to feel her lips going numb while other parts of her body began crying out for more.

His hand still clasped the back of her head, but he'd begun to work her scalp in a way that made her breasts yearn for that same touch. Breasts that were nestled comfortably against him.

But the permission she'd given herself that morning was so new she was a little afraid to let this go any further—despite how much she wanted to—so she teased his tongue with her own a few times and then retreated to let him know that was enough.

She knew he got the message from the low groan that rumbled from his throat. Then he kissed her even more thoroughly before he stopped by slow increments that extended things just a little longer.

When their mouths finally came apart for good he took a deep breath and rested his forehead to hers.

"If this is what comes of feeding you chocolate cake I'm gonna hide the rest of it somewhere and dole it out slice by slice..." he joked.

"I do like cake," she countered. And she liked him. Oh, how much she liked him...

Heaven help her.

They remained the way they were, as if neither of them had any inclination to part more than they already had.

Until Jack jumped up between them with one of the socks they hadn't been able to find in the yard on Wednesday night or when Sutter had looked again in daylight on Thursday.

Then they had to let go of each other and put their attention on the puppy.

"Ah, no wonder we couldn't find that—he must have buried it somewhere," Sutter observed, taking in the sight of the mud-encrusted sock.

"But look what a good dog he is—he brought it back himself."

Sutter laughed. "Uh-huh," he agreed dubiously, collapsing back into the sofa again and picking up the muddy stocking with two fingers to set it aside.

Then, to Kinsey he said, "How does tomorrow sound for the doggy playdate? I think I have it set up."

With the Camdens.

How was it that she was having trouble lately remembering her goal with them?

Luckily Sutter kept her more on task than she did herself.

"A doggy playdate sounds great," she said. "And it'll be good for Jack, too, to see his littermates."

"I talked to everyone about aiming for tomorrow afternoon, when the colonel naps so she won't miss any of us."

"Great! Thank you."

He acknowledged her gratitude with only the raise of that dented chin.

"And then you have Sol coming over tomorrow night for a movie?" he said.

"*I* don't have Sol coming over tomorrow night for a movie—the colonel invited him," Kinsey corrected. "I just volunteered to make a casserole for dinner before and popcorn for during."

"Let me guess. We're watching *Patton*—the colonel's favorite movie that I've seen so many times I can quote the dialogue?"

Kinsey laughed. "Actually, I've never seen it—when your mom heard that, she just had to remedy it."

"And invite Sol, too."

The conversation had occurred that afternoon when they were at the beer garden.

"Think of how much better you'll feel on Saturday nights to come," Kinsey recommended, "when you're back overseas and you can figure Sol is over here watching a movie with the colonel so she isn't alone."

"That better be *all* they're doing," Sutter said.

"Oh, come on, you know deep down you'd love a little brother or sister," Kinsey goaded.

He laughed that laugh she liked as much as she liked him. "Thank God there's no chance of *that* at her age!" he said.

Kinsey took a deep breath and sighed. "It's late—" And she'd been up since before daylight to talk to Conor and Declan. "I should go. I'll check on the colonel and then take off."

Sutter didn't stop her from getting up and going to the colonel's room to poke her head in.

The older woman was sound asleep, lights and television off, her book on her nightstand.

Downstairs once again she found Sutter waiting in the entry for her.

"She's sound asleep—she really was tired."

"Hot Veterans Day dates will do that," he said facetiously.

Kinsey put on her jacket and picked up her purse and satchel.

Sutter had the door open when she got to it and he went out with her, walking her to her car.

"Seems weird that you're always the one leaving and I'm always the one staying," he said.

Only if they were dating, Kinsey thought, but she didn't say it.

Then she opened her car door and tossed in her bags, turning to say good-night to him.

But he didn't seem ready to say goodbye quite yet because he was right there, close by, and he reached his hand into her hair once again, bringing her nearer.

His eyes caught hers and he spent a moment just looking into them before he leaned forward and kissed her again, a kiss that said they hadn't come as far from the thick of that make-out session as it might have seemed.

Then he ended it. But still he kept hold of her as he said "drive safe" in a voice ragged enough to let her know that kissing her affected him as much as it did her. And it rocked her whole world.

Kinsey only nodded and said her good-night, but for another moment he kept her captive, still studying her as if he couldn't take his eyes away.

Then he took what looked to be a steeling breath and simultaneously let her go and stepped back so she could get behind the wheel.

She started the engine and backed out of his driveway under his full scrutiny, wondering as she did just where this *would* go now that she was going to let it run its course.

"I hope you know what you're doing, Kins," she said to herself when she'd gone far enough up his street to lose sight of him in her rearview mirror.

She was a little afraid that she might be playing with fire when it came to her own feelings.

Because guarding against it or not, in the middle of kissing him good-night just now, it had struck her just how much Sutter Knightlinger got to her…

Chapter Eight

"Breakfast and brochures?"

Sutter chuckled at his cousin Beau Camden's alliteration. They were at the Denver Diner predawn on Saturday morning. Open twenty-four hours a day, it was a place that could accommodate that meal for two early-rising marines.

It had been Sutter's suggestion that they meet. "We went to the Veterans Day thing yesterday," he said as their waitress brought them coffee. When she left, he nodded at the stack of pamphlets he'd brought along for Beau and added, "I picked up those at the booths at the festival. I didn't know if you knew what's out there to help returning vets adjust to civilian life but I figured it was good information to have, maybe to put out on display when you have your own stuff going for them at the stores. Get the word out and circulated, you know? For whatever kind of help anybody might need."

"Good idea."

"It's kind of shocked me to find out how much need there is," Sutter said.

"Yeah, you'd think going back to civilian life would be a breeze since every soldier lived at least eighteen years of it before enlisting. But it's not," Beau confessed. "Even for me with plenty waiting for me—work, the whole family. And now with Kyla back in my life. And the baby..." He shook his head. "But it's all still just so different from what I got used to in the service."

Sutter nodded his understanding, feeling as if he, himself, was getting a progressively clearer view of what it was like, of how difficult it could be all the way around.

"We met Louise Turner," he said then, referring to the retired navy captain the Camdens' friend Margaret had put the colonel in touch with. Sutter went on to tell Beau about the navy captain's son's organization to help vets financially.

"Bryan Turner—I had lunch with him yesterday," Beau said. "Seems like a good man. He's thinking what you are—that the programs we set up through the stores could give information on the help he offers vets."

"Are you going to do it?"

"Sure. He helps vets get credit when they can't get it otherwise, I'm all for that. His mother told him about you—a marine with an economics degree. He wanted to know if you were thinking about resigning from the service anytime soon, said he'd like to talk to you about a job, if you were interested."

Sutter laughed. "Did you tell him I'm not resigning?"

"I said I didn't think there were any plans for that in the near future but I'd relay the message," Beau said before changing the subject with a nod at Sutter's injured shoulder. “I see you’re out of the sling already—you’ve been wearing it when you come over to work out so I didn’t think you were at that stage yet.”

Sutter explained what he was doing to wean himself off the apparatus, to regain his strength in that arm.

“How much longer, do you think, before you go back?” Beau inquired when he was finished.

“Don’t know. But not too long. That’s another reason I wanted to talk to you—I’d like for you to be looking out for the colonel when I do. Just an occasional check on her, a phone call here and there?”

“I was planning on that. GiGi and I talked about keeping closer tabs on her—seems like she’s more open to it now. Before your dad died, we’d talk to him. After that the colonel wouldn’t answer or return calls or even come to the door if any of us went over there. But now—”

“I think—I hope—Kinsey is making headway with her, opening her eyes some to seeing that she can’t just hole up, that she needs to get out, to let people in.”

“So as long as she’ll let that happen, GiGi and Margaret will stay on top of her with their bridge club and some other activities. And I’m happy to keep an eye on her, too, if she’ll let me. You know she got pretty mad at me when I resigned. She said to her I was AWOL and needed to get my ass back to where I belonged until I was as old as she was when she retired. But since she spoke to me at Sunday dinner last week, maybe she’s over it and will let me come around, too?”

Sutter flinched at that reminder of the colonel berating Beau about his resignation. But Beau was right—she *had* talked to him at Sunday dinner.

“I think she’s cooled down on that score,” Sutter said hopefully.

"Is Kinsey pulling off that change in her, too?"

Sutter laughed. "I don't know, but Kinsey seems to be like water running over rock—she's somehow wearing the colonel down in a lot of ways without the colonel knowing it's happening."

"You realize that makes her a freaking miracle worker," Beau joked, laughing.

"Oh, yeah," Sutter agreed unequivocally.

Beau smiled slyly and, in a tone full of insinuation, asked, "Is she working any miracles on you?"

"I don't need any miracles worked on me. I am what I am—what needs to change?"

Beau laughed again. "Now *that* sounded like the colonel. And don't forget I know you. And I've seen you with the nurse. There're things going on there."

Plenty. But it was actually unnerving Sutter so much he didn't want to say anything about it and make it any more real than it already was. So he said, "You're dreaming."

"Sure I am," Beau countered facetiously, not dissuaded in the least. "I was at the academy with you—I saw you with Mandy. Four years with her and it wasn't like this. You never looked at her the way you look at this Kinsey. You never looked the *way* you do when you're with the nurse—like you don't even know there are other people around. And there were the British war correspondents the two of us met on leave—you kept up with yours long after I parted ways with mine, and still she never got under your skin. But this one? Way, way, way under your skin..."

The waitress brought their breakfast plates then—bacon, eggs and toast for them both—and that paused the conversation long enough for Sutter to consider whether or not to go on with the denials. His cousin wasn't buying them, so there didn't seem to be a point.

When the waitress left them alone again, Beau picked up where he'd left off and repeated, "Way, waaay under your skin. Like nobody before her, if I'm not mistaken."

He wasn't.

"Maybe," Sutter conceded, seeing Kinsey in his mind's eye—where she seemed to have taken up residence to haunt him even when she wasn't around.

He was suddenly thinking about the night before, when something as guileless and insignificant as scooping frosting off his cake had aroused him more than a pole dance. He didn't have a clue as to why he'd even noticed it.

"But it doesn't change anything," he added.

"I don't know, man, feelings start up…they can make things veer off course."

"Nothing is off course," he insisted.

Although…

He'd meant what he'd said when he'd told Kinsey that if he met someone who wasn't on board with his no-marriage policy—or with anything about him, actually—he steered clear of her. It was what he'd always done after Mandy.

But Kinsey was not on board with anything he was about and still he couldn't seem to make himself steer clear of her.

"And who said there were feelings starting up?" he challenged. Maybe too vehemently because that made Beau laugh, too, at the bark that would have intimidated anyone else.

"Oh, man, it's worse than I thought," his cousin said knowingly.

Sutter's coffee mug was still half full but he raised

it at the waitress to get her to top it off just to buy himself a minute to figure out his response.

He had to acknowledge that Beau was right—he did have it pretty bad for Kinsey. And it had nothing to do with going too long without female companionship. It had begun to sink in a little last night when he'd told her that, at the end of all his relationships, it had been easy to say goodbye.

It *had* been easy—past tense, because even as he'd said the words, it had struck him that saying goodbye to her might not be easy at all. And not because of Mandy-like expectations on her part. Because even saying good-night to Kinsey every night wasn't easy for him.

When the waitress left this time, Beau said, "Looks to me like the colonel isn't the only one who needs to look at some things differently than she has before. You might have to do some rethinking yourself."

Sutter shook his head. "Nothing to rethink," he said, believing that wholeheartedly. Believing, still, what he'd believed all along—marry the military or marry a woman, but not both. And he was married to the military.

"Besides," he added, "Kinsey comes from a military family and she's about as against hooking her wagon up to a military horse as anyone I've ever run across."

But now that he thought about it, since that was the case, why wasn't *she* putting the skids on things between them?

He knew why *he* wasn't—because he couldn't. The minute he set eyes on her or heard her voice or even so much as smelled the sweet, clean scent of her, he was a goner. Everything that happened from then on had a will of its own and took him along for the ride.

But she wasn't pulling away, either.

She knew who and what he was, where he was headed, what he was about—and she still kissed him like she never wanted to stop.

So maybe she was okay with it. Maybe she *was* on board with the idea of a fling that she knew wouldn't go anywhere. It wasn't as if he'd been making out with himself last night, after all…

And if that was the case—that she was okay with having a fling—he didn't have to steer clear of her because he wasn't putting her at any risk of getting hurt.

His breakfast suddenly tasted better.

Maybe he did need to rethink things. Just not the big-picture things. Only the here-and-now things.

Could he really have a little here-and-now with her? he asked himself, more hopeful for that even than he was that the colonel was changing.

Again he thought about the night before, about kissing Kinsey. About making out with her for most of an hour. There was nothing in that that said stop.

Not even knowing full well that anything between them would have an eventual end.

He still felt a hint of worry at the thought of that goodbye, but…

Nah, it was crazy to even entertain the idea that he wouldn't be able to enjoy some time with her and move on as usual.

He was a marine.

He could handle anything.

"Why do you suddenly look like the cat that swallowed the canary?" his cousin asked him.

"I was doing a little *rethinking* after all," he answered.

Just not about what Beau thought he should rethink.

"You're gonna go for it with the nurse," his cousin said as if he could read it on his face.

"But no different than it's ever been with me," he claimed.

"I have a hundred dollars right now that says that's a load of garbage and you just don't know it yet."

"You're on," Sutter took the bet.

Saturday afternoon and evening seemed like one long date to Kinsey—even though she kept telling herself that wasn't the case.

First of all, that was how she was dressed—in another pair of reserved-for-dates jeans and an only-for-special-occasions angora sweater that was a pink mock turtleneck with wooden buttons that ran in an angle from the collar to the front of one shoulder.

And eyeshadow. She'd actually done date-like eye makeup for work today.

It didn't help that Sutter also seemed slightly more dressed up than usual. His jeans were cut better than anything she'd seen him in before, riding his bum to perfection. And on top he had on a torso-hugging V-neck sweater the exact shade of his eyes.

And then there were the events of the afternoon and evening themselves.

They spent the afternoon at Lindie Camden's house for the doggy playdate. Among the couples were Lindie and Sawyer, Lang and Heddy and Dane and Vonni. And while Kinsey did have the opportunity to interact with her half siblings Lindie, Lang and Dane, it had been impossible for it to not seem as if she and Sutter were just a fourth couple.

Plus, in spite of chastising herself for it, she hadn't seized any opportunity to leave Sutter's side to mingle on her own with three of the very people she was there to get to know. Instead she'd done all of her socializing paired with Sutter.

And even though the lingering insecurities from that Sunday dinner were a contributing factor, the real reason she didn't branch off from Sutter was that it was Sutter she wanted to be with today. Sutter's company she couldn't make herself leave behind, even to chat with her half siblings.

Then, at the end of the afternoon, she and Sutter had returned to the Knightlingers' house where Kinsey had prepared dinner. With Sutter's help and company in the kitchen and the easy banter and teasing that they were so good at, the date-like quality had continued.

Then Sol had arrived and it was couples-time again—the colonel and Sol, Kinsey and Sutter—for dinner and then the movie afterward. Where Kinsey was reminding herself for the millionth time today that this was *not* a date. That she was, in fact, at work.

But it didn't make much difference in how she felt.

When the movie ended, the colonel suggested that Kinsey and Sutter take the popcorn and bowls to the kitchen while she walked Sol out. Kinsey had the impression that the older woman wanted a moment alone with the neighbor. Sutter must have had the same impression because he did the chore with a scowl, all the while trying to keep the front door in sight.

But from what Kinsey could see, the parting was nothing more than cordial. The elderly man and woman merely chatted for a short time before saying good-night without so much as a handshake.

As Kinsey helped the colonel get to bed, she and the older woman discussed the movie, which Kinsey had found interesting. Then she got a surprise when she was just about to hand the colonel her nighttime brandy.

Frequently Jack watched them from the doorway and—unless he did something the colonel didn't like—the colonel ignored the puppy. But tonight she patted her mattress to invite Jack up onto the bed.

Kinsey helped the small puppy accomplish it and reserved any comment, but she was happy to see what she considered headway. And happy to see Jack comply without any rambunctiousness, curling up on the foot of the colonel's bed as if that was just what he'd been waiting for.

"Behave yourself and you can stay," the colonel warned the dog before accepting the brandy.

With the nighttime routine finished, Kinsey headed for the door. But before she got there, the colonel said to her, "I was told I could invite someone to the Camdens' dinner tomorrow so I asked Sol. He's coming along."

Ooh, Sutter was going to hate that!

But Kinsey kept quiet on the subject. "That'll be nice for both of you."

"He says Sundays are the longest days of his week, so I thought I'd give him something to look forward to."

Kinsey smiled at the excuse that deflected the fact that the colonel might want her neighbor along for her own sake. "That's nice."

"Sutter won't think so. Take care of that, will you?"

"I'll do what I can," she assured, suppressing a laugh.

Sutter was in the living room when she went downstairs. He was propped on the edge of the sofa doing his physical therapy exercises but stopped when she joined him.

It had been a few days since she'd examined him—in the medical sense anyway—and she'd told him earlier that she wanted to check on his shoulder and maybe add a few new exercises to his regimen. She assumed he was in position for that so she went to stand in front of him to begin.

"Clothes on?" he asked with a crooked and devilish smile.

"Clothes on," she said, resisting the temptation to insist he take off the sweater.

"Too bad," he muttered.

You're telling me? she thought but didn't say it.

Instead she began her exam. "How's it feeling?"

"Better every day. Stronger."

Kinsey tested his range of motion and his strength and found them both improved, though not at a hundred percent yet.

"Have you seen Jack?" Sutter asked as she was working. "Or is he getting into trouble?"

"Your mother is letting him sleep on her bed."

Sutter's eyebrows shot up in surprise. "You're kidding."

"Nope."

"Damn...you think she's warming up to him finally?"

"Looks like it. We just have to hope he doesn't blow it by chewing her sheets or stealing her book...again."

Kinsey paused, then said, "It was the second invitation she extended tonight. Apparently the first was to Sol when she said good-night to him—she asked him to the Camdens' Sunday dinner tomorrow."

The scowl returned. "And you're going to tell me that's progress, too. And that it's all part of what I wanted—companionship for her and backup and a support system and all that—so I should be thrilled about it."

"Do you need me to tell you that?"

Sutter took a deep breath, exhaled, clasped her hand to halt her exam and pulled her down next to him on the couch. "I need you to sit and help me not think about it."

"How would you like me to do that?" she asked with a hint of suggestiveness in her tone.

That only made him smile before he sat back at an angle that faced her and stretched his good arm across the top of the back cushions.

"Satisfy my curiosity," he instructed.

Curiosity was not what she'd been thinking about satisfying…

"Curiosity about what?" Kinsey asked as she made herself more comfortable on the sofa and angled to face him, too.

"About why you're single—you *are* single, right? Or do you have a husband I haven't heard about?"

"Single. Engaged once, but never married," she confirmed.

"Okay. But you're beautiful and smart and sweet and funny. And I get that you don't want anybody in the military. But you're determined to have family—so why not just get married and have one of your own with a nonmilitary guy?"

"Because I don't want to make some rash choice out of loneliness or desperation," she answered frankly.

"And you figure step one is to connect with the Camdens and then you won't be lonely or desperate," he surmised.

"If I have family around me, and a support structure in place, then I'll know that when I meet someone and it feels like I want to be with that someone every minute of the day, it will only be because I want to be with that someone every minute of the day. Not because there's nothing else in my life."

"Has that happened to you before?"

She made a pained face, hating to admit it, and he interpreted it.

"It has."

"There was a guy I met in Northbridge when Hugh got sick, and it lasted until right after Mom died—although it wasn't serious, we never spent the night or anything." She didn't know why she'd felt the need to clarify that but there it was. "Duncan Cain. He was the bank manager there. He would ask me to dinner whenever I was in for a weekend, and that got to be a regular thing—he wanted to move to Denver and liked asking me about living here."

"It was the excuse he used to get to see you," Sutter informed with some humor, as if she'd missed that Duncan's intense interest in Denver had been mostly a ploy.

"Maybe," she conceded. "When I moved there to take care of my mom full-time, he came around more, asked me out more. And he was good with Mom—he'd bring her candy and flowers and she liked that, which was nice."

"But you still never slept with him?"

Kinsey laughed at the tone in his voice that said that was beyond his comprehension. "Because he brought my sick mother candy and flowers?" she said facetiously. "No. I kind of kept him at arm's length even then. There was just no…you know, chemistry. Even though there *should* have been. He was attractive and kind, a decent guy—"

"And a stable, nine-to-fiver like you're looking for."

"Right."

"But?"

"Whenever I was with him..." She made the face again, feeling guilty for this part of her past. "He was really boring and I always felt like I was just going through the motions. Using him a little, I guess, to get out some when I was in Northbridge," she admitted, not proud of it. "But—especially after Mom died and I was *so* alone—he'd call and I'd still say yes to another date just to be with someone."

"To *not* be alone," Sutter said kindly. "Did he know you weren't into him? Or care, if he did know?"

"I don't think he knew—or maybe he thought he was gradually winning me over. At first, when I was just in and out of town, it was pretty casual—friendly dinners, an afternoon at a town festival or something. Then, when I moved to Northbridge, I saw more of him, but he knew I had so much going on with my mom failing and the stress of that, and I think he decided that I just wasn't up for...anything too heavy. So he didn't push me. After my mom died, I was grieving and he knew that, and was understanding..."

Duncan had been so understanding all the way around. Recalling that only made her feel more guilty and it sounded in her voice.

"He kept saying that he was a patient man, that he was willing to wait," she said, not adding that Duncan had said she was worth waiting for.

"Then he got hired at a bank here," she went on. "And he was so happy about it. Not only was he getting a higher position and more pay along with the move he wanted, but he seemed to think that when we both got back to Denver, things would be different and our relationship would kick into high gear."

"Meaning you still hadn't slept with him and he figured that would happen here," Sutter said with a hint of his mother's directness.

"Right." Kinsey made the shame face once more. "And he seemed like such a smart, safe choice that I started to try to talk myself into liking him more than I did. To consider having a future with him, so I could come back here *not* alone and have a white-picket-fence life, a family. I started to try to tell myself that not every marriage has to be based on passionate love. That there are arranged marriages in the world that last forever, based on respect and shared goals. And that at least then I wouldn't be—"

"Alone," he finished for her with that word that kept cropping up over and over again.

"I actually started to think so seriously about it that it scared me a little to realize how simple it would be to just settle for something less than marrying a man I truly loved, how tempted I was."

"What made you not do it?"

"Things my mom had said at the end. About Mitchum Camden. About how much she'd loved him. I wanted that—not with someone else's husband, but that kind of feeling. And what I didn't want was what she had with Hugh."

"Did they have a bad marriage?"

"No, they didn't. I know he was happy enough and I think my mom was…content. But their marriage was more gratitude for him taking us all on than the kind of love a lifetime should be built on. When she was telling me about her feelings for Hugh, compared to her feelings for Mitchum Camden, I couldn't help thinking that poor Hugh had gotten the short end of the stick. It seemed so unfair to him. And it would have been unfair to Duncan if I'd gone through with a committed relationship with him. Plus I didn't want to end up in one of those situations where I was still lonely even with someone in my life—and listening to my mom, I'd had that sense about her."

"So you decided to pursue the Camden connection instead."

She shrugged. "I did. And hopefully things will work out with them. Then, when I meet someone, it will only be about that person and feelings I'll be able to know are real and only for them."

"So Duncan *wasn't* the guy you were engaged to," Sutter said then, a prompt to go on.

"No, I was engaged to someone just before that—Trevor Aimes. I was with him from right out of nursing school until slightly before Hugh got sick—about four years. We were engaged the last six months."

"That must have been the relationship you were in that left you a lot of time on your own to do that pro bono physical therapy for vets."

She'd mentioned that quite a while ago. She was surprised he remembered.

"That would be the one," she confirmed. "Trevor worked for Doctors Without Borders."

"I don't know much about that. Was that his actual job? I sort of thought doctors took time off their everyday practices and just did a stint with that organization here and there."

"It can go either way. Some doctors do it once or twice, some are hired on by the organization." Kinsey sighed. "I met Trevor when he was a month from finishing his residency. He was at the same hospital where I had my first job as a nurse but he'd already interviewed with Doctors Without Borders. He said he wanted to give back for the privilege of his education. I thought that was noble."

"Sure."

"His plan was to do locum tenens when he finished his residency—that's what it's called when doctors substitute for other doctors. Then he'd have a stint with Doctors Without Borders, and when he came back, he'd start his own practice. That didn't send up any red flags for me. But then he came back from the first trip and decided to do locum tenens again until he could do a second stint with Doctors Without Borders. I was still okay, we weren't serious yet. But then he wanted to do it all a third time. And a fourth..."

"Uh-huh..." Sutter said as if he was getting the picture.

"Trevor kept saying just one more trip," Kinsey said. "That then he'd practice here."

"But one more—and one more and one more—wasn't enough."

"No. He decided he wanted to be on staff with them permanently when he came back after the fourth trip. He'd proposed just before that fourth round, swearing that it would be the last time."

"But signing on permanently would be like being deployed over and over again."

"Exactly," Kinsey said.

"Did you ask him not to do it?"

"How could I do that? There was a need for his skills that not that many people can—or are willing to—fill. I have a tremendous respect for the people willing to make that sacrifice." She sighed again. "With my brothers and then with Trevor, I looked at it the way you said your dad looked at his role—staying here, taking care of things here, was my way of serving, of doing good so that they could do what needed to be done."

"I know you took care of your parents, did you have to take care of something for Trevor, too?"

"His family. He was an only child of older parents and his mother had a lot of health problems that his dad couldn't handle alone."

"So you helped out in Trevor's place while he went off and did his stuff. Thinking that it was only going to be for one trip. Then two."

"Because Trevor kept promising that the next trip would be the last. I'd told him why I wouldn't marry anyone in the military, that I wanted someone in my life who would be around, so he knew how I felt."

"But it didn't stop him."

"When he proposed he said that the fourth trip would absolutely be the last. He even wanted to set a wedding date before he left to convince me of that. We settled on seven months away—a month after he was scheduled to come home. I believed him and while he was gone, I did all the planning, all the preparations for the wedding on my own, sure that it was the last thing I would have to do that way. And about the time he got back there was an opening for a position at the hospital. So I suggested that Trevor apply. That was when he said that he intended to do what he was doing forever."

"And there you were, looking at the same kind of life you would have had as a military wife—holding down the fort while he was gone for long periods of time, year after year."

"Yes," she said sadly, revisiting some of the pain and disappointment she'd felt when she'd come to that realization.

"So you ended it rather than asking him to stay home," Sutter said.

"I ended it," she said softly. "I'd been taking care of everything since high school—"

"Back up—what did you have to handle in high school? There was the end-of-life stuff for Hugh and your mom but that wasn't *that* long ago."

"No. But all of my brothers were gone by the time I was fifteen. Even when they were at the academy they rarely came home so they might as well have been overseas. By my junior year it was as if I was an only child—I worked the farm with Hugh, I did all the chores my brothers had done. Then, just after my senior year started, Mom and Hugh were in a car accident that they were lucky to have survived, but they were both in a hospital for weeks and came home needing care, and I was all there was for that, and for running the farm completely on my own."

Sutter flinched. "And you did that, *too*? Senior year when everyone was having a good time, a last hurrah, and even though you had three brothers, you were the only one taking care of injured parents and a farm? Jeez, Kinsey..."

"And it didn't end there. Even after I went to college, even after I was working here, I needed to go back and forth to Northbridge to help out with the farm. And along the way I just started to think—to know deep down—that I didn't want to always be—"

"The only one carrying the full load. Yeah, I can understand that. And it left you with a big, fat, firm *no* to marrying someone in the military—or any other kind of job that would mean your spouse was away most of the time—and ending up in that position for life."

"So when Trevor and I finally hashed things out, I

had to stand my ground when it came to my own future. I made it clear to him that I want someone who comes home at night. Someone I can look forward to weekends with. I want the kind of closeness that comes from being together all the time—because that's a different kind of closeness than what you can have when you're together and then far apart for a long time."

"So you parted ways," Sutter concluded.

"So we parted ways," Kinsey confirmed, suddenly feeling exposed by having said so much.

Sutter smiled a small, knowing smile. "You get to want what you want for your own future, you know? It sounds like you might think there's something selfish about it or something."

He was very perceptive.

"It isn't easy, when someone is out doing good, to complain to them about how hard it is on me," she confessed. "It *does* seem selfish."

The small smile he gave her was kind and understanding. "Still, you've got the right to have your own life be the way you want it to be. And I think you've put in more than your fair share of being the one left behind while other people go off and do good. I think it's earned you the right to say *enough*, that from here on you want someone who sticks around."

Which wasn't Sutter, she reminded herself yet again.

But he was here now…

And now was something, she thought when she looked into those eyes that his sweater made even more vibrant, when she saw that kindness and understanding in them, and—like the previous Sunday at the Camdens—more of the support she was always in such short supply of. It all went to her head and she didn't care that he wouldn't be around forever, she was just glad he was there at that moment.

"I *do* get to say *enough*, I want someone who's around," she reiterated with some audacity, as if she'd been empowered.

That made him smile again. "You get to have whatever the hell you want," he added.

"Except chocolate cake," she joked to get off this topic. "You let the colonel and Sol eat all of that."

"That *was* bad," he agreed. "I turned my back for one minute and it was gone! And I had such good plans for it..."

But Kinsey didn't need any cake to entice her to kiss him and he obviously knew that because his hand came to the back of her head and guided her into the kiss she'd been craving since last night. The kiss she'd been craving far, far more than cake.

There was some familiarity to kissing him now, but that in no way blunted the glory of it. She had to struggle not to lose herself, to keep her wits about her and make sure that kissing him didn't become something she couldn't live without.

She certainly couldn't deny herself kissing him now, though, and so she dissolved into parted lips and the feel of his fingers in her hair and his tongue paying a visit she more than welcomed and eagerly entertained.

Her arms went around him and one of his dropped to her back, where he performed a firm, sensual massage, rubbing in circles that made her feel increasingly pliable the longer it went on. That made her yearn to feel his touch everywhere.

But having his broad, strong back under her own palms was yet another thing to revel in—steely muscles and brawny power.

The longer they kissed, the more heat was generated between them, emboldening Kinsey and inspiring her to slip under that V-neck sweater.

She'd seen him and touched him therapeutically and yet still that initial feel of sleek skin at that moment was different. So sexy. So masculine. So nice.

Mindful of his injured shoulder, she avoided it, but pressed her fingers into him away from it. Working his back like clay, she traveled high, feeling his own tension dissolve under her hands.

She traveled low, to the small of his back, dipping a scant inch below his waistband to tantalize him before she retreated.

She traveled around, under his arms to only the outer sides of those pecs she knew were well defined and wonderful to look at. But she didn't go farther than that, was unable to, given how tightly he was holding her against him as their kisses grew abandoned and all the more fevered. And then that hand at her back began a voyage of its own.

Different from hers, he disappointed her by not finding the hem of her sweater to slip underneath it. But his journey didn't stop at her side when he came in that direction. Instead he brought it all the way around, finally putting space between them to cup her breast.

Oh, she wanted so much more than that!

But she knew he was testing the waters to see if she'd stop him there. And when she didn't, when she swelled slightly into his hand, he got the idea.

There were only a few moments of greeting between hand and angora-covered breast before that hand went where they both wanted it—under her sweater and up to breasts that ached to be set free.

There was only tenderness in that powerful hand as

he worked the contours, as he let her get accustomed to the feel of having him there before he slipped her breast out of the cup and gave her what she really wanted.

Her bare breast nestled in the palm of his hand was a match made in heaven and Kinsey barely managed to suppress the moan that was in her throat.

Mouths opened wider and tongues went wild, and when her hands dug into his back, his at her breast showed a little more force in answer.

Kneading and caressing, teasing her nipple with a soft twist of his fingertips, tormenting her with featherlight strokes round and round that same nipple, until Kinsey didn't think it could get much better.

Which was when he deserted her mouth, braced her back with his other arm and dipped her over it to push her sweater up and replace his hand with his mouth while that hand gave some attention to her other breast.

That was better *and* worse.

Even better than his hand alone, his mouth was warm, velvety magic and his tongue was the magician that drove her to distraction.

But it only made her want even more—want her clothes to come completely off and their naked bodies to press together while hands explored every inch.

And yet in the back of her mind was the fact that his mother was just upstairs.

His mother who was her patient.

And even if it might feel like they were hormonal teenagers frantic for each other, they weren't, and she knew this had to stop.

"We can't..." she whispered in a sort of agony. "The colonel—"

Sutter tugged at her nipple with his teeth and made

her lose complete track of everything but that for a split second before she could go on.

"We aren't kids," she reminded him.

He sighed but stopped.

"Too bad we aren't," he lamented.

But he brought them both to a straighter position, though when his gaze caught on her bare breast, he had to close his eyes and work to regain some control while Kinsey righted her clothes.

When she had, he grabbed her forcefully and kissed her again like there was no tomorrow, causing her to rethink her decision to stop this and actually begin to mentally search for somewhere they could go that would be more private.

But that was crazy and she knew it, so when that kiss ended she said a breathless, "We have to quit."

He surrendered with his hands in the air and fell back against the couch cushions.

That was when he said, "Let's skip dinner tomorrow night."

He wanted to spend the evening with her—alone? The idea sent lightning sizzling through every nerve ending in her body.

"The Camdens' dinner," she said as if it needed clarification.

"I know, I know," Sutter said. "But I swear I'll get you another time with them—I'll invite them to go out one night next week, dinner or clubbing or whatever it takes. But let's let the colonel and Sol go alone tomorrow night and just have dinner on our own. A date."

A date. For real. Where they would honestly be alone…

She wanted time with the Camdens and Sunday dinner was the prime opportunity for that.

But the chance to dress up and go out on a date with Sutter? How many chances would she have at that before he went away again?

Nothing about the Camdens' Sunday dinner could compete with that. Or with how much she wanted it.

"You really will arrange something else to make up for it?" she asked.

"Something that'll give you more contact—if we get all the cousins to a restaurant and we're all sitting at one big table you won't have them milling around and you won't have to compete with other guests the way you do at Sunday dinner."

She didn't actually need to be sold on the idea but it helped her convince herself that she could miss the event without losing her chance to get to know her half siblings.

"Okay," she agreed.

He smiled. "Good," he said before he pulled her down on top of him to kiss her once more.

That kiss went on long enough for her nipples to turn into solid little stones she could feel digging into his chest. Long enough for his hands to go from where he'd grasped her arms to the sides of both breasts again.

When his tongue did some enticing to go along with it, Kinsey knew she was going to have to be the one of them with willpower, so she ended the kiss and sat up straight.

"I'm going," she warned him.

He sighed but got up and offered her a hand to help her stand, too.

He didn't let go of it when she got to her feet, but held it all the way to the entryway where he helped her on with her coat. Then he took her hand again to walk her to her car.

But even with the driver's door unlocked and opened, Kinsey still didn't make it inside because he wrapped her in his arms, pivoted around to lean on her rear door and held her so her body ran the full length of his before he kissed her once more.

"You are not making this easy," she said when she ended the kiss, but he went on holding her close.

"I'm just having a hell of a time thinking about going back in that house without you…"

The colonel's oxygen machine did make a lot of noise...

But despite that fleeting thought that tempted her to let him take her up to his bedroom, Kinsey escaped those arms she had no desire whatsoever to leave and got behind the wheel.

"You'll be gone when I get here tomorrow, won't you," she reminded them both.

"The Broncos game," Sutter verified. "I'll make sure the colonel knows about dinner and I'll arrange for Sol to drive them. So once the colonel is ready to go out, you can leave. Then I'll pick you up at your place for our dinner—at seven?"

"Seven," Kinsey repeated as he stepped up to close her door.

"Seven," he said once more.

The sound of his voice, the way he'd said it, stayed with her while she backed out of the driveway.

And despite the fact that it was nothing more than the agreed-upon time for the next night, she couldn't help feeling as if there had been a world of promise for what was to come in that word.

Chapter Nine

The gruff, pragmatic colonel had a completely out-of-character surprise for Kinsey when Kinsey arrived at the Knightlinger home on Sunday.

She explained that two houses down the street was a hairstylist named Bernadette who had turned her garage into a salon decades ago. The colonel had gone to Bernadette whenever she was in Denver over the years and since retiring had become one of Bernadette's regulars. Bernadette had called the colonel this morning to ask how she was doing and the colonel had persuaded the stylist to open on Sunday solely for Kinsey and the colonel.

"I knew Bernie's husband would be glued to the television for that football game Sutter went to and Bernie hates football. So I asked if she'd like to make a little money this afternoon and open up just for you and me," the colonel informed Kinsey. "I'm having her give me a haircut and a manicure and pedicure. And she'll do whatever you want to your hair, too, if you're willing."

Kinsey wasn't altogether willing.

She liked—and more importantly trusted—her own hairstylist and didn't want to take any chances with someone new. Especially not today of all days, when she was going out with Sutter that evening.

She thought a manicure and pedicure were harmless enough, though, and agreed to have those done.

So after fixing the colonel's lunch, she and the colonel made a slow trek two doors down the street to Bernadette's garage salon where they spent the afternoon.

And to Kinsey's astonishment, it was a lot of fun. The colonel had a ribald sense of humor that came out with the stylist, who clearly knew her well and was comfortable with it. And although it turned into a somewhat raucous three hours, it was a good time that left Kinsey liking the colonel all the more.

It also left her hair an inch shorter because she gave in and let the stylist give her a trim in addition to fire-engine red fingernails and toenails.

Back at the Knightlingers' house again when they were finished, Kinsey helped the colonel dress for the Camdens' Sunday dinner. As she did, the fact that Sutter and Kinsey weren't attending it finally came up.

"So you and my son are ditching Sol and me with the Camdens tonight."

"*Ditching* you? No—"

"Uh-huh..." the colonel muttered dubiously. "He said he wanted to thank you for the extras you've done—with Jack and cooking last night and the rest that doesn't count as my care. But I know what's up with him."

Kinsey had a moment of panic. Had the colonel seen them on the couch last night?

Then the older woman went on. "It's all right. I'm sure Sutter needs proof that I'll go on socializing even when he isn't around. So I'm showing him that I will."

Kinsey breathed a silent sigh of relief. "And will you, even after he actually leaves?" she asked, curious.

"Yes, yes, whatever it takes to keep him where he needs to be."

"And you don't hate it," Kinsey challenged.

The colonel didn't immediately concede to that, but with some reluctance she did finally say, "No, I don't hate it. Before I retired there were always dinners and functions I had to attend. Some socializing Amos arranged for us. But now, between the bother of nonmilitary events and the idea of going without Amos..."

It was the first Kinsey had seen of just how much the colonel really was grieving the loss of her husband because her voice cracked and her eyes welled up.

If the colonel had been a different kind of person, Kinsey would have given her a hug or at least a squeeze of the arm or a pat to comfort her. But she was a little afraid that would offend her.

The show of emotion was fleeting before the elderly woman fought it back and continued in a strong voice. "Without Amos, I just didn't feel like seeing people. But I know my Amos wouldn't have wanted me to sit locked in this house any more than Sutter does, that he would have dragged me kicking and screaming out of it. So for the two of them, I won't do what I was doing."

Kinsey considered pointing out that the colonel should be going out into the world and interacting with people for her own sake, too, but decided that the important thing was that she do what she needed to do, regardless of the reason.

So Kinsey only said, "Good."

"Given any more thought to my son?" the older woman inquired openly then.

I certainly haven't given him any less thought, that's for sure...

Kinsey didn't voice what ran through her head and only said, "More thought to what?"

"To changing his mind about that marriage nonsense he holds on to."

Ah, what the colonel had said after Veterans Day.

"No," Kinsey answered honestly because she didn't ever think about attempting to change Sutter's mind. Nothing changed any of her brothers' minds or Trevor's, so she knew just how futile an endeavor that was.

And she wasn't changing her own mind, either. So even if Sutter decided he *could* be married to the military and to a woman at the same time, she wasn't that woman.

"I think that thank-you business is only an excuse to get some time alone with you," the colonel added.

Kinsey smiled and joked, "You don't think he really appreciates the things I've done?"

"Oh, we both do," the colonel said grumpily, as if she shouldn't have to say something so obvious. "But I still think he wants to get you alone. I know my boy—he likes you. And you could do worse."

"And I have," Kinsey joked again.

"Just so you know, you'd have my seal of approval. I don't mind when you come around every day."

Kinsey was touched and amused at the same time. She knew this was the tough commander's way of telling her she liked her and honestly did appreciate what Kinsey had done for her. But it was such a brusque, backhanded endorsement that it was funny.

She didn't dare laugh, though. The most she showed

was a smile when she said, "Thank you. But that same little, tiny streak of stubbornness you have is alive and well in your son, too."

"Whoever said I was stubborn?" the colonel demanded with a facetious grin that showed her pride in that stubborn streak.

"No one. Not a soul," Kinsey continued the jest.

"Still, stubborn or not, my Amos changed my mind on a lot of things. Sutter might surprise you if you gave it a try."

"I think people have to come to things on their own."

"Well go home and put on something short and see if that might help him come to it on his own."

Kinsey did laugh at that. "Yes, ma'am," she said as if accepting an order.

"But put our Jack here in his crate first, will you? I haven't learned how to get him to go in there yet."

"I will. But getting Jack in the crate isn't hard—you just toss a treat to the back of it and he goes right in," Kinsey explained, also pleased to hear the older woman refer to the puppy more fondly and possessively. Between that and the fact that the colonel had allowed the terrier to sleep on her bed all night, it seemed as if she was finally accepting the dog intended to be her companion.

But still, for her own reassurance, Kinsey asked. "So, is Jack out of the woods? You aren't going to send him back to the breeder?"

"I suppose not," the colonel grumbled as if she were making a great concession.

The doorbell rang just then, making Sol right on time to pick up the colonel.

Since she was ready to go, both she and Kinsey went downstairs to open the door to the neighbor.

After exchanging greetings, the colonel announced she was all set and Kinsey handed her off to the elderly man.

"Have a nice dinner," she said to them as the colonel accepted Sol's help getting down the landing.

"You, too," the colonel said pointedly.

Kinsey was more excited dressing for her date with Sutter when she returned to her apartment than she'd been dressing for her prom in high school.

After a quick shower and shampoo, she let her hair air dry because that was the best way for its natural waves to set in. Then she worked on her face—mainly eyes that she shadowed and lightly lined and mascaraed. Then she dusted on a little blush and topped it with highlighter.

Next came clothes. First a pair of tiny red lace bikini panties and a matching lace demi-cup strapless bra. Then the dress.

She'd bought it—and the underwear—on a whim to cheer herself up after ending things with Trevor. But she'd never worn any of it because once she'd gotten it all home, there hadn't been an occasion to justify it. So the underwear had stayed in a drawer and the dress had gone to the back of the closet.

It was bright red—matching her nail polish—strapless with a sweetheart neck that dipped just enough to show a hint of cleavage, and it hugged every one of her curves. And yes, it was short. Midthigh short.

When her hair dried she brushed it, parted it to the side and let it fall into those waves she'd carefully cultivated. Then she put only bare necessities into a small beaded clutch and took it and a pair of strappy four-inch heels to set near the door so she didn't have to put on the not-so-comfortable shoes until the last minute.

Ready to go, she began to tidy her apartment. Sutter was picking her up tonight, so she wouldn't have her own car. The plan was to go back to the Knightlinger house after dinner so she could help the colonel with the nighttime routine, then he would have to take her home. When that happened, Kinsey had every intention of inviting him in for a nightcap.

So she stashed laundry in the closet and cleared the bathroom counter of creams, lotions, comb, brush and makeup. And as she worked, she recalled her earlier conversation with the colonel about Sutter.

She had honestly never even considered attempting to change his mind about his refusal to marry. Like with her brothers, like with Trevor, she accepted that their minds were made up, that she had no control over the decisions they made, and could only make her own decisions accordingly.

When it came to her brothers, that had meant doing whatever had to be done stateside and making the decision not to dwell on the sacrifices. Not to be bitter or resentful. To view it as serving not only her family, but serving her country, too, by freeing her brothers for their military service.

When it came to Trevor, it had meant ending their engagement and a relationship with a man she'd cared about and had envisioned a future with. It had meant deciding that since she couldn't have the life she wanted with him, she would need to go on searching for someone who would offer her more. And that meant deciding to keep to her own objectives even if that sent the two of them on separate paths. She hadn't tried to convince him to give up the Doctors Without Borders work that meant so much to him—she had simply told him that the choice he had made meant they couldn't be together any longer.

But when it came to Sutter, it occurred to her that while she had no agenda to change his thinking or his objectives or path, in a way, for the first time, she was letting her own decision be interfered with instead.

Because right at that moment, she *should* have been at the Camden family home for Sunday dinner. She *should* have been with the grandmother, cousins and half brothers and half sisters she'd made it her goal to get to know. She *should* have been taking steps to move closer to getting what she wanted.

She hadn't and wouldn't ask Sutter to veer off his course for any reason. But unlike ever before, she was veering off her own. She was wasting precious time and opportunity, losing sight of her own goal just to be alone with Sutter. And all knowing full well that whatever she had with him would be nothing more than a brief interlude.

"And when he's gone, what will you have?" she asked her reflection in the bathroom mirror she was cleaning.

The answer was that she still wouldn't have the one thing she wanted—family here. Family to fall back on. Family to fill the gap in her life. Family that could help provide her with the foundation she felt she needed to make better choices in relationships in the future.

Okay, so Sutter *had* promised to get her another dinner with the Camden cousins later this week, she reasoned. But that still wouldn't be time with GiGi. And there was no guarantee that all the Camdens would be available on another night while the Camden Sunday dinner was a no-miss event. And she was passing it up.

She shouldn't have, she silently chastised herself.

Sutter was clear and unwavering in his own goals and she accepted that.

But she'd wavered in hers.

"It's one thing if you can't resist him, if you let this play out even when you know it won't go anywhere lasting," she told her reflection. "But it's something else if you choose to be alone with him *instead* of doing what you should be doing."

With the bathroom and bedroom straightened up, she went into the combined living, dining, kitchen portion of the place and glanced at the wall clock in her breakfast nook as if it would give her an answer as to how to correct the mistake she'd made.

But it was nearly seven and too late to go to the Camdens' dinner now.

And even though she wanted to kick herself for it, the prospect of dinner alone with Sutter didn't feel like a mistake. It was still something she wanted to do.

"But it has to stop here," she warned herself. After tonight, she would refocus on what she'd set out to do.

Before anything else hindered it.

"So no more pussyfooting around," she said, something she'd heard often from her stepfather when she or her brothers weren't tackling a problem head-on.

Then the knock she was waiting for sounded at her door and she knew that Sutter was just outside.

That's all it took to make her heart beat faster. And to realize that, in that moment, being with him was what she truly wanted to do over and above anything else.

"But starting tomorrow you change back and do what you need to do," she whispered as she slipped her feet into her shoes and picked up the clutch.

Then she reached for the knob to open the door to the man she just couldn't wait to be with.

* * *

"It's too soon, Kinsey."

Sutter had taken her to Morton's Steakhouse in downtown Denver and they'd had a scrumptious dinner. Prosciutto-wrapped mozzarella, lobster bisque, peppercorn-rubbed steaks, baked potatoes and asparagus. She was too full even for chocolate cake—so they'd ordered some to take home with them.

It was while they waited for the cake and the bill that Kinsey had told him her plan. She'd made up her mind to call GiGi first thing in the morning and ask to meet with her. The time had come to discuss the fact that Mitchum Camden was her and her brothers' biological father.

Her announcement had made Sutter frown and respond with the it's-too-soon opinion.

"But when will it ever feel like the right time? It's not the kind of revelation you can ease someone into. It just struck me today that I need to get on with it," Kinsey said. She wasn't—and didn't have any intention of—telling him that the distraction he caused was the reason she was pushing her timetable.

"At least stick to your plan of taking the time to get to know them better as long as I'm here," he went on. "I'll keep getting you in over there, getting you together with them. Tonight was just—"

"I know. You've made good on your word," she said before smiling and goading him a little. "Or was tonight just the beginning of a plot to keep them away from me and my nefarious schemes to swindle them?"

"I know you too well to believe you're working any kind of angle other than trying to connect with your family—if they truly *are* your family. I still don't know whether or not you're really half-Camden and you shouldn't expect anyone to believe it a hundred percent until there's DNA that proves it. But yeah, you could be one of them—I've come over to your side on that. And on thinking that it does need confirmation for your sake and for theirs. But now that I *have* come over to your side, I just think it might go a little more smoothly if you really do let them get to know you well before you do anything."

"It'll be a shock no matter what—unless they somehow already know. But now I'm thinking that the longer I wait, the weirder it will be that I've hung around and *not* told them."

"No, there isn't any chance that it won't be a shock," he said.

"And there's no time like the present," she added with some finality.

Some finality that he ignored.

"What about your brothers? You said they aren't on board. Shouldn't you wait for their sake—since you *are* messing with something that involves them, too?"

"It doesn't have to involve them if they don't want it to. I won't force them to meet anyone or have anything to do with the Camdens. From the beginning this has been something I need to do for myself. I'll let the Camdens know that Conor and Liam and Declan are also out there. It will be up to all of them how far they take anything after that."

The bill and the container with their dessert came then and Sutter didn't say anything as he placed his credit card in the leather-bound folder. But the lines between his eyes let her know he was still troubled.

Then the waiter left again and he said, "Nothing I can say will make you wait?"

Sitting across the table from her, he was dressed in

a dark gray suit and silver-gray shirt with a matching tie that made him look dashing and debonair, and made her wish to go on having this view of him forever.

But she forced herself to remember that regardless of how much she might wish for it, he would not be a constant in her life. Before long, he wouldn't be around to fill the gap.

"No. It's time and I'm going to do it," she said.

"It's not going to be easy."

"I know."

"And it might get ugly," he warned.

"I hope not. But I know that's possible, too."

The waiter returned with his credit card and the receipt for Sutter to sign.

When the waiter left once more, Sutter looked solemnly at her and said, "I don't want you to do it alone."

She laughed lightly at his protectiveness. "You think I'll need a bodyguard?"

His smile was wicked as his lids lowered to half-mast and his gaze dropped to her cleavage for only a split second. "It's a body worth guarding," he murmured. Then he said, "I just don't want you to have to face whatever comes out of this on your own."

"They could welcome me with open arms. The end result could be a celebration," she said hopefully.

His smile at that was kind. "Then I'll be there to celebrate with you."

But she knew he didn't really believe that's the way it would go. And she didn't have any illusions about it herself, despite her show of optimism. Best case scenario, GiGi would be shocked, would need time to process it. There would be no celebrations or warm welcomes right away…even if she hoped they would come in time.

"I'll leave it up to you," he went on. "I can come

with you, be right by your side. Or at least let me drive you over and wait for you in the car so I'm there when you come out."

"You don't have to," she told him. "And if it goes horribly sour you'll be associated with that. It might damage your own relationship with the Camdens—are you sure you're willing to risk that?"

"I'm sure," he said without thinking about it and with conviction.

He just never seemed to take a misstep that could let her like him a little less.

And it did help to think about having a bit more of that support he'd shown her before.

"I think it's something I should do one-on-one with GiGi, but if you want to wait for me outside—"

"Done," he decreed.

He stood then and pulled her chair out slightly so she could get up, too. "But I still think you should wait," he said as she did.

"I know," she answered, saying no more.

Sol was just leaving when Kinsey and Sutter arrived at the Knightlinger house after their dinner. Kinsey kept her coat on over her dress as she took the colonel upstairs to bed—buttoned up and concealing what she had on underneath.

The colonel took note, however, that plenty of leg showed, commended her for it and said nostalgically, "Oh, to have those days back."

From there the elderly woman went through her own routine quickly so that it was only a matter of twenty minutes or so before she was settled into bed with Jack, her brandy, her oxygen, her book, her television remote control and her cell phone in case of emergency.

"Now get out of here and act like your evening didn't get interrupted," the colonel ordered, shooing Kinsey off.

"Want to go have a drink somewhere?" Sutter asked when he and Kinsey were back in his car.

Kinsey considered that. She'd had a nice day with the colonel. She'd had the opportunity to wear the red dress. She'd had a wonderful meal. She was convinced that she'd put herself back on course to achieving her goal by making up her mind and telling Sutter that she was going to contact GiGi Camden first thing in the morning.

But the truth was that from the moment she'd stopped being in Sutter's arms the night before, everything seemed like nothing more than filler to get her to this moment.

And any chance of getting back into those arms.

"How about a drink and our cake at my place?" she countered.

He smiled as if she'd said exactly what he was hoping to hear and headed in that direction.

They were good at small talk and chatted through the short drive to her apartment. They chatted as they walked up the stairs to her door. They were still chatting as she unlocked it and they went in, as she closed and locked it behind them.

But that was as far as the small talk went because before she could turn on a light, he grabbed her and pulled her into a kiss that let her know he'd only been on pause since last night, too.

After basking in that kiss for a while, Kinsey ended it and said, "No drink or cake?"

"No drink or cake," he answered, sounding barely

in control. It made her smile as she took his hand and led him to her bedroom.

Along the way she told herself that this was like a once-in-a-lifetime vacation. She was going to make the most of it, all the while knowing that when it was over, it was over and would never happen again.

But she definitely intended to make the most of it.

Sutter didn't let her turn on any lights in the bedroom either, so there was only the glow of the full moon coming in through her sheer curtains. But it was enough as he spun her into his arms again to restart their kissing with a hunger more intense than she'd ever experienced. A hunger churning inside of her, too.

He took off her coat while she stepped out of her shoes—all with mouths and tongues never missing a beat. Then went his suit coat and tie the same way—shed like chains he couldn't wait to be free of.

Next he unzipped the back of her dress but before peeling it away he paused in kissing her to give it one last appreciative glance. To groan and say, "Oh, that dress…it's been driving me crazy all night."

Then he recaptured her mouth with his and finessed the tight red knit down her curves until it could fall to her feet where she stepped out of it.

That left her in only the matching lace panties and strapless bra. And his clothes against her almost-bare skin was a condition that had to be remedied. She made quick work of unfastening his shirt buttons, of yanking the tails from his waistband, though she was more careful when it came to pulling the material away from his injured shoulder. Then she threw the shirt as far away as she could and went on to his suit pants.

The waistband opened and the zipper slid down with ease, aided by what was burgeoning behind it. But as much as Kinsey wanted those slacks gone, she let them stay to torment him a little.

She wasn't sure he noticed, though, because just then one of his hands dropped to her breasts, insinuating itself inside the demi-cup of her bra to cause a more efficient torment as he caressed and kneaded and teased and held her oh-so-sensitive flesh in that strong hand.

Kinsey nearly writhed with pleasure as he caught her nipple in the web of two fingers. Tugging and squeezing with that gentlest of pressures, he opened wide the door to desires that she'd been trying to bury for what seemed like an eternity.

Desires that couldn't tolerate what was left of his clothes for another minute so she finally let drop everything he had on from the waist down.

Sutter took it from there and pried off his shoes and socks while continuing to plunder her mouth and tantalize her breasts.

And then she was the one overdressed because he had on nothing at all.

Knowing that provoked an even more compelling need to see the entirety of that magnificent body of his. She arched back just enough to take a look downward.

There was no disappointment in store for her there. His upper half was only the prelude to a complete picture of the most impressive masculinity she'd ever laid eyes on.

Then he tipped her face up again with the curve of an index finger beneath her chin so he could return to kissing her, now with something new—a more measured, simmering heat that slowed things down as if to give him the opportunity to savor it all.

Kinsey wasn't sure when or how he'd moved them nearer to her double bed but it was suddenly close enough for him to ease them both down onto it while still kissing her, while still enticing breasts he'd released from the captivity of the bra that he'd tossed aside.

Lying together on her bed she gave herself over to the pure sensations of kissing him, of having his hands on her. She lost herself in how good it all was, finally being with him, being up against his naked body, his mouth hers to play with.

She lost herself in every inch of his muscular back and shoulders and biceps and pecs. In every inch of his rock-hard abs and fabulous derriere. In impressively honed thighs that were the runways to that part of him that was just waiting for her attention.

Like the rest of him it was glorious. Long and thick. And just closing her hand around him drove him wild enough to break away from kissing her to moan, making her smile to have been the cause.

And when he started to kiss her again it wasn't her mouth he found, instead it was the hollow of her neck and the straight path below it to her breasts.

First one, then the other, he drew them in, showing her even more of the talents he possessed with teeth and tongue.

And if that wasn't enough, his hand sluiced down her stomach and underneath the elastic of her bikinis so he could reach between her legs to slip a finger inside of her and make her moan, too.

Then the heat turned up on that simmer and that urgent hunger came out once again.

Sutter suddenly pulled away from her and stood at the foot of the bed, devouring the sight of her as he removed her panties before he retrieved his slacks and took protection from his pocket.

Once that was in place, he came back to her and that

hunger had its day. Mouths met and cavorted in abandon until he rediscovered her breasts with a new concentration. Meanwhile, he sent his hand south again where he worked her into such a frenzy that her legs spread apart in shameless invitation.

He rose over her then, coming into her in one sleek movement that felt so good it brought a tiny sound of primal delight from her throat.

But as he embedded himself deeply into her and she reveled in the weight of him on top of her, she also realized he was bracing his weight on only his good arm.

He was strong and possibly he could have maintained that position but she didn't want him to try. So she wrapped one leg around him and gave him a little nudge.

Sutter got the idea and laughed. "You don't think I'm up to this?" he said with a challenge that revealed no doubt on his part.

Kinsey flexed around him and answered like a tough guy, "I just don't want to hurt you."

He laughed even more at that but rolled her until he was lying flat on the mattress and it was her on top of him instead.

She kissed him once more then, sending her tongue to brazenly play with his while she slid slightly up and then down again. Several times. Using her whole body to further woo his.

Both of his hands went to her hips, holding her firmly to him as he pushed up into her, then pulled slightly away as he helped her meet and match him.

It was all slow at first, like the most sensual of dances. Slow enough to revel in each well-designed thrust and retreat.

Until passion began to grow and speed things up.

Faster and faster, deeper into her he came, while Kinsey clung to him with her thigh muscles that stayed tight around him.

Faster still he went. And if there was any weakness in his injured arm she couldn't tell as both hands gripped her behind and guided her into an explosion of bliss.

Climax must have hit him at the same time because she felt his entire body go rigid and tense. And for one extended, exquisite moment they just rode it together to an end that came inch by inch until they were both completely depleted.

For a while they stayed like that, catching their breath, him inside of her in a way she never wanted to lose.

Weak and spent, it felt to Kinsey as if their bodies completed each other and she marveled not only at the force of what had just happened, but at how flawlessly they fit together.

Apparently small talk was not the only thing they were good at…

Then Sutter rallied and rolled again so that they were both on their sides, nestling her into the protective cove of his big body and kissing the top of her head.

"Is your shoulder okay?" Kinsey asked him, serious now, her forehead between his pecs.

"I am feeling no pain," he assured with a rumble of a laugh deep in his chest. "How about you?"

"A few broken bones but that's all," she said casually.

"You're kidding, right?"

She laughed. "Yes, I'm kidding. I'm fine."

"That's it? Just fine?" He pretended disappointment when she knew he knew full well just how amazing it had been for her.

"Just fine," she lied aloofly. "Maybe you'll try harder next time."

He laughed confidently, hugged her tight and let go of her to disappear into the bathroom for a moment before he returned to drop wearily onto the bed beside her again.

Then he pulled her to his side where she could use his chest as a pillow and raise one of her thighs across his.

"Give me a half-hour nap and I'll see what I can do," he said then.

"Shall I set a timer?"

He moved her thigh higher. "I think this'll do."

It likely would since she could feel him already responding.

Then, in a quiet voice, clear of all humor, he said, "What're you doin' to me, Kinsey Madison…you're kind of rocking my world…"

"Sorry?" she said, not sure what he meant.

"I definitely will be when I have to let go of you and leave this bed," he answered thickly, obviously drifting off.

But he will let go and leave this bed, she emphasized to herself. Because no matter how fantastic it had been, this was only a flash-in-the-pan thing for him.

He wasn't what she needed, and he never would be. And that was why tomorrow she would set the wheels in motion with the Camdens for herself.

But at that moment, against his naked body, one of his arms wrapped around her, his other hand on her bare thigh to hold it to him, Kinsey knew there was going to be more yet tonight.

And that was all she cared about right then.

Chapter Ten

Sutter watched Kinsey walk up to the front door of the Camden family home at four o'clock Monday afternoon. She'd called GiGi this morning asking to meet with her and that was the time the older woman had set.

He went on watching as Kinsey stood facing that door for a while without knocking or ringing the bell. She was visibly nervous and everything in him screamed for him to help her, to rescue her, to at least be by her side.

But that wasn't what she'd asked him to do, so he just sat behind the wheel of his SUV, hating the feeling of helplessness it gave him.

Twice Kinsey raised her finger to the doorbell but hesitated. Then he saw her square her shoulders and do it on the third try.

"Come through for her, GiGi," he said, hoping for the best. But not expecting it.

The Camdens were good people but this wasn't going to be an easy thing for any of them to hear. Or to accept.

The front door opened and he saw the older woman greet Kinsey with a cautious smile. She looked uncertain and leery. But what else could she be with a request for a private meeting from someone she barely knew? Especially considering that the Camdens' position of wealth and power coupled with their history had brought a lot of dangerous things out of the woodwork at various points in the past.

As Sutter continued to watch, GiGi stepped aside and Kinsey went in. The door closed behind her. And Sutter's tension level went up another notch. He was fond of all of the Camdens but no one among them better hurt her…

He sighed, feeling strongly as if he should be in there with her. But difficult for him or not, he had to honor her determination to do this on her own and just be there for her when she came out.

And he *would* be there for her, no matter what the results of this meeting might be.

At least he would be for today and for a while.

But then what?

Then he wouldn't be.

And something about that made his gut wrench like nothing in his life ever had.

From what he'd come to know of Kinsey, she was always there for everyone else. For her family again and again. For the family of that doctor she'd been engaged to. For the Tellers, the last family she'd cared for, including their granddaughter who—according to Livi—Kinsey had doted on, helping and encouraging the grieving little girl who had just lost her parents even though that hadn't been part of her job.

He had no doubt that Kinsey was there in any way she could be for any patient she took on and certainly she'd come through big-time for him and the colonel and even for Jack.

But he hadn't heard a thing about anyone ever being there or coming through for her.

So it was no wonder that she was searching for that in the Camdens.

It was no wonder that when it came to choosing a partner in her life, she didn't want yet another person who *wouldn't* be there for her.

Like him.

And since he wasn't sure the Camdens *would* come through for Kinsey, he knew he should be hoping she'd find a good man who would. A steady, dependable nine-to-fiver. Someone who would love her and care for her and give her everything she wanted and needed and deserved.

But no matter how hard he tried, he couldn't make himself hope for that and it caused him to wonder what it said about him. What the hell kind of a person was he if he couldn't wish for her the one thing she most deserved?

The answer to that was that he was the kind of person who wanted her for himself. Who couldn't stand the thought of her with someone else. With anyone else.

And last night had only made it worse.

Last night and this morning when he'd wanted so badly to just hang on to her and never let go.

He couldn't recall a time when he'd ever felt this possessive. He'd lived too transient a life for that. So this was a new—and not really welcome—feeling for him.

But it went along with a lot of other new feelings he'd found himself having. All of them in regards to Kinsey.

She was just so great. Smart and funny, accomplished, strong and independent, caring and tolerant and…well, she was the whole package. And so beautiful he could hardly keep his eyes off her. Not to mention, so sexy he hadn't been able to keep his hands off her.

And she just had a way about her. Not pushy or insistent or naggy or judgmental or guilt inducing, but still somehow getting the job done.

A way about her that had even influenced the colonel to be a gentler, more cooperative version of herself. A way about her that had not only accomplished what he'd needed accomplished, but had also eased tensions between him and his mother. A way that had made things seem more like when his father had been there to act as a buffer.

And they were just so damn good together, he acknowledged. Even as dog trainers, working and playing with Jack—double-teaming the puppy had actually made some strides with the terrier that Sutter hadn't been making on his own. Enough so that the colonel was beginning to like the dog.

They were definitely good at just being alone, when Kinsey helped him see things—like the colonel's relationship with Sol—in a better light. When she softened his own rough edges and showed him a better perspective to view a lot of things through. When she showed him more subtle methods of achieving what he was after. When time flew and he never wanted it to end and when it did, he felt as if there was an emptiness left behind that wasn't filled again until she was back.

And certainly they were good together when they were in bed. Making love to her had been so much better than sex had ever been before that it had almost been a whole different experience. Something that had

had a new, unique element to it, a deeper sense of closeness, of connection, somehow, that had made it more…

Wow, just more of everything. More explosive and mind-blowing and satisfying in a way that he was having trouble imagining not having as a part of his life from now on.

Oh, hell, who was he kidding? He was having trouble picturing any part of his life now without her in it.

"Damn you, Beau!" he muttered out loud as it occurred to him that his cousin had predicted this. They'd even bet a hundred dollars on it.

He'd believed that Beau was wrong to think that he wouldn't be able to enjoy some time with Kinsey and move on as usual. But now he was coming to realize that Beau was right. When feelings like he was having for Kinsey started up, they made things veer off course.

They made it so that having her only here and now, being with her here and now with the knowledge that he'd soon have to leave her behind, wasn't going to be enough.

But if he wanted to have some kind of future with her, what was he going to be? Just someone else on the long list of men who were in and out of her life?

He didn't think she'd accept that. And even if he could convince her, he didn't think that life would make her happy.

It was long past due for her to have what she wanted.

And he wanted to be the one who gave it to her.

But how was he going to do that when he hadn't changed his mind about marriage? A woman or the marines, but not both—that's how it was for him.

And that was actually how it was for Kinsey, too.

So it was Kinsey or the marines…

That realization—and the fact that he was even entertaining the thought of Kinsey over the marines—hit him harder than the sniper's bullet.

His first reaction was to do what he always did—he straightened his posture and told himself in no uncertain terms that he was a marine, that that's all he'd ever wanted to be, that that's all he ever would be.

But for the first time in his life, he wasn't feeling it. Not if being a marine meant no Kinsey.

And that was when he began to think the unthinkable.

He thought about Beau having left the marines. About the fact that his cousin had served honorably and dutifully and had moved on to a different life afterward—a life of happiness that Sutter could suddenly see as a reward Beau had earned with his service to his country.

He thought about Beau having a woman he was crazy about. A baby. The chance for even more family. And how none of that shadowed the good Beau had done as a marine or how well he'd served. How none of that took away the contribution he'd made.

He thought about having what Beau had now—and having it with Kinsey.

And the longer he sat with those thoughts, the more he surprised himself by beginning to feel as if the time might have come to do what his cousin had done and take a step onto a new track.

But who was he if he wasn't a marine?

What would he do?

The answer came to him in a flash. As a lieutenant colonel, he was responsible for the people under his command. He'd thought that responsibility ended when they finished their periods of service. He'd always assumed that he was sending them back to honor and respect and lives that compensated them for their sacrifices in defending their country.

Now he wasn't so sure.

In fact, now he'd learned that in too many instances he was sending them home to hardship.

Okay, sure, he'd known there would be hardship for the wounded—whether the wound was physical or mental. But he'd also known that he was handing his responsibilities to the injured over to medical personnel who took up the reins.

But the rest?

Trouble finding or getting jobs? Financial and credit problems? Housing issues? Needing aid and assistance and counseling to get them back to being functioning, successful civilians? It was no easy road for too many of them.

And now he felt as if maybe his responsibility could be just as honorably performed if he took care of these people not when they were overseas, but when they were discharged.

If he was actually here to train and guide and lead and protect his people on the home front the way he would do as their commanding officer anywhere else in the world, he could still provide a valuable service.

And thinking about it now, he could easily imagine himself in that role, possibly working with Beau or in the job with Louise Turner's son.

But even if it was a worthy and worthwhile task, it was still a lot for him to come to grips with and he waited for something to tell him he'd lost his mind to even consider leaving the marines.

It didn't come, though.

What did come was the knowledge that the colonel

wouldn't like it. She hadn't liked it when Beau left the corps. She'd like it even less if he did.

But the more Sutter thought about it, the more right it felt to him.

And if he changed his path and took responsibility for marines and other vets in the private sector, it would free the way to try for a real, lasting relationship with Kinsey…

Kinsey, who appeared in the Camdens' doorway just then.

There was no sign of GiGi or anyone else seeing her out. There was just Kinsey stepping outside and closing the door behind her.

Sutter opened his car door and got out.

Her meeting with GiGi couldn't have gone well because her expression was too solemn and forlorn, and her big blue eyes were wide as she blinked repeatedly, clearly trying to hold back tears.

"You don't look like you're walking on air," he said quietly as she drew near.

"We should go," was her only response, short and to the point as she went to the passenger side and got in.

Sutter returned to the driver's side and started the engine, not pressuring her to tell him what went on until he'd driven around the huge center fountain in the front courtyard and was out onto Gaylord Street again.

Then he glanced at her and said, "How'd it go?"

She shook her head. "Not great. I made a copy of my mother's letter to my brothers and me and gave that to GiGi to explain why I was there. She read it and it was weird—I actually saw the color drain out of her face as she went along. By the time she'd finished the letter she looked like she'd aged about ten years right before my eyes."

Sutter nodded. "And then what?"

"I think she was in shock. I started to worry that she was going to have a heart attack or stroke or something. The times I've seen her she's seemed so strong and healthy and youthful—years younger than her actual age. But by the time she'd read the letter she didn't look that way anymore, and I started to think maybe I shouldn't have just laid it on her, alone, like that."

Sutter could hear the alarm in her voice and he was beginning to feel some of it himself. He was fond of GiGi Camden. "Did you call someone? Her husband, Jonah? Margaret or Louie?"

"No. I asked her if I could get her a glass of water but she kind of rallied then. And…well…she didn't get hostile, but there was kind of a scary light in her eyes and she got all formal and stiff and her chin went in the air. She can be a little formidable—I think she could give the colonel a run for her money in that department."

Sutter nodded, knowing that side of GiGi, too, having seen it a time or two when he and Beau had gotten into trouble growing up.

"So there was no sign that she knew anything about Mitchum's affair before this?"

"None. And she either absolutely didn't believe it or at least didn't want to."

"Sure. You were telling her something not too nice about one of her sons. That's bound to bring out some defensiveness."

"I told her I was willing to do DNA testing. That I didn't want anything from them but…family…"

Her voice cracked and hearing it did something extreme to him. His injured arm was in a sling, recovering from the excess use the night before, but his hand on the steering wheel became a tight fist around it.

"Are you okay?" he asked her, not giving a damn about anything but that, but her.

She nodded again but he saw her blink back more tears as he pulled into his driveway, so he didn't believe it.

He turned off the engine and pivoted in her direction, reaching to the back of her neck to squeeze it. "And then what?" he repeated quietly.

She shrugged and laughed humorlessly. "She didn't welcome me with open arms and tell me to call her Grandma."

"Ah, Kinsey..."

"She just said she would have to look into it—"

"*It* being the truth of whether or not Mitchum had the affair with your mom, and whether or not you and your brothers could be her grandchildren," he clarified.

"I guess. And then she sort of shut down and started staring at the letter again. After a while it was like she'd forgotten I was there so I got up and said I was sorry..."

Her voice cracked a second time and he used that hand at her neck to pull her head to his chest where he rested his chin on top of it.

"I'm not sure what I was sorry for," she said in a voice clogged with tears. "But I didn't really know what else to say. And it seemed like I'd done something... bad. So I just left. And I don't know what will happen now. Maybe nothing. Or maybe they'll file a restraining order against me," she joked feebly.

And he loved her all the more for even trying to infuse humor into a situation that he knew was breaking her heart.

"It'll be all right," he whispered into her hair, wondering if this was the time to tell her his own news or the time to leave her in her misery. As badly as he wanted to promise to be by her side for whatever was to come, he thought she was probably too buried in her grief to really hear anything he said right now.

So for a while he just left things as they were and he stroked her hair and didn't say anything.

Then she took a deep breath, exhaled and sat up, more in control. "I know it's dumb, but I had some fantasies about this that were a long way from how it went. My brother Conor warned me about that. But it could have been worse. She could have refused to even entertain the possibility and thrown me out of the house. Then what would I have done? As it is, there's still hope. They just all have to live with it for a while, and maybe have the testing done, and then…we can all see from there."

He smiled at her, loving that spark of optimism in her, too. Just plain loving her.

And he couldn't hold that in any longer.

"So you didn't come away with a family of eleven more. But what would you say to a family of two more?"

Her expression showed complete confusion.

"Well, two and a half if you count Jack."

"You're offering to adopt me?" she joked.

"No, I'm actually asking you—ineptly and without the fanfare you should have for this—to marry me."

Confusion turned to shock of her own. "Marry you? Am I that pathetic?"

"I'm not proposing out of pity. I'm asking you to marry me because I'm that in love with you."

Her eyebrows dipped together in a frown that did not seem like a good sign so he said, "I know this is rotten timing, but I've been doing a lot of thinking—some of it without even realizing where it was leading but—"

He went on to tell her what he'd been thinking about

how the groundwork for his decision had been laid without him even being aware of it as he'd learned what vets went through when they came home. He told her what it had brought him to.

"The thing is," he said then, "it might be time for me to come home for good and serve those who've served. And if I do that—"

"You don't want to stop being a marine," she said as if he was fooling himself. Or trying to fool her.

"Once a marine, always a marine," he said. "It's just time for me to be a marine in a different way. Time for me to have a life I didn't think I wanted but that now I know I do—with you."

"I think you're just sleep deprived after last night—we didn't do much of that, you know."

Oh, he knew. The night had been spent in much better pursuits than sleep. At least it had until she'd insisted he leave at dawn to get home before the colonel woke up. But not sleeping hadn't mattered then and it didn't matter now.

"Last night didn't deprive me of anything. It gave me something that opened my eyes and sealed the deal for me. It's you I want, Kinsey. You and a future with you and a family I come home to at the end of every day. The same things you want."

She shook her head again. "No," she said firmly. "I know what this is—my brothers do it, too. They feel bad or guilty or whatever and they start talking about how maybe they'll come home. I used to believe it. Like I believed Trevor when he said Doctors Without Borders would only be once. Or twice. But I know not to buy into it now. So no," she said even more forcefully. "You're a marine and you don't want to stop being a marine—you couldn't have been more clear about that since the minute I met you and it hasn't changed. *I* haven't changed that."

That seemed to mean something to her that he didn't understand but he said only, "Yeah, you *have* changed that."

"I don't believe it. You'll sleep on it tonight or talk to the colonel or go back to put your papers in and remember that serving overseas is what you want to be doing, where you belong, and I'll just be here dangling by a string, believing I'll get what I want if I'm only patient. Until I face the truth! And no! Not this time! Not even for you!"

"I know that's how it's been for you, Kinsey. But I'm not your brothers or that other guy. Just think about it. Think about what we have. What's between us is amazing enough for me to see everything in a new light. And unless I'm misreading the signs, you feel it, too. So give yourself the chance for your head to clear so you can look at what we could have together, and let go of what you thought before. Because you and I…things are different than either of us planned and worth making a change to have."

"Things *aren't* different!" she insisted, sounding overwhelmed. "No matter how good things are between us, no matter what we *could* have—*you* are the same!"

"I'm not the same as your brothers or Trevor," he said. "And when I say I want something, when I say I'll do something, that's how it is."

He took a breath to inject some calm into what was getting heated and said, "The colonel and I can do dinner on our own. Go back to your place, take some time to sort through what happened with GiGi today. Then think about last night. Think about how it's been with us right from the start. Think about how it can be from here on. And then tell me it isn't what you want, too."

"What I don't want is to be here, alone with a couple of kids, taking care of the colonel while you're gone and telling me *this will be the last time*! And while I'm sorting through what happened today, you go in and put on your uniform, and that'll change your mind right back again about returning overseas. And by the time I come back tonight, you can just tell me I'm right!"

And with that she got out of the car and made a beeline for her sedan in the driveway next to his.

Then she was gone.

And all he could do was hope to God he wasn't the only one of them feeling what he was feeling.

Chapter Eleven

"He took Jack for a walk. They both needed some air," the colonel told Kinsey when she returned to the Knightlinger home later Monday night to help the elderly woman get to bed.

Kinsey hadn't asked where Sutter was as she took the colonel's pulse, listened to her heart and checked her pacemaker. After the meeting with GiGi Camden, after the blowup with Sutter, she was doing the best she could just to be professional and to do her job without breaking down.

But given that the colonel was more terse and cranky than she had been in a while, Kinsey assumed that Sutter had shaken things up here after shaking things up with her. And the elderly woman seemed to want to vent.

"He's leaving the corps," the colonel announced then, sounding grudgingly resigned to it.

"You didn't talk him out of it?" Kinsey said impersonally, trying to give no clue that she was involved as she put her stethoscope away and moved on to the blood pressure cuff.

"What can I say…he's his mother's son. And his own man. Apparently he's made his decision and once that's done, there's no appeals court to send it to."

"Your blood pressure says you put up a good fight."

"You bet I did!"

What Kinsey was betting was that all hell had broken loose here while she was gone. But she didn't say that.

They were in the older woman's bedroom. The colonel already had on her flannel pajamas and was sitting on the edge of her bed while Kinsey set out the morning medications.

"I'll need one more finger of brandy tonight," the colonel decreed.

"Did you have dinner?"

"Takeout from my favorite restaurant. Ordered before my son dropped the bomb—I guess he was trying to soften me up. He should know better," she said caustically, as if there was no chance of that.

"But you did eat."

"I ate just fine," the colonel barked. Then, with some edge to her voice, she went on. "You know, when I told you to change his mind, I meant to change his mind so he'd be a marine *and* have a family. Not change his mind about being in the corps completely."

"In the first place, I didn't try to change anything," Kinsey said somberly. "In the second place, he hasn't really changed his mind. He just thinks he has. Right now he's out there with Jack, rehashing whatever you said to him—which I know had to have been a lot about him staying in the marines—and he's probably changing his mind back as we speak."

It was what Kinsey truly believed.

"You're blind."

"I've had experience with this same thing. It's like someone having a bad day at work—they come home swearing that they're going to quit, that they're going to put in their notice the next day. Then they sleep on it and the urge passes. Everything goes back to the way it has always been."

"It's not a bad day at work. It's that something else has caught his interest that he can't pass up," the colonel countered. "Something that means more to him than being a marine."

Kinsey had no idea what—or how much—Sutter had told his mother. She didn't want to tell the colonel anything she might not already know so she didn't respond at all.

But the outspoken elderly woman continued without encouragement.

"I don't like him leaving the corps," she said flatly. "And don't think for a minute that I do! But he makes a good case for what he can accomplish here to help vets. For not just washing his hands of the people coming home, but taking responsibility for them the same as he's felt responsible for them under his command."

"Sure," Kinsey said noncommittally.

"I don't hate that he'd be here," the colonel admitted, a half-angry confession.

"No, that would be good for you," Kinsey conceded.

"So we argued back and forth—don't think I didn't let him know everything I think—"

Kinsey couldn't help smiling despite her own low spirits. And saying another, "Sure."

"But in the end… He was raised to think for himself. To make decisions—he couldn't have been the decorated officer he's been otherwise. Now he tells me he's made this decision…" The colonel sighed heavily, disgustedly, then she said, "And if the truth be told, I'm grateful to have him at this time of my life. I don't want him to reach my age and find himself all alone."

Kinsey said yet another, "Sure."

"But pour me that extra brandy. Tonight I need it," the colonel concluded.

Kinsey did pour her a small amount more of the liquor, wondering if Sutter had omitted his marriage proposal and her rejection or not. The older woman was letting her know that she'd begrudgingly accepted that he was leaving the marines but nothing else.

If he was leaving the marines, and wasn't already changing his mind.

She helped the colonel with her oxygen tubes and got her situated with her drink, book and remote control as usual. Then she said good-night to the older woman.

It was only as she reached the doorway that the colonel's voice came again, as strong and as firm as it must have sounded handing down judgments from the bench.

"Make him happy. He's earned it."

For the second time Kinsey didn't respond. She just went out of the bedroom and down the stairs.

She could have—should have—left. Her work for the day was done. There was no reason to wait for Sutter. To see Sutter. She'd given him her answer. There was no more to discuss.

But when she got downstairs she spotted the remnants of dinner still on the kitchen table.

Meal cleanup wasn't part of her job. But still, the kitchen was where she went and clean up was what she started doing. All the while telling herself that despite what Sutter had said to his mother, he wasn't really going to leave the marines.

But the colonel had to have been the hardest person on the planet for him to have told his decision. Why would he have tackled that unless he was absolutely certain, absolutely determined? Why poke the bear if there was any doubt, any possibility at all, that he might stay in the marines?

That thought gave Kinsey some pause.

What if he really was planning to stay home for good?

She was so afraid to hope for that that at first she shied away from the idea.

But it had such appeal that she couldn't stay away from it.

What if Sutter became a civilian?

No deployments.

No overseas assignments.

No being stationed in one place after another.

Nothing but a nine-to-five job that he came home from at the end of every day, that he had every weekend free of.

Until that moment Kinsey honestly hadn't entertained the faintest prospect of him going through with the plan. She'd put Sutter in the same category as her brothers, as Trevor, and denied that there was any chance that he would do anything differently.

But the colonel was right—it was she and her son who were alike, and they weren't the type to waver or hesitate once their minds were made up.

Kinsey knew what her brothers were doing when they talked about possibly leaving the military and coming home. They were thinking about it in that moment when there was something tugging at them to stay—a sense of obligation and responsibility to people here, guilt for not being able to help out.

In that moment they were feeling the pull of ties here. But after the fact, faced again with what they'd signed on for, with their call to duty, it was still that pull to serve that won out, making them put off coming home.

She thought that something similar had happened with Trevor. What had begun as a onetime thing he wanted to do to give back had become his calling. But when he finished one trip with Doctors Without Borders and was back with her, it had felt good to him and he'd sworn that the first trip was also his last trip. Only after a few weeks off, he'd felt that call again and couldn't resist answering it, genuinely believing that one more time would be the end until he'd accepted that, for him, it had no end.

So it wasn't as if her brothers or Trevor flat out lied to appease her. They were just torn.

But when it came to the colonel and Sutter?

There were no signs of either of them ever having been of two minds about anything.

Tough and stubborn and strong-willed and straightforward—those were the dominating traits of Knightlinger mother and son.

Knowing that about the colonel, when the colonel had told her that she would continue to socialize with the Camdens, with Sol, with the other retired woman vet and the organization of ex-military women even if Sutter wasn't around to encourage the socialization, Kinsey hadn't doubted that she would. When the colonel began to accept Jack and said she'd keep him, Kinsey hadn't doubted that that was the truth, either.

Yes, these were changes from what the older woman

had been doing before, but it was clear that she was too stubborn to agree to make changes unless she was resolute about seeing them through.

Kinsey had seen the same thing in Sutter when it came to his agreement to give her more contact with the Camdens.

He might have initially been leery of her motives, but he'd done and continued to do what he'd said he would. Even when she'd been distracted from it herself by her attraction to him, he'd persisted. He'd kept his word to her.

And when it came to his marriage-to-the-military-or-marriage-to-a-woman-but-not-to-both philosophy he'd strictly adhered to it. As long as he was married to the military, he'd remained steadfastly single. Now, in considering marriage to her, he'd worked out a plan to leave the marines and serve his country in another fashion.

But she hadn't given what he was telling her a single ounce of credence. Not even for one split second had she believed that he would leave the military for her.

Instead, she'd immediately put up the protective wall she used now to keep her hopes from getting crushed again.

Kinsey stopped filling containers with leftovers and pinched her eyes shut at the realization that she'd done something really unfair to him by clumping him together with the other people in her life who had disappointed her.

And what if she hadn't shot Sutter down? she asked herself when she opened her eyes and took the leftover containers to the refrigerator. What if she'd taken his word along with his proposal?

His *proposal*…

For the first time the reality of what he'd actually done sunk in.

Sutter had *proposed* to her!

He'd told her he loved her. Loved her so much he was willing to alter the course of his life to be with her. That he *wanted* to alter the course of his life to be with her, to have a family with her. To give her what she'd told him she wanted.

But somehow she'd barely even heard that part. It had been secondary to his claim that he would leave the military—a claim she'd judged false.

But Sutter had asked her to *marry* him…

Sutter. Who had knocked her socks off the first time she'd ever set eyes on him. Who she'd been so drawn to that she had been distracted from everything else. Who had been on her mind day and night since she'd met him.

Sutter, who was military strong yet gentle. Who was intelligent and funny and warm and sweet. Who was patient and reasonable. Generous and kind. Who was a man of honor and dignity behind a face and body that took her breath away.

And yes, when he'd said what was between them was amazing, he was right. Since the moment he'd left her bed this morning, her body had ached to be back in his arms. Back in that bed with him.

But.

She took another breath and sighed as she threw away the takeout boxes and asked herself if her feelings for him were real.

Because not only wasn't she coming to this the way she'd wanted to come to another relationship—with a firm foundation of family already filling her life. She was coming to this on the very day that she'd tested the waters with the woman she believed to be her grandmother and not been welcomed with open arms. On the very day that all her brothers' misgivings had been proven accurate, leaving her questioning whether or not she would ever be a part of the Camden family at all.

Which meant that, if not for Sutter, she could very well be looking at more of the solitary, lonely life she was trying to remedy.

So was he the fallback? Was she grasping at something to fill the void? In order to just have *someone*? Was she sure that she wasn't considering settling for a man she'd regret being with down the road?

It was everything she'd worried about since her mother had died, since she'd even considered settling for Duncan right after that. She didn't want to cheat herself out of true happiness with a spouse she loved—and she didn't want to cheat Sutter out of that, either.

Just then the front door opened and Sutter came in with Jack.

Sutter was dressed in a gray hoodie. Jeans. Nothing special. His arm was in the sling.

And all it took was that one look at him to know. To bring tears to her eyes at the realization of just how much she loved him.

This great, wonderful man who had been there for her when she'd had doubts about there being a place for her with the Camdens.

This great, wonderful man who had been there for her again today when she'd confronted GiGi.

This great and wonderful man who was willing to change his entire life to be there for her. Who was everything she'd always wanted.

Had she actually worried she was *settling* for Sutter?

There was no more ridiculous a thought. Except maybe that her feelings for him might not be real.

Yes, her feelings for him had been born at a time when she was lonely, when she still didn't have the foundation she was looking for in the Camdens.

But those feelings had been born without the slightest chance or hope that he'd be the solution to that loneliness. In fact, they'd been born in spite of believing wholeheartedly that there was no future for them.

Only now a future with him was what he was offering.

Except that she'd totally blown it.

And thrown his proposal back at him.

And basically called him a liar.

Sutter didn't see her watching from the distance of the kitchen, but once Jack was off leash the puppy charged her, jumping up on her leg, tail wagging and demanding attention.

She knew she wasn't supposed to reward him for bad behavior but she bent over to pet him just the same.

Then she picked him up to hold him for moral support and found that Sutter had come down the hallway from the entry and now stood in the doorway to the kitchen.

He looked so good. But so drained.

"I'm sorry!" Kinsey blurted out impulsively.

His eyebrows arched. "Okay..." he said. "For?"

"Being a muttonhead this afternoon. I know what you said came from you, but I sort of heard it as if it was coming from other people...if that makes any sense."

She went on to explain what she meant, telling him that she was wrong not to have taken what he'd said on its own merit, to have so easily dismissed it.

"But you actually told the colonel!" she marveled.

"Because it's what I'm going to do, Kinsey. And if you need to wait until it's done—until I've officially ended my service and started working here—before you're convinced, then that's what it takes."

"Meaning you haven't just written me off?"

He laughed a weary laugh and said, "Just because you were a *muttonhead* this afternoon? I think, given all the burdens you've carried alone since you were no more than a kid, on top of what you went through today with GiGi, that you're entitled. But I don't give up that easily. I'm a marine, remember?"

"And you'll forgive me?"

"Anything." He smiled a lopsided smile and nodded at Jack. "Except maybe messing up that mongrel's training."

Kinsey breathed a sigh of relief and set Jack on the floor. Then she closed the distance between her and Sutter and raised a hand to his cheek. "I love you and that should have been what I said this afternoon."

He frowned slightly. "Is there a *but* coming? Because it sounds like there is."

"But it worries me if you're leaving the military *for* me. It worries me that you'll regret it and resent me."

"Then think of it as me leaving the military *for* the vets who need help here at home. That might only be in second place as reasons go, but it still carries weight. And there's the colonel, too. The regrets I have for not being with my dad at the end. I don't want to have those same feelings about the colonel—no matter how damn crabby she can be."

He put his free arm around her, pulling her closer, and her hand dropped from his face to his chest.

"But mostly," he said in a quiet, very serious voice, "I'm leaving the military *for* myself. Because I want a life with you. Kids with you. Looking at the rest of my life *without* you, and thinking about coming to the end of it alone, or with you and a couple of kids and grandkids and the full boat of family, I choose the full boat over the empty one. My choice. So stop worrying."

"And what if this thing I've started with the Camdens goes really, really bad? If you're with me it could affect your relationship with all of them."

"I'll take my chances. I know it won't change anything with Beau, but if it happens with the rest of them, then so be it. No Camden—not even Beau—is as important to me as you are. If being with you makes me an outcast, then okay, I'll be an outcast. As long as I can have you."

Kinsey hoped that didn't happen but she loved him too much, and wanted him too much, not to take him at his word about this.

"So marriage, huh? With the marines as your ex-wife?" she said then.

He laughed. "I never thought about it like that, but yeah, I guess so."

"Then okay."

He grinned down at her. "Okay, you'll marry me?"

"Did *you* want more fanfare?" she asked, referring to what he'd said when he'd proposed.

"Nope. I just want you. I don't need bells or whistles, an *okay* will do just fine."

He kissed her then, a long, slow, sweet kiss that lured her in and quieted any lingering tensions. When he finally pulled away, he looked deeply into her eyes.

"I love you, Kinsey. And from this minute on I will always do my damnedest to be there for you."

Her eyes grew misty again. "I love you, too," she said through a tight throat.

As she worked to gain control over herself, she ran a tender hand over his injured shoulder. "You've had the sling on all day today—did we do damage last night?"

His grin this time was smug. "No, I was letting it rest up. Just in case..."

He kissed her again, a kiss that brought down all the walls and allowed feelings to flood out and take over.

And as Kinsey gave in to it all, the thought passed through her mind that the Camdens might not ever accept her or her brothers as their own.

She still held out hope that things with them might work out. That she could ultimately have Sutter *and* a grandmother and cousins and half brothers and sisters along with Conor and Declan and Liam.

But while it would add to the joy of her wedding, to the happiness of sharing news of a baby to come, of a baby born, while it would add to the love that baby could have...if they never recognized her, it wouldn't lessen any of that happiness or joy for her.

Sutter really was all she needed, all she wanted. Extended family would only be the frosting on the cake.

And at least while the issues with the Camdens worked themselves out, she *would* have Sutter. And the colonel. And Jack.

And a future that she knew would fulfill her every dream.

Right there in Sutter's arms.

* * * * *

Don't miss the next book in Victoria Pade's CAMDEN FAMILY SECRETS *series, coming in August 2017 from Mills & Boon Cherish*

MILLS & BOON®

Cherish™

EXPERIENCE THE ULTIMATE RUSH OF FALLING IN LOVE

A sneak peek at next month's titles...

In stores from 9th March 2017:

- **Reunited by a Baby Bombshell** – Barbara Hannay *and* **From Fortune to Family Man** – Judy Duarte
- **The Spanish Tycoon's Takeover** – Michelle Douglas *and* **Meant to Be Mine** – Marie Ferrarella

In stores from 23rd March 2017:

- **Stranded with the Secret Billionaire** – Marion Lennox *and* **The Princess Problem** – Teri Wilson
- **Miss Prim and the Maverick Millionaire** – Nina Singh *and* **Finding Our Forever** – Brenda Novak

Just can't wait?
Buy our books online before they hit the shops!
www.millsandboon.co.uk

Also available as eBooks.

0317/23

MILLS & BOON®

EXCLUSIVE EXTRACT

Griffin Fletcher never imagined he'd see his childhood sweetheart Eva Hennessey again, but now he's eager to discover her secret—one that will change their worlds forever!

Read on for a sneak preview of
REUNITED BY A BABY BOMBSHELL

A baby. A daughter, given up for adoption.

The stark pain in Eva's face when she'd seen their child. His own huge feelings of isolation and loss.

If only he'd known. If only Eva had told him. He'd deserved to know.

And what would you have done? his conscience whispered.

It was a fair enough question.

Realistically, what would he have done at the age of eighteen? He and Eva had both been so young, scarcely out of school, both ambitious, with all their lives ahead of them. He hadn't been remotely ready to think about settling down, or facing parenthood, let alone lasting love or matrimony.

And yet he'd been hopelessly crazy about Eva, so chances were…

Dragging in a deep breath of sea air, Griff shook his head. It was way too late to trawl through what might have been. There was no point in harbouring regrets.

But what about now?

How was he going to handle this new situation? Laine, a lovely daughter, living in his city, studying law. The thought that she'd been living there all this time, without his knowledge, did his head in.

And Eva, as lovely and hauntingly bewitching as ever, sent his head spinning too, sent his heart taking flight.

He'd never felt so side-swiped. So torn. One minute he wanted to turn on his heel and head straight back to Eva's motel room, to pull her into his arms and taste those enticing lips of hers. To trace the shape of her lithe, tempting body with his hands. To unleash the longing that was raging inside him, driving him crazy.

Next minute he came to his senses and knew that he should just keep on walking. Now. Walk out of the Bay. All the way back to Brisbane.

And then, heaven help him, he was wanting Eva again. Wanting her desperately.

Damn it. He was in for a very long night.

Don't miss

REUNITED BY A BABY BOMBSHELL

by Barbara Hannay

Available April 2017

www.millsandboon.co.uk

Copyright ©2017 Barbara Hannay

CP0317_2

The perfect gift for Mother's Day...

a Mills & Boon subscription

Call Customer Services on

0844 844 1358*

or visit

millsandboon.co.uk/subscriptions

*** This call will cost you 7 pence per minute plus your phone company's price per minute access charge.**

MILLS & BOON®

Congratulations

Carol Marinelli

on your 100th Mills & Boon book!

Read on for an exclusive extract

How did she walk away? Lydia wondered.

How did she go over and kiss that sulky mouth and say goodbye when really she wanted to climb back into bed?

But rather than reveal her thoughts she flicked that internal default switch which had been permanently set to 'polite'.

'Thank you so much for last night.'

'I haven't finished being your tour guide yet.'

He stretched out his arm and held out his hand but Lydia didn't go over. She did not want to let in hope, so she just stood there as Raul spoke.

'It would be remiss of me to let you go home without seeing Venice as it should be seen.'

'Venice?'

'I'm heading there today. Why don't you come with me? Fly home tomorrow instead.'

There was another night between now and then, and Lydia knew that even while he offered her an extension he made it clear there was a cut-off.

Time added on for good behaviour.

And Raul's version of 'good behaviour' was that there would

be no tears or drama as she walked away. Lydia knew that. If she were to accept his offer then she had to remember that.

'I'd like that.' The calm of her voice belied the trembling she felt inside. 'It sounds wonderful.'

'Only if you're sure?' Raul added.

'Of course.'

But how could she be sure of anything now she had set foot in Raul's world?

He made her dizzy.

Disorientated.

Not just her head, but every cell in her body seemed to be spinning as he hauled himself from the bed and unlike Lydia, with her sheet-covered dash to the bathroom, his body was hers to view.

And that blasted default switch was stuck, because Lydia did the right thing and averted her eyes.

Yet he didn't walk past. Instead Raul walked right over to her and stood in front of her.

She could feel the heat—not just from his naked body but her own—and it felt as if her dress might disintegrate.

He put his fingers on her chin, tilted her head so that she met his eyes, and it killed that he did not kiss her, nor drag her back to his bed. Instead he checked again. 'Are you sure?'

'Of course,' Lydia said, and tried to make light of it. 'I never say no to a free trip.'

It was a joke but it put her in an unflattering light. She was about to correct herself, to say that it hadn't come out as she had meant, but then she saw his slight smile and it spelt approval.

A gold-digger he could handle, Lydia realised.

Her emerging feelings for him—perhaps not.

At every turn her world changed, and she fought for a semblance of control. Fought to convince not just Raul but herself that she could handle this.

Don't miss

THE INNOCENT'S SECRET BABY

by Carol Marinelli

OUT NOW

BUY YOUR COPY TODAY

www.millsandboon.co.uk

Copyright ©2017 by Harlequin Books S.A.

CM0317_2

Join Britain's BIGGEST Romance Book Club

- **EXCLUSIVE offers every month**
- **FREE delivery direct to your door**
- **NEVER MISS a title**
- **EARN Bonus Book points**

Call Customer Services

0844 844 1358*

or visit

millsandboon.co.uk/subscriptions

*** This call will cost you 7 pence per minute plus your phone company's price per minute access charge.**